PRA

*THE FIRST V*

"Fans of *The Frozen River* will love *The First Witch of Boston*. Fiery, outspoken Margaret Jones and her husband, Thomas, find themselves outliers in straitlaced Puritan Boston, but trouble back in England leaves them no choice but to make a home in Massachusetts. When Thomas draws the spite of a local widow and Margaret's skill with healing herbs rouses suspicion of black magic, both will find themselves battling witch-hunters in a court case destined to make history. Andrea Catalano draws a tender, intimate portrait of a marriage and a bold defense of an independent woman ahead of her time."

—Kate Quinn, *New York Times* bestselling author of *The Rose Code*

"A sumptuous and heartrending tale of the dark power of fear, loss, and love against all odds, *The First Witch of Boston* is a moving and accomplished debut."

—Heather Webb, *USA Today* bestselling author of *Queens of London*

"I knew I was going to love this novel from the first page, where Andrea Catalano immerses you in the world of seventeenth-century Boston. Her research is impeccable but never gets in the way of a gripping, emotional story. Thomas Jones's love for his outspoken, opinionated wife, Maggie, and hers for him, are beautifully described, and their tragedy is almost Shakespearean. This is a story that will stay with me for a long time."

—Gill Paul, internationally bestselling author of *Scandalous Women*

"Andrea Catalano's *The First Witch of Boston* conjures the treacherous history of witches, women, and injustice in America. Her research is ambitious and beyond impeccable. But it is the exquisite portrayal of a marriage that is the star at the beating heart of this novel, and the best I've read in years."

—Kimberly Brock, bestselling author of *The Fabled Earth* and *The Lost Book of Eleanor Dare*

"Catalano's timely and heart-wrenching treatise about the injustices against women in early America will leave traces etched in the reader's soul. Sensory, sensual, and evocative, *The First Witch of Boston* is the not-to-be-missed historical fiction debut of the season."

—Aimie K. Runyan, bestselling author of *The School for German Brides* and *Mademoiselle Eiffel*

"What a wonderful, moving novel. Catalano's debut is great historical fiction that brings the past alive in an exquisitely human, truly emotional way. I absolutely loved it."

—Megan Chance, bestselling author of *Glamorous Notions*

"A brilliant debut, full of passion, peril, and heartbreak. Between her gorgeous prose and her endearing characters, Andrea Catalano has established herself as one of the most exciting new authors in historical fiction."

—Olivia Hawker, bestselling author of *One for the Blackbird, One for the Crow*

"A rare and powerful debut—one that will hold you in thrall from beginning to end. Catalano gives voice to all the passion, anguish, and injustice surrounding the life and death of a woman who deserved a better fate than the one history dealt her. Lyrically written and impeccably researched, *The First Witch of Boston* settles into the deepest places in your soul, and remains there long after finishing. An artful, important masterpiece of historical fiction."

—Paulette Kennedy, bestselling author of *The Witch of Tin Mountain*

# THE
# FIRST
# WITCH
## OF
# BOSTON

# THE
# FIRST
# WITCH
## OF
# BOSTON

*A Novel*

## ANDREA CATALANO

LAKE UNION
PUBLISHING

Published by Lake Union Publishing, Seattle

www.apub.com

Amazon, the Amazon logo, and Lake Union Publishing are trademarks of Amazon.com, Inc., or its affiliates.

EU product safety contact:
Amazon Media EU S. à r.l.
38, avenue John F. Kennedy, L-1855 Luxembourg
amazonpublishing-gpsr@amazon.com

ISBN-13: 9781662526008 (paperback)
ISBN-13: 9781662525995 (digital)

Cover design by Lisa Amoroso
Cover image: © Nicole Matthews / ArcAngel

Printed in the United States of America

*For Robert,*
*forever my love and best friend.*
*As Anne Bradstreet wrote,*
*"I prize thy love more than whole mines of gold."*

# PROLOGUE

## *Charlestown, Massachusetts Bay Colony*

**June 28, 1648**

As he waited upon the dock, Thomas Jones wanted nothing more than to be rid of Massachusetts.

He wiped the mist from his brow with the back of his hand, surveying his worldly possessions: two trunks and one basket containing a wary-eyed tortoiseshell cat. The cat regarded him with disdain.

"Come, Molly, take that look from your face." He reached down and ruffled the fur of her sizable mane.

"We could use a good mouser aboard."

Thomas stood straight and found himself looking down into the ruddy and perspiring face of the captain of the ship *Welcome*, which awaited him at the end of the dock.

The captain's eyes widened slightly as he took in the height and breadth of Thomas.

Thomas held the brim of his hat and nodded once. "She's a good mouser, she is."

The captain smiled down at the cat. "No doubt she is that, judging by the look of her." The captain held out his hand. "Captain Davies."

"Thomas Jones, sir." He shook the captain's hand but then paused, his blood going cold. Would the captain have heard of him? The fear that followed his introduction of himself was not immediate. There was a slight delay, like when one dashes down a cup of rum and the force and fire of it takes the briefest moment to take hold. It was the same as when someone mentioned his wife, and he thought of her—pictured her in his mind's eye—and then, just when the woman who was his wife became real, tangible, someone who awaited him at home, an icy wind encircled the whole of him and reminded him that she was gone. The surprise was followed precipitously by the feeling of falling from a great height, and the only thing that grounded him once more was the solid and unmoving sadness beneath his feet, reverberating through each weary step.

"And where is it you are headed?" the captain inquired. "New Amsterdam or Virginia?"

"Neither." Thomas cleared his throat, squinting against the sun as he gazed up at the rigging of *Welcome*. "I make my way to Barbados, sir."

"Oh aye? Have you been before?"

Thomas shook his head.

"This time of year, it's as hot as the cauldrons of hell, it is." Captain Davies chuckled at his own remark. "What takes you there? Some business to attend?"

Thomas smoothed the corners of his mustache with his thumb and finger, mulling how best to answer, for Captain Davies was not of Boston, and the answer was a most complicated one. "You could say that, sir. More of a new beginning."

"So I've heard many a man say that, and it always means they are trying to get away from a woman." The captain pulled upon his salt-stained coat lapels and nodded knowingly.

Thomas was at a loss for words, and so he looked down to the cat. Perhaps she might know the proper, witty response. She looked up at him with her peridot-green eyes as though saying, "How dare you think *I* might get you out of this mess?"

2

"Very well, I'll not wrestle any secrets from out of you. Have Smitty here see to your trunks and come aboard. I'll begin passage negotiations at noon."

Thomas mounted the gangplank, his back turned to land and the place that had been his home for the past two years. There was no home without *his* home, his heart, his haven. No sanctuary existed for him any longer now, and this knowledge was like a deadweight upon his shoulders. He was weary from it.

But then he did look over his shoulder and back to land one last time, only to curse it.

"The husband of Margaret Jones, over there."

He heard the whispers while he stood upon the deck, gazing eastward toward the Atlantic's great gray expanse. He had grown accustomed to the hushed tones that had followed him for weeks—they were not unlike rats' scratching upon a wall or door, unnerving in spite of their persistence. "Thomas Jones, there he be."

Thomas turned toward the source. A woman in a crisp-white cap, her boy's hand clasped in hers, her other hand wrapped tightly round the arm of a man, presumably her husband. She gasped when Thomas's eyes met hers, then bid her family to turn away.

*Pious fools.* Boston was infested with them.

Just then, the ship began to lurch starboard side. The wood of the hull groaned like a ferocious, angry beast, only to be drowned out by the shouts and screams of frightened passengers. Thomas took quick hold of nearby rigging to steady himself. The ship listed farther, and he watched helplessly as those who were not so quick to act fell over, tumbling, sliding, like apples spilling from a toppled bushel. Clumsily and frantically, mothers and fathers haphazardly grabbed hold of small children as they slid starboard. Scared young voices rang out, as did the horrified cries of frightened babies. Thomas flung out his arm to catch an elderly man who was beseeching God whilst he lost his cane and tumbled after it. Awkwardly, Thomas dug his fingers into the man's frail, spindly arm, his nails ripping through the worn wool of his coat sleeve.

"Steady, steady!" Thomas shouted through gritted teeth, trying with all of his might to pull the old man toward the rigging so that he might gain a hold himself, but the man thrashed in his fear. Before Thomas lost his grip upon him, the man's cloudy, aged eyes stared into his.

"Jones!" the man exclaimed, recognizing him. And Thomas could not be sure whether it was the fear of falling into the ocean or the fear of his hand upon him that produced a shriek of dread before he rolled away and toward the rest of the starboard passengers.

Sure-footed mariners swore oaths, shouting for the ship hands to climb to the port side to counterbalance the weight of the precarious vessel. Thomas pulled himself to gain better purchase of the rigging, glancing round in confusion. What could cause such dramatic tipping when they were not yet out to sea, when no storm's winds disturbed the day?

"The witch's husband!"

The hairs upon the back of Thomas's neck rose. He turned to his right to see who had uttered the slur and was met with angry stares from men and women, old and young.

"The husband of Margaret Jones! The Devil's hand! The witch hanged two weeks past!!" a voice wailed. A chorus of pathetic prayers and pleas to God followed.

"Get him off the ship! He, too, must serve Satan!"

"Off! Off! He must be thrown overboard to save us from evil!"

What had God wrought upon him now? Had he not endured enough? There were moments when Thomas awoke in a cold sweat from some nightmare, only to stare into the darkness of a reality that was worse than the nightmare from which he had awoken. He now felt as though he might never escape the macabre dream that his life had become.

Mariners scurried here and there, following barked orders from the quartermaster. But some paused in their labors, noticing how the passengers pointed and stared at Thomas.

"What's the trouble?" a young seaman with closely cropped curls asked a young lass.

She pointed at Thomas from her safe place at the doorway of the captain's quarters. "It's him! The husband of Satan's witch, she who was hanged!" she hissed.

Thomas alternately wanted to climb portside and jump ship and wrap his carpenter's hands round the lass's neck and wring, wring, wring until she turned blue and her eyes went red. But his breath caught in his chest, for he remembered gazing down upon his wife as he held her in his arms one last time, her skin blue, her neck blackened, her wide, surprised eyes a mottled, bloodshot explosion. "Sleep now, Lovely," he had said as he drew her eyelids down. "Sleep now."

The pain, the constant agony of it, made him squint and shake his head.

"Look how he denies it!" said the lass.

He stared back, his eyes intent upon hers. "Not ever."

The outraged hisses, the constant ill judgment that followed him like a stench that made him choke to breathe, swirled round him. But he knew his heart well. "I am the witch's husband."

"Thomas Jones." Captain Davies, accompanied by two constables who all climbed whatever they could grab hold of, approached his rigging.

"You've got to go," the captain said, frowning. He shook his head. "The ship won't right itself. We've a good cargo: eighty horses and 120 tons of ballast being evenly distributed. We can't make sense of it. Some of the passengers, they tell me that you be the husband of a witch, and that it's your dark arts at work." The captain labored to take hold of Thomas's rigging and came closer. "I don't believe such nonsense," he said in a low tone to Thomas, glancing warily side to side, "but what work is this?" His eyes darted worriedly round his listing vessel. "This is not natural. You must go, Jones. I cannot lose my ship, my livelihood. You've got to go."

Thomas resigned himself. "I understand completely, Captain Davies."

"You're to be removed from this ship," declared one of the constables, clasping in his grip what Thomas assumed to be a writ from the Boston Court. Unfortunately, he had become familiar with this formality of late.

"I'll not put up any fight. But I shall gather my cat from below deck, and I would like my trunks brought to the dock."

"Aye, they shall, then be on your way, Jones," the captain said before shuffling away and ordering deckhands to retrieve the trunks.

A crowd of passengers was clustered on the port side of the ship in an effort to bring the vessel right. When they caught sight of him, some muttered in prayer. Others gaped as though they looked upon the Devil in the flesh. How very absurd it all was, he thought, as though his presence were the cause of the listing. Madness! The same madness that had taken his wife from him. He did not know whether to weep or to scream. Instead, laughter bubbled up inside him like wretched bile, low, bitter, and angry. "All I want is to be rid of this place," he declared, and never had he heard his voice come so loudly.

The constables shoved him forward toward the gangplank. He made his way down, and when he reached the dock, he placed Molly's basket near his feet and turned. "See you there?" he asked, gesturing with his hand toward the ship. "She has not righted herself, has she now?"

A moment later, four deckhands approached, Thomas's trunks in hand. Quickly they returned his passage fare, placed his worldly possessions before him, and turned to make their way back aboard. But they paused before the gangplank, staring up at *Welcome*.

A chorus of exclamations rang out as the ship suddenly began to tip port-wise. Beseeching unto God turned into a chorus of joyous shouts of relief. Passengers recovered their footing, rising, their mouths agape in wonder. With a great, echoing groan and a surge of waves that splashed upon the docks, the vessel had miraculously righted itself.

The seamen slowly turned and stared at the two trunks they had just hauled to the dock. One, wide eyed, looked at Thomas and stuttered, "What—what have you in your trunks?"

೨ඣ

"Come here, my fine lady." Alice Stratton reached inside the basket and scooped Molly out, cradling her and kissing the top of her head over and over. "I did not think I would ever see you again." She sat down at her table, beside her husband. "So, Thomas, what mischief has befallen you now?"

Thomas, having sold his house the day before, had nowhere to go and take refuge except the home of his dearest friends, the Strattons. Surprised to see him, yet without question, they had welcomed him inside.

"Mischief. I like that choice of word." He smiled at Alice, his wife's dearest friend. But the smile did not reach his eyes. Tears welled up and spilled before he could stop them. He was never a man prone to crying—it was not like him to display his emotions. Things were best kept inside, where he might mull them over, try to understand the meaning behind the pain. But of late, he was like a cup running over.

Alice promptly put Molly down beside her on the bench and reached her hands across the rough-hewn table made smooth by thousands of hours of preparing meals. She took his hands in hers and squeezed tightly. "Come now, friend, tell us—what happened at the docks?"

"I . . . I cannot explain it." He withdrew his hands from hers, studied the patterns of calluses upon his palms. Mountains and plains, mountains and plains. A testament of toil, a source of pleasure to his wife. His breath shuddered as he wove his fingers together. "The ship, it seems, was listing starboard and would not be righted."

"How's that?" asked Samuel. "When I came by you at the docks, the ship looked stable and sound."

"Aye, that's true." Thomas nodded.

Samuel's thick red brows had drawn together as though he were trying to solve a riddle.

"The ship did not right itself until I and my belongings had been ushered back to the dock."

7

There was silence but for the sound of Molly lapping at a bowl of buttermilk upon the floor.

"Come now, you can't be serious." Samuel leaned back from the table, scratching his beard.

Alice's eyes were upon him. "That he is, Husband. Why would he lie?" With a sigh, she rose from the table and made her way to the hearth, where she peered into the kettle and stirred the contents. She stood straight, hands upon the small of her back, stretching herself as she studied the fire. The firelight danced upon her dress and apron. She was a pretty thing but so small and thin. Yet Thomas knew well that her slight build belied the tenacious, stubborn strength within her.

"What was in your trunks, Thomas?" Her gaze did not waver from the hearth. It was as though she sought an answer from the flames. "There must be something, something which you still hold on to from which you must part yourself."

He knew what it was. It lay at the bottom of the trunk, like sunken treasure on the ocean floor, or a secret letter hidden from seeking eyes and fingers: her wedding gown.

Alice turned toward him, and he could see in the quiver of her mouth that she waged war with tears. "You must bring yourself to do it."

Once Samuel and Alice had retired to their bedchamber—the room on the other side of the hearth—Thomas sat in silence, finishing his ale. He studied the pewter tankard by the light of the lone candle on the side table. It was finely crafted, a gift given to the Strattons when they were wed back in England. They had only two, and Alice had always set them before Thomas and his wife when they came to dine. "Come now, pretend you are newlyweds, once again," Alice would say as she placed her beloved tankards before them. His wife would laugh—the sound low and melodic, sweeter than any song he had ever heard.

And he recalled his response to Alice the first time she had performed this kindly gesture. "I need not pretend—she shall always be my bride."

Maggie had moved closer to him upon the bench then, slipped her hand beneath the table and squeezed his thigh tightly as she pressed her lips to his temple. His temple, she loved to kiss him there. "It smells so much like you," she purred softly into his ear as she breathed him in.

He placed the tankard down upon the side table and nearly convulsed at the pleasure of the thought, the pain of the loss.

The last time she had kissed him upon his temple was a fortnight before, within her jail cell. And her words rang through his mind like some Catholic prayer.

"When I am gone, do not be weighed down by sadness. Be lifted by hope—the hope that we have always shared. Be rid of this life, be rid of every vestige of it—of me!"

He had chafed at her words, his despair taking the guise of anger. "Silence, Maggie! Shut your mouth for once! Stop talking nonsense!"

"You heed me!" she had bellowed through lips chapped and cracking. "Every trace of me must be destroyed! Promise me you shall be rid of it all—sell it, burn it, I don't care."

"You talk madness!"

"Nay! I dread the thought of you keeping some part of me and being dragged into some lonely abyss, for innocence . . . a life—your life, to be tainted by this stain upon mine! Swear to me you shall do as I ask. Swear it!"

The ferocity of her words stifled his protest. Reluctantly he nodded once. "I shall."

He had made a vow, a promise to her, the hour before her execution. He swore he would do all that she had asked of him. He did not know how he could go on without her, despite her plea that he do so. But now, at least, with this small action, he could begin to make good on his promise.

9

And so, by the hearth's light, Thomas unlocked the trunk with which he had deceived his wife's last wish. Beneath the carpentry tools and beloved books, his fingers discovered before his eyes might the fine damask fabric. Tenuous in his movements, he removed the folded emerald-green silk. He unfurled it before him upon the hearthrug. Something scratched at his wrist, and he saw that it was a dried sprig of rosemary. Like a flash of lightning, in his mind came the image of his wife on their wedding day in Saint Mary's Church of Uffington. Clad in the emerald-green damask, she had worn a wreath made of rosemary and ivy crowning her mass of unruly dark curls. She had looked like a painting of the Virgin Mary he had seen as a child.

Squinting against the tears, he brought the precious fabric to his nose, hoping to smell some vestige of his wife, but found only the scent of musty felt and leather. His reverie was interrupted by the soft thud of something upon the rug. Moving the fabric aside, he found a small red-leather-bound book. He had never seen the volume before; had it been tucked away in the folds of his wife's gown all this time? He ran his fingers over worn leather binding, then, with his thumb, carefully lifted the cover. He was met with the soothing sounds a book that longed to be opened made—crackles and snaps like a collapsing log in a hearth.

*April 8th, 1646. We have come to Massachusetts to make a new life for ourselves. We have made a home in Charlestown, to the north of Boston, upon the mouth of the River Mystic. The house is good enough. My Love shall improve it with his great skill. Where he is, that is my home. I am blessed. I know this well.*

Thomas's eyes traced the slanted, scratchy scrawl he knew to be his wife's handwriting. He had never known her to record her days. When he saw her scribbling with a quill, he had assumed she worked at account ledgers. He skipped ahead a few pages. Her entries seemed occasional.

*June 1st, 1646. Today I prepared a salve for Goodwife Warren. She requested one for her son, Lemuel, age ten, who suffers from a persistent, wet cough.*

*Base: lard*

*Herbs: 3 parts Hyssop to 1 part Rosemary and 1 part Pennyroyal.*

There was the daily business he had suspected. Also, he noted scraps of papers inserted here and there, what seemed to be bills of purchase and sale, notes of gratitude from those she had healed, had seen through birthing, suffering, dying. But upon turning a page, he noticed that she had also written upon the back side.

*This eve, shall sup on cod, cooked in broth of onion, bay, and thyme, with potato. Shall serve apple slices with honey and cinnamon. Pleases my Love this way.*

"Aye, so it does," he muttered back to the words. And he remembered, the sharp, tart crispness, the flowery-sweet honey, and the cinnamon—so dear but worth every shilling—cinnamon like the Orient upon your tongue. He had eaten like a ravenous child given a sweet treat. She had laughed, low and pleasing, as she wiped a trickle of honey from his chin with the rough pad of her thumb, then put it in her mouth and sucked it clean with a smack of her lips. He sat her upon his knee, put his hand beneath her skirts. She exhaled. She was always ready when he was ready. She had said it was because they had been made for each other, intended from the time they ceased to be stars and took their first breaths in the world of the living.

Aye, they had been intended for one another, it was true. And there, in his hands, leather bound and written in a dancing scrawl, was proof of this truth, this love like purest truth. His treasure, his other half, his life full when it had been incomplete before her, her and everything that she brought: the wisdom, the pleasure, the comfort, the challenge, and now this, the utter loss like falling from a great height and never, never finding the ground.

He ran his fingers over her words absently, then in awe, realizing that this book—diary or journal of hers—was one last secret corner of her heart that he could know intimately.

Sudden anxiety like a cold wind found its way inside him. What if the book contained something, some awful revelation, that would shatter what had been so very good? Did this benign, leather-bound missive actually hold some darkness, some evil, so much so that it had the power to tip a loaded vessel in the harbor? His heart raced. Was this the proof that his Maggie had, indeed, entertained Satan? Did it contain some sinister knowledge, cunning spells? Could this book be the undoing of all he held most dear?

In Thomas's heart, a war waged between icy fear and the warmth of the anticipation, the pleasure of reliving his life with her, his Maggie, his own.

# PART I

## THOMAS

# CHAPTER ONE

*June 21, 1646*

*Pleases my Love this way.*

"Perhaps this time you've put a child in my belly," Maggie said, wrapping her arms round him, her breath hot against the sweat of his neck.

It had become her habit, to say this whilst in the afterglow. At first he had found it sweet, stirring within him pride and the wonder of what magic, what alchemy, might have occurred between them while they were blissfully unaware. But it had been years now, and though the bliss between them had grown, the sense of anticipation—the possibility of creating a child—seemed a far-off dream. But he would not utter this to her, for it would crush her, and what did he have to gain from that?

"Aye, perhaps this time," he said, out of habit, but what he really meant was, "It doesn't matter to me." And there was no malice in that. It didn't matter to him. He had much contentment in his life: His wife was his treasure; his hands and skills had earned them a comfortable living. A man should never get too greedy.

Six weeks later, as they lay in bed together, she took his hand and placed it beneath her navel. She turned her head to him, wearing a giddy grin, her eyes wet with happiness.

He returned her smile—it was such a beautiful sight to behold, her gladness. But he had witnessed it four times before, and had also seen her crumple in grief upon the privy chair, undone by the blood, so much blood. It had shaken his faith in the goodness of the Lord, to have Him play such deceitful tricks upon his Love. He'd rather it be all or nothing, all or nothing.

"It's early still, my Love." He knew his words would disturb her, but he could not stifle his sentiment.

Her smile did not fade. "Aye, it is early. But I know, this time, it is real." Her eyes drifted above him, to the carved headboard. "I dreamed I held a child, and she was the most beautiful creature, so very perfect."

"Have you never dreamed this before?"

Her gaze returned to his. "Nay, not like this."

He knew not to question this, had learned very early on in their marriage that his wife had the ability to dream dreams that would come to be. "A girl?"

"Yes," she said, her smile growing.

He kissed her forehead, his mind's eye creating a little girl, his wife in miniature: a mass of dark curls, big blue eyes, sly smirk that could change to a frown in the blink of an eye. *Lord,* he thought, *let her be more temperate than her mother.*

"What are you thinking about?" she asked him.

"What she will be like."

"Oh yes?"

"Aye. I hope she will be as beautiful and clever as her mother, but without such an incessant mouth."

She shoved against his chest. "Cruel! You knew what you were getting when you took me as your bride."

Oh, it were the truth, and he laughed. It was her boldness that had first caught his attention, some seventeen years gone past.

She laughed too; she always laughed when he laughed, as though one precipitated the other. She placed a hand upon his chest again and ran her long fingers upward through the thatch of dark hair, above the laces of his nightshirt. It always pleased him when she would do this.

After a moment, she spoke. "Where are you off to tomorrow?"

"Tomorrow I go to Boston, to the Widow Hallett."

Maggie's hand paused upon his chest. "The newly widowed Goody Hallett?"

"Aye."

"What is it she requires, Mister Jones, cabinetmaker of great renown?"

He laughed at this. "She would like me to fashion a wardrobe for her."

She toyed with the loose tie of his nightshirt. "Her husband not in the ground a month yet and she already spends his money."

"Come now, do not be unkind, Maggie."

"How am I unkind?"

"You judge too harshly."

"I do not."

"Aye. And what care you? Especially as we stand to profit from her spending her late husband's money, isn't it so?"

"True. I just think it telling, that she mourns so little."

"Perhaps the marriage was arranged."

"True," she said, her fingers sliding beneath the shirt linen, stroking his chest. "Perhaps she did not have much choice upon the matter. He was old enough to be her grandfather."

He reveled in her caress. "Not every woman is as lucky as you, Bride."

She smiled, looking up at him. "I may be lucky but you are more so."

"That is truthful talk." He kissed her forehead. "Come now, turn round so I can hold you close as I sleep."

She turned and fit herself against him. They were like nesting cups, one protectively covering the other. She took hold of his hand and placed it once again beneath her navel.

His fingers were warmed by the heat of her belly, and he kissed her shoulder. "You must rest well, for the babe." He had said it many times before. He silently asked God that this time, He be generous toward his Bride.

᠅

The house upon Milk Street was larger than he had expected. His knock upon the door was answered promptly by a young woman, whom he recognized. Mary Doyle had come to procure various herbs and tinctures from his wife on a number of occasions. She was indentured to the Hallett family, but originally from Ireland. How she had come to be indentured to an East Anglian family was a mystery to him, but not his business to solve.

*"Maidin mhaith, a chara."* Mary smiled, looking down at her apron as she did so.

"And good morning to you, my friend," he replied, warmed by the sound of his native tongue but also setting the course for English. One could never be too careful in Boston.

She showed him into the sitting room. "Please wait here. My mistress is expecting you. I'll get her at once."

As he removed his hat, he surveyed the sitting room. The wood paneling upon the walls was of fine stained oak. The floorboards gleamed as though freshly scrubbed and polished. The mantel above the hearth was the largest he had seen since his arrival in the Bay Colony. The furniture in the room looked to be both locally crafted as well as pieces from the old country, but to be sure, all were newer in condition, well made, and indicative of a man who had been favored by Fortune.

"Mister Jones." Widow Hallett was, indeed, young, perhaps no more than twenty-five. She was clad in black mourning, but his keen eye knew the fabric to be fine chintz. He also was but a man and could not help but take note of the smallness of her waist and the roundness of her bosom rising above a rather low neckline, the style of which he had not seen since leaving London.

When his eyes met hers, she smiled, a slight blush upon her pale cheeks. She wore no cap upon her blond hair, and waves escaped her bun, framing her pleasing face. A widow wealthy, young, and pretty would not remain a widow for long, especially in the Bay Colony.

"I pictured you to look differently," she said.

He did not expect to hear this. "Aye, well, I am sorry to disappoint you." He knew his jest to be presumptuous of him, but he could not take it back now that he had uttered it. It was something his wife would have thoughtlessly said, as she was wont to speak without thinking.

The widow giggled, and he was worldly enough to discern the flirtation beneath. It had been a long while since any woman had deigned to do so; Thomas was no young man, at thirty-seven. But he knew also that his countenance was not unpleasing, and his height allowed him to clearly see the top of many a man's hat. His body was powerful from years of labor, and he still had as much vigor in him as he had when he was twenty years younger. Still, the young widow's outright flirtation took him by surprise. He'd noted that, in this pious corner of the world, lust and desire were secrets kept hidden, locked away from the light of day. They were a long way from London.

"Not at all, Mister Jones. Come now, follow me." She turned with a swirl of skirts and walked out of the sitting room and up the stairway to the second level. He followed behind, realizing that she was taking him to a bedchamber. In his discomfort, he cleared his throat and remained at the threshold.

She gestured toward a wall, across from the bed. "Here is where I would like a wardrobe cabinet, to be about this big." She gestured with her slender arms and small hands.

He knew he had to enter the room in order to take measurement of the wall and learn the size she required. Stepping round her, he produced his measuring twine from his coat pocket and noted the width and height of the cabinet she desired. The piece would be large and costly, and he was glad of both the challenge and the profit. "What sort of wood, madam?"

"What is the best kind?"

"Oak is sturdiest, or cherrywood, which can be varnished to look like Caribbean mahogany, with a reddish hue."

"Oh, yes, cherrywood." She clasped her hands before her and smiled.

"Very well, madam." He delighted at the idea of how he might work the wood. He proceeded to learn what else she required, so far as hidden drawers, knob types, and any embellishment. He quoted a fair price, given the amount of labor and the cost of the wood and African varnish. She accepted immediately, without a haggle.

As she led the way out of the bedchamber, her hand brushed past his thigh, and he felt her fingertips against his skin, through the linsey-woolsey of his brown breeches. The room grew hot. His perspiration dampened his neatly trimmed mustache and goatee. Her game was pleasing, indeed, but equally treacherous, and he was no fool. He began to pity her, her obvious loneliness, her immodest overtures. Such things would heap nothing but trouble upon her in a place such as this. If the Lord were just, He would find this young widow an equally young husband, to tame and quench her passion. And what a lucky man he would be. A smile teased Thomas's lips at the thought.

"Does something amuse you?" she asked with a tilt of her head, a tendril swaying against her pale, graceful neck.

His wife was a graceful woman, too, but powerful, strong enough to lift two fifty-pound sacks of cornmeal, one in each hand. He doubted that the Widow Hallett had ever lifted anything heavier than her skirts. And again he smiled, and he did not hide it.

"Nay, madam. I smile, thinking upon working the wood for your wardrobe."

"Ah," she replied, her gray eyes taking in the whole of him before leading the way back down the stairway.

*Wanton thing,* he thought. *She needs a man soon.* And for the briefest of moments, he envisioned that man as he, taking her against the wall. Oh yes, he knew he could show her what she didn't even know she was seeking. He exhaled, sending the titillating thought away from himself, away. When she opened the door for him, he was glad to be outdoors, in cooler air. He was reluctant to don his hat.

"Mister Jones, when shall you begin?"

He turned to face the Widow Hallett. "In a week's time, I should think. I'll work the pieces in my shop and then assemble them in the room, since the wardrobe is so large. It will be easier in this manner."

"And when can I expect you to return?" Her face was upturned, her eyes searching his. It was as though she spoke to her lover. Such sweetness up for offering, like a kitten seeking a caress. How could a man respond coldly?

"I expect in two weeks' time. Does that suit you?"

She bit her lower lip, her brows drawing together.

"Mayhap you'll be betrothed to another by then," he quipped, then cleared his throat. He had intended to only think the words, but some boldness had caused him to utter them aloud. He chided himself; he must take better care.

She gasped, eyes wide. The players on the stages of London could not outdo her. "I still mourn, Mister Jones."

He busied himself with donning his hat to stifle his laughter. "Aye, indeed."

"Besides," she said, tilting her head as she toyed with the escaped tendril, "a widow must be selective when she remarries."

"As well she should be." In the pit of his stomach, he felt sudden foreboding. She was an artful snare and he must not play the hungry rabbit. "Good day, Widow Hallett."

"That's a kingly piece, that is, with such dimensions." Maggie paused before the hearth, wooden bowl in hand.

"There is much fortune to be made in the Bay Colony, it would seem," he replied.

"Indeed, and you shall share in the bounty, making such a piece," she said as she bent over the pot, ladling cod stew into his bowl. She placed the steaming bowl before him, the pleasing scent of bay leaf, adorned with bright saffron, wafted to his nose. His wife had many talents, and culinary skill was one at which she excelled. She pleased him in so many ways, she knew just how to satisfy his many hungers.

He smiled as he savored the saffron flavor of the stew. She was like saffron; just the smallest pinch, and his meal—his life—was transformed with exotic flavor, the likes of which he had never experienced before, and a flavor unique, singular, and all of her own. And who would have thought such a spice could be found in the depths of a simple autumn crocus? Who would have thought that he would be so lucky as to have such a creature storm into his life?

"What is so funny?"

"Nothing is funny. You please me."

She dipped a piece of bread in her stew, her full mouth playfully smirking in that way so dear to him. "And you, me."

"I know."

"For a quiet man, you lack modesty," she teased before taking a bite of her bread.

"I like to observe the world round me. I'd be a fool if I didn't know I pleased you."

"Less talking, more supping, before your stew gets cold," she said, but he saw she still smiled as she spooned her stew. "So tell me, what is the Widow Hallett like? I've only seen her from a distance."

Some men would choose to lie to their wives when faced with such a question, perhaps make light of another woman's beauty and grace. But Thomas was truthful to a fault, just like his wife. They spoke plainly with one another—it was an unwritten pact. What use lay in dishonesty? Many years ago, before they were husband and wife and when they worked together on the Winship farm in Somerset, he had heard Maggie say to a little girl, "It is best not to lie. For every lie you tell you shall have to tell three more to cover for it, and three for each of those, and soon enough you'll be trapped in your own web of lies times three." He had thought that odd at first, but the more he considered it, the more he had seen the truth in it.

"She's a pretty thing, the widow is."

22

"Aye?"

"Aye, she'll not want for a husband long."

Maggie laughed. "Indeed, I should think not, with such a fortune as she has."

"She would not lack for suitors even if she were poor."

Maggie nodded. "Then she must be very rich in beauty as well. Lucky girl."

"That she is."

"Tell me more."

Thomas took a swig from his ale tankard, then wiped the foam from his mustache with the back of his hand. "She's a small thing, slight, but with a figure men like."

"All men, or just you?"

"All men like what I like."

She laughed a little. "So, what else?"

"She's fair, golden curls, light eyes."

"Ah, an English rose."

"Some may say, but English roses come in many colors. Mine is dark, and I like her above all others."

"You had better."

"As if you need tell me."

He saw her true smile of joy.

"I grow weary of speaking about the widow. Come now," he said, leaning back in his chair, "take your hair down for me, Bride."

Her smile grew as she removed her cap and tossed it upon the table. She unwound her hair, then put her hands upon her scalp and shook. A mass of wild, dark curls swirled about her, spilled down past her bosom, almost to her waist.

He sighed in satisfaction. What a beauty she was.

She rose from her chair, untying her apron and tossing it to the table. She made her way toward the bedchamber, gesturing with her finger for him to follow.

# CHAPTER TWO

*August 10, 1646*

*Goody Carlton come for 10 poultices of cooling spearmint, to keep cool in the heat of the nights of late.*

*Widow Hallett come for ground carnelian and oil of Frankincense.*

*She tells me that she desires a spell to make her irresistible to a suitor. I tell her I am a healer and midwife and have no knowledge of magic and dark arts. I would be daft were I to reveal the depths of the knowledge handed down to me, Grandmum had freely practiced physic as well as dealt in magic potions and tinctures, things said to manifest whatever it was one desired. But these are different days, different times, especially here in New England. They keep so pious here, they see the Devil and his minions in all things lurking. Widow Hallett must seek such things elsewhere.*

*The Widow went to the workshop to view Thomas's progress on her wardrobe. I do not like her presence here. I sense much malice in her.*

"Thomas," called Maggie from the barn entrance. "Here's Widow Hallett come to see your progress."

He straightened, stretching his frame, wiping the sweat from his forehead with the cuff of his rolled sleeve. It was damnably hot, and had been so for a week's time. Never in all of his years had he experienced such heat and air so thick. He imagined that the tropics must be like that, even worse. How did people bear it? And then, here was the impatient Widow Hallett come to see his progress exactly one week to the day he went to take her request. He had only acquired the wood from the lumberyard that morning.

He placed down his tools and made his way to the doorway. Maggie, hands upon her hips, smiled at his approach. She stood some inches taller than the petite Widow Hallett, who was dressed in her fine mourning with a black cap to match. The widow was like a pale spring tulip kissed by the sun, his wife like a bloodred rose in full bloom at dusk.

"Good day, Widow Hallett. How can I be of service?"

There was the flash of a dimple on her right cheek. Her eyes looked him over, and for a moment he fretted over how disheveled he might appear, let alone how he might smell in the heat of the day. Why did he worry? What was it about this woman that made him suddenly ill at ease with himself?

"I wanted to see the cherrywood," she said quickly, like a child. Her eagerness as well as the dimple in her cheek acted upon him, and he smiled.

"Very well. I'll be in the garden," said Maggie.

He looked at Maggie and nodded. Her eyes searched his for a moment, and he noted the crease high upon her forehead—it appeared whenever she was concerned, worried, or having her sense of things, as he liked to say. Did she actually fear that he might dally with the pretty widow? Never had he had any reason to be unfaithful before, and certainly he was not fool enough to be tempted. Maggie should know this; it was her confidence that had always enticed him. Or did Maggie worry about something else, something more?

He led the widow into the barn, past other cabinetry and piles of wood, and to where the cherrywood lay prone, awaiting its transformation.

"The wood arrived just this morning."

Her eyes absently took in the fragrant freshly cut planks. And then she looked up to him, as though awaiting his next word.

Awkwardly he sought something more to say, not because she discomforted him, but because there really was nothing more to say. It was what it was: wood ready to be prepared for the wardrobe. "Have you any questions, madam?"

She stretched her fingers out, leaning over to touch a plank.

"No, madam," he quickly cautioned, "that one has not been finished. You'll likely get a wood splinter. Here," he said, bringing forth the board he had sanded smooth. "This one is safe to touch."

She came closer to him and skimmed her fingertips over the wood's surface. But her gaze was not upon the board and instead upon the laces of his shirt above his work apron. "It is a hot day, indeed, to be laboring." Her eyes moved up to his neck, and then to his face.

In the pit of his stomach, he sensed an unease, akin to when the air grows close and blustery before a lightning storm. Placing the board against the shed wall, he said, "I've much work still to be done, as you can see." He wanted her gone.

"Very well," she said with a tilt of her chin. "Good day to you, Mister Jones."

"Shall I see you out?"

"Do not trouble yourself. I know the way, thank you." She made her way out of the shed with the languid stride of a woman who knew she was being watched. And for that he liked her less.

To be rid of the peculiar feeling the widow had caused, he toiled long and hard, losing sense of the time. He did not know how late it was until Maggie came with a tankard of ale and a wet compress. With gentle fingers, she put the compress upon the back of his neck, beneath his queue. She pressed upon it, and rivulets of water trailed down his back and chest, the clean, pleasing scent of spearmint reaching his nose. Then she removed the linen, pursed her lips, and blew upon his neck. His skin thrilled at the sudden coolness. There was more at work here than just a simple poultice of spearmint. His wife was exceptionally skilled at the healing arts.

"What magic is this?"

She came round to face him. "Nay, no magic, just the will to bring you relief."

"With nothing but spearmint?"

"Aye, and a little something more that is my secret."

He kissed her forehead, tasting her salty perspiration. "Tell me the secret."

"Camphor gum."

"You brought this from London?"

"Yes. There was a Chinaman who procured it from his home, great quantities of tiny white crystals, a resin from the trees."

"What will you do when you run out of camphor? There is no Chinaman to be found here in Boston."

She laughed. "Indeed no. I shall have to go back to London."

A pang of foreboding echoed through him. "We can never go back to London." He grew weary of her longing for England. "You know this. It's too dangerous. This is our home now, Maggie."

"My home is wherever you are." Her eyes would not meet his. Instead, she took his hand in hers and stretched his arm before him, sliding the wet poultice up and down his skin, then blowing upon the dampness.

He shivered at the sensation.

"Perhaps we can go back again in a year's time."

He took firm hold of her chin, raising her face so that he could look into her eyes. "Nay. Not ever. I'll not go back and have you land in a world of trouble."

Her fingers wrapped round his wrist, and her grip was firm. "But I sense more trouble here in Massachusetts."

"What trouble? You speak nonsense." He took his hand away from her chin and turned toward the worktable.

"I do, Thomas, it's true." She came round to the other side of the worktable to face him. "I don't trust that Widow Hallett. I don't like the way she looks at you."

The peculiar feeling of earlier settled in the pit of his belly again, but he tried to shake it off with humor. "Come now, it's not like you to be jealous, Maggie."

She took swift hold of a chisel and threw it across the work shed, where it hit the wall and then clanged to the ground. She gritted her teeth. He had awoken the beast within her, he knew well.

"I am *not* jealous! I am *fearful!* Her presence upon the threshold was like a dark cloud, I swear it. You know not to question this."

"You are jealous and it is unbecoming of you. I am surprised." He went to the corner of the shed to retrieve the chisel, then returned it to the worktable.

She stared at him, and he swore her eyes could have burned his skin with their fury. "She is not the kind you fancy."

"Aye, she is not. I'm glad that you've come to your senses."

"But she houses malice."

He took a deep breath. Maggie's premonitions were not to be slighted. "Perhaps she is a wicked little thing, but she is far less wicked than the trouble that seeks you back in London. You know we can never go back." He shook his head, not so much in disapproval but to rid himself of the frightful thought of Maggie having a price upon her head. "The day you sold that tincture to mad Lady Wembly to help rid her melancholy was the day your time in London was up." The thought still woke a rage in him.

"How was I to know that the Saint John's Wort would send her into a murderous mania against her husband? And even if I had known, how could I have declined a noblewoman's request without heaping trouble upon myself? Are we to unearth this quarrel yet again?"

He shook his head in annoyance. "I'm not the one pining away for London. You are. And we are not going back there, so long as Lady Wembly has a price upon your head. There's naught but trouble when common folk mix with aristocracy. Why should a lady of the peerage take the blame for her own murderous ways when she can simply lay the blame upon a common apothecary?" He spat upon the floor.

"But things have changed back home," she said, moving closer to him, taking hold of his hand. "Parliament's war favors them. Did they not defeat the King's army at Naseby last summer? Parliament shall usher in a new era. Lords and ladies will no longer hold such sway."

He laughed. For such a clever woman, she could be almost childlike in her idealism. "Oh, Maggie, power resides in gold, and gold resides in power. It matters not who sits on the throne or who controls Parliament. This is the way it always has been and the way it always will be."

"Thomas, I don't want to stay here, especially now that there may be a child." Her hand slipped from his and went to her belly.

"Aye, that is *exactly* why we shall stay here, because of the babe."

"But it is like a cloud overhead, this feeling of mine . . ."

"Come," he said, taking her in his arms. He kissed the top of her cap. "The child makes you worry. We've not been here even one year yet. You must give it time."

She placed her ear upon his heart, as she was wont to do when he held her. "I had not imagined this place to be so . . . so stern, so austere."

"It's the Puritan lot here, it's how they are. It's how they create order in the wilderness. As the place grows, as more people like us come to settle, it will become less strict. That's what I believe."

"I hope you are right."

"Besides, we've got good neighbors and friends in the Strattons. They are very much like us."

"This is true."

He moved to look at her. "Come now, I'm famished. Let's have supper."

She smiled, but the crease in her upper forehead remained.

# CHAPTER THREE

*August 30, 1646*

*Three moons have come and gone and I have not bled. My breasts ache, I vomit each morning after I break my fast. For certain, I am with child, Lord bless us. I told Thomas this morning, in his workshop. He had just finished a rocking cradle for Goody Kitchin, and it seemed a fitting time to tell him the news. He is pleased, indeed. A patient man, he is, as the saints of old we no longer speak of. He will come with me today to the fish market, as it is on the way to the Kitchin home and he can deliver the cradle.*

"Are you certain the basket is not too heavy?" Thomas asked Maggie as they strolled through the fish market. He worried for her, being with child. She had lost so many babies early on—neither of them could bear to lose another, once again.

"Of course not, I am not *invalidus*, as the fancy physicians say back in London," she said, laughing a little. "And besides, you've got that cradle to carry still."

"Have you finished here?" Thomas asked, eyeing the sizable codfish, as well as the clams and oysters in the basket.

"Indeed, I've plenty for a nice seafood pie."

"Very good." Thomas loved everything Maggie cooked in their kitchen. And in this new corner of the world, they were blessed to have such a bounty of wonderful fish.

They walked to Market Square, which was bustling with vendors from neighboring farms selling their vegetables and fruits. Maggie stopped at a stall selling freshly milled grain from the Hawkins Mill, which loomed above the town upon Fort Hill. Thomas bid her to await him there whilst he delivered the cradle to the Kitchin home, which sat on the southeast corner of the square. He did not want Maggie to be lifting a heavy sack of wheat flour or cornmeal in her delicate state.

Quickly he dashed past the Meeting House, which sat at the base of Fort Hill, at the northwest corner of the square. He knocked upon the door of a fine burgundy town house. Luckily Goody Kitchin was at home, and she squealed in delight as he delivered the new rocking cradle to her.

"Come, Goodman Jones, to the kitchen, have a cup of ale."

"That is kind of you, Goody Kitchin, but I'm afraid I must be off to meet my wife at the Hawkins stall." He hesitated for a moment to share their news, for he had done so in the past only to have it not come to fruition. But he was happy in this place and on this day and put his caution aside. "My wife is with child, you see."

"Oh how wonderful! Bless you, and her, and the babe, Goodman Jones. I shall pray for Goody Jones's health and an easy birthing. What happy times for us, praise the Lord! My thanks to you again. The Lord has blessed you with such skill and talent. We are blessed to have you here with us. Good day to you!"

She was brimming with blessings, he thought, and it amused him and warmed his heart. "And I am thankful to you and your family. Please give my good regards to your husband. Good day."

He smiled as he strode back across the square in the direction of the Hawkins stall. He tipped his hat to those who greeted him in passing. But just then he slowed, as a small crowd was gathering before the Meeting House. He joined to see what was causing such curiosity.

There were two unfortunates in the pillories—he had not noticed earlier as he passed on his way to the Kitchin house. Maggie was before one of them, speaking to him.

"I pity you, this is harsh punishment," he heard her say to the young man. She was wiping his forehead with a kerchief, for someone had smeared mud upon his face in ridicule.

Thomas moved closer through the crowd, and he heard their whispers.

"What is she doing?"

"She will be reprimanded for this."

"For shame upon her, having pity upon such a wretch."

"I didn't mean to drink so much," muttered the young man, regret in his voice.

"And I were so tired, I forgot it were the Sabbath, you see."

"Of course you did," Maggie sympathized, cupping his cheek.

"I've never felt so hungry in all my life, I swear it," the young man said, then let out a choked sob, obviously embarrassed to have shown his emotion in front of the townspeople.

"Come," she said, reaching into her basket. "Take some strawberries, here. I shall hold them for you, come now."

"You are most kind, Goody Jones. Lord bless you," he said before tearing into the offered berries with his teeth.

"There now, move forward and raise your head as much as you can. We cannot have you choking, you see," Maggie instructed him.

Thomas felt both pity for the poor wretch in the pillory and proud of his Maggie, who, daily, gave out kindness and sympathy for those in pain and suffering. But he grew concerned as he heard the mutterings of the crowd round them again.

"How dare she feed him during his punishment?"

"Who does she think she is?"

"She be like Eve, tempting Adam with Satan's apple," said a loud voice. "Move aside, now." It was the old former governor Endecott, parting the crowd rudely with his walking stick as he made his way to the pillory, where Maggie still fed the imprisoned young man the strawberries. "Woman! Step aside from that criminal this instant! He is a sinner!"

Maggie looked toward Endecott, her eyes sizing up his slight stature, hunched by age. "Oh aye? Did Jesus not say, 'He who is without sin may cast the first stone'? We are all sinners, Mister Endecott, are we not? Only our Lord and Savior is infallible."

"How dare you quote scripture to me! Who are you?" His elderly voice quaked with rage.

Thomas thought to intervene and apologize for his Maggie just to be done with the scene and make peace with the old governor. But before he could, Maggie spoke.

"I am Goodwife Margaret Jones, sir," she said proudly.

"Ah, the cunning woman."

Thomas held his breath at his words. *Cunning woman* was a slur in this part of the world.

"Midwife and apothecary, you mean, sir," she rebutted.

Thomas could not restrain himself any longer. He stepped out of the crowd and toward them. "Mister Endecott, she is my wife and she means no harm." He thought quickly. "You see, sir, she is with child, and she has become in the soft and motherly way, cannot restrain herself from helping those in need: children, animals, even wretches like this one."

Endecott looked Thomas over, then slowly nodded. "Ah, I see." He waved his walking stick between Maggie and the imprisoned man. "No more of this, Goody Jones. Remember your place. Give your ministrations to those more worthy than this sinner. And Goodman Jones, do take your wife in hand. Should this happen again, she will be fined by the court."

"Thank you, sir," Thomas said with a tip of his hat, silently begging Maggie to hold her tongue. Endecott shuffled off into the Meeting House.

The crowd dispersed, went back to their business.

"Goody Jones, please, do not fuss yourself with me any longer," said the young man, struggling to turn his head sideways in the pillory to get a better look at them. "I'll not have such a kind woman be punished on my behalf. Goodman Jones, you are blessed to have such an angel for a wife."

"I thank thee," Thomas replied, feeling sympathy for the poor man. "Lord have mercy on you. 'Tis not pleasant, this."

"'Twas of my own making," muttered the man.

Maggie bent close to his ear. "Try not to drink so much on a Saturday evening. As sure as the sun rises, Saturday will turn into Sunday, you know."

He laughed, in spite of his situation. "True indeed. Bless you, Goody Jones."

"Come now, Wife," Thomas said, ushering her away from the pillory. "Did you require anything at the Hawkins stall?" He could still feel his heart racing from their confrontation with Endecott. "You must be more cautious, Maggie," he whispered into her ear.

"Damn hypocrite, that Endecott," she muttered. "Not a kind bone in his body. Banished a pregnant woman to the wilds."

Thomas knew she meant the poor Anne Hutchinson. Though they had arrived after her banishment, they had heard stories about her many times. A religiously zealous and outspoken midwife, Hutchinson had been deemed a threat to the order of things in Massachusetts Bay. The men in power could not abide by a woman speaking her mind and gaining the admiration of others. And so she had been charged with blasphemy and banished to the wilds. Thomas thought to himself that the sentence handed down by these men spoke volumes of how precarious their control of this little City Upon a Hill might be, that they so feared the words of one woman.

"Maggie, calm yourself. Your anger cannot be good for the babe."

She sighed. "You are right, Thomas. I wish I could be as sensible as you."

Thomas laughed. "You cannot help yourself, you are an Aries, ruled by Mars."

"Ah, to be a gentle Libra, ruled by Venus." She laughed, handing coin to the boy at the stall, who gave Thomas the sacks of wheat flour and cornmeal.

They walked away from Market Square, north toward their home. As they passed the Strattons' house, Maggie of course had to stop to greet their fluffy sheepdog. She could not resist any animal and had to speak to each one as though they were an old friend or a happy child. "Yes, indeed, you are the very best boy, you are!" she said as she rubbed the shaggy fluff of the dog's head. The dog clambered excitedly against the fence separating him from Maggie. He jumped up tall and slobbered his tongue all over her face, which she readily permitted, laughing the whole while.

The Stratton family's front door opened and out stepped Samuel Stratton, who laughed as he beheld the scene. "Longshanks is besotted with your wife, Goodman Jones. I cannot be held responsible for his transgressions with her."

They all laughed at his ribald joke.

"My wife, Alice, and I have been meaning to have you both to dinner at our house. Please join us, in a fortnight, shall you?"

"We would be delighted," Thomas replied with a tip of his hat.

"Very good, very good," Stratton said, waving farewell as he went back inside his house.

"You see, they are not all bad, this lot," Thomas said to Maggie hopefully.

"I long to have friends here, especially now with the babe coming," she said. Maggie was gregarious by nature and had friends aplenty in London.

"You shall, Maggie, I promise," Thomas said, wistfully thinking of their days in London. His mind then went to the incident in the square with Endecott. He tried his best to shake off the ominous feeling that came over him. Thomas had learned in life that it was best to view the balance in one's favor, or the glass as half full, as some said. As he glanced over at his wife, he saw the pink bloom of her cheek, a blush she had acquired with new motherhood. There was much for which to be grateful.

# CHAPTER FOUR

*September 15, 1646*

*The Strattons have invited us to theirs for dinner. I look forward to it. I've prepared a butter pastry filled with wild blueberries, and will serve it with clotted cream.*

Samuel Stratton was a generous man, eager to share his rum with all who sat at his table. He leaned over the table, his portly belly looking as though it might burst through the pewter buttons of his waistcoat, and he replenished the rum cups as soon as they were drunk dry. Thomas knew at that moment that he liked him; he was at ease in his home, at his table, and there was nothing miserly or stingy about him. He was as gregarious as Maggie, always with a good story to tell or joke to share, and always ready to laugh. Humor came easy to him, as it did Maggie, and Thomas had always admired this trait in a person.

Samuel's three sons did not yet have his girth, but all had their parents' red hair. Alice, like Thomas, had no choice but to sit back and admire the great spark of life that was her chosen mate. He knew this sentiment well. When one has such a spouse, one can only study them in awe, then look round at everyone else to see if they were just as awed. And usually they were. And that was a wondrous feeling, a pride that warms and lifts.

Maggie met Samuel story for story, quip for quip, and Samuel's sons looked both thoroughly amused and slightly scandalized. They were too young to remember what society was like back in the old country. They were accustomed only to the womenfolk of Boston, who were another breed altogether from Thomas's wife. Their young wives, too, seemed dumbfounded by Maggie and her animated tales and jokes, for they stared at her, mouths agape, yet could not seem to control the laughter that bubbled up from their bellies.

As it goes when one enjoys oneself, the afternoon quickly turned to evening, and the three Stratton sons and their wives and little ones gathered up to make their journeys homeward. After goodbyes were said and hugs and kisses given round, the four of them were alone.

"It is good that your sons come home for Sundays. Few parents are so fortunate," Thomas said. He had not been home to see his parents since he had been indentured to service at fourteen. He did not mind this, though. His childhood home was not the warm, loving home of the Strattons. His mother gave birth, without fail, every year. Some had died, most had lived, and those that lived were hired out for service as soon as they were of age. One less mouth to feed. His parents had made no secret of their relief to have him off their hands.

"'Tis a blessing, to be certain," said Alice after a sip of rum. "It is one of the good things, living here in the Bay Colony. Family is close by, free to come and go, not indentured at some manor."

"Yes, it's true. Now then," said Samuel, loosening his neck stock, "tell us what brought you here, and how do you like it thus far?" Samuel and Alice looked to Maggie, for she had been the far more talkative one between the two of them. But Maggie turned to Thomas, deferring. Though his wife's loquacious ways, at times, were grating, she was never selfish or overbearing toward him. Thomas loved her for this, though when he was at a loss for the proper words, he wished she would take over the thread. But he was not ill at ease on this evening.

"What brings anyone here but opportunity?" Thomas asked.

"Aye, or adventure," Samuel said with a dramatic sweep of his arm.

Alice and Maggie laughed.

"Judging by the faces in Sunday Service, it seems religious fervor as well," said Maggie.

Thomas inwardly cringed at her words. They did not know the Strattons well enough yet to ascertain how pious they might be. He liked them very much, and it was important to have friends in a foreign place. He did not want to offend them already, or rather, he did not want Maggie to offend them. He gave her knee a slight squeeze under the table, to caution her.

"Of course, I mean no offense by that. I merely make an observation, that's all." She took a sip from her cup, giving Thomas a sideways glance, which he knew meant she disliked his disapproval.

She never apologized to anyone for her blunt remarks, his Maggie. It infuriated him at times, but it was also one of the many reasons he loved her.

"No offense taken, Goody Jones," Samuel cheerfully declared.

"And now I must ask that you stop calling me 'Goody Jones,' and start calling me by my Christian name: Margaret, or Maggie."

"Very good, very good. And likewise, call me Sam." Samuel lifted his cup. "Let us toast, to new friendship."

They drank from their cups, all sighing in satisfaction.

"So, what was it that brought the two of you here?" asked Maggie.

Sam stroked his red beard. "To be honest, it was because I no longer wished to toil on another man's land."

"A good enough reason," Thomas said.

"How did you feel, leaving your home?" asked Maggie, turning to Alice.

She studied her fingers upon the table before her, then looked up. "It were no easy decision for me, but I had two young boys and another on the way. I wanted them to live freely, to have a chance at a better life. I was loath to leave my home, aye." She paused, looking up at her husband beside her. He smiled at her. "But when you are a mother, you think differently. You think beyond yourself. Does this make sense?" she asked Maggie.

Maggie, for once that evening, was not ready with an answer. In fact, at Alice's words, her smile faded, and a shadow of sorts came over her. Knowing that it must be her sadness over the many miscarriages she had suffered, and the fear that it might happen again, to the new baby growing within her, Thomas squeezed her thigh beneath the table again, this time as encouragement. Her hand slid over his.

"It does make sense, even though I am not yet a mother."

There was an uncomfortable silence at the table. Of course it must have seemed strange that a couple their age, so long married, would not have any children.

"We have not been blessed with children," Thomas said, then cleared his throat. "Though she has been with child many times." He paused, looking down into her eyes, giving a little nod. "She is with child now." Instinctively Thomas put his arm round her shoulders.

"Well now! That is happy news, indeed," declared Sam.

Alice stretched her arms across the table, clasping Maggie's hands in hers. "This time, this time you shall have success. I know this."

Maggie laughed a little. "How do you know?"

"Because you are in the New World now. The water is clean, the air is clean, the babe will know this, will sense this within you."

"I've thought something similar," said Maggie. "I believe it shall be different this time, even though I am thirty-three years on this earth."

Alice waved her hand dismissively. "Age means nothing. Why, my eldest sister, Abigail, back in Sussex, she were eight and forty years! Her youngest child was twelve years old, and she fell pregnant again. Remember, Sam?"

"Aye, I do. Poor Jacob, her husband, I thought he would fall dead from the surprise of it!"

"And did she deliver the child?" asked Maggie.

Alice nodded. "Aye, that she did. An easy labor, too, for I was there to help. A big, healthy boy, Daniel. He is twenty years old now, strong as an ox. And to think, she had thought her childbearing years long past."

"A woman's body is a wondrous thing," Thomas said, and he meant it.

Sam nodded vigorously, eyes wide. "Indeed, it is, and thank the Lord for a woman's body."

Alice playfully whacked Sam's shoulder. "Don't be getting rude, Husband."

"Me? Oh, never." He winked at Thomas.

"Do tell the story of how you both met," declared Maggie, who was overly fond of love stories, fairy tales, and legends of chivalric love.

Alice and Sam turned to each other. "Go on," Sam said, giving Alice a quick kiss on the forehead, "you tell the story."

Alice went on to tell the tale of how she was betrothed to another when Samuel had finally worked up the courage to ask for her hand.

"I was dumbstruck," laughed Alice. "Finally, I found some words. I said to him, 'I'm betrothed to another.' And he said, 'I know that, but that's nothing that can't be undone.' And I said, 'Why should I break my betrothal for you?' And he said, 'I'll make all of your dreams come true.'"

Thomas laughed heartily. What boastful confidence!

"Now, I had never had something so wild and romantic happen to me in all of my days, so I was quite impressed. I said to him, 'You'll make all of my dreams come true? Prove it!'"

Alice looked to Sam, who continued. "I got off my knees, and did the thing I had longed to do for years. I took her in my arms and kissed her full upon the mouth."

"I'd never been kissed like that. He decided my fate right there on the common."

"My, that must have been quite a kiss," Thomas said, impressed.

"Oh, aye," Sam said, nodding with pride.

"Does he still kiss you that way?" asked Maggie. Thomas laughed at her. She thrived on romance.

Alice nodded, and Samuel turned her face to his and placed his mouth over hers. Thomas was surprised by the open display of affection, for he'd not seen the likes of it since leaving London. When the two finished, they smiled at each other. Despite years, toil, children, the distance of an ocean, the love was still obvious.

"I love that story," said Maggie, and her eyes glimmered with happiness. "I am so happy that you shared it with me."

"Now we are friends, for certain," laughed Sam.

"Come now, Thomas, you quiet man," said Alice. "Tell us the tale of how you caught this hopeless romantic of a lass."

Thomas looked to the window, "'Tis a very late hour. I'm not sure we've enough time for me to tell the whole of it."

"Go on, then," encouraged Sam.

"Right, then. We both were on contract at the Winship farm, in Berkshire. I had entered into service when I was fourteen, and six years later, I was still there, learning the basics of joining from an elderly man who served at the farm. It was the finest manor in all of Berkshire, well tended and with a goodly master. People many miles away knew of it and many vied for work there."

"It's true," said Maggie. "Thomas came all the way from Bristol."

"So, in my sixth year of service on the manor, this young milkmaid comes into service, and she is immediately the talk of all the servants." He paused, smiling at Maggie as he remembered how her arrival at the Winship manor was as thunderous as a stampede of cattle. "She were this bold creature, looking like some lass come from the Mediterranean. And she had much to say. About everything. Her thoughts—her sentiments—were made plain to all. Isn't it nice to see that some things never change, no matter how much time passes?"

Maggie scrunched her nose and stuck her tongue out at him. That expression hadn't changed either.

"When I first saw her at the servants' supper table, I heard her speaking with another milkmaid about some boy or another, and she did not hide her disdain. I thought to myself, 'Upon my word, she's a beauty but she's got the Devil's tongue in her.'"

The table shared a good laugh over this.

"But I was not dissuaded. I was even more smitten. I had only known coy, reticent women, who never spoke unless spoken to, whose sentiments and inner thoughts were locked away from the world. But this Maggie Drinkwater, she was like a new creature I'd never seen before. And I loved her for it. But, unlike you, bold Sam," he said, nodding to him, "I was too quiet a lad to approach her. She never paid me any heed, so I assumed she had little interest for me. And there were plenty of lads brimming with self-confidence to try their hand at her. And lo, it was like watching men trying to wrestle a bull or tame a wild horse."

"Had you many suitors, Maggie?" asked Alice.

"A few, though many tried," she answered and it was true.

"So," Thomas continued, "the Midsummer celebration approached—"

He was interrupted by a chorus of cheers.

"Midsummer, how fitting," said Sam.

"It were the end of a long day's work, and I were scrubbing myself by the well. And this one, she—" He fell to laughter, remembering the moment. "She snuck up behind me like some ghost, and says loudly, 'You're not taking some lass to the Midsummer faire.' I about jumped out of my skin, she so startled me. And there I am, scared out of my wits, my hair, face and arms soaking wet. I turned to her and say, 'Lass, what is that to you?' And she says to me, 'You'll be taking *me* to the Midsummer faire, that's why.'"

"You did the asking, Maggie," said Sam.

"There were no asking. I *told* him he was taking me. I did not want to take the chance of him telling me he was taking another. I did not want to look the fool, of course."

"So you *did* have your eye on him, then," said Alice.

"Oh, indeed I did," Maggie replied, giving Thomas her sly grin. "How could I not? He was the tallest, strongest lad on the farm, and dark, like me, but with those green eyes. It was his eyes that took hold of me. And his quiet ways. You see, I had only known men who threw their weight and voices round as though they were kings, as though it were their divine right. Most think they know everything and speak like they do, when it is nothing but empty words. They know naught, most of them. And the louder they are, the less they know. The more they boast, the less they have. The more show they put on in front of lasses, the less show they've got for you under the bed linens."

Her bold talk could be infuriating. Sometimes Thomas felt embarrassment for her, but then, that was futile on his part, because what was the use in that if she were not embarrassed too? He feared she might have crossed a line with their new friends.

But Sam and Alice nodded, laughing. "Truer words never spoken," said Alice, to Thomas's surprise.

"I knew, from the time I was a small girl, that I did not want a man like that in my life. I never wanted to be under some boisterous, belligerent man's thumb." Maggie's mood had changed from jovial to indignant in the blink of an eye. "I wanted a man who had enough faith in his own worth, his strength, and his mind that he had no need to put on some absurd stage drama. I wanted a man who was confident enough in himself to handle the likes of me."

Thomas was proud of her, loved her—had always loved her—for her forthright words. He took hold of her hand and firmly pressed her slender yet strong fingers to his lips. "Oh, lass, to speak of yourself as though you are some burden . . ." He did not know how to finish his private thought whilst in the presence of others, so he let it end at that.

"Now, now," said Sam. "What happened on Midsummer?"

The hearth fire had dwindled and the hour was late. "Perhaps another evening we will share that story with you."

"And I shall cook for *you*," Maggie declared, and Thomas knew she eagerly looked forward to doing so, for when she truly liked a person, she wanted nothing more than to please their belly.

❧

Maggie and Thomas had reached the door of their home when they heard someone call out, "Goody Jones!"

A boy of perhaps ten came running down the road toward them. When he caught up to them, he bent over to catch his breath.

"What is it, lad?" Thomas asked.

He stood tall, still breathless. "Goody Jones, my da asked me to fetch you, as my mum's time has come."

"Who is your mum, dear?" Maggie asked, taking hold of his shoulders as she crouched down to look into his face in the darkness of the night.

"Goody Moore. Oh do come quickly. My father is in his cups and my mum is making an awful ruckus, and my little sister is frightened to crying now."

"Very well, I shall just get my tinctures and things. Thomas," she said, straightening as he opened the front door for her, "go back and tell Alice I may need her help." She took a step closer to him and said, low in his ear, "I suspect Goody Moore carries twins, and Mister Moore is a terrible drunkard, he is. I shall need help this night."

"Shall I go too?"

She shook her head as she hurriedly grabbed her basket and her apothecary's box. "Nay, he shall drink himself stupid soon enough I expect."

Thomas had an ill sense about a man who would fall drunk during his wife's travails. As Maggie hurried up the road with the boy, he went back to the Stratton house and knocked upon the door, which Alice answered.

"Maggie has asked for your help at the Moore house. It's Goody Moore's time."

"Oh, bless her, poor thing," she muttered as she removed her apron and collected some linens, placing them in a basket. She shouted to Sam, who was in the next room, that she was headed out. Thomas followed her to the door.

"Alice, if the husband becomes unruly, you be sure to send the boy to get me, yes?"

Alice smiled at him, resting her hand upon his shoulder reassuringly. "Fret not. I know well how to keep a drunkard in hand, Thomas."

The moon was so full and bright that night that it would have woke Thomas with its light fingering its way through the shutters. But he lay awake as it was, for he disliked having the bed to himself—it felt wrongly—and he still fretted over Maggie at the Moore house. He tried to reason with himself that Maggie could handle herself and woe to the man who met with her ire. He decided to think on something more pleasant, like the evening they had just spent with the Strattons. Thomas liked them very much, indeed. They were warm and made no pious pretense.

His mind wandered to the topic of earlier conversation, of how Maggie and he had met. The full moon was much like the moon on that Midsummer's eve.

The Winship manor sat to the west of Vale of White Horse. Each Midsummer, the lord of their manor took charge of leading the other neighboring lords in the hosting of a Midsummer scourging celebration. Their lord liked to boast that Vale of the White Horse had belonged to his family for centuries, as far back as to the time when Saint George slayed the mighty dragon upon the chalk-topped hill they called Dragon Hill.

And so all of the men from the four manors would climb up the downy green slope at sunrise, startling the grazing sheep, and they would commence scouring clean the massive hill carving of the white horse. It was hard labor, but they did not mind, for they took pride in the work, which they reckoned had been done since the ancient times. They sang songs as they toiled through the day and were rewarded with cups of ale and praise from the women who came and went as they cleared the grass and moss from the surface, then scratched and scrubbed with rakes and chisels at the chalk beneath until it gleamed pure white. Thomas could still taste the chalk dust upon his lips—sharp and made milky by his sweat. He could still feel the dry powder of it upon his fingers and palms, the knees of his breeches. He did not mind it; he had worn it with pride as he had the black ash of Ash Wednesday.

And when the sun set that evening, it was a beautiful sight, all orange and red like some rare gem, kissing everything beneath it a golden hue, seeming to imbue the ancient white horse—or dragon, he thought more like—with life.

Down the horse's nose and forelegs the men slid, and then hurriedly made their way to the hill, where the old Roman castle remains could still be seen. And a great feast was brought forth by the women, generously provided by the lords of the manors. They ate and drank their fill beneath the orange-and-red dusk, thankful not to be hungry, to be alive and thriving on that, the longest day of the year. Before the sun had completely descended, the full moon had come up, and it were a magical sight to behold, a fiery red orb. There were two gems in the sky at once, and Thomas marveled at the wonder of it, and he knew then why the ancient men who had carved that white horse up yonder had worshipped the sun, the moon, the earth, and the horse that grazed upon it.

He looked round to see if anyone else was as awestruck as he, and lo, there was Maggie Drinkwater, watching him like a cat watches the guileless bird. And he was glad of it. He pulled her close, delighting at the cinch of her waist and the fullness of her hip beneath his hand. He wanted no other, had not wanted any other from that moment. And he wanted nothing more than her, all of her, and nothing more.

"Beautiful," he whispered into her ear as he grabbed tighter hold of her waist.

"It is," she replied, then wrapped her arms round his waist, laying her head against his chest. And she said nothing more, though he thought for certain she would, as she always had something clever to say.

Everyone else made their way—stumbling, running, rolling—down the castle hill to the green manger between the hills, where bonfires had been lit, minstrels played melodies, and dancing commenced. But Thomas did not want that moment to end. He held her tight against him, his eyes upon the moon as it rose higher and higher, turning from red to orange to gold, then to silvery white. The feel of her body against his was like a wish granted, and he would see how far the granting went.

He took her by the hand and led her back up the hill, to the white horse. He could hear the laughter and murmurs of two lovers who had come to rest in the distance, at the tip of the horse's tail. Thomas followed the line of the horse's head, to where the neck curved to the back, and roughly pulled her down with him to the white chalk surface before she might demure and play some game of run and seek. She did not resist. If she had, the magic would have been ruined, and he would have followed the music to the festival and the drink. But he was in luck.

She kissed him before he could kiss her. Her boldness set a flame in his belly. "Wild," he breathed.

She laughed. "Thomas Jones, I want you to want no other but me. I shall make you forget any other lass."

*"Ná labhair a thuilleadh. Bí ciúin, a bhean." Don't talk anymore. Be quiet, woman.* She charmed from him the Irish he had not spoken since he was a boy.

"Say something more," she said, intrigued.

*"Créatúr fiáin." Wild creature.* Thomas slid his lips over her earlobe and licked. He wanted to devour her. She smelled of bonfire, grass, and something sweet. She dug her fingers into his shoulders and a moan escaped her lips. *"Cat álainn." Beautiful cat.* With his fingers, he tipped her head back so that he might kiss the whole of her throat.

*"Capall galánta."* *Graceful horse.* Her breath came quick as her eyes looked to the moon. His hands traveled over her body. *"Déanfaidh mé thú a chomhlánú." I will make you complete.*

Thomas was slow, deliberately slow so that she could make him stop if she chose to make him stop. But she did not want him to stop. She lay down upon the curve of the great horse's neck and helped him lift her skirts.

*"Tá grá agam duit, tá grá agam duit,"* he said, bracing himself over her.

"I love you," she said, as though she knew the meaning of his words.

In a fever he became one with her and she cried out. He had done this before and none had cried out in such a way. He stopped moving, cradling her. *"Ná bí ag caoineadh." Do not cry.*

She clung to him as though he were all she had in the world. It was then he realized, perhaps no other had been here before. He gasped with the sudden knowledge, as though he'd been shown a treasure. But then he felt her body quivering, like a cornered rabbit. She were afraid, and not because it was her first time. Thomas was no fool. He had calmed beaten dogs and horses in the past and had brought them back, back to where they could trust a man again. And there were no sight more heartening than the gaze and devotion of a creature who had realized there was something of kindness in the world. Nay, he were not a fool. He sensed it, in the way she'd become deadly silent, in the look of her wide, wet eyes like dark, endless wells. Maggie had been used ill. And now Maggie was even more of a treasure to him, for he would show her what it was to be gently and steadfastly loved. He would renew her faith in man. It was every ounce of his will that kept him from wild abandon. Finally he moaned, "Oh, my sweet," and moved farther within her depths, and she moved with him. Such pleasure! Ecstatic, he was more alive than he had ever been. And when he met his end, he opened his eyes and the world was more beautiful than it had been before.

*"Bí i mo bhean chéile.* Maggie, be my wife." Thomas did not ask, but told. He lay down beside her and crushed her against him. He was breathless, reborn. "Let me be your *Rí,* your king." It was nonsense to speak in so dramatic a fashion, but he wanted it. She made him feel like

a king. He wanted to be her king, he wanted to rule over her and give her a kingdom, give her everything he could possibly give her. She had his life in her fist, which grasped the linen of his shirt over his chest. She kissed his heart, aye, his heart, for he felt her lips through his skin and upon the beating vessel within him.

"I will be your wife, if you will be my husband." She kissed the down of hair upon his chest. He felt her breath upon his skin. "I will be your queen."

*"Banríon."* Queen.

They kissed into the night. He stroked her thighs, nestled her neck, muttered all the sweetest Irish words he knew in the softest, lowest voice, like when he would calm a startled mare in the stables. He would bring her back, he would show her how this was the truest love and not a violent act. He would show her beauty, her own beauty, see that she would come to embrace it and celebrate it, not fear it. He coaxed her atop him, showed her how it was done, and, as he knew she would, she found her own pleasure and oh, it were as though he died a thousand times and were brought back to life over and over. It was some magic, some force. Could it have been the ancient magic of the Vale? Or was it the magic of two hearts finding destiny?

They slept upon the white horse's mane and woke with the hazy dawn, as dewy as the chalk and grass. He helped her to her feet, seeing how her hair had come free of its braid. What a wild mane! All dark and curly, unruly and lush. His heart beat faster at the sight of such beauty. He thought he might cry with happiness, and so he busied himself with dusting the chalk from her skirts so that he could gain control of himself.

For one so given to talk, she was very quiet.

He took her hands in his, looking down into her dark-blue eyes.

"You make me happy," she said, then burrowed her face against his chest.

"Come now," he said, feeling like the king of the Vale. "Let's head back, tell the master of our news."

The sun was rising when she returned home. Thomas woke to the sound of water trickling in the wash bucket, the wet cloth sliding over her arms.

"How did it go?"

"Twins, just as I thought. One boy and one girl, both healthy but small. I gave her hops tea to help bring the milk on quickly. Poor woman with two newborns and two older children to care for and a husband about as useful as a stone in her shoe."

"Did he give much trouble?"

"Not after I dosed him with poppy."

"Be careful, lass." He laughed, shaking his head.

She was in her chemise, drying herself as she turned toward their bed. She smiled at him. She often smiled when he laughed. "Be careful of what?"

"Be careful with the poppy tincture."

She tisked. "Oh, aye, who do you take me for? I'm no fool." She tipped her head to the side. "Really, Thomas."

He reached a lazy arm toward her and beckoned. "Come here," he said, rubbing the sleep from his eyes with his other hand.

"I am so tired," she whimpered.

"I'll make you feel better."

She shook her head and laughed. "You are always the same. Do you ever grow tired of me, after all these years?"

He took her hand and pulled her toward the bed. "I know you feel what I feel."

"So modest, my husband."

"Truth."

"Aye, truth." She ran her hands over his chest, pressing her lips to his heart.

"*Banríon*, always."

# CHAPTER FIVE

*December 29, 1646*

*I am now about six months with child. I dream of a girl.
I shall name her Elizabeth, after the great and powerful
Queen, for I feel her strength within me. She dances in my
belly for hours each day.*

There were no Yule or Christmas celebrations permitted in Massachusetts. The overlords did not allow such pagan, Papist festivities, though Thomas didn't see how they could prevent what went on within the privacy of a man's home.

And there was much to celebrate in their home. Maggie was very round with child and more radiant and beautiful than ever. Thomas admired the new, full curve of her body, helped her spread the wool fat spiked with sandalwood oil over her belly, to prevent the stretch scars, she said, though he thought more than anything it were soothing to her, his touch and the warm scent of precious sandalwood from the Orient. Her breasts, always generous, had swollen to round orbs. Her hair, always so wild and unruly, had grown even more so, and the skin of her cheeks was kissed rosy. What a beautiful mother-to-be.

But Maggie was also even more of a force than she was before. If she disagreed with him, her temper would flare inordinately. There were many broken bowls and cups that could lay testament to this. Not only did her temper become magnified but also her tears, her moments of sadness, of fear, of worry for the baby inside her. "I've not felt her move since this morning," she would fret, and always she referred to the babe as a girl. Thomas did not question this, nor did he mind. He was happy to have either a boy or a girl, so long as the child be healthy and survive. He was happy that, after all these years of marriage, his wife was rounder with child than she had ever been before. He prayed, prayed that they finally be blessed with a child come into the world. Maggie's worry was usually all for naught, for she would later be unable to sleep, the child within her dancing and kicking into the wee hours of dawn.

Maggie's intuition, about others, their illnesses, their troubles, be they physical or of the mind, became a thing of wonder. Folk would come calling on her for tinctures, poultices, mithridates, and she would know, before they spoke, what it was they needed. She knew with nothing more than a quick glance at them or the sound of worry within their words. It was unnerving at times, and when Thomas happened to be round when a customer would come calling, he would see the surprise and perhaps fear in their wide eyes when Maggie would say, "Goody Proctor, I know, you require fennel seed and parsley root to help your father pass water." Or "Goody Alcott, I know you desire more than just clary sage for your son's cough. You've not slept of late, I sense this. 'Tis the women's change. You need a tea of Damask rose and valerian root."

Oftentimes she would offend when she offered up her insights. Thomas happened to be at the house, washing some sawdust from his eyes, when he overheard Goodman Mason bellow out, "How dare you, Goody Jones, pretend to know what might ail my wife? Why, she is perfectly fine, and *content*." With the stress upon the last word, Thomas knew that Maggie's intuitive mind was at work and her mouth was speaking before she might consider her words.

"I mean no disrespect or offense, Goodman Mason, I only have a sense of things and believe your wife might find this of use, and therefore you shall, as well."

"For such impertinence, you shall give me a sample of the oil for free."

"Oh aye, I shall. For you shall find that I know of which I speak and you shall come back for more." Maggie produced a small blue glass vial and then counted ten drops into it from the glass pipette of a larger bottle. She stopped it with cork, then presented the bottle to the man. "A sample, of oil of sandalwood. Spread three drops below your wife's *umbilicus* and you shall see what transpires."

Thomas entered the main room of the house, which served as Maggie's apothecary shop during the day, just in time to see Goodman Mason snatch the glass vial out of Maggie's hand, muttering something unintelligible, before storming out the door.

"Woman, what on earth have you done now to offend?"

"Before that poor man set foot inside the door, I sensed his frustration. And I see Goody Mason, so pinched in her face, like a hungry mouse." She paused for demonstration, sucking in her cheeks and making her lips small, squinting her eyes. "Those two need to resume their wifely and husbandly duties."

Thomas stared at her. "You must mind your tongue." Pregnancy was perhaps addling her brain to madness.

"Why, Thomas?" She slammed down a box of herbs upon the table. "I am glad I spoke because did he *not* take the vial? If such were not the case, he would have spit on the floor and been off without a word."

She glared at him, hands upon her hips. Her wild hair was spilling free of her cap and bun, but she cared not a fig. Thomas thought her both slightly mad and beautiful. And this angered him, that even when she was being absurd, he still found her fetching. It was his weakness, and he tried his best to fight it.

"Woman, are you mad? You can't simply go round giving out intimate advice to those you think might benefit from it, whether it be true or not. And a *man*, no less! Do you want him to think you some base, cunning trollop?"

Her eyes narrowed. "*What* did you just call me?"

"You must stop and think for a moment—something that has never come naturally to you, I know."

"Don't you *dare* talk to me that way! I'm sorry that I'm not as perfect as you, Thomas. I'm sorry I don't stand about, silently considering every word that comes to my mouth before I utter it, letting others think I might be dumb or stupid whilst they wait in my silence!"

He threw the linen cloth he'd been using to wipe his eyes down upon the table. "What are you saying, Maggie? Are you trying to say that people think me stupid?" The realization of her meaning was like a hot poker jabbed into his belly. It hurt and it burned. And he was angry for it. "This is a revelation to me. Why did you never say this before? Why does this just come out now? You've never been one to hide anything from me, that's for certain. Lord knows you could talk me to death if you so wished!"

"Shut your mouth!" She turned and made her way toward the bed chamber. "I'm tired."

He went to her and grabbed tight hold of her arm. "Nay, lass, you can't say such a hurtful thing and then plead your belly. I'll not stand for that. You tell me now what you mean with your words. Are you saying I look dumb to others?"

She glared at his hand upon her arm, then looked at him, and he swore she looked as though she might spit fire. But then her face crumpled as she looked down at the floor. "The Devil got hold of my tongue."

"Likely excuse," Thomas said, letting go of her arm. "Blame the Devil rather than your own self." He'd had enough. If he lingered, he would lose his temper with her, and he was better than that. He would not be that man, the kind of man that both Maggie and he despised. "I'll be in the workshop."

She took hold of his hand, then lay her head upon his chest and wept. "You are right. You are always right. I don't know what's wrong with me. I don't know why I don't think before I speak. It is like some wild force speaks through me sometimes, before I have a chance to consider. It is my weakness. I hate myself and my mouth."

There were moments in their years of marriage when Maggie would admit her shortcomings, her wrongdoing. It happened seldom, but when it did, it were like a deluge, like she had been holding back the rain clouds of doubt and self-loathing inside herself until finally the clouds broke and there was no holding the rain back. And there was no need for it, such self-deprecation. And who was he to criticize her for having the spirit for which he loved her, the spirit of which he needed more?

"No tears, lass. *Gan deora, a chailín.*" He kissed the top of her cap.

"I am sorry, Thomas. Please do not be cross with me. I love you more than anything in the world. Please, please, don't be cross with me." And she broke into fresh sobs, dampening his shirt.

"I am not cross, *Banríon*. But you must be careful. You must think before you speak, before you upset others. Do not give them cause to dislike you. Be mindful that you don't get yourself into a pot of trouble as you did in London, yes?"

She sniffed. "Yes, I will try."

That Sunday, as Thomas and Maggie exited the Meeting House with the rest of the townspeople, someone called to Maggie.

"Goody Jones, do wait up!"

They turned round to see Goody Mason quickly approaching, holding tight to her shawl on the blustery day. Goodman Mason followed behind his wife, holding on to his hat. Goody Mason reached Maggie and laid her gloved hand upon her arm, squeezing. "Thank you," she whispered, then flashed a big, long-toothed grin Thomas never had thought she possessed. She giggled as she sauntered away, clasping tight hold of her husband's arm. He looked over his wife's capped head, and tipped his hat to Maggie, and lo and behold, he gave her a wink.

Maggie and Thomas walked in silence for a moment, both surprised by the very public display of rather giddy gratitude.

"I told you," said Maggie. "I'm always right."

"Well now, it would seem you've done a very good deed," Thomas said.

Soon Maggie was called upon by many in Charlestown as well as Boston, Cambridge, and Dorchester. They called her a "healer," though Sam told Thomas that he overheard some in the public house call her a "cunning woman." This unsettled Thomas, because "cunning woman" was one step shy of "witch," and "witch" was most certainly a name to fear. There was nothing but bad luck that followed that word, whether it be back in Old England or New. He, like most others, had heard about the Lancaster witches some years before. Why, just in these last couple of years, there had been word of the witch trials over in East Anglia. These Puritans who had established the Massachusetts Colony, they had brought their fervor with them from the old country. Thomas had heard the stories in the pub, of the two women, Hutchinson and Dyer, who had been banished from Massachusetts for heresy, as "instruments of the Devil," who had given birth to "monstrous creatures." He gave little credence to that last bit of the story, but Thomas knew this: When a woman caused too much trouble or spoke too plainly, it seemed, there were those who would take umbrage and use piety as excuse and reason to take her in hand. He knew this firsthand, after Maggie had been accused of aiding in the murder of Lord Wembly, simply because she had given mad Lady Wembly a tincture of Saint John's Wort. A woman skilled in herbals and physic was always a woman both admired and feared.

Maggie fretted that she would lose her heightened intuition once the baby arrived. Thomas told her she often borrowed trouble. There's enough trouble in a day's work, he would say, without heaping on trouble that doesn't even exist. But her business flourished, and she had to send away to London for more supplies, hoping that they would arrive in eight weeks rather than sixteen, depending upon the whim of the Atlantic's currents and winds.

She began to waddle as her time approached, and Thomas found it endearing. There could be no doubt at that late hour, he would soon, finally, be a father. The idea was somewhat frightening—he had lived decades having to care only for himself and then his wife, but she was strong and required little from him. He knew that all that was familiar in his life—all that he had known—would be upheaved like a virgin meadow plowed fresh. It would be like working against the grain of the wood. But he assured himself that, though it would be difficult at first, eventually it would not, and with time, something beautiful would come from the effort.

Thomas worried more that he might lose his Maggie. He had never himself known a woman to die in childbed; his mother had survived fourteen birthings, and Maggie, in all her time at midwifery, had never lost a woman. But he knew the threat was real. His wife had tended many women in their time of need and had done so successfully. Who would tend to his wife in her time?

"Alice, of course. Go get Alice," Maggie said as she paced the floorboards of their bedchamber in her chemise, running her hands to and fro over her belly, swollen and as hard as marble. The wrinkle upon her forehead deepened like it had never done before.

"Who else?" Thomas asked, pausing in the doorway.

She braced the bedpost, teeth clenching as she breathed loudly through her nose, like a mad raccoon he had once spied at the edge of the woodland. He went to her, placing his hands upon her shoulders, his heart beating inside his throat. *I could lose her. No no no no no, don't think it.*

"It passes now," she sighed, but then gasped. Thomas heard the sound of water upon floorboards and looked down to see rivulets running over her bare feet.

"Thank the Lord," she said, a hint of relief in her smile. "The barrier has broken, it is most certainly my time now. Please, get Alice."

Thomas flew down the stairs and out the door. "Alice! Alice!" he yelled as he tripped over his own feet in his attempt to reach the Stratton house.

# CHAPTER SIX

*March 30, 1647*

*I have become a mother. Praise Be. The child is healthy.*

Memory clouds often in the most poignant moments. It is as though even Memory knows it must watch what momentous thing is transpiring and forgets to record the details. But then, like clouds parting after a fierce storm, the sun shines through and it seems more clear and vibrant than ever before. And so Thomas recalled how that day was the first springlike day of the year, the air fragrant with sweet, damp earth coming back to life. The taste of rum and bile upon his tongue, his stomach tying itself into knots in his fear. He heard his boots shuffling upon the floor beneath the table each time his wife cried out in pain, and the cry, so angry, like a warrior who would stare down death.

And she did.

She labored for ten hours. The child was stubborn to come into the world, perhaps preferring the warmth of her mother's womb. In the end, Thomas was gripped by a fear so fierce, he was undone to tears, for the bedchamber had gone quiet. He pulled at his hair. "For the love of God, Alice! Let me in!" He banged upon the bedchamber door like a madman, like a boy seeking his mother. And still he could taste the linseed oil and maple wood of the bedchamber door as he pressed his face against it. He could have opened the door, he could have, but he would not, for the fear had paralyzed his hand, like a dead, unmoving weight upon the latch.

And then the sound, so perfect, so beautiful, he was not sure at first if it were contrived by his mind. He stopped breathing, waiting for the sound. There it was again, and stronger, and never did a bird sing sweeter, never did a melody move him like that one sound, the plaintive cry of a bewildered newborn, followed by the sound of his wife, exclaiming, "Oh! Oh!" over and over. He exhaled, the fear rushing out of him like a bucket of water turned over, and opened the door.

When a child is birthed, a man is as useful as a newborn foal to a cart. Thomas was a bumbling idiot in a room of women who knew more than he could ever begin to know, no matter if he had read all the books contained in the colleges of both Oxford and Cambridge combined. Like a confused child he went to the bedside and stared down at Maggie, who was drenched in sweat, her hair a mass of tangled black vines surrounding her face, flushed, her lips, cracked and bleeding. She was his wife, his Maggie, and something even more now.

She looked up at him, smiling with her eyes because she was too tired to do so with her mouth. He bent over her and kissed her forehead. "I love you."

"Please, I want to hold her," she pleaded.

Alice and her daughter-in-law Sarah were busy wiping down the babe and swaddling it. The babe howled, not wanting to be restrained in the blanket.

"Please!" Maggie begged, her voice surprisingly loud and shrill.

"Give her the child!" Thomas shouted, wanting nothing more than to end her longing.

Swiftly Alice came to Maggie, passing the bundled babe into her arms.

"Oh," Maggie said through her tears. "Welcome, little one."

And Thomas watched as his daughter turned her swollen, newly opened blue eyes and looked directly into her mother's face. Life is a wondrous thing, beyond the compass of mere words. At that moment,

Thomas was nothing and the tiny creature was everything, the sun, the moon, the whole sky, the heart beating wildly within his chest.

"Oh, she looks at you as though she knows you," he said, marveling.

"Aye, she knows me well. She has danced a ceaseless jig against my right rib for months now."

Alice waited beside the bed, wringing her hands as though she were uncomfortable to have to interrupt the moment. "Maggie, we ought to finish our work here."

As though she were woken from a dream, Maggie replied, "Yes, you're right." She kissed the babe upon its forehead. "Thomas, please, hold the babe for now, until I am done here. There is the afterbirth—"

"Right." If he heard any more detail of the women's work, he knew he would be overwhelmed. Gently and tenuously, he took the babe from her arms, amazed at how light she was.

Before Thomas exited the room, he saw Alice and Sarah lift Maggie's legs and swing them over the side of the bed. "The chair, I'll hold tight to the back of it," Maggie said in a voice hoarse with effort.

Thomas carried the child, cradled in his arms, over to the window so that he might see her better. Swollen nosed, she now slept, her tiny red-bow lips turning down at the corners, as though the world, so soon, did not meet with her lofty standards. *Proud like her mother.* With one hand Thomas peeked beneath the blanket to see the top of her head, which was covered in thick black hair, like both her parents. He could not help but kiss her forehead, for he was filled with a longing—an urge—to do so. As he kissed, he placed his hand beneath her head and gasped—he had not noticed how elongated the tiny head was, like a cone. His heart constricted—would the child live with such a defect?

The bedchamber door opened and Alice stood in the doorway. "You can come back in, Thomas."

Quickly he made his way to her. "Alice, speak truthfully. Will the child live?"

Her smile faded. "Thomas, only the Lord can answer that question. Certainly not I."

"But the child's head! Surely you noticed?"

She approached him and the bundle in his arms, looking down at the babe, placing her hand upon her head. She then giggled. "Oh Thomas, you've not spent much time round newborns, have you? Their heads are malleable, so that they can be passed through the womb. Her head will not stay this shape, you fool." She laughed again. "It will be perfectly round in just a few days, you wait and see."

Relief flooded him. "Oh thank the Lord," he said, then laughed at his own stupidity.

"Go to her, now," Alice said, putting her arm round his back and guiding him into the bedchamber.

Maggie was in bed again, eyes closed, but when she heard Thomas's boots upon the floor, she looked to him, her eyes wide, bewildered and sagacious all at once. The afternoon sunlight came through the diamond-paned glass of the window, caressing his wife with its glow.

"She is an afternoon baby," she said in a hoarse voice, as though she read his thoughts. "Surely she will be blessed with Leo in ascendance in her sky."

Thomas stood beside the bed, holding their child.

"Please," she beckoned, holding her arms out to take the babe.

He passed her the child as he might a fine glass figurine.

"My love," she cooed, touching her fingertip to the babe's perfect lips. The child instantly sucked. Thomas watched, amazed by every tiny action.

Maggie untied the laces of her chemise and brought the child to her breast, and the child knew what to do.

"Should it hurt?" she asked Alice.

Alice approached and studied the newborn as she suckled. "No, let me show you." She put a finger between Maggie's breast and the baby's mouth. Then, placing one hand behind the child's head, she took Maggie's breast in her other and repositioned the baby upon it. Thomas felt as though he watched something very intimate and beyond himself. Once again, he felt like a useless ornament—superfluous.

"That's better, now, isn't it?" asked Alice.

"Aye, it is," said Maggie, staring down at her daughter.

"It takes getting used to. It's not as easy as some might let on. But the girls are much better at latching than the boys."

"Ah, the girls are more clever, right from the start," said Maggie, smiling.

Both looked at Thomas at the same time, smiling as though they pitied him. But he did not mind. Knowing at what his wife had labored for the past day, he would not protest. Instead, he sat himself down beside her, putting his arm gently over her shoulders.

"What shall we name her?" he asked.

"Elizabeth," replied Maggie.

"Very well. Elizabeth Jones, our daughter." He kissed Maggie's damp cheek. He took gentle hold of the babe's tiny foot, poking out from the blanket. *"Taisce."*

"What does that mean, my Irishman?"

"Treasure."

# CHAPTER SEVEN

*May 17, 1647*

*I get little sleep. Elizabeth is always hungry, but I am glad. She thrives! My milk flows plenty, for I have taken a tea of hops and fennel seed. And now parsley grows in the garden, for April was warm, thank the Lord. Parsley makes for good milk.*

*Thomas has been so kind, bringing me tea, ale, and water during the night so that I never thirst. He is so patient, more so than I, for there are moments when I weep in my exhaustion and wonder when I will ever get sleep. There are moments when, just as I begin to sleep, she wakes, demanding milk, and I want to tell her to look elsewhere. But Thomas tells me not to fret, this trying time shall pass, and our beautiful, plump babe is proof of my mother's love. I want to believe him, but I am so very tired. My babe deserves a better mother than I.*

"Thomas, I am a terrible mother," Maggie muttered before covering her face with her hands, weeping profusely. "She is never satisfied! I cannot satisfy her hunger!"

"You talk nonsense," Thomas said, cradling Elizabeth in his arms. "Look at all these plump rolls upon her arms and thighs. She is plenty satisfied. She just grows." He put his little finger in her mouth and she sucked mightily upon it. To think, Maggie must endure this on her breasts for hours, the poor lass. "You are exhausted, that is why you speak so."

"Yes, it is because I get little sleep. Yes, you must be right. I am just not myself."

He watched as Maggie washed herself at the basin, running the wet cloth over her neck and shoulders and under her arms. It had been almost seven weeks since Elizabeth, or Bess, as they had begun calling her, had come into their lives. Maggie's body had already slimmed. She was almost back to her size before becoming a mother, and he found this remarkable. But her breasts, which had always been full, were even more so now. She was a sight to behold, and he desired her more than ever. It had been months since he had been inside her. He was like a man starved, and she were like a roasted haunch of venison. He could have sunk his teeth into her, she looked so delectable to him.

"I want you so badly, *Banríon*."

She stopped in her washing and looked at him over her shoulder. "Do you, truly?"

"Good God in Heaven, Maggie. I long to be inside you."

She giggled, and there was the Maggie he knew and loved.

"Oh, say yes." He rose from the chair, Bess in his arms, still sucking upon his finger. "I'll bring Bess to Alice, just for an hour—"

Maggie's smile faded, her eyes wide with anxiety.

"A half hour. Not even. Ten minutes, ten minutes and I will be the happiest man you ever saw."

She laughed heartily at this, and oh, it made his heart glad to hear her laugh so once again. She turned to face him, her hands over her lower body, where the skin of her belly was loose from having held a child within.

"You think I don't find you beautiful any longer? You are *more* beautiful to me." He came closer to her. "'Tis true, lass."

She gestured with a tip of her chin to the Moses basket upon the table. "Go on then. If ten minutes is all that you need, then Bess will be fine in the basket."

Never did a man move faster. "Aye, well, maybe fifteen minutes, for your sake." Thomas gingerly placed Bess in the basket, replacing his finger with her thumb. *Why have I not thought to do that sooner?*

When they were abed, he brought her to satisfaction quickly with his tongue, and God above, she tasted sweeter than ever. And when they were one, she clung to him as she had the first time, many years before, upon the white horse. After he came, he was so happy he almost cried, for he was home once more.

"Do I still please you?" she asked.

"What do you think? Were you not just with me a moment ago? I could have sworn it were you beneath me."

She slapped his shoulder and laughed.

"The better question, do I still please you?"

"What do you think?" Her fingers worked at his chest hair again in that manner he loved so dearly. She looked up at him, fluttering her thick black lashes.

"I know it," he said. And he did. Her body could say more than her words.

She gave him a knowing smile.

"Look at me like that, and I'll be ready to take you again."

"You've worn me out enough for a day."

Just then, as though she understood their words, Bess broke into howls.

"Her Majesty beckons," Thomas said, rising from the bed and donning his breeches. "Stay there." He picked up Bess, cooing in her ear as he brought her to her mother's arms. *"Mo thaisce."* *My treasure.*

Bess would have none of his sweet talk. She did not stop her howling until she attached herself to Maggie.

Whilst Maggie nursed Bess, Thomas dressed himself. As he bent over to put on his boots, he could smell Maggie's scent upon him and it was enough to quicken his blood again. But he quelled it, thinking of the work that needed done in the workshop. There was more business than he could handle, and he'd had to turn some away—the sort of problem of which many a London craftsman dreamed.

"Have you had your fill, my love?" Maggie asked Bess as she began to burp her upon her lap. Bess answered with a hearty belch, and Thomas and Maggie both laughed in delight. Bess turned her head to look at her mother and she smiled a big, toothless grin—her very first. "Oh!" Maggie exclaimed, as though she had received a divine revelation.

"And you think yourself a poorly mother," Thomas said, shaking his head. "Then you do not see what I see each day."

Maggie broke into tears.

He went to her. "What's wrong now, woman?"

"She smiles at me!" she said through her sobs. "How beautiful!"

He rolled his eyes. What a tempest was his wife. But he kissed her atop her head. "I must be off to the workshop."

It felt good to be alive, to work at the wood, to break into a sweat, to create something from nothing, to think of his wife holding their child. He whistled a melody as he sanded an oak board.

"What song might that be?"

He leapt at the sound of the voice, quickly turning round, startled out of his wits. And there stood the Widow Hallett, no longer in mourning attire, but in somber gray. Her hands were upon her hips and she took full appraisal of him from his boots to the top of his head.

He cleared his throat, surprised by such boldness. He was tempted to ask the brazen thing if she liked what she saw. "I did not see you come in, Goody Hallett."

She bit her lip, swaying to and fro upon her heel like a country lass at a dance. "I just followed the sound of your whistling."

He wiped his brow with a cloth. "How can I be of service?"

"I've something else I'd like you to make for my house." She made her way toward him with slow steps.

He was wary of this woman, like a man ought to be wary of a dog he did not know. He had even hired two day laborers to deliver her completed wardrobe, just so he might avoid her.

"And what might that be?" he asked, looking down into her gray eyes.

She fluttered her lashes, the artful lass. "I would like a bed. One larger than the one I have now."

He nodded. "I'll not be able to start on that for about a month's time."

"Why not?" She looked cross, as though he had greatly inconvenienced her.

"Well, the reason being that I've many requests. My workshop flourishes. And I'm trying to catch up on the work I missed some weeks back."

She put her fingers to her lips in surprise. "Pray, Mister Jones, you were not ill, were you?"

He found her feigned concern ridiculous. He busied himself with sorting his chisels in order of size. "Nay, Widow Hallett, I am in sound health, better than I've ever been. I am newly become a father."

She put her hands upon her hips, and a knowing smile spread over her lips. "Ah, yes, how could I have forgotten. Blessings upon you and your wife, the cunning woman."

He stopped what he was doing, caught by her words. "What did you call my wife?"

His eyes bored into hers and he saw her lashes flutter, her skin go flush. He had caught her in her bold pretense.

"Why, I mean no harm in saying—that is . . ."

"Widow Hallett, my goodwife Margaret is a healer, apothecary, and midwife. And she has yet to lose one woman to childbirth. She is skilled at her work, and she is no purveyor of potions and magic. I'll not have you thinking otherwise."

"You are fond of her."

*Daft cow!* "As sure as day will turn to night, Widow Hallett. Now, if you'll simply tell me what size bed you require, and what wood you favor, then I'll carry on with my work here in peace."

She bit her lip and looked down at the wood shavings upon the shop floor. He had spoken very harshly, and he did not regret it. After making suggestions of wood so that he might be rid of her, she gave him the desired dimensions for the bed—one so large that he had not made the likes of since leaving London.

"My word, are you certain?"

"Indeed, Mister Jones."

"Are you to be married again?"

She laughed, the music of it contrived. "Perhaps. We shall see if the man can be convinced."

He shook his head at such an absurd notion. "If a man needs convincing, he is not worth the trouble."

"Well," she said, fingering the weave of her shawl, "if only all men were as forthright and sure-footed as you are, Mister Jones."

Still she lingered and he wanted her gone. He did not like the way her eyes gazed at him as though he were some confection made for her relish only. "Very well, Widow Hallett. I've work to do. Good day to you." He turned his back to her and resumed his original task.

"Good day, Mister Jones," she said in a singsong voice, and he heard her footsteps fade out of the workshop.

Lord forgive him, he thought, but that woman needed to be mightily fucked. And if the Lord were just, He would find her a husband as young as she.

# CHAPTER EIGHT

*July 14, 1647*

*I worry. The pretty Widow Hallett come by, asking for water of rose geranium for her skin. She complains that she suffers from blemishes, but her skin is the envy of the parish, and the vain thing must know this.*

*Before she left, she went to Bess and touched her cheek, calling her a sweet poppet. Ever since Bess has been ill tempered. I shall not take chances. I made a sachet from a scrap of silk, filled it with dried Rue, which is an herb of the sign Leo, Bess's ascendant sign. I tied it with a cord and put it round Bess's waist so that she cannot put it into her mouth. My grandmum swore that Rue would protect against the Evil Eye. And I do like my grandmum, taking Sage-infused oil and rubbing over Bess's forehead, and I recite the old chant. Lord let this keep my sweet Bess safe from harm.*

"What are you doing with Bess?" Thomas asked, sitting down to supper.

Maggie was muttering something over the child in her Moses basket as she moved her fingers upon her head. She then paused, dipping her fingers in a small dish of oil. The mildly green, musky smell filled the air. She resumed, dancing her fingers over Bess's now glistening forehead as she muttered some sort of prayer. Bess cooed, obviously enjoying the soothing touch and warm oil upon her forehead.

Occasionally Thomas had seen Maggie dabble at superstitious things, such as the hanging of certain herbs to ward off bad and welcome good. But he had never seen anything like this, and he found it ridiculous.

"What on earth do you play at?"

She wiped her fingers upon her apron, then busied herself with dishing out the suppertime stew. "I worry that someone has cast the Evil Eye upon our Bess."

Thomas mulled over her words. "Why do you think this? Why would someone want to harm Bess?" It made no sense.

"She has fussed now for two days, as you know."

"Aye. Perhaps she cuts a tooth?"

"She has fussed since Widow Hallett touched her cheek two days ago."

He had not known Widow Hallett had visited Maggie. "Why was the widow here?"

"She wanted some water of rose geranium. For her face."

"I don't see why she would want to harm Bess. That's a ridiculous notion and you know it, Maggie."

Maggie quickly turned from the washing to face him. "Don't be calling me ridiculous, Thomas! I'll not stand for it!"

Misfortune, to wake the beast of Maggie's temper. He put his hand upon her arm. "Come now, please. Sit and talk with me, *Banríon*. Why do you think such thoughts?"

She considered for a moment, then acquiesced, seating herself. "I do not like the widow. I sense much malice in her."

"I think you give her more import than she deserves. She's nothing but a silly thing who ought to be married soon. She needs a man's presence."

"Really." Maggie raised her brows, scrutinizing him. "She 'needs a man's presence,' does she?"

He should have kept the thought to himself. Maggie was a shrewd thing. "I mean that if she is not married soon, she is the sort that will find herself in a heap of trouble."

"How so?"

"Trust me, Maggie. The lass is in need of a good fucking."

Maggie burst into laughter. "And I suppose you think yourself the one who should be giving it?"

Thomas shook his head as he stirred his stew. "Daft woman, who do you take me for? You know I want none other but you. Don't talk nonsense."

"But it's true," she said, her voice softening. "You could give it to her if you wished to, and you know it. I have seen how the pretty thing looks at you, eyes like a doe in heat."

He grunted, shoveling his meal into his mouth. He was not sure what she was playing at. Could she be jealous? It was not becoming, and he would not give credence to it.

"Do you ever think about it," she asked, playfully fingering the rolled cuff of his linen shirt, "what you could do to the widow if you so desired?"

For a brief instant, Thomas pictured again what he had pictured in his mind before, the young, petite widow in his arms, her legs wrapped round his waist, and him rutting her against the wall at the top of her stairway. He could feel her panting against his neck, her breath coming quicker and quicker as he brought her to a place she'd never been before. He took a long swig from his tankard of ale and slammed it down, trying to rid himself of the treacherous thought.

Maggie studied Thomas as she leaned back in her chair. Her fingers drummed upon the table. "Aye, I see it. I see it in the way your eyes go black. I know you well. In your thoughts you feel her breath upon you—"

He shot up from his chair, knocking it over. "What is the meaning of this, woman?" It unnerved him that she knew his mind as well as her own.

Bess, startled, began to howl. Before she could go to her Thomas grabbed tight hold of Maggie's wrist. She looked up at him with scared eyes.

"What's gotten into you, woman? Why do you so desire to torment me? How have I been cruel to you?"

She did not reply, but only hardened her jaw as she returned his probing gaze.

"I asked you, Maggie, have I ever been cruel to you? Have I ever been untrue to you?"

She shook her head. "Nay, you've never been cruel to me."

He let go of her wrist. "And I have never been untrue to you."

"Aye, I know," she said, lifting Bess from the basket. She untied her bodice and brought the babe to her breast. "But maybe you think about it, with such a pretty thing making eyes at you."

Thomas sat down again. "Maggie, I've never lied to you, and I won't begin to do so now. Aye, I've thought about it. I'm but a man, after all. And I know you have thought of it with others too. I remember, back in London, that Irish harpist who came to you for the tincture to help keep him awake so that he might play for Charles's court until the wee hours of the morning."

Maggie did not respond, but busied herself with examining Bess's fingernails in the candlelight.

"You've always had a penchant for us Irish, dark-haired ones with large noses and an artistic way. See? I know your type as well."

"*You* are my type," she shot at him.

"Aye, I know it," he said, leaning back and taking in his fill of her. "But don't play innocent. You thought about that fine Irish harpist long after he kissed those lips of yours a little too long in farewell at the shop door."

"I never lied to you. I told you he had kissed me."

Thomas nodded. "You were young and spirited, too much spirit for one man alone to handle, and I had neglected you whilst working long hours. Playing the mouse in absence of the cat."

"This mouse never played, beyond a kiss."

"I don't doubt it. You're too honest to lie."

Her gaze left his, her lids fluttering as she looked down at Bess.

"But I know you must have dreamt about that dark Irishman coaxing notes from your body as he did his harp."

"I'm but a woman, after all. And men and women are no different when it comes to tempting thoughts. At least, *this* woman is no different." She smiled at him, then coyly turned her gaze to Bess, still drinking.

"As if that harpist ever could have made you sing as I do."

Her smile grew. Her gaze swept over his chest and shoulders. "As if that little flaxen-haired strumpet ever could do to you what I can do."

Thomas rose from his chair, wiping his mouth with the back of his hand. "I'll be in the bedchamber, waiting for you."

"Bess sleeps well," Maggie whispered into his chest.

It was morning and he unfurled himself from her, retrieved his shirt and breeches cast haphazardly upon the floor the night before, and dressed himself. He approached Bess's cradle, saw her breathing steadily in deep sleep. Her thumb had slipped from her mouth, yet her sweet little lips still worked away as though it were still there.

"Ah, lo!" Thomas said to Maggie. "She is cutting a bottom tooth."

Maggie rose from the bed and bent to peer into the cradle. She straightened, her fingers over her lips, stifling a happy giggle. "How wonderful, and she's not yet four months!"

"She is singular in every way." He kissed her forehead. "*Banríon*, there is no need to fret, you see?"

Thomas took the horse and cart to the lumberyard by the Mystic. It was a beautiful summer's day, the sun shining, the air sweet with pepperbush and tall phlox. He whistled as he guided the horses to a hitch post already teeming with other carts. There was chattering and laughter coming from inside the mill, and the scent as dear as that of his own wife—freshly cut lumber—wafted to greet him.

He paused to make small talk with the other men, commenting on the fine day, the houses being built in Charlestown, Cambridge, and Boston town.

"Keeping busy, as usual, Jones?" asked Goodman Willby, the mill owner.

"Oh aye, so busy I have to turn business over to the likes of Jacob Tallum, here."

"Ay, easy now, Jones," said Jacob, but he was laughing with the rest of them.

"Who is in need of furniture from you these days?" asked Willby.

"Well, let's see. I am quite late on a request for a mighty large bed from the Widow Hallett."

"Hmm," Willby replied, nodding. "Fine woman, the widow."

"Aye, indeed," muttered the others.

Thomas had to look down at his boots to hide the amusement springing to his lips. Back in old England, this conversation amongst men surely would have devolved. But here in pious Massachusetts, men chose instead to keep their filthy thoughts to themselves.

"She ought to be married by now," Thomas said, and he knew it were bold of him, but it were true.

"Perhaps she still mourns," said Goodman Reed, an elderly carpenter.

"Come now, Reed," said Willby. "Goodman Hallett was as ancient as you. Why would she still mourn for a man who was long past his prime?"

Thomas could not stifle his laughter, and it precipitated a raucous response from the group, as though he had given them permission to laugh too.

"What she needs is a young man, like Tallum here."

He, no more than twenty years himself, looked up, eyes wide, as though he had just been named heir to a great fortune. "Me?"

"Aye, why not?"

"Has she mentioned me?"

"Of course not."

Amidst the merriment at his expense, his brows drew together in confusion. "Then why me?"

"Why not?" Willby asked, giving the lad a hearty pat upon the back. "You're in need of a woman, she's in need of a man. Are you up to the task?"

The laughter was interrupted by someone clearing their throat in an obvious, disapproving manner. The men round Thomas ceased as though they'd been caught pissing upon the steps of the Meeting House.

Thomas turned to see that Governor Winthrop and former governor Dudley had entered the mill. They did not look amused.

"Surely there is no need for such bawdy talk. We are better than that, are we not?" asked the governor in that pedantic way of his Thomas had greatly disliked since he had first heard him speak at the Meeting House some months before.

"Goodman Jones," said Dudley, his small, watery eyes taking study of Thomas, "you must rein in that wife of yours."

"Come again, sir?" He was taken by surprise.

"Really, Jones. She chided my wife for not coming to see her to take one of her remedies, told her that if she did not, then she would suffer worse than she does." Dudley shook his head slowly. "What sort of Christian woman makes such threats? It's as though the Devil takes hold of her tongue."

All eyes were wary, upon Thomas, awaiting some reaction, some explanation. Bewildered, he searched for an answer that would be lighthearted, to dispel the ominous feeling within the millhouse. "Goodman Dudley, my wife has always spoken freely and plainly. It is what makes her an astute healer."

"Perhaps, as her husband, you should take that matter into hand, yes?" His ratlike eyes seemed to challenge Thomas, dared him to say something untoward.

Thomas thought about spitting on his doublet but thought better of it. "Unlike some men, I derive no pleasure from cruelty." Reflexively Thomas balked at such talk. He had seen men beat their wives and children, and if sparing them the rod spoilt the character, the using of it broke the spirit.

Winthrop inspected some of the lumber. "As well you should not. We have set laws down in this place against wife beating. Surely Dudley did not mean to imply violence, nor should you, Jones, infer such a base notion."

The governor was the sort who claimed to want to create a new society, a beacon of hope and peace, a "City Upon a Hill," like some new Jerusalem. But really he was not so different from the wealthy landed gentry of the old country, the sort who rely on the preservation of order and station, where men—and women—knew their "place" beneath him and his wealth. Thomas had no use for such hypocrisy. Mayhap he was more like those Agitators back in England, who wished to turn the world they knew upside down.

Before Thomas made his exit, he heard the governor call out, "Jones."

Thomas paused, glancing over his shoulder.

"Do keep that wife of yours in line. A cunning woman is easily made the handmaiden of the Devil."

Thomas donned his hat and spat upon the ground.

"She's got a good look about her, you see?" Sam said, patting the haunches of the yearling goat.

They stood in his barn, for Thomas had agreed to purchase a young goat from him so that Maggie and he might eventually have goat's milk and then raise goats of their own.

"Sam, the way you go on, I'd think you were sweet on the goat."

They shared a laugh.

"So, what is it about the look of the goat that tells you she'll be a good one?"

"The eyes," Sam said immediately, as though Thomas were a fool not to know. "They are large and heavily fringed. She has the look of a mother about her."

"Does the same rule apply to women?"

"Oh, aye, and you and I have done well for ourselves."

"I'll lift a tankard to that."

Sam gave the goat a pat on the rump, sending her skipping away to a pile of hay. "Speaking of wives, I've been meaning to speak to you upon a matter."

"Go on then."

"Aye, well," Sam said, pausing as he stroked his red beard. "I'm not rightly sure how to say it."

"Come now, Sam, you are never at a loss for words. Between you and my wife, I'm surprised my ears don't bleed each night upon my pillow."

Sam only smiled a little at Thomas's jest. "Aye, well, you've touched on it there."

"Something to do with my wife?"

"Alice and I worry, that is all, you see?"

"See what?"

"Maggie, she must be more cautious in what she says to people. Why, she told Alice that our Daniel's Sarah was with child, and there was no way she could have known, for it was so soon and even Sarah herself was not yet certain."

Thomas leaned against one of the horse's pens, felt the creature's hot breath on his neck as she sniffed him. "She is skilled at healing," he said with a shrug.

"Aye, I know this, she has a gift, to be certain," Sam agreed. He looked down at his boot as he worked his heel into a clod of mud. "But she has more than one gift. She can see and know things that are impossible to know. She is cunning, indeed."

Thomas nodded. "This I know."

"I know there are some women that have that talent. There was an old widow in my home village who was blind yet knew which horses would foal long before they showed any sign—long before they were even bred. I know that is the way with some women, and I know there is no malice in it. But when people cannot understand something, when they can't make sense of a thing, they always become fearful. People fear what they do not understand, you see?"

Thomas crossed his arms over his chest, unsure of how to respond because he knew his friend was right.

"Alice and I worry. Alice has heard some of the other women of town say that Maggie has a tongue that works for Lucifer. And once the hens start making a ruckus, the cocks soon get involved in the frenzy."

"You know my Maggie, Sam. She's got a wild streak."

"Aye, I know it. She's like my kin, she is. And I know that's why you chose her for a wife, don't deny it. You like the wildness in her."

"You know me well." The horse penned behind Thomas licked the back of his neck and he moved away, only to bump into the goat, who had returned and leaned against his legs. "The wild ones like me. See, even your filly here is sweet on me, and your goat too."

"Look, Tom," Sam said, clasping his hand upon his shoulder. "Maggie needs to know she is a long way from London. London is teeming with all kinds of folks, like one lively festival. And I don't care who holds power: a king, a parliament, or the Lord knows what else they might invent when this ends. In London you get lost in the crowd, but not in this place. We are under the watchful gaze of powerful and pious men who think themselves the eyes of the Lord. Of course, that bit stays between us, yes?"

"Sam, you should know better than to ask me of all people such a question."

"Aye, I know it." He nodded. "But do have a word with Maggie. Even if she can see into the hearts and minds of others, tell her to keep it to herself unless she is called upon to provide it. I would hate to see any misfortune befall the both of you. We finally have the friends we have long desired—don't want to lose them so soon."

Sam scooped up the goat in his arms, holding her against his portly belly. He then passed her to Thomas.

The sweet-natured creature did not even fight, but rather busied herself with chewing on the shoulder of his jacket. "Come now, Sam, don't say such dire things."

"These are strange times, these are. As much as I thrive here in Massachusetts, there are moments I long for old England. I grow weary of everything being so pious, everything reverting back to God. I am as God-fearing as most men, but when I take a piss I don't thank God for it. Enough is enough, do you not agree?"

"Indeed I do."

They stepped outside into the cool evening dusk. "Tell me, Tom, have you ever considered going back to London? A good joiner is always in demand, no matter where he is." Sam heaved a sigh. "There are moments when I wonder, was it for the best, to bring my family to the edge of the world? Make no mistake, I know I have prospered here, far better than I would have back home. But it's the zealots, Tom. The zealots often make life dreary." He came closer to Thomas, and dropped to a hushed voice. "Even Christmas. They've outlawed Christmas!"

He was probably the dearest friend Thomas had since leaving the Winship farm, but he did not want to burden Sam with a twisting tale of his and Maggie's arrival in Massachusetts. "I don't disagree, Sam. But we thrive here. Maggie is convinced it is the clean air and water that allowed us to have Bess, finally."

"And she may well be right. I certainly would never question your Maggie's opinion on matters of health."

# CHAPTER NINE

*October 22, 1647*

*A busy day. I helped Goodwife Morris birth her first, a healthy boy with more hair than I have ever seen upon a newborn. I made her smile and laugh, despite her long labor, joking that the father must have been a Spaniard. Her mother-in-law scowled, the old cow.*

*I hear Goodwife Weston's young son crouping, and know the sure remedy and tell her so. She says she will not visit "a cunning woman who deals with dark arts." Foolish woman. I tell her she risks her son's health because of her ignorance. The boy should not suffer when I surely can help him.*

*Bess has begun crawling—what a wonder to see! My heart is glad, seeing how she grows each day. Next week will be her seventh month.*

"Where are you off to?" Thomas asked Maggie, watching her pack various bottles and sachets of herbs into her apothecary's basket.

"I've received word to go see the Westons' son, Jacob. They certainly took long enough," she muttered, shaking out her shawl and draping it round her shoulders. "There's supper in the pot, and watch out for Bess—she's off in the blink of an eye, the artful sprite."

Thomas scooped up Bess, who had already made her way to the table. She let out a howl of protest, chagrined that he had interrupted her explorations. He placated her by raising her gown, placing his lips upon her round belly, and blowing upon it, letting out a loud, rude sound. Her shrill, delighted laughter echoed through the house. Thomas could not help but laugh too.

"Don't be long, *Banríon*," he called to Maggie before she closed the door.

"Worry not," she shouted.

Thomas busied himself with singing to Bess as he fed her tiny morsels of cornbread soaked in goose stew. She especially loved the goose fat that rose to the top of the bowl, clever thing. She smacked her lips and hummed, "Mmm, mmm, mmm," as her lids lowered in pleasure. She was her mother's daughter, to be sure. He kissed her dark ringlets that smelled of fresh egg whites. As Thomas took a spoon of stew for himself, her dimpled hands grabbed for another piece of cornbread. Instead of bringing it to her lips, she held it up before him, her eyes questioning his, then gestured toward the bowl of stew.

"*Banphrionsa*, Princess, your wish is my command." Thomas took the morsel from her fingers and submerged it in his stew, breaking it up, and serving her once again.

After supper he wiped her face and hands, then decided to bundle Bess up and take her for an evening stroll to the docks, to see the ocean. He wrapped her tightly in a wool blanket, and then a bearskin Maggie had procured from a Pawtucket woman by trading herbs. Maggie had said many times that cold air was beneficial to a babe, strengthening their lungs, so Thomas thought the walk would do them both some good. He braced her against him, and she felt like a plump, fluffy creature in his arms.

In the cold autumn twilight they walked down to the Charlestown docks, looking north across the Mystic River to Winnisimmet. Then he looked due east, toward Noddle's Island, owned by Samuel Maverick. Maverick's plantation had been boarded up, for he had traveled south to the Carolinas for the year, and taken his family—and his slaves—with him. Maverick was a greed-driven landowner who had settled there years before the Puritans had arrived in Boston. He was a thorn in the General Court's side, as he was a loyal subject to King Charles. Ever the mercenary, he was off to seek fortune for a time elsewhere, and he would by no means take the chance of leaving behind his Africans, for fear they would flee. And who might blame them? Thomas spat upon the ground, considering the audacity and cruelty of a man who kept humans like livestock, if not worse, for the livestock still had the freedom to roam about the island whilst their master was away.

Knowing the cruelty that possibly occurred upon that strip of land sent a shiver of foreboding up Thomas's spine. He shook himself free of the ominous feeling, then glanced south toward Boston.

"Bos-ton," he said to Bess. "Bos-ton."

She squealed in delight.

He laughed. "Clever girl!"

Some passing seamen laughed. "Good girl," one shouted, well into his cups.

Before turning to head back home, Bess managed to free her tiny, mittened hand from the blankets, and pointed toward the east, uttering some little sound that only she understood.

"Aye, that's England across the ocean. Eng-land."

"Eee!"

Thomas lifted her to his lips and kissed the top of her cap. "So clever. I love thee."

"Eee!" she exclaimed again, gesturing to the black expanse of the Atlantic beyond Noddle's Island.

Thomas sighed, his breath taking form in the cold October night. Was England home? Was London? Was England or was Massachusetts? Nay, home was upon this land, with his daughter held against him. Home was beneath the roof where he lay his head down beside his wife's. He had left Ireland as a young boy with his family and had little recollection of the place. He had only known England: Bristol as a boy, the Berkshire countryside as laborer turned joiner, and the busy, crowded streets of London as an apprentice cabinetmaker who went on to establish his own thriving business. As newlyweds, Maggie and he had delighted in the anonymity and opportunity of London. They would spend evenings walking along Cheapside, and they would admire beautiful faces from round the world: Africa, Asia Minor, the Far East, with exotic clothing, headdresses, and mouths full of sounds they had never heard before. It was a wonderful place to be young, and he had been loath to leave it. But there was no going back to England—certainly not London.

When Thomas returned home, he changed Bess's wet clout for a clean and dry one, still fumbling in the process, though becoming more skilled than he'd once been. He tucked her into her cradle—a cradle he had made from maple wood and trimmed with carved ivy vines, then stained with varnish. Maggie had proudly shown the cradle to some womenfolk. "Look how skilled my husband is. Come, place your fingers upon the wood and see for yourself." She could sell an empty sack of wine for full price, that one could. Thomas had crafted eight cradles like this one since then.

He rocked the cradle to and fro with his foot, singing a melody his mother once sang to him. That memory was one of the few he had that was shared between just she and him; a mother who had borne fourteen children could not afford to hand out individual kindnesses. Bess cooed, looking up at him and smiling. She then put her thumb between her lips and, try as she might to fight it, her eyelids became too heavy and soon she breathed evenly, sucking upon her thumb, in the arms of some sweet dream.

Never did Thomas grow weary of staring at that sweet little face. Such wonderment would fill him, each time he looked upon her, as though he were seeing her for the first time all over again. He still could not fathom that he had helped create something so beautiful and perfect. Even when she threw a fit and cried angry tears, she was still the loveliest creature he had ever beheld. Maggie had once quipped that it must be so, else no baby would survive, for if they were not so beautiful and perfect, no one would put up with their nonsense otherwise. He laughed to himself, thinking of her words, for though it was the thing that no mother should utter, it were the very truth. But that was his Maggie, always brutal in her honesty. Some who did not know her might think her cold to say such a thing, but they did not see her in the early hours of the morning, when she would press her lips to Bess's apple cheek, breathe in the scent of her, and hum some little melody in the child's ear. They did not see the serene smoothness of Maggie's brow, the contented set of her lips, which Thomas knew could only be bestowed upon her by this tiny little creature.

In the darkness of night, Thomas could hear the quick, soft singing of laces being pulled loose upon Maggie's corset.

"Why so late?" he asked.

She sighed as she settled next to him in the bed. Her hair carried the scent of cold, salty air and sage smoke. "It was a struggle with the Weston boy. Well, rather, I should say it was a struggle with the mother."

Thomas waited for her to continue as she slid her leg over his, as she was wont to do when she faced him in bed.

"I treated the boy, Jacob, well and good. Got his lungs purged out so he could breathe easily again. I then told Goody Weston that we must open the window to the cold night air, to loosen the croup, to be rid of her son's ill humors. Goodman Weston did not see the trouble with it, but oh, that Goody Weston. She acted as though I were inviting Satan into the room."

A nervousness bubbled in his gut. "Was it necessary for you to worry about ill humors? Could you not have kept things simple and just treated the boy's croup?"

Suddenly Maggie raised herself upon her elbow to study his face in the dark. "What are you trying to say, Thomas?"

"What do you mean?"

"Spit it out. Say what it is that you mean."

"Shush, you'll wake Bess."

"Tell me," she hissed, "what you're trying to say."

"You know full well what I'm trying to say. You complain that people think you a cunning woman and you wish they would regard you as a healer and apothecary. Well, when you go about speaking of ill humors and throwing windows open to the cold night's air, you give mean, narrow-minded folk the wrong impression."

There was silence as she considered his words. "So I bring trouble upon myself when I speak the truth?"

He sighed. "Just try to consider your words before you speak—"

She rose from the bed and stormed out of the room before he could finish.

"Wild thing," Thomas muttered, and not in the endearing way he usually did. He was tired. He had cared for the babe in her absence. And now because she was careless and did not think before speaking or acting, she brought trouble down upon herself. Selfish thing! Let her storm off into the common room. He would not go after her. He would sleep.

And so he did, until the early morning, when he rolled over and realized the bed was still empty. He got up and went out to the common room. There, sitting in a chair by the hearth, covered in a blanket, was Maggie, her eyes wide open, her sleepless night showing in the dark circles beneath them.

"Maggie, what are you trying to prove?" he asked.

She did not answer.

Her silence was more provoking than her ranting. "You will answer me, woman."

Her eyes met his and narrowed. "I'll answer to no one."

This happened sometimes, when he could only assume that she were so deeply embedded in her thoughts, like a rabbit in its den, that she could not see what was going on above the ground, here in the real world. It was when she turned from wordy to wordless.

"Have it your way, then, stubborn woman." Thomas went to the cupboard and angrily tore a piece off the loaf of day-old cornbread. "I've work to do. Should you finally decide to speak to me, you'll know where to find me."

But she did not come that morning, and it infuriated him. He could not concentrate on his work, and bloodied his thumb with the chisel, yelling out an oath as he cast it aside. It would not do, to let this anger fester and ferment. Thomas went out of the barn, to find her in the garden foraging for any last herbs that had survived recent frost. Bess, bundled up in layers, sat upon the ground and fingered a large rock as though it were the most fascinating thing she had ever seen. She looked up at him and smiled, babbling.

Maggie froze, then slowly straightened and turned to see Thomas, as though she were a child expecting a scolding.

"Come now, in the house."

She sighed as though annoyed with the interruption, then scooped up Bess, who howled in displeasure, reaching toward the beloved rock. Thomas followed them inside. Maggie sat and placed Bess before her upon the table. Bess continued to protest.

"See now, are you pleased with yourself? You've gone and upset Bess."

He threw his hat down upon the table. "You shall listen to me now, woman," he said in a low, slow voice, trying to keep his anger under control. "I've had enough of your tantrum. You're no better than the babe when you act this way."

Maggie glared at him.

"I simply warned you last night. Sam says that he and Alice hear talk in the town, that many call you the Devil's hand. Do you want to bring this sort of trouble down upon yourself? Is this really what you desire? Because we are a long way from London—"

She guffawed. "Don't I know it."

Thomas paused, surprised by her words. "Aye, and you ought to know it, since it was because of you we had to make haste and leave."

Bess's howling grew, and Maggie shot out of her chair, going to the cupboard and returning with a spoonful of honey for Bess. Bess immediately ceased protesting and greedily grabbed the spoon in her fist and sucked upon it. Maggie looked at Thomas, and he saw tears upon her face.

"Must you remind me? I know, it was all my doing, all my fault. And not a day goes by that I don't regret it. So you need not make me feel any more guilty upon that matter, for I heap plenty of guilt upon myself as it is."

His anger drained. "This place is the opposite of London. In this place, everything one does, says, every laugh, every quarrel, every act of lust, it's all watched and it's all collected, I can only assume, so that the powers that be can control this tiny corner of the world. Don't you see?" He reached for her hand, taking it in his. "You're a healer, a midwife, an apothecary. You're a woman with knowledge and skill. And you are clever enough to know what misfortune can befall skilled women when they anger the wrong people—people who profess their godliness. I don't need to remind you what happened a few years ago in East Anglia, or what happened here to the Hutchinson woman. Take care, Maggie."

She wiped at her tears with her apron, nodding.

"So when you tell me that you speak of ill humors and upset a wealthy matron, aye, I'll get concerned and I'll be nervous about it."

"I know, you're right. I'm a stupid cow!"

"Hush now, you're no such thing." He went to her and embraced her.

"I hate how pious, how zealously pious they all are . . ." she muttered.

He sighed. "You chose New England."

"Nay, the astrologer said it was predestined."

He rolled his eyes above her head, thinking of the old astrologer whose eyes were so clouded it was a wonder he could even read the star charts spread out before him. "Aye, the astrologer." He pulled away to look at her, smoothing away from her lashes the wild curls that had escaped her cap. "We could always go to New Amsterdam or Maryland."

She suddenly smiled. "What about the tropics?" she asked breathily, like an excited child.

Thomas shook his head. "We will have to save more coin for such a journey. Besides, what do you know of rum making?"

"Nothing, but I'm a quick learner."

"Aye, that you are," he said, kissing her forehead.

"And you are clever too," she said, fiddling with the strings of her cap. "And everyone takes a liking to you the moment they meet you, unlike me."

"Because I know when to keep my mouth shut."

She slapped his arm. "Then you ought to shut it now."

Thomas took her in his arms again. He loved it when she toyed with him. "Come now, let me love you. Please." He took hold of her earlobe between his teeth. She moaned, pressing herself closer to him. "Don't make me beg," he spoke softly. "You know I'll make it worth your while."

She pushed him away. "Nay, Bess is here, watching."

He looked over at Bess, who stared at them curiously, honey spoon absently suspended between her lips. She was so perfect, like a fine porcelain doll he had once seen in a shop window in Cheapside. His arousal quickly waned. "Aye, it wouldn't be right."

"Later," Maggie said, grabbing a handful of his backside.

"Indeed," he replied, taking her hand in his and kissing her knuckles.

"Jones, a word, please."

The voice startled Thomas from his work. He had been making great progress that afternoon upon a cupboard for the young couple Lovell, newly married. He had even added extra flourish: a carved grapevine along the top trim. Thomas would not charge them for the handiwork, for he liked the young couple and wished for them the same fruitful, joyful, and fulfilling marriage that he had with his own wife. Let their love be as fruitful as this vine he manifested from the maple wood.

Thomas looked up from his work, squinting as he looked toward the workshop door. His new goat pranced in front of a figure he did not immediately recognize. "Aye? How can I help?"

The figure approached, and finally Thomas realized that it was Goodman Weston. He removed his hat, sheepishly glancing at some of Thomas's work in the barn, in its various stages of completion. Weston nibbled at his thin lower lip as though he were uncomfortable, searching for words.

Thomas wiped his brow with his coat sleeve. "What brings you out on this cold day? Can I be of service?" Thomas did not like for others to feel nervous in his presence. Why, there were no need for it.

"Oh, no, Jones, not at this time, but I thank thee. I come to speak to you about your wife."

Thomas's stomach turned. "Aye? I hear she come to help your son last night. I hope he fares better this day, the young Master Weston."

"Aye, he does, thanks be to God."

Thomas noticed how Weston's right hand instinctively went to his forehead and then his heart, as though to make the sign of the cross, but he quickly went to scratch his sideburn instead.

"I am glad to hear he mends," Thomas said, surprised by the gesture. Goodman Weston had just revealed much about himself. Like Thomas, he had once been—or still was—a Papist.

"But your wife greatly upset my wife, speaking of ill humors at work within the house. What sort of ill humors could she mean, Jones?"

Before answering, Thomas studied his face. He did not spy malice or cunning. He saw only the inquisitive lift of his brow, and eyes wide with a nervous fear.

"I know not, Goodman Weston. My wife has always had a strong intuition of ill humors. That is why she is so skilled at healing."

"Indeed," Weston replied, though Thomas could tell he was not satisfied with this answer. His eyes still questioned.

"Perhaps it would be best if I were to fetch my wife, and then you might ask her yourself?" Thomas regretted his suggestion as soon as he had uttered it, hoping that Maggie would have enough sense not to become overly dramatic or animated. He would have to warn her and hope that she would heed him.

"Very well, Jones, if you would not mind?"

"Nay, of course not. Give me just a moment, if you please."

He nodded and Thomas left the workshop, crossing the yard and opening the back door. By the hearth, in the common room, Maggie sang a ribald Cheapside ditty as she mended Bess's stockings. Bess sat by her feet, smiling as she held two poppets who danced along to the song.

"Maggie?"

She stopped in her singing and looked up at Thomas, smiling.

"*Banríon*, come. Goodman Weston is in the barn, and he would like to speak with you."

Her smile faded, and a look of fear took hold. She visibly swallowed.

"Come now, he is a goodly man. And I'll be with you. Just be sure to allay his fears about 'ill humors,' will you now?"

"Aye, of course," she said as she quickly placed her darning aside and scooped Bess from the floor.

"Let me hold her," Thomas said, and she passed her into his arms.

As they crossed the yard to the barn, Thomas noticed the sun was already crashing down into the skeletal arms of distant trees to the southwest. The sky was decorated with magnificent hues of gold, crimson, purple. As he followed Maggie to the barn, he watched her long, purposeful stride, her head held high as though she were some force, some royal priestess. Thomas followed, holding Bess, who silently studied the poppets in her hands, as though she sensed some great import in the moment. The air was still and cold upon his cheeks, as though the wind held its breath, too, in that very moment.

"Good day, Goodman Weston!" Maggie said cheerfully. She gave him a beaming smile and bobbed a curtsy. "I do hope that young Master Weston fares better today?"

"Oh, yes indeed, Goody Jones, that he does." Perhaps it was Maggie's wild, bold beauty that caused him to forget to make the sign of the cross, for he stared at her as though she were a rare jewel, rather than with fear.

"I'm glad to hear it. Now, how can I help?"

"Well, uh, you see, you spoke of ill humors in our house, and my wife and I are quite unsettled by this accusation. What, exactly, did you mean by such a thing?"

"Goodman Jones, the world is filled with good and ill humors, the same which cause imbalance within our bodies, do you see?"

"Well, yes, of course, but—"

"Did you not say that Master Weston fares better today?" She looked to him with wide eyes, placing one hand upon the worktable, the other hand upon her hip.

Goodman Weston was captivated. Thomas could see it in how his eyes went to the hand on her hip and lingered. Maggie was a natural force, Thomas knew it well.

"Why yes, Goody Jones, I see your meaning now. Of course, you banished the ill humors from our home and I thank you for it."

"You tell your goodwife that she need not worry. Her son mends, and is that not what matters most?"

Bess suddenly yelled from Thomas's arms, reaching toward Maggie. Even she was under the persuasive spell of her mother at that moment.

"Bess, my sweetest pea," she replied, going to Thomas and taking Bess into her arms.

Bess burrowed her face into Maggie's neck.

"How very much like her mother she is," said Goodman Weston.

"Aye," Thomas replied. "I'm doubly blessed."

As Goodman Weston bid them good evening and went on his way, Thomas kissed Maggie's cheek. *"Banríon,"* he breathed into her ear.

"I am," she replied with a knowing smile.

# CHAPTER TEN

*December 2, 1647*

*A sad day it was today. It were the first time in all of my midwifery years that I lost a babe. I know not how long the babe were being strangled by the cord within Goody Hall's womb, but when she were finally delivered, the babe were cold and blue. There was naught I could do. So sorrowful a sight for the mother, who has lost three babes in their infancy in the past five years. May the Lord ease her sorrow at so dark an hour.*

*And if this day were not terrible enough, the Widow Hallett came to me, begging of me my silence. I tell her there is no need, all good healers are beholden to the Hippocratic oath. She seeks "aphrodesia." I ask in what manner she means aphrodesia. She says something to seduce a man, so that he is overcome with desire. Such an artful strumpet! I tell her she comes to the wrong apothecary, for I do not deal in such tinctures or mixtures. And I think to myself that even if I did, I would never, ever provide such to such a one as her. "Surely," she said, "you must have in your coffers some satyrion root, blister beetles." I shudder at the thought of the harm that can come from Spanish fly when used for such a purpose. Such sins and tragedy which can result from the powder of blister beetle, I know these firsthand. I tell her I have none of these things she seeks. She tells me then that she will seek out the Old Merrymount Squaw, a medicine woman down in Braintree. I have heard of her, one who cavorted with Thomas Morton some years hence at his colony which the Plymouth settlers claimed was a heathenous place of licentiousness and paganism. I wish her Godspeed and see her out. Her presence is like a storm cloud—how I loathe the Widow Hallett.*

*To be rid of her malice, I shall go out in search of Black Willow Bark, which cures the fever of many. When alone in Nature, amidst God's bounty, I am happiest.*

Thomas tapped the sawdust from his boots before entering the house. Inside, Maggie sat at the table, her head resting upon her arms before her. For a moment, Thomas did not know whether she slept, but then he heard a muffled sniffle.

"Maggie?"

She lifted her head, her face ruddy and wet with tears. "Goody Hall, she lost the babe."

A sudden sense of relief washed over him that no harm had come to his wife or child, but then he inwardly censured himself that he might find any satisfaction in another's sorrow. Thomas took the chair beside Maggie's and sat, placing his hand upon her shoulder.

She continued. "The babe was born strangled by the mother's cord. There was naught I could do."

"Nay, of course not." He caressed her shoulder.

She sniffed again, wiping tears with her fingers. "How horrible it was, to have to tell Goody Hall that the babe was still. I hope I never have to do so again, so long as I birth babies."

"Indeed, may the Lord forbid it."

"The poor woman has now birthed four babes, yet has no living children."

"Lord have mercy upon her and her husband."

There was silence for a moment, but for the crackling of burning wood in the hearth.

"I told Goodman Hall that I would not accept payment for my service. It would seem unjust, don't you think?"

Thomas nodded. If only all midwives were as kind as his wife.

"I offered the Saint John's tincture for Goody Hall, but she would accept nothing more from me." A shiver went up Thomas's spine at the mention of the Saint John's tincture. It was the same that had caused their flight from London. He knew it had helped many, but it had also heaped much trouble upon them.

She rose from the table. "I ought to go get Bess from Alice."

Thomas put his hand upon hers. "Nay, I shall go. You rest, take some brandy."

She nodded. "You are sweet to me, Thomas." She pressed her lips to his forehead.

❧

"Come, Thomas, have some ale," Alice said, pulling out a chair for him at her table.

"I thank you, Alice." He sat down, smiling at Bess, who sat upon Sam's knee and happily sucked upon a biscuit.

"How I miss having a little one round," said Sam, bouncing Bess. "Come, Alice, shall we have another?"

Thomas was caught by surprise by his comment, and he laughed heartily.

Alice turned round from the cupboard, tankard of ale in hand. "What, pray tell, is so funny, Thomas?"

He bit his lip, stifling his smile.

"Aye, best to stay silent," she said, placing the tankard before him.

"But you've not yet answered me, wife," said Sam, who would not give up the jest.

"You'll have to seek out a younger wife if you want little ones, for it seems you'll not get any more from this one!"

"Ah, all is well, all is well, my love. Besides, I shall have another grandchild soon."

Alice sat down at the table. "How fared Goody Hall?"

Thomas swallowed the ale, heady with wheat and honey. Alice made the best ale, that was for certain. "Not well. She lost the babe."

Alice gasped. "Oh but I'm sorry to hear it."

"A pity," muttered Sam, who then bounced Bess upon his knee again.

"Aye, Maggie says the babe was born strangled by the mother's cord."

Alice shook her head. "There was naught she could do about that."

"Maggie said the same."

"This is the first babe Maggie has lost in her midwifery, isn't it?"

Thomas nodded before taking a sip of ale.

Bess exclaimed, holding her arms out to Thomas, soggy biscuit still in hand. He rose and took her from Sam's lap. *"Banphrionsa."*

"Aye, of course you prefer your da with his Irish endearments. Those damn Irishmen and their way with words and song," he laughed.

Bess wrapped her arms round Thomas and nestled her face against his neck, just as her mother was wont to do.

"Well," said Alice as she got up to stir the kettle, "I do hope that Goody Hall mends soon, and sees that it was God's will, for there is no other way to see it."

"I hope she does not make trouble for Maggie," Thomas said, giving voice to the nagging worry in the back of his mind.

"No, no, of course she won't," said Sam. "Has not Maggie delivered her of two other babes that lived?"

"Aye, but none survived infancy," said Alice, and Thomas could tell from the low tone of her voice that she had the same fear as him.

"Surely Goodman Hall will speak reason to his wife," said Sam, nodding as though he were certain of this. "He seems a decent man."

As Thomas, Maggie, and Bess emerged from the Meeting House, the sun warmed their faces despite the chill of the air. Thomas took a deep breath through his nose, detecting the faint yet sweet smell of snow. "Mmm," he muttered. It felt so very good to be free of the confines of the Meeting House with its scent of damp wool and stale bodies. It reminded him of something he missed about the Catholic Mass of his youth; at least the Papists burned warm, heady frankincense at the altar so that it were a pleasing place for the senses. The Papists were very good at that sort of thing.

"Ah, look," Maggie said, pausing. "There is Goody Hall with her husband."

Thomas looked to see the Halls leaving the Meeting House. Goody Hall's face was pallid and mournful, poor woman. Her husband guided her as though she were an elderly matron, yet she was thirty at most.

Just then Sam and Alice joined Maggie and Thomas.

"I ought to speak to her," Maggie said.

"To Goody Hall?" asked Alice. "Is it too soon?"

Thomas noted the worried crease in Alice's forehead.

"It has been three weeks, and look, she has come to Sunday Service."

"But Maggie—"

Maggie strode with purpose toward the Halls before Alice could finish her thought.

"Oh, dear," muttered Alice, watching Maggie make her way.

There was a sinking feeling in Thomas's belly as he clutched Bess more tightly against himself.

They watched as Maggie came before the Halls, reaching out to clasp Goody Hall's hand in hers.

Goody Hall pulled her hand and body well away from Maggie, as though she carried some pox. Instinctively Thomas took a step toward them, but he stopped himself. It would not do to interfere, to bring more attention to what was transpiring.

"Do not touch me! Do not come near me!" yelled Goody Hall for all in the churchyard to hear. "How can you show your face to me, you cunning woman? You are nothing but the Devil's hand!"

The congregation stopped and stared at the scene unfolding. The trepidation in Thomas turned quickly to anger. He handed Bess over to Sam and made his way to Maggie with a determined stride.

"You are upset, still, and rightfully so," Maggie said after a long pause. She said this in a deliberately loud voice, knowing that all of Charlestown was bearing witness to this moment and the ugly accusation now hanging in the air. "You still mourn, and you speak out of anguish and sadness. You do not mean what you say, Goody Hall."

"Oh yes I do!" Goody Hall shouted in a voice crackling with anger. Thomas saw her face contorted with pain.

Thomas took tight hold of Maggie's arm. "Come, Wife. You've upset Goody Hall. Let her husband tend to her. Goodman Hall," he said, nodding his head to him.

Goodman Hall gritted his teeth, pulling his wife against him. "Leave us be, Goodman Jones. Your wife has caused enough misfortune."

Though his wife's anger was jarring, it was not unexpected. But Goodman Hall's behavior was like a fist to the stomach, taking Thomas by surprise.

"Come, Maggie," Thomas said, turning her round and marching back toward the Strattons and Bess.

The whole of the congregation watched their procession as though they were ghosts come to walk the earth again. Never in his life had Thomas felt his skin crawl under the scrutiny of so many. He wanted nothing more than to disappear, to be clean of the judgment being thrown upon his head like filth upon the condemned criminals placed in the stocks in Cheapside.

But as they made their way back home and shuttered themselves in the house, safe and away from judging stares, Thomas still could not be free of the horrible feeling of dread.

"Maggie, we must leave this place," he said, for once appearing to be the more rash of the two.

She turned round from hanging her cloak upon the wall hook, her hands upon her hips. "I shall do no such thing! I'll not keep running away as though I am guilty. I've done nothing wrong."

Thomas placed Bess down upon the hearthrug, then made his way to Maggie, his finger in her face. "I know this, but trouble seeks you out like a lover."

She scoffed at him. "Calm thyself, Thomas."

He grabbed her shoulders. "This is no time to mock me or make light of things, woman! Did you not hear Goody Hall's accusation, voiced so all could hear?"

She shook herself free of his grasp. "Aye, I did. And everyone will know she speaks out of grief. Is it my fault she gives birth to weakling babies? Nay! How many healthy babies have I delivered in our years here? This be the first I've lost. One loss versus a hundred living, breathing babies. Her argument means naught. No one will heed such foolish, hysterical words. They will only pity her in her feeble state."

He knew Maggie spoke the truth. How could one loss amidst so many healthy births be proof of some nonsensical claim? He was being much too hasty in his fear—there was no need to flee like guilty criminals on the run. But he knew also that Maggie could not afford any more mistrust or scrutiny.

"Heed me now, Maggie. You must tread much more cautiously now. Do not speak of ill humors, do not meddle in others' affairs. Keep hold of that sharp tongue of yours, do you hear me?"

She raised her chin in challenge. "I shall speak as I see fit. I'll not let some hysterical cow stop me from uttering what I believe to be true. And you'll not tell me what and what not to say!"

Her defiance in the face of such danger lit a spark beneath his rage. Why would she suddenly be so audacious? He longed to strike her stubborn face. He had to fight the heady desire to do so. He took a deep breath and stormed out of the house and out to the workshop, where he proceeded to chop wood needlessly in his anger.

His wife vexed him to no end.

# CHAPTER ELEVEN

*January 16, 1648*

*Thomas is angry with me. He will not speak with me beyond simple exchange. It has been three weeks now. He has never stayed vexed for so long.*

*But I will not apologize. I have done nothing wrong. I will not give in.*

Thomas threw himself into his work. He would begin well before sunrise and labor the day through, until twilight, until his insides ferociously growled in hunger. He avoided Maggie at all costs. He saw her scowl at his approach, her stubborn, luscious pout set firm. There were no smiles or kisses for him. There was no sweetness for the having, and that were fine with him—it made perfect environs in which his anger could fester and grow.

And there was much work to be done. Never had Thomas been so inundated with requests. Settlers desperate for furniture to fill their bare homes came to his workshop throughout the day, offering to pay more if he could move their requests to the top of his list. But he knew well that, despite the lure of their offers, it was bad business to show precedence. He had in his possession a copy of Honest John Lilburne's pamphlet, *London's Liberty In Chains Discovered*, which had stirred his heart and opened his eyes to what might be possible if "free-born Englishmen" came together, in protest, to demand the liberties of which they had been long deprived. One must always seek justice, renounce corruption, and deal honestly. Thomas were no statesman or man of law, but in his own way, in his own realm, he could be fair and just.

These mid-January days brought a sudden thaw, the slightest gift of mild air. A man indoors by a hearth would not notice such small change. But Thomas in his workshop with the doors swung wide, breathing heavily with the labor of the saw, he felt the gathering warmth, the teasing of spring. He was glad of it; winter was a bone-wearying cold in this remote corner of the world, far more bitter than any January day in London. The promise of spring breathed vigor into his body, made him feel younger than his years. He knew it was fleeting, that winter in the New World could last well into April, and this was folly on the part of Nature, but he would take it and enjoy it, however brief it might be. If only his wife were not so vexing—he longed to have her ride him astride. But he would not give in to her stubborn tantrum, selfish thing. Also, she did not seek love from him, and he was no man who derived satisfaction from forcing himself upon a woman. Men who did so, Thomas believed, were not men but beasts. He knew his wife had been ill used by another before him. Some men might claim it to be the marriage right, he knew this well, but he was no beast. After all, Thomas knew, half the pleasure is in the giving.

"Goodman Jones?"

His name was a song, carried by a tinkling, pleasing voice. He jolted upright at the sound, wiping at his brow with the cuff of his shirt. "Aye?"

The Widow Hallett came on tiptoe over the threshold of the shop, then paused by the freshly varnished headboard of Goodman Page's new bed stand. She studied it intently, sliding her delicate white fingertips over the carved acorns and filigree work at its trim.

"How fine," she said, turning her eyes to him, regarding him from boots to face.

*Curious tart.* He grew hot under her gaze. How could such a young, delicious, and eager thing still be without a husband? "Good day, Widow Hallett. Have you come to share happy news of a pending betrothal?" *Lord, have it be so, have mercy upon her.*

Her eyes went wide and her pert mouth went agape. "Goodman Jones! Nay, I've no such news. Shame upon you—I still mourn."

Thomas could not stifle the laugh that came from him. "Aye, of course, you still mourn." He turned back to the saw so that she not see the amusement upon his face.

"Are you mocking me?"

He vigorously shook his head. "Nay, nay, of course not. I mean no disrespect, madam."

"Then why do you laugh?"

He was in no mood to make excuses, tired, vexed, and hungry as he was. "I laugh because I think you ought to get yourself a husband soon. Enough of mourning. Life is fleeting, you should enjoy it while you are young. Your late husband would not want you to waste your days. That is what I think."

He put the saw aside, put his hands upon his hips, and awaited her challenge. This were an amusing game they played.

She bit her lip as though contemplating something witty to say in response. The effect was charming upon her.

"You speak plainly, Goodman Jones."

"Aye."

"There is no rush for me to marry. I have been provided for, I am not in need."

"True, you are not in monetary need."

"So what other need is there that would force me to stand before the minister again?"

It was his turn to regard her, and he did so. Her cheeks flushed beneath his gaze. She liked his eyes upon her. He liked that she liked this. This game was as pleasing as a glass of fine cognac. "There are other needs, madam."

She tipped her head to the side, a smile playing upon her lips. "Which are . . . ?"

"Do you not desire children?"

She shrugged. "I suppose so, though it seems it is nothing but a hardship for a woman, the suffering she must bear."

*Cunning fox.* She was luring him into her lair. He was no fool. If she wanted frank words, she would have them from him. "The pleasure is worth the suffering."

She breathed through her nose. He had upped the stakes of her cribbage game.

"Yes, a child's love is worth the suffering."

He regarded her a moment more, smiling. "Aye, that, too."

She smiled back.

"Now, Widow Hallett, I am a busy man, as you can see. What is it you seek? Certainly not my advice on your marital state."

She giggled, and it were genuine, a mix of both elation and nervousness. He did not like the sound, but liked that he had unnerved her. *Tricky minx.*

"I require a new dining table."

"Indeed? Very well, but it shall be a month's wait, at least. Will this suit you?"

"I shall pay double to have it done as soon as possible."

He gently pulled at his goatee. He had a sudden desire to be cruel. "Nay."

"Please, oh please. How much do you desire?"

If Thomas were a different man, he would have cast aside his conscience, his awareness of the life he had built for himself, for one sweet, fleeting, meaningless moment of gratification. And given the current animosity that brewed in his own marriage bed, he would be a liar if he were to claim he did not consider so rash a deed.

He went to his worktable and fiddled with the organized tools upon it. He steadied his breathing. He was a fair-dealing craftsman, but he was also a romantic, he knew, and could not deny such a lovely lass. He would not be cruel, but he would not be ensnared in her web. "Two weeks' time. What dimensions do you require?"

"I . . . I know not. You will have to come to my house and measure. Will you do this?"

*And what an elaborate web she weaves.* "Aye. Tomorrow."

❧

Maggie tossed a bowl of stew before him, the contents slopping over the side in her haste.

"What is this?" Thomas asked, trying to sound unbothered.

"The same as yesterday and the day before," she shot at him. From the wall hook, she grabbed her cloak and threw it on.

"You're not eating?"

"Does it look like I am?" She gave him an annoyed look.

"Where are you off to then?"

"Been called to Goodman Page's house. He suffers from gout."

"Tell him that I shall deliver his bed stand tomorrow."

"Tell him yourself." And with a resounding bang of the door, she was gone.

"Damned woman," he muttered as he tore a piece of bread and dipped it in the stew.

Just then, Bess pulled herself up to standing against the cupboard, as she often did. He watched her. He could not be cross with her just because her mother vexed him.

"Come, Bess," he said, holding his hands out to her, coaxing her to let go and step toward him.

She smiled, her wild black curls bobbing. She took a step, reaching a hand toward him, her other hand still upon the cupboard.

"Come, now."

She giggled and let go, taking one, two, three steps toward him, wobbling and clumsy like a drunk seaman. He gasped and caught hold of her. "There you are, my big girl! There you are, come on your own."

She beamed with pride, and Thomas kissed her apple cheeks over and over. He held her close, savoring the scent of her, the satisfaction of it like hunger sated, but even more.

After he cleaned his bowl, Thomas took Bess next door so that she might show her newfound skill to Sam and Alice. She happily obliged, holding her head high as she repeated her feat over and over, much to everyone's delight and cheers.

"What a wonder you are!" exclaimed Sam.

"A wonder, indeed. Just shy of ten months old!" Alice gave Bess a lump of sugar to suck upon as reward for her hard work.

"Just like her mother. What a lucky man you are, Thomas." Sam gave Thomas a hearty pat on the back.

"I don't know about that," he muttered as he scooped Bess up and put her upon his knee.

"Lovers still quarrel, eh? What's it been now, about a month?" Sam said, chuckling. "It'll pass. You both have weathered much, I'll wager."

He was right, Maggie and Thomas had been through good times and bad, but never had a quarrel lasted so long and bitterly. And never had Thomas been so disappointed with her behavior.

"Sam, don't pry into others' affairs," said Alice, who sat down across from Thomas at the table and studied him, her brow creased. "It's to do with what happened in front of the Meeting House, with the Halls, isn't it?"

Sam guffawed. "And she tells *me* to mind my own business."

"Aye, it is." Thomas shook his head. "She's a stubborn, rash thing. She will not curb her tongue."

"And that's why you love her," said Alice.

"I'm not feeling much tenderness of late, truth be told. Maggie will not speak to me."

"She will come round," said Sam with an assuring nod.

Alice raised her brows at him as though she doubted his words. "If you want to mend things, you will have to speak first. But that is just my opinion."

"You're right. But I'll not do it this time. She owes me an apology."

"You're not the sort who is likely to hold a grudge, I don't think," Alice said reaching over the table to wipe Bess's chin with a cloth.

"Perhaps I need to this time. Maggie does not realize the weight of Goody Hall's words."

Neither Sam nor Alice replied, but only nodded. They knew it to be true too. Why his wife did not, Thomas could not know or understand.

"Have a seat, please, Mister Jones." Mary, Widow Hallett's servant, gestured toward an ornately carved chair in the main room, close to the hearth and beside a fine table with a candle perched atop.

Thomas did as she bid him.

"Mistress will be down shortly. She bid me give you this to drink." Mary placed a tankard of ale beside him.

"Many thanks," he said as he regarded the condensation beading upon the side of the tankard. As Mary left he took the drink—a hearty stout with something sweet and smoky about it. He had not broken his fast that morning, so the stout was welcome to his empty belly.

He studied the candle on the table beside him, burning within a fine glass lantern. It was not a tallow candle—he could tell this because there was little soot upon the lantern's rim, and the scent was distinctly sweet. It was a fine home that could afford to burn beeswax candles in an empty room during the daylight hours. It seemed as frivolous to him as tossing coin into the sea.

The sea. The flame atop the candle began to waver and take the shape of a little illuminated boat, bobbing upon the tide. *How odd,* Thomas considered as he rubbed at his forehead. He was not feeling himself. True he had drunk stout on an empty stomach, but he had taken ale at breakfast for as long as he could remember. He would ask Mary what her recipe might be, perhaps it was fortified. For a moment then, he glanced round at his surroundings. Where was he, again? What was he here about?

"Mary, go and purchase more tea from the merchant." He heard Widow Hallett's voice outside the great room. *Oh yes, the widow and her desire for a table.* He chuckled aloud at his foggy-headed musings.

She entered and he rose from the chair. "Good day, Widow Hallett." The room slightly undulated beneath his feet, but then he gained his bearings.

She summoned him with a curl of her finger. "Come, follow me to the dining room."

He did as she bid. It was a large, richly paneled room with a finely built table at its center.

"This is a good table," Thomas said, leaning to the side so that he might get a better look at its legs. He put a hand upon the edge to steady himself. "Dutch?"

"You are astute, Goodman Jones. Yes, my late husband had it made in New Amsterdam."

"Why are you in need of another?"

"Because I want something new."

The idea were as frivolous as the beeswax candle in the great room. It said much about the Widow Hallett. Long had he suspected her to be a silly thing. This proved it.

"Very well, do you want it to be the same size as this?"

"Oh, no. It must be bigger."

Thomas raised his brows. "Are you hosting a large feast soon?"

She giggled. "Not that I know of, but maybe in the future, yes."

Thomas took the measurements based on her gestures of where she would like the new table to begin and end. He wiped at the sweat on his brow—he felt unusually hot. What had been in that stout? He then bent down to take a look beneath the table, to get a better look at the leg work. "Do you desire a similar style of leg?"

She crouched beside him. "I believe so, yes."

He stood, feeling unsure again of where he was, then offered his hand to help her stand. When she took it, he was struck by how small and soft it was. Never had he held so fine a hand in his. Curious, he studied it.

She took the brief moment to step closer to him. "What is it, Goodman Jones?"

"You've fine fingers, madam," he replied before he could think. He was not himself.

"As do you," she replied, then guided his hand to her tiny waist.

He cleared his throat, about to make protest, but she put those fine fingers of hers upon his lips, and the words on his tongue were obliterated.

"Don't speak," she whispered, removing her fingers from his mouth. Then she slipped her hand round his neck, coaxing him to bend and meet her lips.

His mind, his reason, disappeared. Her lips were questioning, begging, and it was the natural instinct of him to give, to give in. Her mouth was like silk he once fingered furtively in his youth in a shop in Bristol, the heat of her breath stoking the hunger within him. Lord, it had been too long. *Maggie, Maggie, it has been so very long.* Yes, it was his Maggie he was kissing. It was her scent filling his nose, her deep moan against his lips. His arousal was instant, straining against his breeches. Maggie was in his arms now, finally. He tightened his grip upon her waist, trying to ground himself, trying to figure out if this were real. He pressed her body against his, so that she would know this was no game, that he was in no mood for games. Where was his mind? No reason existed in that moment. He would have his Maggie.

But was she Maggie? Where was that mane of dark, unruly curls? She were more petite, smaller, not as voluptuous and strong. The cunning fox was in his sights. She was new to him, and the thrill of the newness was like a roast to a man starved, like stumbling upon a purse filled with coin. Her hands slid over his shirt, her soft fingers tenuously finding their way between the laces and beneath the linen, coyly stroking the hair beneath. It was too much. "Don't," he said, but it sounded weak, like it came from someone else.

"Please," she pleaded. "Show me."

"Don't say such things," he said hoarsely, in a voice that didn't sound like it came from him, yet he gripped her waist tighter. So fine, oh, so very fine. She was Maggie again, in their younger days, when she knew nothing and he thrilled with showing her everything, when he would watch in awe as she discovered that of which her body was capable.

"Teach me," she said, her words ending in a moan of pure desire as her fingers found his nipple.

"Ah, no!" he said, arching into her touch. "You don't want this." But he knew she did. Maggie always wanted his affections.

"I want this, more than anything, since I first saw you. Don't speak of Hell. I don't care. I want this. Teach me." Her other hand went down, past his navel, taking tight hold of the arousal he could not control.

He was someone else, the he of his younger days, before Maggie, days when he was free and he toyed with dairymaids and house wenches and gave coin to the tavern keeper's daughter because she would, she would, she would.

And she would, his Maggie, his own, and he put her atop the fine table from New Amsterdam that he could never re-create. She pulled her skirts up. He touched her and he knew how to touch her and he'd teach her how it was and how it could be and he would show her things she never knew of, and she would never be the same for knowing them. Yes, he was teaching his Maggie once again. And he was glad. Soon it would be Imbolc, but it felt like Beltane, like early May and the depths of spring. He wanted to ruin her and exalt her all at once, and he did it with his tenacious touch, he worked on her the thing she sought, the thing she never knew how to find. His Maggie, his own, and her eyes rolled back into her head and went all white and she gasped like she glimpsed something ever so beautiful.

"Oh, yes, that's it! More."

And like any man with any willing woman, he freed himself and entered her, because none of this seemed real any longer. Who was she? *My Maggie, my own.* She yelped in surprise, or pain, he did not know. He paused, she pressed her legs more tightly round him.

"Do you want this?" he asked before he descended, before he would completely lose any more of himself.

"Yes! Take me."

She was fine and tight and he took his sweet time, slow, slow, his heart racing, faster, faster, her breath heavy, quick, her hips instinctively knowing how to tilt just so.

He felt like some wild creature. As he quickened, he smiled, watching her climb and climb, his Maggie, and he felt like some other being, animalic, and how sweet it was, to watch her climb, to reach for the thing most good, so very good. And she was so hungry for it, his Maggie, starved for it, and she reached for it and then he moved just so and raised her there. And when she shuddered and pulsed within, he got there, too, to the place so very good.

But then he came to, came back, and he sank low. *Oh God, no.* He pulled away, pulled her legs from round him, freed himself from her hands clutching his shoulders. His mind felt cloudy and he shook his head, disbelieving. It was Widow Hallett, not his Maggie. What depravity was this?

"Oh, God no." The room was undulating beneath them. She had been his Maggie, and then she no longer was his Maggie. Some force had had him in its clutches.

She did not notice, or she did not want to notice. She panted, smiling, eyes closed, her fingers going to where he had just left. "Yes, oh yes!"

The utter disgust that flooded him was physical. His gut soured, there was bile upon his tongue. He grabbed her hand away from her quim. "Stop. I don't even know your damn Christian name. Oh God, what have I done?"

She looked as though he had startled her awake from a deep sleep. "It's Jane. Jane."

"Jane, this should not have happened. What unnaturalness is at work here?" He squinted his eyes shut, feeling as though they were at sea.

She studied his face as she slowly lowered her skirts over her thighs. "You are afraid of Hell."

He laughed, a bitter laugh. "I'm afraid of nothing but that I might have gotten you with child, and that I have done something I can never undo."

"A child," she said, and not in the thoughtful, wishful way so often sighed by women, but with dread. "So quickly?"

"You really know nothing."

She began to cry. He shook his head. "Don't start that. No tears. You knew what was transpiring, you cunning thing. You had a hand in this, too, I'd say. You worked some trickery here, you wanton thing." He put his hand beneath her quivering chin. "Come now, be a woman about this." He gasped for air. "You were woman enough a moment ago."

Her tearful eyes met his and she smiled. "You made me a woman."

He shook his head, grunting as he took tight hold of the table's edge to steady himself. "Nay, your late husband made you a woman. You were no maid."

"But you showed me . . ."

"Aye," he said, not knowing what else to say, for it was true, and lo, did he regret it now. He thought of Maggie and the pain of it was like a fist to the belly.

"What shall we do now?"

"This won't happen again."

She looked stricken.

"Don't look at me so. I'll not let this happen again." He fastened his breeches, his hands still shaking.

"But you wanted it too."

"That does not make it right. And you muddled my mind with something, some taint added to the ale, I'll guess." He could taste a lingering bitterness on the back of his tongue.

She did not heed him. "But what shall I do?"

"Find yourself a young husband, as I've been saying to you."

"I don't want a young husband. I want you," she said, reaching for his cheek.

He evaded her touch. "You cannot have me. I am married. What was in that tankard?"

Her face darkened. "Leave her."

"For what?"

She looked aghast. "For me!"

"Foolish thing."

"I am not!"

"Aye, you are, and you'll shut your mouth this moment. You speak like the Devil's whore. Have you poisoned me, you cunning thing?"

It had the right effect, for she got to her feet and smoothed her skirts. "Of course not!" Then she bit her lip. "What shall I do if I am with child?"

"Find yourself a husband quickly."

"Aside from that?"

He got her meaning. His wife was an herbalist, he knew plenty enough about such things. "Pennyroyal."

"Pennyroyal," she repeated as though it were a formula.

"You're better served to find a husband. Make some man happy."

"I don't want *some* man. No man can show me what you showed me."

"Oh aye, it's no secret, this business."

"Then how come my husband could not show me?"

"Because he was an old man of the gentry. Find a young man who works at the docks or at a forge. That's the sort of man you need."

She looked sullen.

"Do you really want the table?" he asked, gulping for air, longing to be away from this scene of his damnation, longing to be away from this evil.

"Nay, I've no use for it."

"Very well. Leave me be, wicked thing." He made his way toward the door.

She caught up to him, taking hold of his arm. "How can I, after this?"

There was a moment when he longed to strike her face over and over, this artful fox. But he knew he was complicit, that it had been just as much his own doing as hers, despite feeling as though some elixir had muddled his mind, for he could have sworn in the fever of the moment that it had been his Maggie in his arms. And he just had to teach her, just had to show her. He was Eve to her Adam. His eyes grew bleary. He was heated yet shook with chills. He pulled her hands from his arm. "Come now, this was a terrible mistake, and we must forget it ever happened. We must. I must be gone now." An acrid, sticky-sweet taste filled his mouth.

"As you wish," she acquiesced. Then she smiled as though she'd won a game of cribbage. "But you won't get very far."

Two steps into the foyer, his vision went black as he simultaneously uttered an oath and fell to the floor.

# CHAPTER TWELVE

*January 17, 1648*

*Bess has taken ill. A pestilence in the throat, perhaps. She burns, despite taking the Willow Bark tea. My arts have failed thus far. I am fearful. I feel a dark presence lurking at my threshold.*

Thomas heard the murmur of Irish in his ear. Was it his mother? Had he crossed to the spirit world?

His vision blurred, but soon his eyes focused on a human form hovering above him. And the formidable stench of hartshorn salt wafted into his nose, acting like a fist upon his forehead. He shot upright, not remembering where he was. He looked down to see he lay upon a finely crafted daybed. And the Irish voice was not his mother's.

"*Bí fós anois. Laghdaíonn an nimh, buíochas le Dia.* Be still now. The poison wanes, thank God."

"Mary?" he asked feebly, his tongue feeling swollen and numb.

"Drink," she said, holding a cup of milk to his lips.

He did as he was told, but the milk upon his tongue nauseated him. He pushed her hand with the cup away.

"What did you say before?"

"Hush." She put a finger over his lips, her eyes going to the foyer. She then looked to him. "She's gone now but not for long."

"What has happened?" He rubbed at his eyes. *This is Mary Doyle, servant to Widow Hallett.* "How did I—"

"The mistress and I, we both dragged you and pulled you up onto the chaise. Was no easy task, pulling the likes of you."

"Oh God, no," he groaned, remembering what had transpired before he had hit the floor.

"*Mo Chara.* My friend," Mary whispered, continuing in a quick pace of the Irish they shared in common. "I found the posit, in the kitchen, after she had soaked it in the ale. I would have never given it to you otherwise, I swear it."

"What posit? Ah, no, the ale!"

"Aye, the ale. She put a chaa pouch in it. I know naught what it was made of. I found the dampened cheesecloth with some sharp-smelling muck of herbs within it. The cow thought I wouldn't suspect anything. She thinks I am dumb, calls me 'idiot.' I'm no idiot, Mister Jones."

"A posit? A poison?"

"She told me you were unwell, had shown up here to take measurements full well within your cups. She bid me tell no one, to get you back on your feet and out as soon as you woke, so as not to cause a scandal."

"My god, what devilry—"

"I am a good girl, Mister Jones. But I am not an idiot. I know things. I know when you came here you were not in your cups. I also know a man cannot rut if he's too far into his cups." Mary looked down at her feet, her face turning crimson.

"Oh God, Mary, I am horrible." He covered his face in his hands, wishing away the past hours of his life.

"No, sir, heed me. She put a poison in your ale. An aphrodisiac or some sort of spell, I swear it! This was not your doing."

He took in her words, remembering the earthy-sweet ale, the undulating room, the watching of his own self as another being took over. "I was not myself, Mary." He recalled the triumphant smile upon the strumpet's face as his vision went black and he hit the floor. "Aye, she poisoned me."

Mary nodded quickly, wringing her hands.

"Mary!" He grabbed hold of her wringing hands. "Swear to me you will not tell a soul of this, you hear?"

"Aye, I swear it! *I swear é!*"

"*Geall dom!* Promise me!" He squeezed her hands, pleading, tears in his eyes, disgusted with himself, the guilt like the weight of the world.

"Thomas Jones, *geallaim*, I promise!" She snatched her hand away to make the sign of the cross.

The weight was crippling. He sobbed. Mary brought his head to her apron, cradling him. "You're a good man, Thomas Jones. You are one of my people. I won't let you down. *Tógfaidh mé seo go dtí m'uaigh*, I will take this to my grave. *Is fuath liom í*, I hate her. I should tell the magistrate of her witchery."

Thomas composed himself, wiping his eyes upon his sleeve. He shook his head. "Mary, no, they'll never believe you. They'll never take the word of an Irish indentured servant over a daughter of fortune, you know this." He exhaled as he gingerly rose from the daybed. "And what proof could you give? That she poisoned and seduced me?" He laughed bitterly. "She could have any man in Boston with that pretty face and comely figure. They would laugh and then they would find a way to take my wife and I down as quickly as possible."

Mary followed Thomas as he made his way to the door. "Her day of reckoning will come. It must." She opened the door for him, peering out. "It's good that night has come. Go quickly, now."

"Mary, I thank thee for your friendship."

"*Téigh le Dia,*" she murmured. "Go with God."

It was three nights past a new moon, the sky inky black but for a tiny crescent of light. Thomas lit the lanterns within the shop for he could not bring himself to go inside, to face her, to face his guilt and shame. He would work until he couldn't stand, make himself weary to the bone. She would be asleep when he would roll his weight into bed.

But his hands were rendered useless, fumbling in attempts to shape, to curve, to embellish wood. In frustration he worked at sanding new planks of maple wood. To and fro, more like a gristmill, less like a man. The sand and the sod covered his clothes, stuck to his skin, filled his eyes, which shed tears, to soothe, to wash away the debris, the anger, the dread of what he had done.

"Thomas!"

"Aye!" He bolted upright, startled by the sound of her voice. Through blurred eyes he saw Maggie standing on the threshold of the shop, clutching her apron within her fists.

"It's Bess. Do come."

There was no anger in her voice. A pang within his belly told him that something was amiss.

He followed her out of the shop, across the yard to the house, pausing at the back door to wash his face and arms in the well bucket.

Inside he was met by the sound of Bess's strangled sobs and a barking, high-pitched cough. The stench of burning clary sage and boiling rosemary oil thickened the air within the house. But there was another scent, of sour sweat, of illness.

"What ails Bess?" Thomas asked, going to Bess, who lay on the small trundle bed he had crafted for her. He took a nearby candle and held it above the child. His breath left him in a great rush, for he could not believe what he saw before him.

"Maggie?" he asked in a small, frightened voice.

Bess's once plump and creamy cheeks were covered in an angry, blotchy red rash.

"Maggie!" This time he shouted in alarm.

Maggie took the candle from his hand, illuminating her own face. He saw the fear written in her wide eyes, her quivering lips.

"Scarlatina," she said.

"What can we do?"

"I've done all I can."

"Should she be bled?"

"No!"

"Why did you not come find me sooner?"

"You were away, I did not know you were back in the shop."

"Good God almighty. Please, God . . ."

"I have prayed too."

"Is there anyone else who can help?"

"Nay. Most would have sent for me."

"What tricks do you have, Maggie? What secrets from the Chinaman in Cheapside? Tell me," Thomas said, taking hold of her forearms, shaking her to coax some knowledge, some remedy from her. A cold sweat trickled upon his neck, down his back.

She then scooped Bess into her arms and placed her in a washbasin of warm water that smelled of mint and something earthy and green, cascading the water over Bess's skin with a small cup. The child's sobs subsided into sniffles and whimpers. The sudden change startled Thomas and gave him hope.

"Is she better?" he asked, and knew he sounded like a boy asking for something impossible.

"I know not. Just pray with me, please."

He followed her lead, reciting the old Catholic Hail Mary over and over. It was embedded in him from childhood—no amount of Protestant reform could erase the impression of the words learned so early on, words so dear.

They continued to recite the rosary in a low murmur as Maggie dried Bess and swaddled her in clean linen. As soon as Bess was back upon her bed, she was asleep.

"Can she be mending?" Thomas asked in a hushed voice as Maggie and he stared down at the child who no longer resembled his child.

"The fever subsides, but this can be misleading."

"So we must watch over her," he said.

Maggie nodded, slipping her hand into his by his side. He clutched it tightly and brought it to his lips, kissing it over and over.

"I knew she were not well, remember?" She looked up at him with questioning, moist eyes. "We thought it was because she cut a tooth, but I knew in the pit of me, I felt it."

"Aye."

"We are being punished, for some misdeed. I know it."

# CHAPTER THIRTEEN

*January 24, 1648*

*She has gone, my life, my heart.*

Thomas lifted the latch, the bedchamber door singing as he swung it open. She stood by the window, her fingers tracing the diamond-shaped lead pane, the sunshine filtering through as though it could not resist touching her. She turned round to greet him. Her smile stole the breath from his chest.

How could this beautiful creature be his? How was it possible that he had some hand in her making? He bit the inside of his cheek to fight the emotion welling up within him. "Ready?" he asked, holding his hand out toward her.

She wore burgundy wool, and the color brought out the rose of her lips, her cheek. Her hair was a wild mass of black curls. She was her mother as a young lass, yet there was some of him in there, too, in the eyes that never gave a wary glance, eyes that regarded the world with wonder and delight.

She crossed the room and put her hand in his. "Da."

"My wonder and delight. My wonder and delight."

His wonder and delight.

The hand clasped his more firmly, shaking him. "Thomas! Thomas!"

His eyes opened to the dim bedchamber, to Maggie looming over him. He sat up, pushing the bedclothes aside. "Bess!"

They went to the trundle bed, freshly carved and stained, intended for her, to last until she grew too tall for it, intended for her until she reached womanhood. But it would not be so. For she were still, she would grow no more. She would not speak, her voice stolen from the world, trapped in some secret place he knew he would seek and seek and go mad with the seeking. The sweet milk breath never warm upon his cheek again. Never would she sip milk again, never would he fetch her the richest cream from atop the goat's milk and wipe her lip clean with the pad of his thumb. Warm lips cold. Who had taken his Bess? This was not his Bess. This was some creature put in her place, some trickery. He searched round the room. "Bess!"

Maggie screamed over and over, crumpling over the child. The screaming turned to moans of pain, then back to screaming, back to shrieks.

Her pain brought him to, brought him out of the dark place. He wrapped himself round her as she wrapped herself round the child.

"No, no, Bess, no!" she wailed. Her body convulsed and shook against his.

"Hush, Maggie," he pleaded, his words muffled against her back. The wool of her dress grew damp beneath him. "Hush now."

He knew not how long they remained there. He lost account of time. What did it matter? Time was of no consequence to him. When he was able to separate Maggie from Bess, he brought her to their bed, where she said she thought she may die from the pain. He asked if she might take brandy, she asked for the mithridate of poppy. He measured it as she bid him, then did the same for himself. He held her in his arms until the whole of him, his body, sank into the earth beneath the wood floorboards, where he was cool and made of rocks and the rocks were impenetrable, and he no longer felt the loss like a knife in his heart twisted over and over, over and over. His heart was a lump of granite, he had turned to stone. And when Bess as a woman came to him and touched his cheek, she gasped, for he was a statue, much like those smashed to pieces by Protestants. But he was too hardened to be broken. No one's god could destroy him.

Thomas rose from the bed to see it was early morning. The whole of him ached, his head throbbed mightily, as though he had drunk a butt of brandy on his own. He cursed the poppy mithridate. He looked down at his Maggie, whose dark-blue eyes were upon him, searching, frightened like a deer's.

"Rise, *Banríon*."

"Nay."

"Come now," he said, holding his hand out to her. "She deserves better of us."

She rose, her motions slow, purposeless, as though she did not bid herself but was bidden by him, and he knew then that they would never be the same again.

# CHAPTER FOURTEEN

*January 27, 1648*

*Bess were laid to rest today in the churchyard.*

*But she is still with me.*

It was a balmy, springlike day, though spring was still many weeks away. The air was brimming with life, the unmistakable sweet scent both intoxicating and cruel, making a mockery of him, of this.

The coffin was of his making; never would he permit another to have such an honor. Thomas had worked on it the night through, hewn the oak, carved it with the sort of filigree one found round the vestibule of the old churches, much to the dismay of the minister. He had raised his brows when he spied the heart—her heart, Thomas's heart—within the center. Thomas had sliced his palm open and mixed his blood into the varnish. His Bess's coffin was fit for a princess, his princess.

There were no more tears that could be shed. His grief had molded into something else, something hot and red like the blood varnish. What sort of God takes away a child so dear? How dare He? The cruelty was unbearable.

As the elf-like coffin were lowered into the earth, Thomas heard Maggie whisper, "Look, Bess, there it goes." He took her hand in his and squeezed tight. He thought that it could only have been heard by his ears, as he was beside her, but when he looked round, there were several parishioners who stared at Maggie, wide eyed. Let them, he thought. Let the poor mother grieve as she saw fit. They could all be damned.

⧖

Alice brought them supper that evening and each evening a fortnight following, bless her. She would serve them and then quickly make her exit, leaving Maggie and him alone in their silence, in their shared fog.

There are moments with a child when one desires nothing more than for them to be silent, be at peace, so that one might have one blessed moment to collect one's thoughts, or at least form a thought without the interruption of some nonsensical outburst. But now, now the silence was far worse. He cursed himself for all the times he had told Bess to hush. How selfish of him, for look now, look how bleak it be without the nonsense that was everything, though he had been too shortsighted to know.

His somber musings were interrupted by a slight giggle from Maggie. The sound was so foreign and strange that it did not seem to come from her.

"Maggie?"

She shook her head, her lips spreading into a smile. "Of course," she said, rising from her chair and going to the cupboard. She snipped a lump of sugar from the loaf, returned to the table with it, and put it before Bess's place.

"What is that for?" Thomas asked.

She gave him a sideways glance and drew her brows together. "For Bess, of course," she said as though he were a simpleton.

"Aye," he replied, for what else could he say? If it pleased his wife to leave offerings to their departed child, if it helped to ease her pain, who was he to criticize?

But when another fortnight had passed, and she did the same each night, when she told Bess fairy tales and sang her songs, reaching to stroke a cheek visible only to her, Thomas grew concerned. This was not right. Reluctantly he confided in Alice, for he had no other he trusted as he did she.

"This will pass, Thomas," she said, placing her hand upon his shoulder and giving a squeeze. "It is less than five weeks since Bess's passing. She will mend." Alice nodded her head to reassure him, but the furrowed crease across her forehead did not go unnoticed by him.

Nature continued to mock his grief and anger, for March came in glorious, warm and bursting with splendid color. Their garden flourished, and sometimes he would spy Maggie working in the rows, upon her knees. She would be rattling on to nobody but herself, but it wasn't herself in her mind, he knew. At first he made light of it, would say such things as "And how do the two of you fare this day?" And she would smile up at him and for the briefest of moments he would glimpse his Maggie again. The sight would so gladden him, he asked himself, could he not just play along with her madness, for the sake of seeing her smile like that once again?

How easy it would have been to slip into the warm bath of irrational denial, to take the draft of the imaginary, to walk through a door and leave behind the real, the hurt, the pain like a knife through the ribs. But time and life marched onward, and they mustn't be left behind, they mustn't pretend that they were no longer governed by the Great Wheel of Fortune, which forever spun on and often landed upon loss. Who were they to take a bow and leave this stage? Would it not be akin to the taking of one's own life? And were it not agreed upon by all religious creeds that he who took his own life affronted God, who gave that life as a precious gift, and risked eternal damnation in flame? Thomas was no coward, he was not a fool who believed that life should be naught but sweetness. The wind blew both fragrant and warm as well as blustery and piercing cold. Both came and went, both were born from the same horizon as surely as the sun rose and set each day without fail.

Maggie did not show this madness much outside the home. But often, when patrons would come to seek her medicine and advice, she would be caught in the act, looking down to the worn stool beside the table as she worked her cures upon the mortar. "Hush now," she would mutter, and Thomas would catch glimpse of the confusion written upon a patron's face. They were unsure of whether she spoke to them, herself, or some unseen person.

"What now?" asked Goodman Mason, who had come again to procure the beloved sandalwood oil that had transformed his wife from a pinched shrew to an open bloom.

"Hmm?" Maggie glanced up at him, a serene look upon her visage.

"Did you tell me to hush?"

"Oh, no, sir. I was speaking to the child."

Thomas was in the corner, finishing a draft of ale before heading back to the workshop. He froze, fearful of what Goodman Mason's response might be.

Goodman Mason's eyes quickly darted round the room, then back to Maggie. His brow smoothed and he sighed, giving her a reassuring nod as though he had come to some realization. "Poor thing, you still grieve your child."

Maggie shook her head. "Nay, sir, there is no grieving here. My child is always with me." She hummed a melody as she corked the tiny cobalt bottle and handed it to Goodman Mason.

After Goodman Mason bid Maggie good day and exited their home, Thomas followed him outdoors.

"Goodman Mason, might I have a word?"

He turned round and nodded. "Of course, Goodman Jones. How might I help?"

Were it not for the fact that Thomas's wife had helped transform Goody Mason and create a blissful marriage bed for Goodman Mason, Thomas would not have deigned to speak so frankly with him. But

Thomas knew him to be praiseworthy of Maggie and one of her most loyal patrons. Thomas came close and spoke in a low tone. "Do not pay much heed to my wife. She still struggles with the loss, in her way . . ."

"Mmm-hmm, yes, of course she does. 'Tis no light matter, the loss of a mother's only child. Of course she still struggles. She would be a heartless, Godless creature if she did not, aye?"

"Aye, well said."

He nodded, then clasped Thomas's shoulder. "Best cure for such melancholy would be to put your seed in her again. Give her another child to love and fuss over, aye?"

Thomas would not tell him that it had been months now since he had made love to his wife, or that it mattered not in the past how many times and how passionately they had made love, that his wife had great difficulty getting with child. He had shared enough of his private world with Goodman Mason that day, and he had seen enough of it too. Thomas only mustered a smile. "Aye, it's my intention."

Mason nodded. "Very good. See to God's plan." He departed with a salute.

Thomas turned and went back inside. Maggie still hummed the same melody as she dusted her shelves full of bottles with the turkey feather brush she had crafted herself.

Thomas hesitated, watching her as she stretched high to the top shelf, one hand upon her hip. Just then he had the desire to take her waist within his hands and squeeze tight. And so he did.

She exclaimed, turning round, her brows drawn together, her hands pushing against his chest. "Thomas, no! Not in front of Bess."

There was a surge of both the anger and the guilt and sadness within him. It took him a moment to find his words, for he was so overcome with the heady mix of sentiment. "She isn't here, Maggie."

She stared at him blankly.

"Bess is no longer here."

"Stop it, Thomas!" She shoved him away.

He would put a stop to this madness, before it drew him in. "Maggie, you must see reason. Must I take you to the churchyard?"

She crumpled over the table as though he had punched her in the stomach.

In that moment, he felt like some cruel monster, as though he had, indeed, taken his fist to her.

Thomas placed his hand upon her back. "Maggie, please, I'm sorry."

Her back quivered against his hand, as though she fought against something within her, some instinct. She then straightened and turned back to her dusting as though nothing had transpired between them.

"Maggie?"

Without looking at him, she spoke. "You are horrible, to say such things, when Bess is here. I'll not abide by it. Leave us be."

They had quarreled for so long. He had betrayed her, and now they paid for it, he reasoned. The guilt was like a chain round his waist. Perhaps this was what his sin had wrought. His insides felt as though he had run for many miles and there were no stamina or strength left in him to keep running. At a loss, he left the house and crossed the garden to the workshop, where he knew he could drown his despair in the sweat of his labors.

That evening Thomas still toiled, reluctant to return to the house. He paused for a moment, wiping the sweat from his brow with the cuff of his sleeve. Looking toward the open doors of the workshop, he realized the daylight was quickly fading. There was only so much work he could do by candlelight, so he cast more sand upon the birchwood before him. He would work until he could no longer see through the darkness, then hope that Maggie would be asleep by the time he retired. He was far too exhausted to navigate her flights of fancy that night.

As he sanded, he daydreamed fondly of days gone past, when it were just Maggie and him and no ghosts. He drowned his ire in the warmth of mirth remembered, in the glow of past passions quenched without thought but instinctive gladness. It was a pleasing place to hide, the memories of what now he knew were simpler times. Thomas missed that Maggie. He wanted her back.

As though his dreamings were answered, arms wrapped round his waist, taking him by surprise. Hands then caressed upward, along the planes of his torso, which were covered by his damp shirt linen. His breath caught in his throat, and he closed his eyes, giving in to the sensation. It was like a dream come true, and he dared not ruin it by opening his eyes. She had done this in the past, crept up behind him to touch, to coax, to distract him mad with desire. Thomas stood tall, reveling in the feel. Her hands then slowly descended, past his navel, sliding deftly beneath the ties of his breeches. A throaty moan of satisfaction and happiness rumbled from his lips. Her hands met with what they sought and what she had wrought with nothing but her touch.

She gasped, and that one simple sound shattered the dream. She was not Maggie.

Thomas dashed her hands away and turned. Widow Hallett wore a look of delight upon her face. Without thinking, he grabbed her wrists, taking a tight hold, and pinned her against the birchwood. "Who do you think you are, taking me by surprise like this, eh?"

Her lashes fluttered and she deigned to move closer to him. "You want me, look how your body responds to me."

He squeezed her wrists. "Answer me, you fox of a thing," he hissed, struggling to control the volume of his voice.

She winced at his grip, making him aware of his fury. Thomas let go quickly, disgusted with her, with himself.

"No, I like it when you grab me, like you want to possess me," she said. "No one has ever done so with me."

He turned away from her, trying to get his thoughts in order, control his fury. "Aye, that's the problem with you. You don't know your place. You take too much, like a child."

"I love you," she declared, loudly, placing her hands over her heart like some bard in a tavern, playing for a shilling.

Thomas turned back round and put his fingers to her lips. "Hush, you silly cow. You've caused enough trouble and mischief."

She boldly kissed his fingers.

He took firm hold of her chin. "You shall listen closely to me, do you understand?"

She nodded, wide eyed.

"I do not return your affections. I am married. I want nothing to do with your devilry, for that's what it be. I know what you slipped in my ale. I'm no fool. My wife is an herbalist, I know these things." He would not loosen his grip upon her chin. "Hear me now. You shall leave me be. You shall from this moment forward never set foot upon my land. You shall leave my wife and I be."

She guffawed. "Your wife is a madwoman."

Thomas tightened his grip and she winced. "You shall leave my wife and I be. You're an evil thing who has no compassion, no conscience. You're the Devil's hand. And if you should bother me again, or bother my wife, I shall have your good name ruined forever. Do you understand?" He let go of her chin, pushing her away from him. "We have suffered enough. We lost our baby girl, little do you care."

"Run away with me," she said, grabbing hold of his upper arm. "There is nothing to hold you back now. I will make you a happy man. I'll give you everything you desire. I'll give you a house full of babies. You won't give another thought to this life, to her and the baby."

"You don't know when to stop, do you?" He shook his head, pulling his arm from her hands, and spat on the ground. "Your mouth is insufferable. You cannot accept that I don't want what you offer up? You're like a cat in heat. Go find some other tom to sate you, you little minx."

She exclaimed, "You don't know what you're giving up!"

"I mean what I say. Go."

She turned quickly round upon her heel and exited the workshop. In the distance he heard the sound of her cart's wheels upon the road. It was not until the sound was gone that he closed up the workshop and headed to the house.

The air had grown close. The sky to the west turned to a ghostly glow of dusk as storm clouds from the east roiled and rolled inland. Lightning flashed, followed by the low growl of thunder. It was as though the heavens mirrored his insides, his life, his predicament.

# CHAPTER FIFTEEN

*March 3, 1648*

*I was requested to attend the former Governor Bellingham at his hunting lodge in Winnisimmet yesterday Eve. A fine home within a great wood, far finer than any lodge. There I was greeted by Goodwife Bellingham, a very young and comely lass who greeted me like family. I was entreated to a fine supper at their table. After much jovial conversation I inquired as to why I had been summoned. The amiable Governor Bellingham informed me with much humor that he suffered from acute gout in his right toe, which I readily treated. He then demanded I stay as his guest for the night and depart for Charlestown in the morning. In the morning I broke fast with his young wife, who then paid me handsomely for my services before returning on the ferry to Charlestown.*

*I like them, indeed. They were kind to me and most generous and I would happily provide physic to them again should they require it.*

As Thomas approached the back door, it swung open. Maggie held her apothecary basket in one hand, her shawl in the other. She stopped abruptly when she saw him. "You're quite late."

"Where are you off to?" he asked, trying to shake the uneasiness from moments ago.

"I've been summoned to the former governor's hunting lodge, in Winnisimmet."

"Bellingham?" This took Thomas by surprise. "How is it he knows of your physic?"

She shrugged. "Word travels, Thomas. I'm skilled at what I do."

He could not help but smile. That was the confident Maggie he admired and loved. "Indeed, you are."

She approached him, smiling, reaching up to place her palm upon his cheek. "Be sure to look after Bess."

The breath within him disappeared, like a ship mired at sea.

"Aye," he replied, not knowing what else to say.

And she was off toward the road, where a carriage drawn by two black horses awaited her.

Later, as he supped upon the stew and cornbread that Maggie had left for him, there was a knock upon the door. Thomas opened it to see a young man with whom he was unacquainted. "Good evening, sir, is Goody Jones at home?"

"No, she is not."

"Fie!" the young, wiry man spat out, gritting his teeth.

"I'm sorry, do I know you?"

He looked round as though to be sure no one spied him. "May I come in for a moment, sir?"

Reluctantly Thomas ushered him in.

He removed his hat, catching his breath, perspiring heavily. "My name is Daniel Spence. I've come from Dorchester."

"My, that's a long way. How do you know of my wife?"

"Sir, if I may speak directly, everyone knows of Goody Jones. I was told to see her for my, uh, affliction."

"What ails you?"

"Ah, well." The young man's eyes searched wildly round the room. "I'm sure you don't want to hear of my travails."

Thomas gestured toward a chair. "Indeed I do. My wife's business is my own business, as well."

"Oh, aye, of course sir."

"Go on then."

He hesitated. "Ah, well, I'm recently wed."

Thomas nodded. "My congratulations to you, young man."

"Many thanks."

"So what's that to do with my wife?"

"Ah, well, yes, I sought her help, in perhaps, assisting me in my husbandly duties." He grimaced in embarrassment at his own words, scratching his neck, staring at the floor.

"How so?" Thomas's temper flared. *What could he be trying to say?*

"Oh, sir, let me explain," he said, holding his hands before Thomas at the sound of irritation in his voice. "What I mean to say is, I sought out her physic, to help me, uh, um, last longer, in my husbandly duties, so that I might please my wife, you see?" The poor youngster had turned three shades of red.

"I see, you sought out a mithridate or salve? To help you in your endeavors, shall we say?"

"Aye, that." He nodded, relieved that Thomas understood his meaning.

"Did my wife provide you with something?"

"That she did, sir, and it worked so well that my wife bid me to go and get more, immediately. Today. This day. So I am here."

"Indeed, I'm happy to hear my wife was able to help you."

"You must know of it? The salve, it is miraculous! You apply it to the nether regions and it has a cooling sensation, then a warming sensation, which helps a man to, well, last longer, and please his wife."

Thomas knew Maggie to be skilled at concocting remedies, and knew this one to be one of her best sellers back in Cheapside. But he did not know that she still was mixing this magical balm in this new corner of the world.

"Sir, if I may speak plainly, it works almost too well."

"How so?"

"Well, I'm able to last for hours!"

"Is that a bad thing?"

"Not if you were to ask my wife, sir," he said, sitting straighter, putting his hand to his hip.

Thomas could not help but smile at his youthful pride. "Well then, good on you."

"Indeed, sir. Although it frightens me sometimes, as though I'm insatiable."

Thomas felt a pang of warning. "Love can make a man that way. You are blessed to find that within the marriage bed."

"Aye, but it makes my wife a wild thing."

"This is upsetting to you? I should think that makes you fortunate indeed."

"Oh aye, sir, to speak plainly, yes." He grinned stupidly. But Thomas saw the fear in his eyes. "But is such a thing God's will?"

Foreboding entered the room. "I cannot speak of what God's will might be. I know my wife deals in herbal remedies and tinctures that are as old as time, and created by God Himself if He chose to put them on this earth."

"Aye." He did not sound convinced.

"So is it fear or concern that brings you here?"

"No, sir, I desire more of it."

Thomas could see the pull of good and bad, right and wrong, or what he had been taught was right and wrong, written plainly on his visage. He grew uneasy. "Well, Daniel, my wife has departed for the evening to see a patient across the river." Thomas could have told him it was the former governor to impress him, and perhaps assuage his fears, but that would be compromising to the former governor, who himself was shrouded in a sinful nature, what with the business of marrying the young lady who was a guest at his lodge and conducting the ceremony himself despite the laws of betrothal.

"Aye, that's unfortunate. And I suppose you don't know how to mix it up?"

"Lad, I'm a carpenter and joiner, not a midwife and healer. That's my wife's expertise."

"Of course. Well, I shall tell my wife she must wait."

Thomas walked with him to the door. "Aye. Also, it helps to think of all and sundry."

"How do you mean, sir?"

"Think of something mundane, whilst . . . in bed with your wife, like your day's work, the ebb and flow of the tide, that sort of thing."

"Aye, I've tried that. Lucky for you that works. Not so much for me."

"Give it time." Thomas stifled his laughter as he opened the door for him. "Good evening, Daniel."

Thomas laughed to himself, shaking his head as he returned to the kitchen to pour another cup of ale. Soon he found himself very weary from the day, and took himself to the bedroom. He fell quickly asleep, yet his sleep was disturbed by nightmares. He dreamed of angry faces shouting at Maggie and him as they walked down the street. "You gave me a medicine that worked! You turned my wife into a wanton!" yelled Daniel. A crowd grew round them, and soon enough they swept Maggie away from him, and try as he might, he could not get back to her.

He awoke with a start, sitting upright. It was dawn, and Maggie was washing her hands and face at the basin. She turned to him. "Thomas, I didn't mean to give you a fright, my darling."

"No, Bride, I had a terrible fright of a dream."

"Ah, well, was just your mind playing tricks on you."

"Have you only just arrived home from Winnisimmet?"

"Yes, Goody Bellingham insisted I stay the night, and I acquiesced, only if I might arrive home at dawn. I've much work to do today."

Thomas ran his hands through his hair, trying to shake sleep. He watched as she removed her apron from a peg on the wall and tied it round herself. "Tell me about your call on your wealthy patron."

"Very well," Maggie said, running a comb through the tangled ends of her wild curls. "Bellingham's city carriage took me to the Mystic River ferry. The ferryman took me northeast from there, round the mouth of the river, into the creek between the mainland and Noddle's Island. He left me upon Bellingham's private dock, a fine structure within the tall cattails of marshland. There I was met by Bellingham's manservant, who took me by horseback up to the great hunting lodge. Thomas, this be no ordinary hunting lodge; it's a fine home, indeed."

"I would expect nothing less for a former governor of the colony," Thomas said.

"Indeed," agreed Maggie. "The mistress of the house—whom, of course you know, is quite young—was very jovial, insisting that I join them at supper. A very fine meal, with fine claret to accompany."

"Lucky girl!" They both laughed.

"I then inquired as to why I had been summoned, and the governor announced he suffered from a bad case of gout, which he then showed to me after removing his stocking and placing his foot upon the dining table. His young wife howled with laughter, and I could not help but join her. The governor was brought to his bed, where I mixed a salve of milk thistle and made a poultice for his afflicted toe. I made him promise to refrain from drinking wine or ale for two days, and only freshly squeezed lemon juice. He joked he did not suffer from scurvy, but I explained to my gracious host that lemon juice purges the kidneys, which will alleviate the pain in his toe."

"Clever woman."

"I am, it's true."

"And modest, as well."

She laughed, hitting his arm playfully. "They then insisted I spend the evening as their guest. They put me up in a fine room on the upper floor. It had a lovely view, looking southward, toward Noddle's Island, Charlestown, and Boston. A lovely sight."

"It sounds as though you've made new friends." He was so glad to see his wife like her old self again—enterprising, gregarious, jolly.

Maggie toyed with the edges of her apron, looking pensive. "I am like most in this place aware of the governor's scandal, and how he came to marry his young bride. They are unlike the other members of gentry here in Boston. They remind me of them back in London who would patronize my apothecary and who would see Clive the tarot reader next door. They are of the old ways."

Thomas rose and pissed into the chamber pot. "They are quite scandalous, the governor and his young wife, what with that oddly rushed marriage some years ago."

"Indeed. They seem very much in love, in fact smitten I would say. Can't seem to keep their hands off each other. Such attraction explains the rushed marriage." She stood on her toes to kiss his cheek.

It was all the encouragement he needed. He took her in his arms. "I've missed you."

"Have you checked on Bess?"

His heart sank like a rock thrown in the ocean.

"Have you?"

"Maggie, please." Thomas wrapped his arms tighter round her. "I've missed you," he muttered into her hair, squinting his eyes shut, not wanting the moment to disappear.

"Mmmm," she muttered, turning round in his arms, pressing her backside into his growing arousal. She tossed that coy look he loved over her shoulder. "What are you waiting for?"

Never in his life had Thomas hiked up Maggie's skirts and undone his breeches in such haste. It was over quickly, as they both urgently sought their pleasure. Unlike poor Daniel, Thomas had a wife who did not require so many overtures.

"Do you want more?" he asked, his nose filling with the scent of them as he trailed his fingers along her thighs and buttocks.

"More?" she laughed. "Are you able?"

"I'm able to taste you and bring you there again." He spoke in a low voice in her ear.

She laughed again, the sound like a sweet melody. *My God, it has been too long.* He would do her bidding all day if she would have him, to prove his love, to make amends for the sin he so regretted, the sin he would take to his grave. He would lick her the whole day through and never come up for air, he so adored the taste of her on his tongue, he so missed the taste of her.

"Nay, Thomas, I've much work to do," she said in a lazy, sensual voice as she rose and reluctantly straightened her skirts.

"Aye, same," Thomas said wearily.

She wrapped her arms round him and kissed his lips. "I'll go see to Bess now."

Again, he felt the breath in him disappear. "Maggie, she's not here," he said, shaking his head.

Her brows drew together. "You're right, she isn't here right now."

"Aye, my love. She's an angel watching over us now."

Slowly she nodded her head. "Aye."

Thomas was flooded with hope. Perhaps now, finally, his Maggie was coming to her senses. He kissed her forehead.

"But sometimes, she comes to me again, she does."

He looked down at her, stroking her cheek, waiting to see if she might continue.

"Sometimes she is really here with me, Thomas. I am not daft. I see her. She comes to me and waits for me patiently." A tear rolled from her eye, down to his hand. "And then sometimes I look for her and she is gone."

"'Tis how you mourn, my Bride."

"No, Thomas, 'tis the truth. She comes and goes."

There was a knock upon the door, shaking them from the dreamlike state. "I do believe you'll have your hands full today," he said. "Some came looking for you last night."

"Ah, such is the way of it, when your remedies work well," she said confidently as she exited the bedroom and went down the stairs to the door.

As Thomas made his way down the stairs, he heard a terse voice. "This instant! I require it immediately!"

It was Goody Tanner, her cap askew, looking a fright.

"Calm yourself, it shall take me a few minutes to mix up the salve."

"I don't have a few minutes! His cough is frightful, sounds like he is barking, my poor baby."

Thomas watched as Maggie pulled various bottles and wooden tubs from her shelves, slamming them upon the table as she did so. "Oh aye? Is that so? Just as I told you would happen two days ago when you sought my advice and declined my remedy, do you remember?"

"Steady, Maggie," Thomas said beneath his breath as he walked past to the kitchen.

"'Twas a threat! That's what it was! I believe you cursed my son out of spite!"

This stopped him in his tracks. Immediately he turned round and went back to the room.

Maggie threw her head back and had a hearty laugh. "It's naught to do with cursing and everything with you being a foolish cow who would not heed my advice out of your own parsimoniousness!"

Goody Tanner's mouth was agape.

It was time for his intervention, to control the damage that Maggie was wreaking all about her. "Maggie, hold your tongue and provide Goody Tanner what she needs for her son. Put it down as my gift to her on the ledger."

This had the desired effect on Goody Tanner, whose face relaxed into a glad smile. "My thanks to you, Goodman Jones."

"Oh, so that's to be the way of it?" Maggie demanded of Thomas, her hands upon her hips. "I must eat the cost simply to appease this miser who would pinch a penny till it bled?"

"Maggie, come with me," he said, quickly ushering her into the kitchen, shutting the door behind them.

"Get your hands off me!" She tried to shake off his grip.

He took hold of her shoulders. "Would you hold that viper's tongue of yours for one moment? Listen to reason. You're most intemperate!"

She glared at him. "Go on, give me my lecture, Husband!"

"Did you not hear what Goody Tanner accused you of just moments ago? A curse!"

"Fie! Nonsense it is!"

"Indeed, it is, but would it be nonsense before the magistrates? She's wealthy, the wife of a barrister. She comes from landed gentry back in England. You've ridiculed her while she is distraught over her sick child. Have a care, woman!"

Thomas could see the reason of his words sink into her, like dry earth absorbing the rain. Her eyes downcast, her breathing slowing.

"Aye, maybe you're right."

"I *am* right. And I don't give a fig about Goody Tanner, but I know you've no need for her ill will."

She nodded.

"Go back out there and make right the wrong your viper's tongue wreaked. Give her the physic she needs for her son. Offer to look in on him. Besides, it's not the poor lad's fault that his mother be a miserly cow."

Maggie laughed. "True, that is, poor lad."

"Go on then."

She went back out to the parlor, and Thomas stayed to listen at the door.

"I'll make up the salve with haste, Goody Tanner, and it's my gift to you. And I'd be happy to look in on your boy if need be. Also, here is a vial of oil of hyssop. Put a few drops in a bowl of steaming water, put the boy's head over the bowl, and cover him with a blanket, let him breathe in the steam. Hyssop will help him cough up the bad humors. And honey, give him honey off a spoon before he sleeps, will soothe him."

"I thank thee, Goody Jones," the woman said coldly. "But I do not want you to look in on him, thank you very much."

There was silence but for the sound of Maggie working upon the salve, the uncorking and corking of various bottles.

"I bid you good day," said Maggie.

The door slammed shut.

# CHAPTER SIXTEEN

*March 28, 1648*

*Of late, the former Governor Bellingham has requested I bring him various oils, herbals. He does not ask that I make him any physic, but he and his wife seem to make these of their own accord.*

*Town gossip has it that the Widow Hallett has married the new preacher come from England by the name of Longfellow. I am glad of it. I hope it means she leaves off bothering Thomas. The minister is young and I dearly hope he can quench her desires, so that she stop casting those doe eyes upon my husband.*

"And here's to the matrimony of Reverend Longfellow and his lovely bride, the Widow Hallett," said Samuel as he lifted his tankard above the table.

Of course Thomas had heard the news while about in town, but still, the mention of Jane Hallett was like a thunderclap within his belly. He had not expected Sam to make mention of her.

Alice broke into laughter, toasting her husband.

"God be praised!" shouted Maggie.

"Cheers to that," Thomas said, with true relief.

"I do hope that the Reverend lives up to his name, and quenches that maid's longing," declared Maggie. She was well into her cups.

The table laughed at her ribald jest.

"Well, I don't know about that," said Samuel. "Young man looks like a milksop to me."

"He can't help that, he's from the Fens, is he not? The folk are all fey and inbred from that way, they say," Thomas quipped, in hopes that his jest would quell his unease.

"Don't let the Governor Winthrop hear you say that," said Alice.

"There's nothing of the milksop about *that* one. He's dark, he is," said Maggie with a pensive look on her face.

"Indeed, he's quite swarthy, isn't he?" said Alice.

"Hush, Alice," mocked Samuel. "Don't be talking about the governor that way. I'll start to think you're sweet on him."

"Ugh, no!" protested Alice, falling into laughter.

"You like the dark ones, my Bride," Thomas teased. "Have you taken a fancy to Winthrop?"

"Oh nay, when I say he's dark, I don't mean just his visage. There is something dark about him."

The table went silent, mulling over her words.

"Ambition, that's what it be," declared Samuel before he took a hearty swig from his tankard.

"But Winthrop the Younger," said Maggie, with a tilt of her head, "now he's a handsome one, I do declare. Very dark, with a pleasing visage. And a clever scientist, too, they say."

"Oh, aye, that he is," Alice agreed.

"Right," Samuel said, rising suddenly from his seat, stretching his arms in the air, "Thomas, let's be off to find this Winthrop the Younger and deliver a warning to him before he might seduce these fawning maids of ours."

The room erupted in laughter at his bawdy joke.

There was a knock upon the door, and Samuel immediately answered it. There stood Goodman Storey, his next-door neighbor, looking mightily agitated.

"Storey! Do come in and join us for a draft."

"I've no time for such, Stratton. Come see what your goat has done!"

They all went out into the dusk to see what Storey spoke of. In the Strattons' side garden stood one of Storey's cows, munching away at Alice's onions.

"How on earth did she end up in my garden?" asked Alice.

"See for yourself, your dolt of a goat knocked a path through the fence and coaxed my cow into your land!" Storey gestured toward a gaping hole in the low wooden fence line separating his property from the Strattons'. "Now you've got to repair the fence, and now my cow's milk shall be spoilt by those onion shoots!"

"Easy now, Storey," said Samuel as he held up his hands. "Worry not about the fence, I'll see to it in the morning. And let us help you get the girl back to your yard now."

"That'll not be enough!" declared Storey. "You shall reimburse me for the spoilt milk she'll be making these next few days!"

"Pray, Goodman Storey, it's not our fault that the cow chose to eat my onions," said Alice. Laughing she continued, "Why, I could easily ask for reimbursement for those onions she ate!"

"Stratton, you ought to send your wife back inside," said Storey. "She's inebriated and not fit to be in public."

Samuel's mouth fell open. Before he could utter a rebuttal, Maggie spoke.

"Goodman Storey, what nerve you have, telling another's wife where she should go. And nerve to ask for reimbursement for 'spoilt milk.'" Maggie guffawed. "It's ridiculous to think such might happen after she ate some onion greens. And your cow's an idiot for following a goat through the fence!"

"Maggie, please," Thomas cautioned her, placing his hand upon her shoulder.

"Did you just speak ill of my cow?" asked Storey.

"Indeed, sir, I did!"

"I'll remember that, you cunning woman!"

Alice led Maggie quickly back inside the house, and Thomas followed.

"Maggie," Alice said, "you must be careful with what you say to those as ornery and judgmental as Goodman Storey. He has been unkind since he moved here from Boston."

"Pious fool," said Maggie. "He should have stayed back in Boston with the rest of the lot. He should have known he'd be with more regular folk here in Charlestown."

"But Alice speaks wisely," Thomas said. "You'll heap nothing but judgment and ill will upon yourself if you don't hold your tongue. I tell you this time and again."

"I'm so tired of your lecturing me, Thomas, as though you are holier than thou!" Maggie made for the door. "I must go check on Bess now." And with that, she was gone.

Thomas turned to Alice, searching her face. "I have tried to reason with her, Alice. She told me that Bess comes and goes from her. Do you think it madness?"

Alice laid a hand on his arm. "I think she still mourns in her own way. Maggie is different than most. She feels things more deeply. I know not how else to say it. She is very insightful but also she must learn to hold that tongue of hers."

But as Thomas met her eye, he knew she, too, believed that Maggie never would.

# CHAPTER SEVENTEEN

*March 30, 1648*

*This day is Bess's first birthday. Instead of me giving her a gift, she has given me a gift. This day, whilst at work in the garden, the Great Wheel of Fortune turned and decided to bestow upon me a most beautiful, majestic creature. A cat, with a fluffy coat of all colors, black, brown, red, and gold. She is splendid and loving. I shall name her Molly, as she be as vibrant as the painted mistresses of the gentry back in London.*

*She has chosen me. She, too, can see Bess. She looks to her, watches over her like a sentinel. She is also a great huntress, my Molly. She caught a mouse trying to get into the cellar. Of this I am most thankful. I love my Molly cat.*

The day had been most sorrowful for Thomas, who shed some tears upon his woodwork, knowing that on that day, his Bess would have celebrated her first birthday. Had it been his fault? Had her death been his penance for his great sin? He still wondered about this, often waking in the middle of the night with the guilt upon him like some sinister being pressing upon his chest. And then there was Maggie, growing more intemperate with each passing day with that Devil's tongue of hers, with her insisting that Bess was still with them. And then there were the days that she would weep inconsolably, muttering over and over that Bess's death was her atonement for all of her sins of the past. Thomas's heart would break at this, both with the weight of his own guilt, and because never was there so devoted a mother as Maggie. He would ask her, "What nonsense are you speaking of? You are no sinner." And she would turn her back to him and sob and heave, as though she did not hear his words.

After Thomas washed at the well, he entered the kitchen to sup with Maggie, only to hear her chattering away. His heart dropped, assuming that she be in one of her moods where she spoke to Bess. But he heard an answer to her chatter, which took him by surprise. It was the raspy, loud, and low meow of a cat.

"Pray, who do we have here?" Thomas asked, going round the table to see the creature. And there she was, the fluffiest, largest ball of a cat he had ever laid eyes on. Her coat was many colors and reminded him of the hue of a polished tiger's eye stone he had once seen in London. She turned to him, eyeing him with bright eyes as green as peridot gems.

"Who is this most beautiful puss?" he asked, instantly in her thrall as he bent before her and offered his hand.

"This is the Mistress Molly, this is," answered Maggie with a delighted giggle.

Mistress Molly deigned to have a sniff at his hand, then seemed to approve of him, as she licked his fingers and brushed her fine whiskers against his palm.

"She has deemed me worthy," Thomas said with a laugh. He had always been fond of cats and regretted that they had not taken one with them on the journey from London, as there were still few to be found here in Massachusetts.

"Come, supper's ready," said Maggie, filling a bowl and gesturing for Thomas to join her at the table. Molly jumped onto the bench beside Maggie and sat, lording over all that transpired at the table between them.

"She's an imperious thing, is she not?" Thomas said as he dunked his bread into the oxtail stew.

"What puss is not imperious? We are all their subjects," said Maggie, giving Molly a scratch beneath the chin, which was half black, half gold.

Thomas laughed, happy to see Maggie fussing over something, someone real and tangible, happy that they both had not descended into their grief, given the day.

"And how did you come to find Molly, or how did she find you, I should say?"

"I was in the garden this morning, splitting and replanting rosemary shoots. I felt someone's eyes on me. I looked northward toward the hedges, and sure enough I saw those gem-green eyes looking at me from the depths of the bush. I said, 'Come, my beauty, I've salt cod for you,' and it were as though she understood my words. She came right out, strutting over to me like some bold Cheapside doxy, her hips swaying this way and that."

They laughed. Mistress Molly gave them both a slow blink.

"There's those love eyes that cats give," Thomas said.

"We shall keep her."

"She has readily kept us, it seems. Salt cod, indeed! No wonder she bestowed her favors upon you."

"Ah." Maggie waved her hand dismissively. "She would have come to me without the promise of fish. I believe she was sent to me."

A cold finger went up Thomas's spine. "How so?"

"Someone is looking out for me."

"Bess is looking out for her ma, she is."

Maggie's eyes darted to where Bess had sat at the table. She did not respond.

"Maggie?" Thomas said, trying to coax her back to him.

She placed her fingers over her lips, and he knew she tried to still their quiver of sadness.

Molly let out a low, gravelly meow, looking at Maggie, and put her paw up, gesturing toward Maggie's hand on her mouth, as though she wanted to banish her sadness. It was the most remarkable interaction Thomas had ever seen transpire between a cat and a human. How could she understand so well? What magic was at work here?

Molly's gesture called Maggie back to the present moment, and her fingers fell from her mouth to Molly's great, fluffy mane. She smiled, looking down at the cat, then laughed. "Clever thing! You know my heart. Indeed, you've been sent to me."

"Indeed. But keep that knowledge to yourself, my Bride. You know as well as I do that that sort of chatter won't go over well with the pious lot here."

"Aye, I know that." Maggie dismissed him, dipping her spoon into her bowl.

"The stew is mightily good," Thomas said, tucking into his bowl. His wife's skill at the art of cooking never wavered.

"Oxtail, I know you like it. I think it's the currants I stew in there, then pound to a pulp and stir back into the stew. Gives it the sweetness," Maggie said with a nod.

"Oh? I always thought it was given its sweetness by you," he said, giving her a wink.

"That, too, my Love." She blew him a kiss.

Mistress Molly put her great mitt of a paw upon the table, as though impatient to be served.

"Oh, aye, your ladyship, how could I forget thee?" Maggie rose from the table, getting a morsel of meat from the kettle, which she put on a small saucer, then broke into smaller pieces with the kettle spoon. "Here you are, my lady," she said, placing the saucer down on the floor beside the table.

Molly readily jumped down from her spot at the table and went to her dish. She were no fool, the cat. And Thomas was thankful for her. She was something real to take the place of Bess in some very small way. He would have to tell the creature when they were alone how grateful he was that she had chosen to bestow her happy nature on them.

Indeed, there would be many instances in the days following where he would gladly tell and show Molly his affection for her. Maggie was right in her comparison to a Cheapside doxy, for the cat gave her affections freely with them and any who might enter their house or shop whom she deemed worthy. The cat became something of an attraction, much like a traveling minstrel. Children adored her, and she was very good with them, unlike most felines. She would allow them to stroke her downy, silky coat. She would rub against the legs and skirts of Maggie's better patrons. Clever puss! But as well known as she had become for her size, beauty, and friendly nature, she was also reviled by others.

"Shoo!" Goodwife Pierce had yelled at Molly one day before the cat had even made a move toward her. Unwise of her, for Molly was not one to be chided. The cat leered at Goody Pierce through slit eyes, letting out a low, nasty growl.

"Did that beast just growl at me?" Goody Pierce asked, her eyes wide with outrage.

"That she did, Goody Pierce," readily answered Maggie as she mixed up a salve for sciatica in her mortar and pestle.

The sharp green herbal note of pounded savory leaves filled the room. Thomas had come inside to have a snack of cornbread in the midafternoon. The door to the front parlor was ajar so he could not help but watch the interaction.

"That beast is intemperate, ought to be drowned in the harbor in a sack with a stone," declared Goody Pierce.

"And you wonder why the cat growls at you, with such thoughts as those floating about in your head?" asked Maggie with a bitter laugh.

"Are you claiming that the heathen creature can read my thoughts? What nonsense!"

"They are far more clever than you think," warned Maggie as she grabbed the bag of wheat flour, adding a small amount to the mixture in her mortar.

"Hold your tongue, else I shall think the Devil has it, Goody Jones! I ought to leave this instant!"

Maggie's concentration did not leave her mortar and pestle. "But you'll not leave, because no one makes a poultice for your sciatica like I do, and you know it to be true."

*Oh, Maggie, must you prod the baited bear?* She had always been one to speak plainly, but when Bess left this world, Maggie's couth—her gentle manner—left with her.

With a grunt, Goody Pierce acquiesced. "'Tis true, your poultices are my only relief from the pain. Your skill at herbs is indeed good. Too good, I worry, sometimes."

There, once again, went the icy fingers of foreboding up Thomas's spine. Goody Pierce insinuated that Maggie had power that went beyond that of the herbs. Power like that was power to be feared in this part of the world.

"There now," said Maggie as she smeared the mud-like mixture onto a piece of linen, which she neatly folded into a sizable poultice. "That ought to fit the likes of your haunch, don't you think?"

Thomas groaned under his breath but also had to stifle his smile. How cutting his bride could be with her insults. She took it to a level of artistry few could.

Hurriedly Goody Pierce slapped her coin upon the table. "Give me the thing so I can be rid of you, Goody Jones!"

As the woman opened the door to exit, Maggie chimed out, "I'll see you the next time your haunch pain returns!"

"Do you dare curse me?"

At this, Thomas would not remain silent. He entered the room with haste, to hear Maggie shout, "'Tis no curse but the truth! That pain will come again the more damp and cool the weather gets, when fall comes round again, and the more you sit and fill your belly!"

"Maggie!" Thomas said, surprised at her brutally frank words.

"Goodman Jones." Goody Pierce turned at the door to address him. "You ought to take her devilish talk into hand!" And with that, she slammed the door shut behind her.

"Ha!" Maggie grabbed her mortar and pestle and headed to the kitchen to rinse them clean. "As though anyone might tell me how to speak," she muttered beneath her breath as she poured hot water from the kettle upon the mortar and pestle in the washbasin.

"Maggie," Thomas shouted, irritated with her thoughtless interactions with a woman whom he could guess would readily accuse his wife of true devilry.

"What?" she shouted back, hands on her hips. "I suppose you're about to take Goody Pierce's words to heart and give me a lashing for the things I said?"

"I ought to, for you might drive me to it. How could you be so foolish, to provoke the likes of Goody Pierce in such a manner? What do you hope to achieve by this? Do you yearn to defend yourself in a court of law? Do you want to play at being your own barrister?"

She tilted her head and looked skyward as though she contemplated his words. "I'd make an excellent barrister, I'd wager."

Thomas slammed his fist upon the kitchen table and she jumped.

"'Tis no time for jesting, Maggie. We aren't in London anymore. The Roundheads might still be at battle with the King back in England, but they've won the war here in Massachusetts. You must learn to bide yourself, woman!" He searched her face, which was flush, her eyes wide, her brows drawing together in that way they did when she suddenly realized her folly.

"The words come out before I can stifle them," she said in little more than a whisper. "It's like a bonfire spreading to the nearby trees—I can't rein it in, Thomas, I can't. I'm so sorry, you're right." She sank down upon the bench at the table. "Oh, Thomas, I'm not fit for the likes of you. You always know the right things to say and do. I fumble like an idiot, a child."

There had been instances like this in the past, when suddenly Maggie would see the error in her ways and come tumbling down off her high and confident perch in a most dramatic way. Thomas had seen it before, and it always caused him to feel a pang of guilt, as though he had taken down a bird from the sky with a single musket shot, and watched it descend lifelessly to the ground and waiting hound below. But this time, he did not feel the guilt. He did not feel as though he had taken the life of a bird in flight, but rather as though he had put a hissing badger back in its crate. It served her right, before she did more damage.

"Do as I say, Maggie—*think!*" He searched her downcast face. "This is a dangerous place."

Suddenly she took hold of his hand and looked up into his eyes. "Let's leave this place, Thomas. Please, I beg you, let's make a fresh start elsewhere."

Thomas would have been dishonest if he were to say that the notion had not crossed his own mind more often of late. But here in Boston, they had become far more prosperous than they ever had in London. And the air, though cold and damp, was sweet with ocean and pine. The wind was cleansing, unlike in London, where the wind always seemed to carry pestilence. He was reluctant to leave their new home. It would be a good place in which to prosper and grow old, if only his intemperate wife would rein herself in.

He shook his head. "No, my Bride, no more running, no more uprooting. We prosper here."

She must have seen the resignation in his face, as she turned her gaze away and let go of his hand. "Aye. I've made you uproot time and again. I'll not force you yet another time."

"Come now, Maggie. Every decision we have made has been made together."

"I loved London," she said, her voice firm and quaking with anger.

"Aye, but London didn't love you back. The Great Wheel of Fortune in the sky did not favor you. You were beset with ill luck in the end."

"Damn that stupid cow for taking that Saint John's Wort tincture as though it were ale."

Thomas rolled his eyes, not wishing to revisit that unfortunate moment in their lives—the first time he thought he might lose his Maggie. "Come, lass, there's work to be done still today. Do your best to bide your tongue and all this shall blow over."

"I pray it does, my Love."

# CHAPTER EIGHTEEN

*April 17, 1648*

*This day I went by horseback, headed Cambridge-bound, toward Willis Creek. There I hoped to find some wild cranberries, as they are wondrous good for the treatment of scurvy, which is prevalent amongst those poor souls still walking upon sea legs. Alas I did not, and will have to pay dearly for those brought up from Plymouth. But I did come upon a wise, old woman, of the Winnisimmet tribe. She were merry and was keen enough to observe I were a healer in search of quarry, and she spoke English well enough to ask what it was I sought. When I told her, she waved me closer and said Lo, here is something else. I crouched beside her in the muck of the wetland beside the creek, and there she gestured to a bright green, leafy plant, some call it Indian White Hellebore, always the first harbinger of spring in these wetlands. She wrapped her gnarled fingers round it, twisted, and pulled upward. She showed me the white roots and explained that her people dry them, and grind to a powder. The powder is beneficial in the healing of wounds, and abates the pain of a rotten tooth. I thanked her kindly for sharing her knowledge.*

*As I was thanking her, there came up The Governor himself, Winthrop, and his son the Younger. Caught by surprise, I curtsied like a foolish maid. The old woman stayed crouched in the mud, paying no heed. The Governor studied me warily, but the Younger was friendly indeed and curious to learn about the plant. He smiled at me and asked my name. His father answered for me before I might. He spoke my name as though it were unsavory. The Younger did not seem to notice, but instead made conversation. My, but the Younger is a handsome man. Soon his father The Governor interrupted, bidding me not to trust in the ways of the Savages, for they were heathen. Challenged thus, I said to him, Oh, aye, but they were not so savage and heathen to you when they offered you corn when you and your people were starving, or when they trade you beaver pelts for wampum. Are we not all children of God? He quaked with anger, bidding me not to speak thus, that no woman should ever presume to know the ways of God. He then ushered his son onward, without a good-day to me.*

As Maggie related her meeting with the Winthrops, Thomas could not help but feel a shadow cast over his evening. He had little affinity for the governor. And, of course, his Maggie could not hold her tongue, and must always speak forthrightly, even with the likes of the most powerful man in Massachusetts.

"Must you always speak your mind? Even with the governor, of all people?"

She turned round from the hearth to look at him. "And why shouldn't I? Did he not come here to build a New Jerusalem, where all are equal under the eyes of God?"

"Aye, but he conveniently forgot about that when dealing with the likes of Anne Hutchinson, did he not?"

She sighed, her eyes going back to the pot she stirred. "'Tis a pity that the austere governor won't return to England for the rest of his days, let his son take charge as governor," she said.

"Soon, hopefully," said Thomas as he rose from the table and went to the hearth, turning one of the logs with the poker. "He is a member of the Assembly after all. Though he does travel much back and forth between Boston and his colony at Connecticut. He may well end up there permanently."

"I wonder," Maggie said as she poured a pot of boiling water carefully over the dishes and bowls in the washing trough. "Do you think the other settlements are . . . less rigid?"

He knew her meaning. He had wondered the same himself and had made some inquiries since the incident with Goody Pierce. Maggie had stirred to life old fears within him. Mayhap this was not the place for them, despite their prosperity. Perhaps they could not conform enough to what was expected of the Massachusetts settlers. William Pynchon's Springfield was much too far inland for his tastes—on the very edge of the known world, it seemed to him. And Connecticut, he learned, had its own share of troubles.

"Some months back, I heard a woman were hanged for witchcraft in Hartford, a Goodwife Young was her name." He watched as Maggie rinsed the bowls clean, silently sloshing the steaming hot water over them. "I think it not likely the other English settlements are any less rigid, as you put it."

She reached for a linen cloth to dry a bowl. "Poor Goody Young . . . I suppose there's always New Amsterdam," she said, a hopeful note in her voice.

"Aye," he replied, for they had mentioned it before, and as time wore on in the Bay Colony, the idea had taken root in his mind. Would it be better for them to uproot their lives again, in a new land, where few would even speak their language? At one time the notion seemed too burdensome. But perhaps it was worth the effort, the work, to pursue it?

A week later, at Sunday Service, the new minister, Longfellow, took the pulpit for the first time to deliver the sermon. Tall and lean, young and pale, he paused in his preachings often to clear his throat. He wiped at his nose with a handkerchief. He looked as though a brisk wind from the harbor might carry him off. Samuel was not wrong—the young minister looked like a milksop in a preacher's livery. A few times he stumbled over his words, and Thomas noticed out of the corner of his eye how some of the young lads had to stifle their laughter in the crooks of their arms. A most difficult predicament that can be, to be struck with a fit of humor whilst in the pews. Thomas smiled to himself—how sweet youth is.

When the service finally concluded, Minister Longfellow and his new bride, the former Widow Hallett, stood by the church steps to receive their parishioners. She looked well pleased with herself, holding her lovely chin high, looking down that delicate nose of hers as though to say, "Look where I have arrived now." Thomas felt a mix of both hilarity and anger—if one believed that the Devil took servants and made them his tools, here be one, no doubt.

Maggie stared at the minister's wife. She was quiet for a moment. "She is with child already," she said in a quiet voice.

Samuel and Alice looked toward Goody Longfellow. "How can you tell this? She looks no different to me," said Samuel.

"Aye," said Alice, "but Maggie here has a keen sense of these matters. I don't doubt her for a moment."

Maggie's eyes narrowed as she studied Goody Longfellow. "I should say that he put that babe in her belly before their hands were joined, by the looks of her."

Thomas's stomach churned, his mouth went dry. It took much effort for him to stutter out, "Come, Maggie, don't be inventing mean gossip."

"Aye, leave the newlyweds be," said Samuel. "Why, I care not what the governor says, there's naught wrong with young lovers betrothed consummating before their marriage ceremony. Why, the whole lot of us would be found guilty if that be the case, isn't it so, Alice?" he said, wrapping his arm round his tiny wife, giving her a hearty squeeze.

Alice playfully whacked at his arm. "Shame on you, Husband!" She fell to giggling.

"Fie shame! I'll have none of it. Here we are some decades later, with three young men to call sons and our marriage bed still a warm and happy place."

"Oh, Samuel, that's enough, really."

"Come along, my Bride. Let's make haste out of the cold." Samuel hurried his wife along to their horse and hitch. "Blessed Sabbath to you, Joneses," he said to them with a tip of the hat.

They watched them go their way. "Shall we?" Thomas asked, longing to be away from Goodwife Longfellow, her presence like a storm cloud looming above.

Maggie hesitated, a crease between her brows. Her gaze went to Thomas, as though she were foraging for some rare herb or mushroom in the woods. She blinked twice. Could she read his mind? He took a deep breath to steady his nerves. He tried to find something clever to say.

"Surely you don't want to be received by the minister, do you?"

As though he had woken her from her contemplations, she vehemently shook her head. "Heavens, no. Her presence is like black ink from a squid."

Again, Thomas felt the bile rise to his throat. *Could it actually be? Let it not be so, God, no.*

As he ushered Maggie to their hitch and helped her up, he turned round and looked back at Goody Longfellow.

Her eyes were on him like a hawk's upon the rabbit.

175

# CHAPTER NINETEEN

*May 4, 1648*

*This day Mary Doyle, the indentured servant of Goody Longfellow, the former Widow Hallett newly married, came to me. She brought with her a tiny poppet she found within the chemises of her mistress. The poppet is fashioned with unfurled black wool upon its head, a mass of curls. And within its lower belly were embedded 13 straight pins. I shall take it upon myself to confront Goody Longfellow this day. I believe this poppet was fashioned to be me, and she has cursed my womb.*

"Thomas!" Maggie shouted his name from the threshold of the workshop.

"Aye!" he answered peevishly, for he disliked being disrupted whilst in detail work. He ceased his filigree work upon the cabinet corner, wiping his brow, his gaze focused upon her.

Immediately he noticed the flush upon her cheeks and neck, her eyes wide with outrage. For a moment his heart stopped—had she discovered his secret? He froze in fear like a deer caught in the sight of a musket barrel.

"Look what Mary Doyle has brought to me."

He didn't move as she made her way across the workshop, Molly unfailingly trotting by her side. Maggie held out her hand before him. He looked down to see a small poppet or doll of some sort, and finally allowed himself to breathe. "Pray, what is this nonsense?"

"Look upon it!" she demanded.

He placed his chisel down on the bench between them and looked more closely. "It's a doll. Aye?"

"The hair, Thomas! Does it not remind you of mine?"

"I suppose?"

"Look at its womb and count the pins."

Pins? He knew then it were no simple toy. He took it from Maggie's hand, and as he counted, eleven, twelve, thirteen pins, Molly jumped up upon the bench and swiped with her plump paw at the poppet. It dropped to the bench and Molly immediately set upon it with her fangs, shaking the thing violently as though it were some delicious prey she were lucky enough to surprise.

"Come, Molly," said Maggie, snatching the poppet away from her. Molly let out a gravelly meow of protest.

"You say Mary Doyle brought this to you? Is it hers?" Thomas tried to understand.

"Nay! She tells me she discovered it whilst straightening the chemises in the widow's wardrobe. Come now, it is me! She dabbles in the dark arts, making a poppet of me and sticking thirteen pins within my womb. To harm me? To harm our Bess? She is a demon!" Maggie spat out.

"You speak of superstition," Thomas said dismissively, though he was equally disturbed by this. First Jane Longfellow née Hallett had used some poison upon him, now this. His wife was called a cunning woman and worse, all the while the minister's wife was the one consorting with Satan. The thought of that evil thing somehow bringing about Bess's sudden illness and death? It was too much to bear. He tried to shake the notion—it was folly to believe in such nonsense. But all the while, he wanted nothing more than to find Goody Longfellow and wring her neck until she met her Dark Lord in Hell. But certainly it was all a trap, was it not? If they were to confront Goody Longfellow, it would only speed their ruination.

"She's nothing but a silly strumpet, Maggie. Pay her no heed." He took up his chisel again, hoping to end the discussion.

"We must go and confront her," declared Maggie.

"Absolutely not. Are you mad?" He slammed the chisel back down upon the bench. "What evidence do you have that it belongs to Goody Longfellow? The word of her Papist indentured servant? Do you think that her words will hold any weight against the minister's new wife, a daughter of fortune?"

"They ought to!"

"Indeed, but an idiot you are if you think they might." He ran his hand roughly through his hair. "You've nothing except a poppet. She has power and money and a town full of religious zealots behind her, many of which would jump at the opportunity to take the likes of you down, Margaret the cunning woman."

He was fully prepared for his pugnacious wife to lash him with her fiery tongue. He would have to bear it until she finally saw the truth of the matter.

But she did not rail at him. She heaved a sigh, taking the poppet in her hand again, studying it. "You are most likely right."

"I'm happy you see it," he said, giving Molly a scratch under the chin and a caress before crossing his arms in front of his chest and nodding in approval. He knew he had been spared from another battle with his wife, and hopefully saved the two of them from worse peril.

She lingered, chewing on her lower lip.

"Best get back to work, Maggie," he said, longing to be alone again.

"Aye, to the garden I go."

❧

One evening, a week later, Thomas was surprised to find that supper was a hasty cornbread, cheese, sliced apples, and a few meager pieces of salt cod.

"Busy day?" he asked, taking in the table's contents.

Maggie occupied herself with filling tankards with ale. "Aye, it was."

"Many customers?"

"Some," she replied tentatively as she placed the tankards upon the table and sat across from him.

He chewed in silence, waiting for her to speak about her day.

She took a hearty sip from her tankard and placed it down carefully. "The minister's wife put on quite a show today in the square."

His heart stopped. "How so?" He endeavored to sound unbothered.

"She was strolling with her husband, purchasing some odds and ends from the farmwives. I was there to buy some beetroot. I'm sure she could feel the heat of my stare, wretched slut! When she turned and looked at me, she dropped her basket and exclaimed, covering her mouth with her hands, as though I were some ghost or phantom." Maggie stopped to laugh. "Then she fell into a faint, into her husband's arms."

"What?"

"Aye, so I went to her, of course, to offer my assistance—though I desired nothing more than to strike her perfect little face—and when I approached, the little slut screamed and said that I had cast some evil spell upon her and that her head ached, and she bid he make me leave, for a dark presence came with me and caused her pain. And then she feigned a swoon!" Maggie stopped to laugh again. "Can you believe the audacity? Why, it was all I could do to silence myself. I had to bite my tongue, for I wanted nothing more than to confront her with that poppet Mary found in her wardrobe. But I knew I must not make mention of it."

He could not bring himself to meet her gaze. He focused on the pewter plate before him with his unfinished supper, noted the crumbs of the cornbread. "And then what?"

"Of course that weakling of a minister bid me to leave. I was happy to do just that."

"Lord help us," he muttered, shaking his head, tremors coming over him. He knew that, at that moment, he had been saved from his secret coming to light. But he also knew that Maggie had been cast in a new light—or darkness—by the slut's dramatics. "Maggie, they've damned you. They might as well have issued your arrest warrant."

"Nonsense," she said with a guffaw, followed by silence.

When he sat up and met her eyes, he saw how they were wide with realization and fear. Her lower lip quivered. "You jest, don't you?"

He closed his eyes as the sensation of blood rushing to his head came over him. Like a flash of lightning, he saw his Maggie in chains. He saw his Maggie standing before a rope. He shook his head. *No no no no no! Be gone!*

"Thomas?" she asked meekly.

He rose from the table and took her hand, leading her to the bedchamber. There, she circled her arms round his waist and cried silently upon his chest.

It was as though she had traded with him her intuition for his silence. He knew it would come as sure as night fell and day dawned. For a brief second, he thought of how they might escape in the night, head for New Amsterdam. The journey would take four or five days by land. They would be caught in Connecticut for certain. By sea, there were no way they wouldn't be found leaving the docks. There was not the time to come up with a plan to hide themselves. And at that moment, he could think of nothing but the fact that soon she would be taken from him. Nothing else crossed his mind but that one thought, that she would be taken.

He knew it could be the last time he held her close, and the thought made him like a starved creature. Hastily he removed his clothes, then hers. At first he was eager and rough with her, forcing her down upon the bed and pressing her legs apart with his hips. She gasped as he entered, her fingers digging into his shoulders. He looked upon her to see a tear spill, as it had their first time together, so many years before, a lifetime before. It had been a different life, far more pleasing and hopeful than this life in which they were now held captive. He slowed his pace, his fingers sliding up her thigh and to her hip. Her skin was as soft and silky as that night upon the White Horse of Uffington. He vaguely realized that they might have come full circle, that their Great Wheel of Fortune might now be complete.

No! He could not let it happen. He must fight the will of the Great Wheel. He must tear it apart with his own bare hands and his own desire. Like those who bellowed into their tankards of ale in Cheapside pubs, singing, "Kill a thousand men or a Town regain, we will give thanks and praise amain. The wine pot shall clinke, we will feast and drinke. And then strange motions will abound. Yet let's be content and the times lament, you see the world turn'd upside down." Like the Bible psalm sung by those who wanted a leveling, on the streets of London and out upon the bloodied moors of Marston and Naseby: "Let God arise, let his enemies be scattered: let them also that hate him flee before him. As smoke is driven away, so drive them away: as wax melteth before the fire, so let the wicked perish." Likewise, he would tear down the sky for his Love, this Love, the very heart of him that beat madly within his chest.

"*Mo Rí*, my king," she sighed.

And now it was he who cried. It was he who had been taken. "*Mo bhanríon*, my queen."

# CHAPTER TWENTY

*May 12, 1648*

*This day I have been served with a warrant for my arrest. They say I am accused of witchcraft, dealings with Satan, having familiars, doing harm to others in Satan's name. I have been given one half hour to see my things in order and say goodbye to my husband and child. I will be held in the Boston jail until my summons to stand before the General Court's magistrates.*

*I fear for my life, for my husband, for my Bess. I know the time has come, to atone, for perhaps the Devil does indeed reside in me. I have been a poor sinner the whole of my life. And now I shall be held accountable, though never have I sought to harm others, even when they might vex me mightily, and even when they may have been deserving of my malice. I have only sought to help and to heal, to atone for my life as a sinner.*

The air were close that day, like it can be when a storm of lightning and hailstone looms overhead. It added to Thomas's sense of anxiety. Hastily he dressed and headed to the kitchen.

Maggie was already up, had cooked a pot of corn mush, and had a cup of fresh cream awaiting upon the table. She did not look up to greet him, but scribbled away furiously at what looked to be a letter.

"What are you writing?"

She gasped, looking up wide eyed. He'd taken her by surprise. She leaned closer to the letter. "It doesn't concern you."

He raised his brows. "No need to be upset, I was only curious."

"'Tis a business matter," she muttered as she went back to writing. "There's corn mush and cream."

Thomas quickly served himself and ate his breakfast, watching with foreboding as she wrote.

She glanced at him again. "Have you no work? For I have plenty."

"Aye, true. I'll not linger." He wiped his mouth with the back of his hand and went to the workshop.

Some hours later, above the sound of his saw at work, Thomas heard a bellow of a shout. He paused in his labors, listening. He could make out the voices of his wife and that of a man unfamiliar to him. Thomas dropped the saw, running out of the workshop and toward the back door of the house. His first thought was that someone had attacked his wife, some drunkard or some low-life mariner just come to port after months at sea. Barging through the door, Thomas saw his wife's hands being bound with rope by two constables. A barrister read loudly from a paper he held before him that housed a large black wax seal.

"What is this?" Thomas demanded, talking over him.

All three men stopped and stared at him.

"Might you be Goodman Jones, joiner?" one asked.

"Aye, that's me. Unhand my wife this instant," Thomas said in a low, calm voice. He had learned, as most did early on, that it was best to use a calm voice when addressing men of the law, else more misfortune might befall you.

"You heard him!" shouted Maggie, squirming away at the ropes, her wrists going red and raw against the cord.

"Goodman Jones," bellowed the constable with the paper. "Your wife has been accused of the following: witchcraft, dealings with Satan, working with Him through the use of a familiar, bringing harm upon many with the use of tinctures created with dark arts, for casting malignant curses upon many in the community, and for the hexing of one Goodman Storey's late cow."

"What?" shouted Maggie, before she guffawed. "You jest!"

"Goodman Storey brought evidence before the court that you put a curse upon his cow after she ate Goodwife Stratton's onion patch."

"That's absurd!" she shouted. "I called the cow an idiot for following a goat into the Strattons' garden! If that be a curse, then the whole of Boston would be cursed time and again for the ignorance that abounds!"

"Maggie!" Thomas hissed, his heart racing as he saw the constable take note upon a small paper with a wrapped graphite stick.

"Accused made mention of another familiar in the form of a goat . . ."

"Horse shit!" Maggie railed, struggling again against the cord, the two constables keeping a tight grip upon her.

"Constable, please." Thomas tried to steady the quiver of nervousness in his voice. He must bring a halt to this. He knew what had happened to Anne Hutchinson and Mary Dyer. He knew what had happened in East Anglia, some twenty-odd women found guilty and hanged. He knew he must stop the precipitous injustice barreling toward them. "This is some misunderstanding, you must hear me—"

"'Tis not for me to decide the matter, Jones. I am but the servant of the court and governor, I execute his bidding. Goody Jones is to be held at Boston jail until her arraignment and trial, in two weeks' time."

"Thomas," Maggie pleaded, tears streaming down her face. "Please, go see to Bess, comfort her, please."

The constable looked round to see of whom Maggie might be speaking. "Who is Bess?"

Thomas felt as though his stomach dropped to his feet. "Our daughter."

"The daughter passed some months ago, I believe," said one of the constables holding on to Maggie.

Immediately she spat upon his face.

"No, Maggie, control thyself!" Thomas shouted, knowing she damned herself further with every moment.

Again the constable jotted notes down upon his paper. "Accused addresses a ghost, spits upon constable . . ."

Thomas slapped his hand to his forehead, wishing that all this might be some macabre dream he might wake from. "What is it you require from us, Constable? Is it apologies to those who have been affronted by my wife somehow?"

"No, sir," the constable answered calmly as he put the small bit of paper and his graphite back in his coat pocket, then rolled up his official warrant.

Thomas was a desperate man. "Is it money? I have coin, I can pay any fine levied upon us by the General Court—"

"Jones, do you mean to entice me to take a bribe?" asked the constable, looking as though Thomas had slandered his name. "I shall make the court aware of your line of questioning, indeed."

Thomas followed helplessly as the three constables and Maggie exited through the front door of the house, to an awaiting constable's wagon pulled by two horses. Within the confines of the wooden holding cage, there sat Salty, the homeless old drunkard who spent all his days on the front stoops of the Charlestown waterfront taverns. Not a week went by that he was not arrested, only to be released again, back to drink himself stupid at the docks.

"Good day, Jones!" he slurred, tipping an imaginary hat.

Like a stunned drunkard himself, Thomas watched as they unlocked the holding cage and placed Maggie inside, across from Salty. The padlock was put in place, and the constables went back round to the front of the wagon and took their seats.

"Goody Jones!" said Salty. "It must be my lucky day, to be with such a comely lass."

Maggie said nothing, gazing down at the rope that bound her hands.

"Pray," Salty continued to slur, "might you have something to help with the drunkard's shakes?"

"Not this day, Salty," she said sadly, not bothering to look up at him.

"Ah, that's a pity," he said, slouching back against the wooden cage rails, closing his eyes. "She be the very best physic in this part of the world, Goody Jones is! She be an angel, taking away my shakes when I have to go without drink. She be the only one who can do it with . . . what is it you use to take my pain away?"

"Liquid from the poppy," she whispered, and Thomas was glad the constables did not hear of that.

"Save your chattering, Salty," called the head constable. "Mayhap you can serve as a witness in Goody Jones's defense?" The two constables fell to laughing as they carried on their way to Boston, Thomas's bride a captive in their hold.

Following behind the wagon was Molly. She would not be separated from her beloved mistress. She ran at a quick pace, jumping up to the side of the wagon and making her way into the hold. Thomas knew she would be safe, for she were a cunning, brilliant little creature and she would hide herself well. He had faith in her.

"Witnesses, aye, that's what I need," Thomas said, suddenly awakened from his shocked stupor.

"Thomas." Alice was by his side; he had not noticed. "Come with me, inside. We've much work to do."

Thomas followed her like a child. Samuel stood at the front doorway of his house, thick arms crossed in front of him, a look of disgust upon his face as he watched the constable's wagon move along the street.

"Who will vouch for her, aside from us, of course?" asked Samuel as he, Alice, and Thomas sat at his table, heads bowed together over parchment, quill, and ink. "Let's list them, Alice."

Together they thought of all those whom had been loyal customers and patrons of Maggie's since she set up her apothecary shop in this part of the world. The list was long, for Maggie had helped so many, had brought so many babies into the world successfully. Alice quickly jotted down all the names they could think of, though at times they were forced to cross a name off the list, thinking of some instance or manner in which Maggie had caused affront or insult. Despite those cases, the list was long. The three of them read it over.

"Who of these is someone who might have sway over the magistrates?" asked Samuel.

"Without a doubt, the former governor—Bellingham," quickly answered Alice.

A sudden feeling of hope took hold of Thomas. "Aye! Many an evening he has sent his carriage for Maggie, so that she might see to him and his wife at the hunting lodge across the Mystic."

"Odd one, that Bellingham," muttered Samuel.

"Odd he might be, but he is still a former governor, a founder of the Charter, and still sits upon the court of magistrates," said Alice. "He is your ace in your faro cards, Thomas."

"I must go to him and his wife and plead for them to vouch for Maggie," Thomas said, jumping up from his seat at the table and grabbing his hat.

"Not without me you won't," said Samuel, rising from the table and taking his hat from the peg by the front door.

Thomas and Samuel reached the north-facing dock, where Bellingham's ferry service awaited.

"What's your business, Stratton, Jones?" asked the ferryman with a tip of his worn hat.

"We would like an audience with Governor Bellingham. Misfortune has befallen my wife, who as you well know has been the governor's apothecary and physician these past months."

"Aye, Goody Jones. Skilled and cunning she be. The governor thinks most highly of her, this I know." The ferryman paused to take a puff of his pipe, the scent of heady clove and tobacco rising between them. "Trouble is, men, the governor is a most private man, he is. I'll need to bring word to him that you request audience before I take you over."

"Very well," Thomas said, eager to be done with the task at hand. "I'll pay you to take us to the other side, and we shall wait while you ask him, save some time that way?"

He removed the pipe from his lips. "You've coin?"

Thomas produced the sack of coin tied to his belt. He had been paid in full by a customer that morning. "I'll pay you what I'd pay the ferryman to take me to Cambridge town."

His lips pursed together and he nodded approvingly. "Very well then, come aboard, men." He put the pipe back in his mouth, turned round, and jumped inside the simple-yet-sturdy rowboat.

They followed, settling themselves onto the boat benches.

"I'll take these oars and help, to make the crossing quicker," Thomas said, taking hold of the oars at the opposite end.

"Very well, I thank you for that," the ferryman said whilst gripping his pipe between his teeth.

Northward they rowed, across the deep, cold, and dark waters where the River Mystic meets the Atlantic. Winnisimmet was not far off, but Bellingham's hunting lodge was farther east, across the narrow from Noddle's Island, where Samuel Maverick's plantation stood. Bellingham had purchased the land at Winnisimmet from him some years past.

Soon enough Thomas spied a dock, extending over a sandy slip of beach. The towering white pines lay beyond, fairly shrouding the road that led to the Bellingham hunting lodge. When they disembarked upon the dock, Thomas could see to the east where the Winnisimmet creek flowed out to sea. Beyond, to the northeast, above the cattails, he saw the brown-and-green marshland extending for a mile or so before reaching a huge stretch of sandy beachhead. Indeed, it was easy to forget, while dwelling in town, just how breathtakingly beautiful this New World could be. His insides suddenly churned—but it was not so beautiful, this New World, if his wife be taken from him.

"Now, do stay here while I go to the governor, please," said the ferryman. He untied a waiting horse by the side of the road, which must have been tethered there for that main purpose. He was off in a gallop, up the road that disappeared into the depths of the wood.

"How fine it must be, to have all this to call your own," said Samuel, pacing along the dock with his hands behind his back, surveying the forest before him, the beach below the dock.

"Samuel," Thomas said, "I fear for Maggie."

He turned his gaze to Thomas, nodding. "As you should, Thomas. You're no fool, and neither is she, which is why she's in this mess. Seems that when a woman has too much knowledge or skill, or speaks her mind freely, these Puritans take great offense."

"It wasn't like this in London."

"Aye, of course it wasn't. London is a city of the people, all people, scraping a living, hoping to give their children a more comfortable life than their own. That is, until the gentry and royalty take umbrage."

Had it not been for Maggie's misfortune in London, they would still be there this day. But trouble seemed to follow his Maggie, as though she paid for some great sin. And did she not say, in her moments of reverie, that she was a base sinner? Maggie had always been a faithful wife, of this Thomas was certain. There was but that one time she kissed the Irish harpist, but who was Thomas to cast judgment on that? She was a passionate creature, and he was a skilled musician, and he were dark and Irish like himself, and she lost her head for a moment. Was this the sin? Thomas did not see it as so egregious.

Thomas stepped off the dock and walked along the small stretch of beach, kicking the mussel and oyster shells aside with the tip of his boot. Maggie was not the sinner. The sinner was he. And he had kept it from her. He kept from her how he had been tricked and deceived and drugged to play the fool and lover to the damned Widow Hallett, now Goody Longfellow, who paraded about, secretly holding a child in her belly he feared was his own doing. What a mess. Thomas swore at himself as he kicked roughly at a stone, which flew into the lapping waves upon the sand. He must tell her. Because if she might—nay, he would not think of it. No, no, no. He wouldn't because it was impossible and ridiculous. His wife was no witch. She was cunning and skilled to be sure. And most intuitive, knowing a man's true nature long before Thomas could discern for his own self. Some women, he had known, had something like a third eye that could see and sense beyond the two. It was a gift, but Thomas saw nothing devilish in Maggie. She did not go about reading palms or gazing at the tarot cards, divining futures for those who asked. She had a healing touch, it was true. No one knew how to concoct a tincture, a salve, a mithridate like his Maggie. But she was his Maggie. There was no sin. He had known her and loved her since he first saw her, all those years ago. He had made her his in the Vale of White Horse. She was sharp-tongued, witty, clever, and without pretense; with Maggie there was nothing stifled or hidden. And here Thomas had been, hiding the darkest secret from her. He must confess to her the first moment he got. Because he might lose her—*nay!* Thomas would not think the thought. He would not.

"A carriage approaches," said Samuel, who had remained upon the dock.

"A good sign," Thomas said, hopping back up to the dock and making his way to the roadside.

The ferryman came to a halt by them, pipe still in mouth. "Come on, then. The governor says he shall give you an audience."

They got in and made their way, away from the water's edge and through the dense wood. The canopy above let in a patchwork of sunlight on all below it, and the light danced with the winds. The scent of pine and moss was heady. The road began to slightly incline upward, and eventually they emerged into a clearing in the forest, a hilltop, where a great two-level wood-framed manor greeted them, a sizable barn nearby. When they disembarked the carriage and walked up the granite-block steps to the front door, Thomas looked round, amazed by the unobstructed view of the sea, the harbor, the river, Noddle's Island, Charlestown, with Boston and its Beacon Hill looming beyond. The view was fit for a king. For the briefest moment, Thomas considered, were King Charles himself to come here and stand before this view, would he be so quick to give grants away to these Puritans, these men who so despised him?

They were shown in by a short, portly manservant, who took them from the great foyer into a sitting room, which housed a great hearth, walls finely paneled with dark wood, wide pine-planked floors, and many pieces of furniture of quality. In the center of the room stood a well-liveried man past midlife, who Thomas assumed to be the governor. Beside him stood a much younger, pretty lass in a blue dress the style of which Thomas had not seen since leaving London. She smiled warmly at them, as though she had been expecting their arrival. Quickly Thomas and Samuel made their introductions.

"Your wife is an exceedingly skilled healer and herbalist, Goodman Jones," said Bellingham as he shook Thomas's hand. "Please, come, have a seat, take some brandy with us."

"I thank you kindly, Governor," said Samuel as he sat.

"Pray, sir, I do not have very long to visit, unfortunately. I've come on a pressing matter," Thomas said, wanting to get to the point of his visit as quickly as possible.

Goodwife Bellingham offered him a cobalt-blue glass filled with fragrant apple brandy. "We know," she said, a look of both concern and sympathy on her face. "They have arrested her, haven't they?"

"Yes. How is it you've come to know?" Thomas asked before taking a hearty sip of the brandy, hoping it would steady his nervousness.

"I'm briefed daily on all the court's business whilst I'm here," said the governor. "I learned yesterday evening that a warrant had been issued for Goody Jones's arrest."

"Is there anything that can be done, sir?" Thomas asked loudly, sitting at the edge of his chair.

"I'm afraid not," the governor said. "You see, I'm no longer governor, so I have no executive privilege to issue a pardon."

"But can you not vouch for her character, as a presiding member of the General Court?"

"Indeed I already have vouched for her good character, Jones." He shook his head. "They'll have none of it. They have made up their minds, and many powerful members of the parish have come forward demanding this arrest and trial."

"Wouldn't your word count for more than a parishioner's?" Thomas demanded, for surely he must have more power and influence than he pretended.

"Alas, my word does not hold so much weight any longer with the likes of Winthrop. He conceives of me as ungodly since my marriage to my loving wife," Bellingham said, reaching over to the arm of his wife's chair, taking her hand in his.

"For shame, for them to judge our marriage so cruelly," said his wife, with something of a sulky pout, like a child upset when denied a treat.

"Then may I impress upon you to bear witness in her defense?" Thomas asked. "I know very well that she has come to your assistance on many an occasion."

"Indeed she has, and I would trust none other with my apothecary needs," replied Bellingham. "And it was exactly that which I pleaded in her case. But I cannot become entangled in the trial, I'm afraid."

"Whyever not?" Thomas knew his question was demanding and bold, but he did not care one bit.

Bellingham looked to his wife, as though trying to come up with the words. She squeezed his hand. "I would not wish to bring further scrutiny upon my dear wife and myself. We live a very private life here in Winnisimmet. We do entertain guests on occasion. But mostly, we treasure our solitude, and the freedom to pursue our . . . interests in private."

Goody Bellingham took her gaze from his and looked to Thomas with pleading eyes. "My husband, you see, is much enthralled with the nature of herbalism, and your wife was very kind to provide him with the supplies he required. I would not want my husband to fall victim to further scrutiny from the parish."

"Dearest, it isn't so much 'herbalism' that interests me, but how certain humors and ailments are governed by the movement of the heavens, the planets and stars, you see," explained Bellingham as though he were making his own case.

"Astrology, is it?" put forward Samuel.

"In some manner, yes, as well as how elements interact with each other to produce new compounds."

"Alchemy," Thomas labeled it, for he had known many of both amateur and professional alchemists during his time in London.

"Aye, so?" asked Samuel. "There be no harm in that scientific pursuit."

"Stratton, your intelligence is most obvious," said Bellingham with a slight bow of his head. "Why, even Governor Winthrop's son is an avid student of alchemy."

Thomas grew agitated with the slowing discussion. "Then if that be the case, why are you so concerned with the governor's knowing of your alchemic studies? You speak in circles, sir."

"Have you ever had the pleasure of meeting Governor Winthrop, Jones?" He did not wait for an answer from Thomas. "Above all else, the man desires power and clout. He cannot help himself—none of these Suffolk landed gentry can. He is both intelligent *and* clever. What would seem benign, and even pleasing to God, when associated with his eldest son he could most quickly and unapologetically portray as dark arts when dealing with any political adversary. Friends," Bellingham said, raising his finger in the air, "I caution you: Never underestimate how deeply power can corrupt even the most godly. And I shall declare I do not deal in any dark arts," Bellingham qualified at a deliberately slow pace.

"And neither does my wife!" Thomas tossed the rest of the brandy down his throat, placing the glass upon the side table and rising from his seat. "I'll not take up any more of your time or my own, Governor. I'll bid you both good evening."

The governor rose from his seat, putting his hands before him as though to slow an approaching horse. "Now listen to me, Jones. If there were a way I might help you, I would—"

"Aye, but not if it means a possible compromising of your own well-being," Thomas challenged. He knew it were wrong to speak so to a man of such influence, but his world was turning upside down further for each moment he wasted dallying with the likes of him.

"I am sorry you view it in such a manner, I really am," Bellingham said in a calm tone, as though he were a father speaking to an intemperate son. "I would urge you to implore your wife to remain calm, to speak little, and to appear penitent—regretful, even—of any misdeeds of which she has been accused. A contrite woman upon the court's stand stands a far better chance of survival. She will have to submit to the legal examination of her body."

"Her body? How do you mean?" asked Thomas.

"Of course. This is how it's done now, in English courts, according to Matthew Hopkins's methodology."

"Who is Matthew Hopkins?" Thomas shot.

"A witch hunter," answered Samuel. "He who hunted in East Anglia a few years ago."

"Indeed, and he has written a guide to see to the discovering of witches. I am certain that his instructions shall be used in the proceedings against your wife."

"Samuel, we must be on our way," Thomas said, now in a panic of what might befall Maggie while she awaited trial. "I must see to Maggie."

They made their way to the door, followed by the governor and his wife. "Remember, Goodman Jones, to tell your dear wife to be temperate and contrite whilst standing before the court," Bellingham said.

"Oh, indeed, Mister Jones," said Goody Bellingham. "And tell Goody Jones that I shall pray for her, light a candle for her."

Her last comment took Thomas by surprise. He turned to look at her, as did Samuel and Bellingham.

"Ah, she means that figuratively, that she shall light a candle for the Lord with the vehemence of her prayers," Bellingham said with a nervous laugh.

They said their goodbyes and the ferryman was summoned to bring his carriage and return Thomas and Samuel to town.

"Papist?" muttered Samuel to Thomas as they rode toward the dock. "You might be able to use that to your advantage."

"And a hypocrite I would be if I were to do so, to slander another whilst the same is done to my wife? You forget as well that my blood is from Ireland. I could never do what you ask, Samuel."

"Indeed, I take all of that back, should never have suggested it," he said, looking down at his hands upon his knees.

Few words were exchanged between them as they arrived back to the dock and boarded the ferry for Charlestown. It was dusk, and the sky eastward over the ocean had darkened, whilst to the west over Cambridge, it still glowed with the last rays of the day. Again Thomas took up the task of taking the other set of oars so that they might make haste back to town, so that he might go to the jail and see Maggie.

Alice awaited them on the ferry dock at Charlestown, her brow creased in worry.

"Alice," said Samuel, embracing her at the dock and kissing her forehead. With her, he was home.

With Maggie, Thomas was home. But she had been taken from him, and he felt like a boat unmoored, a rabbit without a burrow, a man without a name. She was his other half, the half that made him whole and complete. His life before her had been like a spring day devoid of green. Who was that man, the one he was before her? He was like a stuffed, mounted beast, bereft of a beating heart, a shadow of the creature he could be. The ground beneath Thomas's feet felt as though it undulated. He paused, bending over, hands upon his knees, and retched upon the side of the road. He could not lose her, he must not.

Alice wrapped a slender arm round his bent shoulders. "Come now, you need to eat and you need rest."

"I cannot rest, Alice, until I see her."

"I've already gone to see her at the jail, Thomas."

He stood straight, looking down at her. "How was she?"

"Like a wildcat in a snare, that's what she's like," she said with a bitter laugh. "I told the jailers that they held an innocent woman."

"Alice," warned Samuel. "You must be mindful, for there's nothing to stop them from doing the same to you."

"Pfft!" She waved her hand in the air. "They've got nothing on me. I've angered and offended none. I'm the little goodwife of Samuel Stratton, nothing more."

Thomas sensed a note of bitterness in her. He studied her face, waiting for more.

Despite the darkening sky, Thomas could still make out the sprinkling of freckles over her cheeks and the bridge of her nose. "My friend Maggie," she declared in a low voice made raspy by anger and sadness, "dared to be a woman with a profession, a talent, and a sharp tongue. Heaven forbid such a thing, in a woman." And she spat upon the ground.

Thomas knew Alice to be a woman of strong convictions and loyalties. But it was the first time he had ever heard her speak so vehemently.

"I shall go to her," Thomas said, turning toward the Charlestown-Boston ferry dock.

"Thomas, they'll not let you see her at this hour. And you're liable to say or do something rash that will get you in a world of trouble yourself. Now come," said Samuel, gesturing with his arm. "Sup with us, drink with us, and then rest for the morning."

Thomas knew he spoke sense, but still he lingered.

"Maggie asked that I look after you, she did," said Alice. "She worries for you."

"For me? Folly!" Thomas laughed bitterly. What a silly thing, to fret over him whilst she spends the night on a bed of mildewing hay in a jail cell.

"Do as she bids this night, Thomas," said Alice. "There's nothing else you can do."

Thomas ate little and drank much that night. He sobbed in his tankard and even began to speak in his native tongue. Alice patted his shoulder and cooed, "There, there, I know."

"Do you understand him?" muttered Samuel, thinking Thomas could not hear him.

"Aye, she's Irish like me, aren't you, Alice?" Thomas paused for another sip of rum. "With that red hair and those freckles like the stars upon your face."

She laughed a little at his expense. "Nay, I don't understand a word, Samuel."

"Right." Samuel rose from his place at the table and pulled Thomas to his feet. "'Tis time for you to sleep it off, you filthy Irishman, before you go charming my wife with that magical tongue."

Thomas had many witty responses at the ready, but he could not walk and speak at the same time, so he just laughed. He was a man unmoored.

He remembered little else from that night. He awoke face down upon the bed, clothes and boots still upon him. The sun was just beginning to rise. He reached his arm out, but Maggie was not there. Startled, he jumped up, remembering where she was—in the Boston jail. The room spun round him as it did after too much rum. He retched in the chamber pot, splashed cold water on his face, and smacked himself hard to wake from the stupor, to punish himself for drowning his sorrows while his wife awaited her trial in a prison cell. *How dare I?* Despite the heat of the day, he shook as though chilled. He donned his better cloak of black wool and firmly placed his black felt capotain upon his head. He stepped out of his home, squinting at the startling morning sun as though he squinted against a blizzard. Indeed, he felt as though he were making his way through a blizzard—every step labored and forced as he fought against the dread. The dread was in his heart, upon the brim of his hat, pushing at him like the winds and tides come off the Atlantic. When he reached the ferry dock, he saw three constables disembarking. He knew immediately for whom they had come.

"Jones! You've made our task much easier this day!" It were the same constable who had jotted notes about Maggie at the time of her arrest. "You are under arrest, by warrant issued by the General Court."

The townspeople stepped clear of Thomas, watching him go by as though he were the king. A king instilled fear, and it seemed as though his wife's imprisonment had the same effect. He saw the fear in their eyes as he dared them to meet his gaze before they faltered and cast their eyes downward, as though his stare alone could bring the wrath of Hell upon them. He offered up his wrists to the constables for shackling. He cared not. Let them take him. He had nothing to fear, he did not entertain Satan. Now he would be closer to his Love.

*Good, for see what they have wrought through their fear: the damnation of my wife, my heart, my happiness. Good, let them all be damned.*

# PART II

MAGGIE

# CHAPTER TWENTY-ONE

*The evidence against her was, 1. That she was found to have such a malignant touch, as many persons, (men, women, and children) whom she stroked or touched with any affection or displeasure, or, etc., were taken with deafness, or vomiting, or other violent pains or sickness.*

*—John Winthrop, Governor of Massachusetts Bay Colony, journal entry*

I could feel the crawl of lice and fleas upon me as I stood before the court, but I would not allow them to see me scratch. I would rise above, above, from this place, this folly, this nightmare come true.

The last time I had felt so filthy was on the voyage to this colony, far flung to the edges of the world. And I saw some divine meaning in this, that I might exit this place just as filthy as I had been when I entered it. I rued the day we put our futures into the hands of this part of the world. Damn this place. Damn them, damn them all.

The shackles round my wrists, after two days, had worn my skin raw. It was best not to struggle against them. The less I moved, the less they hurt. Alice had brought me some salve of duck fat and chamomile—a better friend none has ever had than my Alice—but it had worn away the day before, leaving nothing but the scent of a roasted duck's rendered fat and the sweet, bright note of steeping chamomile in a steaming bowl. Now, I rested my hands upon the polished wood of the witness stand's banister, hoping that they might remain there, unmoving, until this whole debacle be done.

The nine magistrates of the General Court took their places before the room. I knew all nine of them—everyone in Boston and its surroundings knew these nine powerful, wealthy men: Governor Winthrop, Deputy Governor Thomas Dudley, and Assistant Governors John Endecott, Increase Nowell, Simon Bradstreet, William Hibbins, William Pynchon (come all the way from Springfield settlement), John Winthrop the Younger, and my patron, Richard Bellingham. Nine magistrates stared down at me, a woman, denied the right to a defense barrister.

The first charge was read aloud by Dudley, and I laughed because it didn't seem real. It seemed as though I watched a pantomime in Cheapside, and I was waiting for the moment the comedian came swooping in to make us all laugh at the folly of it.

All eyes turned to me. If they were daggers, I would have been drained of blood in an instant. Deputy Governor Dudley cleared his throat deliberately, as though chastising a boisterous child, and continued with the description of my "malignant touch." Malignant! The stupidity! Why would any midwife and physic endeavor to harm her charges? What would be the gain in that? If nothing else, it made no sense at all when speaking on business matters. Surely that would be a quick way to lose all patrons and money. Business wouldn't remain solvent. What would be the use in that?

Dudley said that when I stroked anyone, they would become ill. Again, I laughed in disbelief, shaking my head. In my mind's eye I saw long hours, through days and nights, countless times, of feeling pulses in wrists, stroking foreheads burning with fevers, of laying my ear gently upon heaving chests that struggled like drowning men. I recalled the setting right of displaced shoulders, broken fingers and toes. I pictured my hands, gripping tight and smacking the backs and bottoms of newborns so that they might take their first breaths in this world. I thought of the heels of my palms, firmly massaging the bellies of mothers newly delivered, to be sure the afterbirth did not remain within their wombs and fester. I remembered bloodstained fingers deftly and swiftly sewing up quims ripped by babies' heads. How many women had told me in private what nice work I had done, how they had gained more pleasure after becoming mothers because of my skill with the needle? Where were those women now? Where were those men whom I saved from drowning in their own lungs-made-oceans by ill humors? Where were the little girls and boys whose foreheads I stroked while I sang and rubbed camphor and mint tinctures, banishing the evil humors away, away, to the corners of the room, to the windows I would open wide so that they would be gone?

I closed my eyes, wishing with all of my might that I could will open all the windows in the courthouse, so that this malignance of a trial could be sent away, away.

I opened my eyes. I had not succeeded.

I turned my gaze to the magistrates, seated above the General Court as though they were the royals for whom they espoused hatred. I shook my head and smiled. What a farce.

You see, I had figured out by a very young age something about men. The lot of them are not to be trusted. Indeed, I had learned in a most brutal manner, one that returned to me as a palpable nightmare each night I'd spent in the jail cell. Men are governed by their whims and passions far more than us women, yet they ascribe such traits to us. It is the purest form of hypocrisy there is. It has existed since the dawn of our time. Think of Adam and Eve. Oh aye, the Devil tempted Eve with knowledge, and she thought to better herself. And so she took the bait, and then Adam grew curious and envious and wanted a piece of it all. Just like a selfish child. But go ahead and tell me again how man is governed by his mind and woman by her heart. They have lied to us from the beginning.

Some men, though, are better than the lot. My eyes looked over the galley. I saw there Samuel Stratton. He is a rock, solid and devoted to my best friend, Alice. He is like my Love, my husband, Thomas.

Thomas was not there. He could not be, for they held him in the jail now and he awaited the same fate as me. Never was there a man so grounded to the earth as my Thomas. He was a part of the earth, an extension of it, like a towering great white pine. To think that the court might try to link him to the supernatural, to Satan, was absurd. I shook my head again, caring not that the magistrates and galley watched and scrutinized my every move, and saw the Devil present in every aspect of my being.

The call for the first witness broke through my mad musings.

It was young Jacob Weston. They saw fit to call a boy as their first witness against me. Truly, this was a farce.

Weston tentatively took to the witness pulpit before the magistrates. His chubby cheeks were flushed in his nervousness. I spied the quiver of his hand and his lips as he swore upon the Bible to tell the truth. I thought to myself, This should be interesting, that they should choose as first witness a boy whom I had healed so that he stood before all today, alive and breathing. Is not his being present the proof of my innocence?

"Tell us, Young Weston, of your experience with the accused," spoke Dudley.

The boy stuttered a little. "S-s-sir?"

"The accused being Goody Jones."

"Oh, right." Jacob Weston licked his lips as he pondered how to begin. "Some months ago, I was struck with an illness. I burned with a fever and my lungs labored to breathe. By the third day, my mother sent for Goody Jones to attend to me."

"And what happened then?"

Jacob Weston visibly swallowed. "Uh, I don't remember what exactly she said while she tended to me, for I was not well, you see." He paused, looking to the magistrate with wide, questioning eyes.

"Go on," Dudley urged.

"I recall she placed a cooling poultice upon my forehead that caused me to shiver most mightily. It was not pleasant. She then spread a salve upon my bare chest that burned my skin."

"All of these things do not sound beneficial to one in sickness, Mister Weston."

"Aye, well, no, I suppose."

"Proceed."

"I recall she then threw the windows of the bedchamber open. It were a cold night and the wind chilled me to the bone. I shivered and begged her to close the windows, but she—"

"She being the accused?" interrupted Dudley.

"Aye, she would not listen. She muttered words over me, all the while making with her hands as though she were pulling something invisible from me and casting it out the window."

"What did she mutter, Mister Weston? What did she say?"

"I cannot recall, for I shivered so that my teeth clattered together and I could not hear over the sound of them."

"Not a word?"

"Aye, sir, no."

"Proceed. What transpired next?"

"After a short while, I felt as though my chest heaved against my will." His eyes cast upward as though he searched for words in the corners of the courthouse. "I know not else how to describe it."

"Was it as though another force took possession of your body? A malignant, dark force?"

The galley members gasped, then began to chatter.

"Order!" yelled the constable, who stood beside me and banged mightily with his silver-tipped staff upon the floorboard.

When the galley had quieted, Dudley spoke. "Answer the question, Young Weston."

"I can't be quite sure, but aye, it was as though I were no longer the master of my own body. It were like my lungs were no longer under my own control."

"Were you frightened by this?"

"Aye, I was. I felt as though I might die."

Again, murmurs from the galley.

"And what happened next?"

"Then Goody Jones pulled me by the shoulders up to a seated position. She went behind me and whacked me hard upon the back."

"This does not seem the way one should treat an invalid child, does it?" Dudley posed to the room. "Proceed."

"She did this a few times, and then I coughed up a great deal of phlegm and slime, brownish, green, putrid in color. It came forth from me with each cough, until a great deal of it filled a bowl she held before me."

"And then what happened?"

"Well, sir, I could breathe properly again."

The audience murmured, as did the seated magistrates. Dudley looked frustrated by this admission, for his brow furrowed and he paced slightly. "And what then happened?"

"I recall she cast the contents of the bowl out the window and shouted 'Be gone, ill humors!'" Jacob Weston considered this. "It struck me as odd, at the time."

"Ill humors!" Dudley looked round the room knowingly. "What kind of woman can recognize and ward off ill humors?" He turned back to Weston. "Did you suffer any illness after that?"

"No, sir, I had been cured. It was as though when Goody Jones put her hands upon my back that the humors left me."

"Humors!" Dudley shouted, pointing his finger skyward as though he had made some great discovery. "Do you believe, Mister Weston, that perhaps Goody Jones consorted with some dark power in order to purge the ill humors and illness from you?"

"I can't say I know, sir, but aye, it were remarkable how quickly the sickness was gone and I could breathe again."

"Perhaps, my fellow magistrates, Goody Jones consorted with the Devil himself so that she could purge young Mister Weston of his ill humors so violently!"

I could not help myself, for I had stood there quietly for so long, listening, waiting for this tale to be twisted to their whims, and so I laughed aloud. All eyes were upon me. "Or perhaps, *Magistrates*, I merely did what was asked of me, what is asked of any herbalist, midwife, and healer? Perhaps I rid the boy of his ailment, so that he be able to stand before you today and bear witness?" I laughed again. "Is this what is to transpire in this *trial*? Are we to listen to witnesses tell all the stories of how I healed them? And then see this as some mark of evil upon me?"

"Silence!" yelled the constable, who pounded on the floorboard beneath me with his staff so that it rattled the chains that bound me.

The presiding magistrates studied me. John Winthrop, the great, self-important, and pious governor, stroked at his mustache and goatee, his eyes squinting at me as though I were a beast of burden for which he considered the price. "You are most intemperate, Goody Jones. I suggest you remain silent whilst we consider your fate."

"Oh, aye, it's just my life in your hands, is all. I should remain silent and not defend myself, aye?" I asked in little more than a whisper.

But he had heard me, I could see it in his eyes. He stroked at his fine goatee again. "Dismiss the witness and present the next."

I did not let go of his gaze. He knew I spoke the truth.

"Goody Weston, please rise and face the court," called the constable.

As her son left the witness stand and she made her way to it, she reached out and patted his shoulder as though he were a good dog. She took hold of her skirts and lifted her large frame up to the witness box. Folding her hands piously before her matronly torso, she cast her gaze up to the magistrates, nodding in greeting to them with a hint of a smile. What could this shrew have to say about me now?

I watched all the formalities of her swearing to tell something that she claimed was the truth. I raised my brows, questioningly, appraising her as her jowls quivered as she swore her oath. I turned my gaze to the magistrates and noticed they were more intent on me, seeming to watch me for any false move.

"Tell us, Goody Weston, about your interaction with the accused."

She took a deep gulp of air. "As you have heard from my dear son, Goody Jones did come to our home to see to Jacob in his time of illness."

"Indeed, and was there anything in your interaction with her that caused suspicion of any kind?"

She nodded quickly. "Oh yes, as Jacob said, she uttered some chant for ill humors to be gone, telling them to leave through the open windows."

"Did this frighten you?"

"Oh aye!" She glanced over at me but couldn't meet my eyes. "I was very alarmed, as though I were in the presence of some sort of sorceress!"

"Ha!" The laugh of disbelief escaped me before I could even reconsider.

All eyes turned to me; a gasp went up among the congregated.

"Such a sorceress, that I cured your son of the croup with naught but a poultice of ground mustard seed and hyssop, and opened the windows to the cool night air so that he could expunge the ill humors in his lungs. How evil of me." I fell to laughter again. If they chose to drag me down, I would not go down easily. I would not go down without a fight and without revealing the absurdity of it all.

The constable urged order.

"Goody Jones, you shall not speak until you are ordered to do so." Dudley turned to Goody Weston again. "Has your son been well since Goody Jones saw to him?"

She was reticent to answer, coyly tipping her head to the side. "Well, yes." Her voice had gone quiet. "But I do believe she deals in dark arts, I do."

"Thank you, Goody Weston, that will be all for now."

As she made her way past me, back to the galley, she could not bring her eyes to mine. She knew it were all folly too.

"The court now summons Goodman Proctor. Please take the witness stand."

After a shuffle amongst the congregation, there came old Proctor with his walking stick. It took him some time to make his way to the witness box, being well past seventy and suffering from reumatik legs. Again I wondered why, why on earth old Proctor might take umbrage with me. I was kind to him and his spinster daughter, had provided them with tinctures and teas to ease the stones from his bladder, to alleviate the pain in his joints. They had been some of my most reliable and regular customers.

"Goodman Proctor, please tell the court of how you know the accused and your interaction with her."

"Aye, sir." He paused to clear his gravelly throat of phlegm. "My daughter Martha and I would purchase herbs, teas, and tinctures from Goody Jones to help with my aches and pains, and . . ."

"Go on, sir."

He wiped his hand over his mouth and great beard, considering his next words. "When I could not relieve myself, you see, she could help with that."

There was a bit of chuckling from the congregation.

"Do you mean, sir, with your bowels?"

"No, sir, when I could not piss."

Again, there was some laughter from the congregation, but not from me. I had seen the pain caused by bladder stones and I could say with much authority that it could often be more painful than childbirth. I recalled the last time I visited old Proctor at his home, witnessed the poor man crawling upon the floor in sheer agony. To be sure, it was nothing to laugh about.

"And how did Goody Jones help in this matter?"

"She advised that I regularly drink a tea made from dyer's bloom, gooseberry leaves, parsley, and cleavers. It seemed to get things moving back along, most of the time."

"You do seem to remember well the physic she used."

"Aye, sir, you would, too, if you ever suffered from the piss blockage as I did." Old Proctor, bless him, stood taller and stared down the magistrate.

"Tell us about the time, this past winter, when Goody Jones came to call on you in your time of . . . discomfort."

"Aye, the pain was like nothing I'd ever had. The piss would not come from me, no matter how I struggled. My good daughter, most startled by my state, went and fetched Goody Jones. Jones came readily, herbs at the ready to brew a very strong tea. She had me drink great quantities of it. She asked me where the pain was in my body. It seemed to be everywhere, but especially in my back, round here." Proctor reached round and pointed to the midpoint of his back. "Goody Jones then lifted my shirt and began to rub some sort of foul-smelling, warm oil upon my back. Her touch was very firm, to the point of most painful."

"What did you do, Goodman Proctor?"

"I begged her to stop, but she yelled at me to keep quiet. She then began to mutter something as she continued to beat upon my back, something like, 'Be gone, be gone!'"

"Did this frighten you? Did you feel something evil in this?"

"The only evil I felt was the thing blocking my piss! Indeed, I began to chant with her, for I wanted the thing to be gone too!"

The congregation laughed at old Proctor's humorous nature, and even I could not help but smile. He was a good man. I sensed no malice from him, even as he stood witness against me.

"Tell us then what transpired."

"Goody Jones brought the piss pot to me and bid me to piss."

"Did the accused avert her eyes?"

"No, sir, she was waiting to see what happened."

"Did this not unnerve you, Goodman Proctor? Did it not seem wrong of a woman to watch you . . . relieve yourself?"

"Lord, no, sir. At that moment I was in such pain and so grateful for her help in my hour of need, I cared not what she saw of me. She is a healer, after all." At this, he turned to me, and his cloudy, aged eyes met mine. He tipped his head in thanks.

My heart was warmed. I felt a flicker of hope within me.

"Were you able to urinate?"

"I did, sir. Never in my life did I experience such pain as in that moment the piss finally came from me. All the while she pressed her thumbs into my back, muttering her chant."

"After you relieved yourself, what happened?"

"I believe I passed out from the pain, did I not, Goody Jones?" He looked to me questioningly.

I nodded. "Aye, Goodman Proctor. I caught you before you hit the floor, and your daughter and I brought you to your bed."

"Aye, so it was! I woke in my bed, and you presented me with this." From out of his coat pocket, old Proctor pulled a tiny black pouch. He gestured for Dudley to come forward. "Give me your hand."

The magistrate reluctantly did as he was told. Old Proctor tipped the black pouch and emptied the contents into his palm.

Everyone in the courtroom, including the seated magistrates, strained to get a look at what it might be, but I knew, and smiled.

"What is it, Magistrate Dudley?" asked Winthrop.

"It appears to be two pebbles," said Dudley. "One about the size of a small pea, the other the size of a sunflower seed."

Old Proctor nodded knowingly, looking round at the court. "Those right there, those came from me as I pissed, as Goody Jones pressed my back. She was kind enough to save them for me. I carry them with me wherever I go, to remind me of how our Lord God works in most mysterious ways. I am forever humbled, forever His servant."

Mutters of approval came from the congregation.

"Goodman Proctor, have you anything else to add?" Dudley asked as he handed the stones back to him.

As he gingerly replaced the stones in their little sack, old Proctor drew his brows together. "Magistrates, the rest of this assembly, I know not why Goody Jones is accused of consorting with Satan. I know her only as the angel who saved me in my time of desperate need."

"That will be all, Goodman Proctor," Dudley interrupted in a curt voice. He was obviously not expecting to hear that from old Proctor.

As old Proctor left the witness stand and made his way slowly and stiffly back to the congregation, he looked up at me and lifted a hand in salute.

"May the Lord look after you, Proctor," I said in a strained voice. I would not allow the court to see me soften, and so I had to fight the tears as best I could.

"Martha Proctor, please take the witness stand."

Martha Proctor went through the formalities. A spinster at forty-seven, she had accompanied her father to the New World and had been his caretaker. She was a quiet, shy little mouse of a woman who kept to herself. I was puzzled as to what she might be able to add to her father's testimony.

"Miss Proctor, please tell the magistrates and the court of your interaction with the accused."

"Yes, sir, I shall." She spoke in a soft voice so timid that all seemed to lean closer to pick up her words. "I often did procure herbs and such for my father, to help him relieve himself and to help with his rheumatism."

"Did you find these herbs to be of help to your father?"

"Yes, sir."

"Except for the day he described to the court, when he was in horrible pain and could not relieve himself."

"Yes, sir, that was a most frightful day. I did not know how to help him so I sent for Goody Jones."

"You trusted her."

"Aye, I did, sir."

"Did you witness anything dark in her dealings with your father that day?"

"I was most scared, sir, for my father seemed as though he were possessed by a dark humor, the way he did howl and crawl about in pain. And when I witnessed Goody Jones working so harshly upon his back, and the way my father howled in pain, it were as though we were in the presence of something very evil, coming from him."

Stupid, deceitful cow! It was always the mousy ones that could take you by surprise. I shook my head and laughed. "Aye, it was something evil! It were two stones come through his cock! I'd say that's as evil as things can get!"

The courtroom reacted to my words. Some laughed. The constable banged upon the floor and called for order as he stared at me.

"You shall not speak, Goody Jones, unless ordered to by this court!" yelled Dudley. He turned back to Martha Proctor. "Proceed, Miss Proctor."

"Sir, it is true that my father carries round these stones which came from him. He often shows them to me and to others he encounters. But when I look upon the stones, I see evil visages upon them."

"Ridiculous," I said, staring at Martha as though she had gone mad.

Some in the court shrieked in fear.

"Goodman Proctor," called Governor Winthrop from his seat. "Bring forth these stones again."

The court turned to where old Proctor sat. Reluctantly, he passed forth the pouch to the constable, shaking his head in disbelief. "I know not what my daughter rails about."

The pouch was taken to the magistrates. Each in turn inspected the stones and passed them along as Martha Proctor continued. "I see upon the stones, the ridges, that is, seem to look like demon faces to me. They haunt me in my sleep. I fear they were sent from the Devil."

"Likely you have a wild imagination, Miss Proctor, to come up with such a fanciful idea," I said.

"Order!"

The court held its breath as the magistrates passed the stones to each other. Two of them nodded. Old Endecott looked upon them and gasped, averting his gaze as he quickly passed them to Governor Winthrop. Winthrop inspected them up close, then held them at a distance. "I suppose to see a visage in an object is subjective, dependent upon the eye of the person considering," he said.

"You say these demon faces upon the stones haunt your dreams, Miss Proctor."

At this point her shoulders began to shake and she sniffed. "Yes, sir. There be evil all round us. And I believe that Goody Jones is able to commune with such evil."

"Utter horse shit!" yelled her father from his place. "Now give me back my stones this instant!"

The call for order was made again.

"We shall hold these stones as evidence in this trial, Goodman Proctor."

"Bah! Blast the lot of you!"

"One more word from you, Goodman Proctor, and you shall be put in chains," warned the constable.

"Miss Proctor," said Dudley, "have you anything else to tell the court regarding the accused?"

"No, sir, I have said my piece."

"Then you may go now, thank you," said Dudley as though he spoke to a little girl.

My eyes were upon Martha Proctor as she walked past me. She would not meet my eyes, until she suddenly paused and looked up at me. "You always thought yourself better than the rest of us," she muttered, then spat on the floor.

If evil did exist among us in Boston, this duplicity of Martha Proctor was sure proof.

# CHAPTER TWENTY-TWO

*2. She practicing physic, and her medicines being such things as (by her own confession) were harmless, as aniseed, liquors, etc., yet had extraordinary violent effects.*

—*John Winthrop, journal*

The court called for a recess for dinner. I was roughly taken from the stand and escorted—more like dragged—back to the jail across King Street. A crowd gathered to watch, some gawking, others leering. There were some mutters of prayer, "Lord save us from evil" and the like. An old man some paces away yelled, "Satan's whore!"

Before we reached the door of the jail, I felt something crash against the back of my shoulder, leaving a wet trail as it slowly slid off my linen dress. The stench quickly followed—dog shit.

"Keep order!" yelled one of the constables who dragged me along.

The other constable chuckled. "A fine lady you appear now, Goody Jones."

Did they all really think that dog shit would be the undoing of me? Did they think it would bring me low and cause me to confess to some ridiculous accusation? Idiots, the lot of them. I stared right back into the laughing constable's eyes as he awaited the door to be unlocked. A slow, knowing smile spread over my lips. His laughter quickly abated. He remembered who exactly I was and what I had been accused of. He thought better of laughing at my expense.

I was placed back in my cell for the time being, where I was given a grimy cup of water and a chunk of stale bread. I ate and drank, for I would do whatever I could to keep up my strength. I would not let them see me grow weak or falter. When the constables came to bring me back to the courthouse, I told them to wait a moment, then went to the corner and pissed in the privy bucket. At first they stared in curiosity like two dogs. I stared right back at them, for I'd nothing to be ashamed of. They would not make me feel dehumanized. They averted their gazes as I finished. I laughed to myself. Perhaps I was far more powerful than I had thought.

As we made our way back up the stairs of the jail, a magistrate was stepping inside. Former governor Bellingham—I knew that neatly trimmed mustache and goatee, the bemused set of his brows and slightly hooded eyes. I knew him well. For a brief moment I thought that perhaps he had come to vindicate my character. I looked to him hopefully, not wanting to hide my eagerness. He looked upon me, his brow creasing and his lips drawing together as though he were filled with pity.

"Guards, find Goody Jones another dress to wear this instant. She cannot go into the courthouse smeared with dog excrement. That is an insult to the court."

I bowed my head to him. "I am most grateful, Governor."

Quickly I was whisked away, unchained, and allowed to change into an ill-fitting frock. The bodice was not ample enough, and so I laced it as best I could, knowing now that I looked the strumpet with my breasts swelling above the neckline. Perhaps that is what they wanted of me, to better look the part of the fallen woman.

As we exited the jail and crossed King Street, Bellingham donned his magistrate's cap and walked before us. His presence parted the sea of spectators like Moses in the Red Sea. All were silent. Again, I was most grateful to him. I had not lost hope that he might come to my defense.

Once inside the courthouse, I was again brought to the stand in shackles. I scanned the courtroom, looking down with all the dignity I could muster, ignoring the stares at my breasts in my ill-fitting dress. Let them degrade themselves. Dogs.

And then I saw him, my Thomas! He were there, beside Samuel and Alice Stratton. "Thomas!" My heart was so full, knowing that he was free of the jail now. I saw it as a divine sign, that if the Lord saw fit to grant Thomas freedom, He may well do so for me as well. Thomas mustered a little smile, then put his finger to his lips, urging me to be quiet.

I turned to the constable beside me. "Sir, pray tell, was Thomas Jones, my husband, freed from the jail this day?"

He did not turn to meet my gaze, but stared straight forward at the magistrates taking their seats. "Aye," he said in a quiet voice. "There was no evidence against him. Bellingham and the Reverend Longfellow argued that he could not be kept imprisoned without any evidence."

Longfellow. Immediately my eyes sought out the lanky, pale minister. There he was, with a front-row seat, his cunning fox of a wife at his side. She caught my eye and smirked. If we had been in a tavern or out of doors rather than in this courtroom, I would have struck that smug look right from her face. But then I realized, it were she—not Longfellow, not Bellingham—who had lobbied for Thomas's freedom. She wanted Thomas. She was in heat for him like a street cat, and all the more so because she was with child. She thought she would win. My shackled hand pressed against the pocket tied round my waist, beneath my ill-fitting dress. There it was, the poppet. I had kept it close to me this whole time, within my pocket. If I had to use it, I most certainly would. But not until the right moment.

Order was called. I was most glad of all that my Thomas were there. My Love, my dearest friend. Never was there such a forthright man, and he were mine. And I was undeserving. I had brought this shame upon him, had done so before in London. And I had never been worthy of his love. I knew this, but I held on to it despite knowing this. A drunkard knew he should not have another bottle of wine, yet he did, because he could not imagine his life without its sweetness.

The constable called out, "The court does summon Goodman Spence of Dorchester. Please come to the witness stand."

Spence, Spence. I could not remember the name. But when I saw the tall young man approach the witness stand I remembered the lad. He came to me once for something to help him stay virile for his young wife. Apparently he was too zealous and quick in his lovemaking to suit her, poor thing. It was out of sympathy for his young wife whom I didn't even know that I concocted the warming balm for his cock. And here he was now to stand witness against me? Would he confess to what it was he procured from me? If so, I admired his audacity—perhaps my balm had grown his balls as well as preserved his cock.

After Spence swore to tell the truth, Dudley began his interrogation. "Tell us of your interaction with the accused, please."

He cleared his throat, looking directly at the presiding magistrates. "I did seek out physic from Goody Jones, some months ago."

"And what was it that you sought, or rather, what was the ailment or ill humor from which you suffered?"

"Aye, well, I went at my wife's bidding."

"Answer the question, Goodman Spence. For what did you require Goody Jones's physic?"

"Ah, well, you see, we were newly married, and new to the marriage bed, you see. And so my wife desired that I procure something to help, uh, prolong our . . . conjugal . . . activities."

It was too much, I laughed aloud. And not only did I, but much of the courtroom did as well. I searched to see if there were a young lady in the congregation shrinking in humiliation, for most certainly that would be the lusty Goody Spence, but did not see one. I even noted Bellingham look down and hide his mouth behind his hand as his shoulders shook. Winthrop would not crack a smile, but a sudden guffaw burst forth from him. Old Endecott did not see any humor in the matter, and he called for order.

"Do proceed, Goodman Spence," urged Dudley.

But lo and behold, young Spence showed no shame or embarrassment. In fact, he looked more willing to complete the task at hand. "So I explained my dilemma to Goody Jones, and she reassured me that she had just the physic to help me, a 'proprietary recipe' she called it, that she had brought to Boston from London." He paused, seeming unsure of how much more he would be required to say.

"Was this physic a drink? A tea? A salve of some sort?"

"A kind of oil, sir."

"And did you ingest this oil?"

"No, sir." Spence shifted uncomfortably on his feet.

"Elaborate, Goodman Spence, for the magistrates."

He took a breath of air, then continued, "It was an oil, to be administered to my manhood."

Gasps and giggles rumbled throughout the court.

"And what effect did it have upon you?"

"It created a warming sensation upon my manhood, then it became numbing in a way."

"And this was beneficial, you say? How?"

Spence looked at the magistrate like he were an idiot. "Why, it helped me to . . . prolong the act of lovemaking, sir."

"And why would this be necessary, Goodman Spence? It is God's will that man and wife make children."

"Aye, but I have been told that a child can only be made if the woman finds her pleasure, also."

The court erupted in ribald shouts, giggles, and laughter.

"If only that were true," I muttered. I found Spence's naivety endearing, until I remembered where I was and that his testimony would be held against me.

"Order!"

The courtroom settled, held captive by what was quite possibly the most informative and entertaining drama they had ever withheld.

"So, Goodman Spence, without speaking further upon such private matters," Dudley said, clearing his throat, "the physic Goody Jones made for you was effective."

Spence seemed to grow taller upon the stand, as though this was the moment he had been so patiently waiting for. "Aye, it worked. I would say it worked *too* well."

"How so?"

"It turned my wife into a wanton woman. She constantly wanted my affections."

"Why thank you, Goodman Spence. You shall make me a rich woman indeed!" I laughed.

"Silence, Goody Jones."

"How can there be evil in this?" I could not help but pose to the magistrates. I knew I would be scolded, threatened with the stocks even, but I could not see the logic in their line of questioning. "How can it be wrong that a young married couple enjoy each other's affections? Is that not God's will?"

"Goody Jones! You are not to question the court!" shot old Endecott. "And you are not to speak of God's will either. You are not one of the Elect, woman!"

"Oh aye, indeed I'm not or I wouldn't stand here accused of evil deeds."

"One more outburst, Goody Jones," warned Winthrop, "and you shall spend the night in the stocks."

"Goodman Spence, proceed. Did Goody Jones's physic cause harm in some way?"

"Indeed it did. My wife, she wanted to be abed with me constantly. She were like a cat in heat! So much so that one day while I was at my daily tasks, she left."

Again, the audience rumbled with surprise.

"Left? How so?"

"She left me, Magistrate. She left me!" The anger—and the anguish—was clearly written upon his pained visage, and the way he punched his finger into his chest. I had not seen this coming, indeed I did not. The pit of my stomach dropped.

"She has left her husband's home? Has she gone back to her family?"

"No!" shouted Spence, outraged. "She was last seen upon the Long Wharf, arm in arm with a Spaniard headed to Hispaniola. She has left me for a life of sin! I am here"—he pointed again to his chest, turning to address the whole of the courtroom—"here, telling you the most private details of my life, because I am a heartbroken man!"

His vehemence was startling to me. I actually pitied him.

"My wife, Lydia Spence, became a wanton *slut*, ruled by her quim!" His face grew red, his mouth quivered. He cared not that the constable banged his staff and called for order while the courtroom erupted. "It was because of this woman, Goody Jones," he yelled, pointing at me, "who is an evil hand of Satan in our midst! It was her magic that took possession of my wife, turned her into Satan's whore!"

"Have you any more to tell the magistrates, Goodman Spence?"

He shook his head, seeming suddenly drained of his outrage. "No, sir, I've said my piece."

He left the witness stand and did not go back to the congregation, but made his way out the courtroom door, head bowed.

As the magistrates waited for the court to quiet, I looked over to Thomas. His eyes were upon me, and he sat as still and unmoving as a cat. I saw the crease of worry upon his brow, and the manner in which his chest rose and fell with bated breath. He knew as well as I that this might be the first nail hammered into my coffin.

The magistrates spoke amongst themselves, then requested to leave the courtroom so that they might discuss Goodman Spence's testimony. The rest of us were required to remain. It seemed an eternity before they returned to the courtroom. All the while I had to endure the vicious stares and heated words of the congregation. I stood tall, staring straight ahead at the chamber door. I would not let them see me weak. Was it my fault that young Spence's wife suddenly discovered that there was more to life than being an obedient Puritan wife in Dorchester? Who knows what she might have endured as his wife; perhaps he were cruel to her, perhaps he was often in his cups? That might explain the need for the physic. But then again, mayhap she were nothing more than a woman who knew she would never find her satisfaction within his bed. Perhaps she knew there was a far greater love awaiting her elsewhere? And what if it were with that Spaniard? Who are we to judge? Who are we to say? Or maybe she was just a wanton whore. Only Goody Spence and the Lord knew what lay within her heart.

The magistrates took their seats again.

"Goody Jones," called Winthrop, "the court desires to question you further upon the testimony of Goodman Spence."

"Very good, Governor," I said with a nod, for I was grateful that I be able to tell my side of the story.

"Goody Jones," said Bellingham, leaning forward in his chair, "pray tell, what was the physic you provided to Goodman Spence?"

I had to stifle the smile that came to me, for I found it most humorous—and predictable—that it be the ever-curious alchemist Governor Bellingham to ask this question.

"It was an oil, Governor Bellingham, used for the purpose for which Goodman Spence sought."

"We gather this," said Bellingham. "But of what was this physic comprised?"

I laughed a little. "Wouldn't every man in this courtroom like to know."

"Goody Jones," scolded Winthrop. "This is not a theater, but the General Court of the Massachusetts Bay Colony. Answer the question posed to you."

"Very well, I shall. The base oil, or the carrier oil, is derived from walnuts. This I procure from a native woman, from the Winnisimmet tribe, who sells her wares now by the docks. I then mix into the walnut oil ground clove and the tiniest pinch of ginny pepper, the hot red pepper from Guinea. Finally, some drops of anise seed extract are added, which helps the clove and cayenne to blend more efficiently, as well as create a more pleasing scent. The three combine to produce both a warming and a numbing sensation upon the nether regions of a man, so that he not finish his conjugal duties too quickly."

The magistrates pondered my words, some stroking their beards as they considered.

"Then, Goody Jones," continued Bellingham, "you do not use that most evil and vile tincture sold throughout Europe as Spanish fly?"

"No, Governor Bellingham, not for this particular physic." I was surprised that he knew of Spanish fly, but then again, when I thought of the marital bliss between himself and his much-younger wife, things began to make more sense.

"But you use that most vile tincture in other physic of yours?"

"Governor Bellingham, perhaps you are unaware, but the ground powder of the Spanish green beetle, mixed with hard spirit, is a most useful way to bring about blistering upon the skin."

"And why, Goody Jones," asked Winthrop, "would you be required to blister anyone?"

"Quite obviously, Governor Winthrop, blistering is the very best way to be rid of warts of any kind," I replied, raising my chin. I was ready to answer each and every apothecary question they might pose to me. I had been trained with herbs by my grandmum from the time I could walk.

"So then," said Bellingham, "you do then have in your possession this Spanish fly powder?"

"Indeed, sir, most skilled apothecaries would have at least a small amount, for the purpose of blistering the skin."

"But not, of course, for the vile practice of seduction," posed Winthrop.

"There is a fine line, which an apothecary precariously treads, whilst mixing green blister beetle dust with anise seed extract for the purpose of creating a *tinctura aphrodesia*. Just the smallest amount too much, and the patient is not only driven to insatiable desire but also to vomiting and death."

The whole of the courthouse seemed most impressed with the knowledge I was imparting. Even the magistrates were being educated, it seemed. I saw Winthrop stroke his dark goatee as his eyes went to the neckline of my gown. He might be one of the Elect, but he was also a man, simple as a dog. His son, on the other hand, looked upon me with fascination, as though I were some wildflower newly discovered.

"Goody Jones, pray tell," said Governor Winthrop. "How did you come to be an apothecary, midwife, and physic? How did you come by such knowledge?"

I looked to Thomas for a brief moment, unsure of how much to tell the court. "I was trained by my grandmother, who was a midwife and healer in the village of Reading, back in England. And then I sought more knowledge in London, where I worked as an assistant to an established apothecary for five years. You see, my husband, Goodman Jones, was also serving an apprenticeship with a cabinetmaker. I'm sure all here are well acquainted with my husband's craftsmanship. He has made many a fine piece of furniture for the good citizens of Charlestown and surrounding." I had skirted our past life in London, and purposely sought to bring attention back to this side of the Atlantic.

The courtroom muttered, for many knew my dear Thomas well.

"But Goody Jones," croaked old Endecott, "will you confess to consorting in some dark arts, that your physic act most powerfully that it might turn the wife of Goodman Spence from devoted wife to wanton strumpet at the docks?"

"Governor Endecott, I cannot speak to why Goody Spence left her husband. I had no hand in that matter, I can assure you. If anything, I sought to help Goodman Spence keep his wife satisfied."

"Most ribald talk from a woman!" shouted old Endecott. "What sort of healer or apothecary has such a physic within her repertoire, to aid in acts of carnal sin?"

"I reckon that most apothecaries worth their weight have recipes for such physic. After all, as apothecaries, we follow the oath of Hippocrates, to help any and all in need of our knowledge and physic."

"I declare it evil knowledge! Much like Eve with her apple of temptation for Adam."

"If only such physic were as simple as prescribing a mere apple," I muttered, and some in the courtroom chuckled.

"Blasphemy!" shouted old Endecott as he struggled to be out of his chair. "We shall adjourn for the day, before Goody Jones speaks any more sinful words!"

"Is this the best you can muster, to accuse me of witchery and dalliance with Satan?"

"Indeed no, Goody Jones," said Dudley as though speaking to a simple child. "Why, we have more testimonies to hear tomorrow, followed, of course, by a thorough watching and examination of your body tomorrow evening, the method invented by the Witchfinder General Matthew Hopkins, which is now used by the English courts. We, too, have his treatise, *The Discovery of Witches*, and shall employ it as is done by Parliament."

A sudden sensation of icy fingers went up my spine. I did not like the sound of this examination one fig.

# CHAPTER TWENTY-THREE

*3. She would use to tell such as would not make use of her physic, that they would never be healed, and accordingly their diseases and hurts continued, with relapse against the ordinary course, and beyond the apprehension of all physicians and surgeons.*

—*John Winthrop, journal*

As I greedily wiped the bowl of porridge clean with my tongue, I heard footsteps descending the stairs and down the jail hallway. I put down the bowl and wiped my mouth, certain that it was someone come to look in on me. I sat up tall upon the pile of hay that served as both my only chair and my bed in this cell that was now my home. I straightened my worn skirts, for I would not let them see me without pride and dignity.

The jail guard approached, keys in hand, followed by Governor Bellingham and Thomas. The sight of my beloved caused my heart to leap in joy, caused me to forget the troubles and misfortune of the moment. He was everything that was good and worthy in my life, aside from Bess.

The guard unlocked the cell door and made way for Bellingham and Thomas to pass.

"Good evening, Goody Jones," said Bellingham, as casually as if we sat in his dining room drinking port. "I've brought you a gift."

I got to my feet, smiling, going to embrace my husband, forgetting that my wrists were shackled and I could not spread my arms wide enough to do so. Pretending not to notice, Thomas cocooned me in the warmth of his large frame. Immediately I wept. There was no shame in a woman showing gladness. He stroked my hair, kissed the top of my head.

"Come now, lass, no tears," he said, and I knew it was not to comfort me but more to prevent himself from weeping.

Remembering that we were not alone, I turned to Bellingham. "I cannot thank you enough, Governor, for allowing my husband to visit me."

He nodded, smiling.

"Have you any good news for us, sir?" I asked him, hopeful.

His brows drew together. "I'm afraid not, madam. It was most difficult for me to arrange this meeting with your husband, no less." He looked down at the cell floor, seeming to search for words. "I was able to persuade them by saying that perhaps your husband could speak reason to you so that you might confess, and save yourself the examination on Monday the eighteenth."

"Confess?" I looked to Thomas, then back to Bellingham. "Confess to what?"

"Why, to the charges of witchcraft leveled against you, of course."

I looked again to Thomas, looking for an answer from him. His eyes would not meet mine. "What is the meaning of this, Thomas?"

"I wish to save you from the disgrace of the examination," he said, finally bringing his gaze to mine.

I tried to make sense of his words, then scoffed. "Thomas, you know what sort of woman I am. No amount of questioning from the likes of them can disgrace me. I've nothing to be ashamed of."

"If I may, Goody Jones," interrupted Bellingham. "I don't think you understand the enormity of the examination."

"Then, please, educate me, Governor."

"According to current English law," he said, pacing the cell, "you shall be observed overnight. You will have to sit upon the floor, legs crossed, and you will not be allowed to sleep. Not at all."

"How can that be? That's impossible, to pass the night without any sleep. Why is this?"

"It is how they can discover if Satan will come to you, often in the guise of an animal or imp."

I laughed at the stupidity of it. "You jest, Governor."

He stopped in his pacing. "Indeed I do not. This is the law. And on Monday the eighteenth, you will be stripped of your clothes and your body shall be examined and searched for any mark of the Beast, any sign that you nurse a demon."

"My body shall be examined," I repeated, trying to comprehend the absurdity of it.

"Even your most intimate areas shall be searched," he informed me.

"You see now, Maggie," Thomas said, placing his hand upon my shoulder. "You see now why you might confess."

"I've nothing to hide, Thomas. I have no mark of the Beast upon me, whatever foolishness that might be. Indeed, they can search me all they want. I'll not confess to a falsehood."

"I know it's a falsehood," Thomas agreed. "But perhaps if you confess, you shall be given some leniency?"

The two of us turned to look at the governor for a sign that there might be some truth to this. His face was inscrutable. "Now that, that I cannot promise, Jones."

"Absolutely not, I'll not confess," I said, the shackles shaking as I expressed my disgust. "They can look upon me all they'd like, I care not. Did not the Lord create Adam and Eve without clothing, and were they not innocent in His eyes and each other's eyes before Lucifer tempted them with the apple? I do not fear my nakedness. I do not fear for them to see my nakedness."

Thomas shook his head slightly, a rueful smile playing at his mouth. "Nay, of course you don't, my wild Maggie, always proud as a lioness."

"I beg of you, Goody Jones, to think upon the matter," said Bellingham.

"Whilst I beg of *you*, Governor Bellingham, magistrate of the General Court," I spat, "that you plead my case, that you stand in defense of my character, of me who helped you on many occasion with your own ailments."

He heaved a sigh, placing his hat upon his head, moving to exit the cell. "That I cannot do, Goody Jones, not at this time."

"Then my blood shall be upon your hands for all eternity, Governor Bellingham. Can you live with that in good conscience?"

"Maggie, please," Thomas said, wanting me to curtail my talk, as he often did.

After exiting the cell, Bellingham turned round to face us. "I've made arrangements with the jail deputies. Goodman Jones has one hour with you before he must leave. I hope that perhaps he might convince you to reason, Goody Jones. Good evening." And with that he left.

The jail guard locked the cell door behind him. "In one hour's time, I'll be back to get Jones." He then followed Bellingham back up the stairs of the jail.

"Who has Bess?" I asked. I knew, of course, that she was no longer made of flesh and bone. But I knew, also, that she still came to me, stood beside me, holding my skirts, her presence never truly gone from me. How could it be otherwise? She who was a part of me, she could not just disappear. Aye, for certain, she was a heavenly creature now. And I, too, believed that God possessed the power to send angels to walk here amongst us. How could such life—such love—disappear?

Impossible, that it could be extinguished—smothered—by earthly death.

But Bess had not graced me with her presence for some days. Perhaps she was with Thomas? And if so, could he see?

Thomas sighed. "She is safe. Worry not."

I believed him. Thomas never lied to me.

"I'll not do it, Thomas, I will not. I'll not lie for the sake of a lie."

We sat upon the hay pile, side by side, our backs against the cold, damp stone wall of the cell. I stared down at my shackled hands before me, watching as Thomas slipped his fingers within them, against my chafed wrists, as though he hoped to protect me from further injury. A wife as blessed as I, there never was.

"Aye, I know you won't. I knew you would not agree to it, but I told Bellingham I would try to convince you, knowing it would buy me an hour with you, to hold you."

"Because I am such a lovely wife? I'm sure I look a fright." There was no need for pretense, for with him I was my truest self. Or at least as true as I could let myself be.

"Mind your words, Maggie. I could very well have my way with you in this jail cell," he said, kissing my temple.

I had a good laugh at this. "You'd wind up covered in fleas and lice. How romantic."

We both laughed. For what else was there to do?

"Maggie, what of the heart-shaped mark upon your upper thigh?" Thomas asked, and I could hear the nervousness in the hoarseness of his voice.

"Oh, aye, I've not forgotten about it," I said, thinking of the dark-brown, heart-shaped spot, no bigger than a pea, that had been upon my upper-inner thigh the whole of my life. "Could it be seen as 'The Beast's Mark'? I don't see how, I was born with it. If this be the case, then every woman and man who walks the earth might be charged with consorting with the Devil. Does there exist anyone without some unique mark, spot, freckle?"

Thomas nodded slowly. "Aye, true that. But it is you who shall be examined tomorrow, not the rest of the world."

❧

When sleep did come to me, upon the lousy pile of hay, it came carrying the same nightmare again, or rather, the same memory I wished dearly to forget.

It was the first of May, Beltane, and I was three months shy of my fifteenth birthday. I worked away in my grandmum's garden—the most resplendent, verdant, magical garden I have ever known. It had been her mother's and her mother's before that, for so many years and generations that my grandmum would say "back, into darker times." It was my most favorite place to be, that garden, and whenever someone would mention "home," it was the garden that came first to my mind.

I heard two horses approach my grandmum's cottage. They stopped, dismounted, tethering their steeds to the old hitching post by the moss-covered stone wall. The cottage blocked my view, but I knew it to be two men, for I heard their low voices, and then one of them laughed—a pleasing laugh that immediately stirred something within me, something like elation, warmth, and fear all wrapped together. Never had I felt this way before.

I heard their knock upon the cottage door, and the loud complaint of the hinges as my grandmum welcomed her guests inside our humble home. I sat up, leaning back upon my heels, pausing in my weeding round the hyssop so that I might hear what the men wanted from my grandmum. It was not uncommon for people to travel many miles to our thatched-roof cottage, to seek physic or tinctures from my grandmum. She was known far and wide for her skill, which she had passed down to me.

Despite the back door being open, I could not make out their conversation—I heard only occasional laughter from my grandmum, who was easily humored and very jovial. Curiosity got the best of me.

I rose from the dirt, shaking out my skirts. I removed my straw bonnet as I made my way toward the house. In the kitchen I cast aside my soiled apron. I went to the cracked old looking glass that hung over the washing trough, inspecting my visage. The messy braid would not do. Something within me compelled me to unplait my hair and shake it out so that it were a wild mass of dark curls. I liked my curls, they were untamable and unpredictable. Every day with curls was like an adventure all in itself, it was.

The face staring back at me from the mirror appeared new, more mature, more like a woman's than a girl's. I liked it. I felt a surge of power from the knowledge, and an eagerness to wield this power and see what might come of it. I heard the muffled voices on the other side of the door, in the front room that served as our sitting room and apothecary's shop. I took a deep breath, my heart racing in anticipation, and opened the door. "Might I help you, Grandmum?"

She was already at work, grinding away with her mortar and pestle at some potent-smelling chaa or mithridate. "Ah, there's my girl, my Maggie. Be a dear, fetch me two cheesecloth sachets from the cupboard."

I paused in my tracks, and stared at the two men seated at my grandmum's table. Not just men, they were clearly *gentlemen*. Their clothing was made of rich velvets and brocades. They wore fine leather riding boots, and upon the table before them were their hats— resplendent black beaver felt adorned with lush, colorful plumage. I observed the gentlemen's faces: one in middle age, the other, young, perhaps midtwenties. Time stopped; I could hear nothing but the beat of my racing heart within my ears. My breathing suspended, as though Fortune herself presented me with a ribbon-bound gift and beckoned me to open, come see.

"Good day, Maggie," the younger man said, and when he spoke it were like a siren's song, and I could not help but come closer, as though pulled by some other force.

"Good day," I managed to muster, and my voice sounded lower, huskier than it ever had before.

His dark-blond hair cascaded in silky waves to his shoulders, a neatly plaited lovelock, tied with a robin's egg–blue ribbon, framed the side of his face. His skin was sun kissed, his jaw angular and masculine. His eyes were a golden hazel. He smiled, revealing even white teeth with a sudden sparkle of a gold cap upon his incisor. And at that moment, I was overcome with elation, desire, and I was utterly at his mercy, his servant, like a mortal in the presence of a deity.

"This is my granddaughter, Maggie. She's a good girl, she is," declared Grandmum, sounding both proud and wary.

"I'm sure she's a very good girl, lovely lass," said the elder gentleman with a hearty laugh. I did not see him—my eyes were captivated by the young man before me.

"Where is your mother, Maggie?" the young man asked.

I tried to answer but could not find the words.

"Her mother is long gone, she is."

"Dead?" asked the elder man.

"Nay, nay, gone and run off when this one was barely walking. Nothing but a wanton trollop, she is."

"Tisk tisk, what a pity," the elder one said again, but I heard no sadness in his voice.

"So, it's just you and your grandma here, lass?" asked the young man.

"Yes," I said, drawing closer.

"Come, sit with us," he said, kicking a chair away from the table for me.

I did as he bid me, the closeness of him, the sharp bay and petitgrain of his perfume, causing the air between us to hum, or so it seemed to me.

There was silence as Grandmum ground away with her mortar and pestle. She stopped and uncorked a cobalt bottle. As she poured from it into the mortar, I gasped. Small dried beetle carcasses, green and shining like peridot gems, spilled into the mortar.

"What is this, Grandmum?" I asked, for in all of her teaching, never had I seen these beetles.

As she gently ground the carcasses with her pestle, there were silence but for a sickening, quiet crunch. "'Tis the green fly from Spain, lass."

"And for what is its medicinal purpose?"

At this the gentlemen laughed, and I felt embarrassed, chagrined as a fool.

"I will teach you someday," she said reluctantly, her mouth hard set as she worked.

"It makes a man's cock hard as stone!" exclaimed the elder man, slapping his hand upon the table and having a good laugh.

"Oh," I said, feeling the blush spread to my neck and cheeks as I looked down at the table. But I felt the younger man's eyes on me, and I could not help but meet his gaze.

"It makes the pleasure sweeter," he said, his eyes going to my lips, and when they did, I swore I could feel the heat of his kiss.

"Maggie," my grandmother said sharply, and I could tell she wanted to be rid of her customers. "I told ye, fetch me the sachets."

I jumped up and did as she bid me.

"Now, child, hold them open for me so that I can spoon in the powder, and then tie them fast and tight."

I watched as she carefully moved, scooping from the mortar with a tiny silver spoon. The powder was both acrid and earthy-sweet at the same time, and seemed to sparkle and glow with its own light. She filled one sachet, which I fastened, and then we finished the second.

"There you are, good sirs. Now, be most careful with it, do not use too much of it at once, else your innards shall grow inflamed and death is possible."

"Aye, we know this, old woman," said the elder, swiping up the sachets in his plump ham hock of a hand.

"It mixes best with the liquor made from anise seed," she added as the gentlemen rose from their seats.

The younger threw down a gold coin. "For your work, and for your silence too."

Grandmum snatched up the coin, biting it. She nodded. "Worry not. I thank you for your patronage, good sirs." But I did not sense candor in her words.

Without thinking, in a daze, I followed the gentlemen to the doorway, and outside to the hitching post. Transfixed, I watched as they untethered their horses' reins. The elder gentleman mounted with a groan, then looked me over as though I were a curious creature.

"Come, Lucius, you dawdle. Make haste," he said over his shoulder as he cantered down the path.

The young man, Lucius, approached me, taking my hand in his and bringing it to his fine mouth. His lips lingered upon my knuckles, and then he licked with the tip of his tongue and I felt my knees go weak. He looked me in the eyes knowingly as he let go of my hand with a roguish grin.

"Maggie, 'tis Beltane."

I managed to find my voice. "Aye, it is."

"At dusk, come and find me at the Fox and Crown Inn, down the road in Reading village. I'll be waiting for you, and I will have a very special gift for you, my love."

I could not contain the giddy smile that came to me. *He called me his love!* "For me?"

"Indeed, lass. Do as I ask, and do not tell your grandmum, you understand? 'Tis our secret."

In a trance, I watched him mount his white horse. He tipped his fine plumed hat, then galloped away after the elder gentleman.

I watched them go, until the path meandered south and I could no longer see them. I then exhaled, not realizing I had been holding my breath all the while, and leaned against the stone wall, my hands pressed to my heart, which felt as though it would burst from within my chest.

"Maggie, come inside now," called Grandmum from the doorway, a crease of worry between her brows. "Men like them are trouble, do not concern yourself with them."

I felt as though there were air between my feet and the ground. Floating, I made my way back inside, slamming the door shut behind me. "How could such gentlemen be trouble?"

"Little do you know, lass," she muttered as she cleaned her work.

"Oh, but did you see *him*, Grandmum? His name is Lucius . . . *Lucius*," I said, sighing as I sunk into the chair in which he had sat. I breathed deeply through my nose, for his scent still lingered.

"Hmph, I saw him, and I saw how he looked at you as though you were a haunch of roast venison he longed to sink his teeth into."

"Did he?" I was delighted.

"Have you gone daft, lass?" she said, the crease of worry growing between her brows.

"He was the most beautiful man I have ever seen."

"Rotten to the core, they were," she muttered, corking bottles and placing them back upon the shelves.

"Why do you say so?"

"Any man who comes to my door looking for the green fly dust is no good."

"But surely it was for the elder man, for he was the one who took the sachets. A young man would not have any need for such a thing."

"Oh aye? And how do you have knowledge of such things?"

I opened my mouth to answer, but then closed it. I had no rebuttal.

"You're nothing but a child," she said with a firm nod of her head.

"I am not a child. I'm a woman now. I began my monthly bleeding this past winter. You yourself said that makes me a woman now."

"A woman in body but with a child's mind."

"You shall see, Grandmum, I am no fool. Someday I shall fall in love with a gentleman and be a fine lady with a home full of chubby babies." I gestured wide with my arms.

She fell into hearty laughter, so much so that she had a coughing spell. I loathed the sound of her raspy, wet coughing. It happened more often than not.

"That proves that you know nothing of the world, lass. Now, go get back to work in the garden, before the sun sets." She gathered up the mortar and pestle and went into the kitchen.

I followed, donning my apron and straw bonnet as she worked at the washing trough. "Grandmum, I'll not be like my mother. I promise you." She stopped in her washing, turning round to face me, and I noticed she cried, her mouth trembling.

"Aye, I know you'll not be like your mother. But I know not how much longer I can keep you innocent."

I did not fully understand her, but I went to her and gave her a rough hug, squeezing her plump sides. "Come on, Grandmum, don't grow sulky."

"Oh hush up." She shoved me away. "Get to your chores now."

I went and finished my daily chores, lost in dreams and fantasies of Lucius upon his white steed, the feel of his lips upon my knuckles, the flick of his tongue that made me tremble, caused me to grow damp between my thighs. This was all new to me, and it were thrilling. I was so overcome with my daydreams that I mistakenly pulled up the chives, thinking they were grass sprouts within the garden. "Oh blast," I muttered, quickly trying to replant the clump of roots.

When I finished, I rose, stretching my back. Looking westward, I saw that dusk approached. Quickly I went to the well and drew a bucket, scrubbing my hands, my face, behind my ears, my neck. I went inside and checked myself again in the looking glass, and I was pleased with the image that peered back at me. "This is what love looks like," I said in a whisper. Giddily I cast aside my apron. I placed my ear to the door, heard my grandmother speaking with our neighbor, Mrs. Hathaway. I knew they would be chattering away for the next two hours and would never notice my absence. On my way out the door, I grabbed a fistful of fresh mint leaves. Sneaking round the back of the house to the path that led to town, I moved like a sly fox. Once I was round the bend, I stood proudly as I walked, listening to the dusk song of birds, chewing the fresh mint leaves so that my breath would be sweet when I saw Lucius again.

The sun had set by the time I reached the Fox and Crown. Town was abustle with farmers bringing in milk and cheese for the evening, the coaches coming and going, to and from London town. I walked proudly inside the inn and tavern, approaching the innkeeper, my head held high.

The balding man did a double take of me, his eyes growing wide. "Good evening, lass! How is it I can assist you?" His tone was much too sweet, and within my gut I felt a rush of foreboding.

It must be nervousness, I thought, ignoring the sensation. "I am here to meet a gentleman by the name of Lucius."

The innkeeper's eyes looked me over with newer interest and familiarity. "Oh aye? He and his uncle are just there, by the hearth. Lord Lucius," he bellowed out across the crowded, smoke-filled tavern. "A young lass here is asking for you, she is!" He fell to chuckling, as all eyes in the tavern turned toward me.

I cringed, feeling as though I stood in nothing but my chemise. It were not a pleasing feeling, and for a moment I thought to turn right round and run back home. Grandmum was right, there were nothing but trouble here.

Lucius rose from his seat and approached me, that roguish grin upon his face. "Aye, she's my little sister come to meet me!"

The tavern erupted in laughter, and I knew it were at my expense, but when he embraced me and took my arm through his, nothing mattered anymore. I was his servant, completely, utterly.

"Come, sister, let us go up to my chambers. We have much catching up to do," he said loudly, and the laughter followed us as we made our way up the stairs and down a corridor to a room at the end. He ushered me inside, closing the door behind us. The room was heady with his perfume, and I found it intoxicating. The inn was shabby and worn, not fit for the likes of such a gentleman as Lucius, but his presence was like the sun, casting everything in gold.

"I am so glad you've come, Maggie," he said, taking hold of my hands in his, pressing kisses into each palm, then placing them over his chest. I could feel his heartbeat, and it raced in time to mine. "Do you feel what I feel?"

"Aye," I said, breathless.

"'Tis Beltane. This was meant to be. This night was destined for us."
Driven by a hunger and need, I slid my hands up his chest, round
his neck. Standing on tiptoe, I boldly pressed my lips against his. I did
not know how to kiss. A sound like pleading came from within me.

He roughly pulled me away, exhaling, looking down at me as
though I were the fox he had sought the whole day long. "Good, sweet
lass. Come," he said, making quick work of my corset laces before I
even had time to consider. Foreboding brewed in my belly. He drew
me down upon the bed, leaning over me as his hand slid beneath my
loosened stays and chemise, taking hold of my breast.

A moan of delight came from within me, and I arched against him.
The foreboding was banished by the fire lit within me. Never had I felt
such a sensation, and I had to have more, I hungered for more.

"That's the way, sweet thing. I knew you were meant for me."

His mouth descended upon mine, his kiss tasted of port wine, his
tongue artfully playing with mine. As he did so, his free hand went from
my breast, lifting my skirts, his fingers deftly going between my thighs,
where I was drenched with the wanting I had never known before. His
touch was gentle, yet demanding. Skillfully he moved his fingers, and
I panted and moaned into his mouth, thrashing and arching against
him. I was like candlewax, melting and pooling and hot and burning.
I wanted more and more, I was wild.

He pulled his mouth from mine, gazing down at me triumphantly
as his fingers worked away.

"Oh God! Give me more!" I didn't know what the more was, but I
knew I wasn't complete, that there was something, just waiting for me
to discover it.

"Sweet, wanton thing! I've possessed you."

I took no note of his threat, for with nothing but a quick turn of
his wrist and a flick of his finger, my eyes rolled back into my head and
I let out a great moan of pleasure, my body pulsating in burning waves,
over and over. It was like some divine revelation, but it had nothing

to do with prayer. When I looked up at him, his pupils were huge and he panted.

"Gods, you wicked thing!"

I didn't want him to speak, and I hungrily took his mouth in mine as the burning waves ebbed away. I could think of nothing else but him. He had me completely.

He rose from the bed, unlacing his breeches. In the darkness his form loomed over me, like some specter, something I ought to fear. But I was so overcome with the revelation, with what he had shown me, I could not think. He must have known this. In an instant, his body was on top of mine, he braced his arms on either side of my head, and I felt the press of something impossible between my thighs.

"You're so ready for me, sweet, wicked thing," he said between breaths. And with that he took my wrists in his hands and pinned them to the bed, and he thrust between my thighs and my waning pleasure turned to piercing pain.

"No! Please! It hurts!" I yelled. The fear took hold, for I knew now what was happening and that there was no turning back and that I had brought this down upon myself. "Please stop, Lucius, it hurts." I began to cry. I struggled against him, to no avail.

My protests seemed to encourage him. "My Beltane maid, my virgin sacrifice," he hissed into my ear.

I closed my eyes against the pain and breathed deeply, willing him to be done, to complete his task, his deed. "Devil take me!" he gasped, his mouth open in rapture, the color of it like the bloodred of a freshly killed deer's heart. He moaned aloud, and I knew he felt what I had felt some moments before, before he had raped me.

He collapsed upon me, the weight of him bruising, his breath hot upon my ear.

The door opened, then closed, and I heard the sound of an amused chuckle. "Already done? For shame, Lucius, you should last longer than that."

I froze beneath him, tensing. Lucius rose from me. "She's too sweet, much too sweet."

The elder man groaned. "Move away, it's my turn now."

I bolted up, pulling down my skirts, looking to Lucius. "Please, no, let me go home. I thought you loved me!"

"Aye, for a moment, I did." He laced his breeches, then reached for my chin, tilting my face to meet his kiss. I felt bile rise to my throat. What a stupid, stupid girl I was.

"Goodbye, Maggie," he said, going out the door, slamming it closed behind him. He whistled as he walked away.

A sob escaped from me, for I was most fearful.

"Aw, no, no tears, no crying, now!" ordered the elder man as he unlaced his breeches. "If you must cry, then get on hands and knees so I don't have to look at you."

I did not make it back home until dawn. Grandmum met me halfway, upon the road. I did not need to tell her. She knew. She said nothing, but put her arm round me and kissed my forehead fervently. She and I wept silently the whole way home. Once inside, she got out the great washbasin, filled it with steaming hot water from the hearth. She stirred in dried chamomile, calendula, and sheep's milk, and bid me take my clothes off and sit and wash my cunny with the sponge until the water cooled. It hurt mightily at first, but eventually the pain eased. After I dried myself, I vomited. She helped me dress and put me to bed.

I woke in a fevered sweat, the hay beneath me sticking to my neck, to my face where my tears had spilled. I heaved, then felt the bile rising. I rolled to my hands and knees and retched the little that was left in me. My heart pounded and I swore, I swore I could feel the aching within my cunny, as hot, burning, and painful as it had been that day.

"Lord forgive me," I muttered. "This is my great sin." And I knew, I knew Thomas knew, he had said long ago that he knew he wasn't my first, that I hadn't been a virgin, and it meant nothing to him. He had said that in his mind I had been only his, for he had shown me love and I had come to see the beauty in love. And it were true! He had shown me how to love myself, to love the act of love, and to take my power in it. Lord but I had been blessed in love, indeed. I did not deserve Thomas. And he did not deserve me, the trouble I brought down upon us, and the greatest shame I could not share with him.

"The General Court calls upon Goodwife Pierce. Please take the witness stand."

I groaned aloud, rolling my eyes. Still this seemed a farce to me and I'd yet to see how anyone could prove me guilty of consorting with the Devil. Goody Pierce? That cat-hating cow? Let her come. Let her speak. I did not fear her.

Goody Pierce placed her hand upon the Bible, swearing to tell the truth, then looked down at me as though I were a filthy beggar come to bother her. I laughed aloud. "You've come by your own fruition, Goody Pierce. 'Tis not my fault that you've been inconvenienced this day."

I found that I could no longer concentrate on the proceedings. I cared not what stupid Goody Pierce had to say about me and my tinctures. I drifted off into dreary thought, my insides still aching from my nightmare from the prior evening.

But I awoke from my thoughts, to hear Goody Pierce.

"I was frightened of Goody Jones."

"But did you not seek her out for her assistance?" asked Dudley. "Why were you frightened?"

"I did, but when I called upon her to purchase the balm, I was frightened by her beastly cat."

*Cat-hating cow!*

"Her cat?"

"Aye."

"Can you describe the animal to the court, Goody Pierce?"

"Indeed. It is large, very large, with a huge fluffy coat, and a mane like a lion."

"What color is the creature?"

"'Tis all a muddle of colors: black, brown, orange, and gold."

"And why did the animal frighten you?"

"Because it appeared out of nowhere, it seemed to just manifest itself upon Goody Jones's counter, it did."

I scoffed. "She jumped up. She was curious to see you."

"Quiet, Jones," warned Winthrop.

"What else about the creature frightened you?"

"Well, sir, cats are known to be evil creatures, Satan's pawns. They do as they please, unlike dogs. They cannot be trained, they are evil by their nature."

I shook my head and looked to the ceiling. What utter nonsense. What more idiocy must I suffer to hear?

"And then what happened, Goody Pierce?"

"The animal stared at me, leered with those eyes of hers. I told Goody Jones that I did not much care for cats, and she crassly ridiculed me. We began to quarrel, and then Goodman Jones interrupted us, kindly offering to provide me with the balm free of charge for my troubles with his unruly wife." She gave me a side glance. "Everyone in town knows she is unruly, that Goodman Jones does not keep her in check. Poor man, to be married to such a shrew."

This stirred much mumbling from the court.

"Do you have anything else to add, Goody Pierce?"

"Aye, I do," she said, casting another disdainful glance my way. "As I left the shop, Goody Jones told me that if I did not use the balm she had mixed, then my pain would grow twofold. She then also insulted me, commenting that it was my size that was the cause of my pain." She paused at this, reddening, mulling over her next words. "'Tis not true, for my mother was bigger than I and did not suffer from such pain. And so it came to be! I did not use the balm, for I had been so frightened by Goody Jones and her beast of a cat, and then I awoke the next day with such pain I could barely stand. Isn't it so, Husband?" She looked out onto the galley.

"Aye, she could not stand!" supported Goodman Pierce.

"And everyone in this town knows that that beast of a cat of hers, it trails her wherever she might go. Why, I'm surprised the cat isn't present here in this courtroom, unable to separate itself from its witch of a mistress!"

At this, the court went into an uproar. The constable called for order over and over, banging the staff.

"Goody Pierce, I ask that you refrain from slandering the accused. Please let the testimony and evidence speak for itself."

"Goody Jones," said Governor Winthrop, "is it true you keep a familiar?"

I shook my head in disbelief at how ridiculous this trial had become. "If by 'familiar,' you mean a good and loyal cat that keeps the mice from out of our thatch and my husband's workshop, then aye, I do!" I spat. "But if by 'familiar,' you mean something dark and nefarious, then I'm afraid I've no such beast." How dare they bring my Molly into this.

"See? She does indeed!" exclaimed Goody Pierce as she pointed toward me.

Amidst the din of the courtroom, Goody Pierce was released from the witness stand. She spat upon the floorboards before me as she walked past.

I sought out Thomas again, and there he was, eyes steady upon me, giving me a reassuring nod. My Thomas, my own.

"The court summons Goody Hall to take the witness stand."

My heart dropped and panic rose up from my belly. I looked quickly to Thomas. He met my gaze, then looked down at his hat he held in his hands. I saw the clench of his jaw, which he was in the habit of doing anytime he worried over a matter. This I knew was when the scale would truly tip to my misfortune.

"Goody Hall, please tell the court how you are acquainted with the accused."

She nodded her wan face, a small tendril of graying hair escaping free from her cap. "This past winter, I lost my child while birthing him. Goody Jones was the midwife present."

"I am sorry to hear of your loss, Goody Hall, but the Lord giveth and He taketh away, does He not? How can this tragedy be the doing of Goody Jones?"

"Because she is the hand of Satan!" Goody Hall shouted as she quaked. I jumped at the ferocity of her response, as did most of the court.

"How, pray tell, is she the hand of Satan?"

"I know she killed my baby! Goody Jones has delivered all four of my children and none of them have lived to see their first birthday! Four children, Magistrates! Four! How can all four perish?"

The court was silent.

I cleared my throat. "If I may, Magistrates, I can tell you about what happened in Goody Hall's birthing." My voice was meek, for I, too, was devastated to have lost Goody Hall's baby, the only baby I'd ever lost in all my years as midwife.

"Proceed," said Winthrop with a gesture of his hand.

"Goody Hall labored for many hours. The babe was breech within her womb. As you know, if the babe cannot be turned whilst still within the womb, it shall most often perish, along with the mother."

"True," said Bellingham.

"Indeed, I was able to turn the babe after many long hours, by use of massage upon Goody Hall's belly and within her womb, you see."

At this, Goody Hall let out a wail, covering her face as though I had shamed her in public.

"Goody Hall, 'tis nothing to be ashamed of," I said, to assuage her. I felt such pity for her.

"Do not speak to me, witch!" she spat at me. Her sharp rebuke was like a blow to the face.

"Continue, Goody Jones," Bellingham said, eager to hear how the babe left the world.

"After I was able to turn the babe, I got Goody Hall to walk, and then she requested the birthing chair, but I do not like birthing chairs, so I urged her to squat by the bedpost, for better leverage, you see?"

Again Goody Hall hid her face in her hands as she wept. The magistrates fidgeted in their seats, obviously discomforted by my detail.

"She was reluctant to do so, but finally agreed. And when she went down by the bed and pushed, the babe came forth, but immediately I knew that the child was no longer with us, that the Lord had taken him."

"Don't you dare speak of the Lord!" Goody Hall screamed at me like a wild thing. The courtroom broke into chatter. But the constable did not call for order.

"Continue, Goody Jones," urged Winthrop the Younger. It was the first time he had spoken during the whole of the trial. His voice was soft, encouraging.

"You see, Magistrates, the navel string, it were wrapped round the babe's neck, and it had choked to death within the womb."

"It were because she pushed the babe with her hands upon my belly, and she put her evil fingers within my womb!" cried out Goody Hall.

"Is this true?" asked Endecott.

Stupid, stupid men. Even one so handsomely educated did not understand the workings of a woman's body. "Is what true, Magistrate?"

"Is it true you put her hands within her womb?"

I could not stifle the pitying grin that came to my mouth. "Indeed, any woman here who has birthed a child will tell you that the midwife must often put her fingers to the womb, to see how the child progresses, to assist in its delivery. It is only the lucky few who are easily delivered of a babe without assistance. 'Tis the curse of Eve, isn't that what we have been taught?"

I turned to face the assembly. A great number of women nodded and affirmed my words, and I were most grateful to them.

"No!" shouted Goody Hall. "It were her evil fingers that worked the cord round my child's neck, I am certain. She muttered some sort of chant as she did so, some evil chant!"

"Indeed I uttered the Lord's Prayer, nothing more," I said. I would not admit to reciting the Hail Mary. That would immediately bring guilt upon me, I knew.

"Then why have all four of my children perished?" She pointed at me, her face twisted in anger. "Four children dead! And she the only midwife!"

"Have you anything to say in your defense, Goody Jones?" asked Bellingham with a note of hopefulness in his voice.

"I cannot be held accountable for God's will, no more than anyone else in this courtroom."

"Indeed, no," agreed the governor.

"I will say one last word in my defense of this charge. Goody Hall's fourth baby was the first and only child I have lost in all my years of midwifery, both here in Massachusetts and back in England. I have delivered babes since I was eighteen and apprenticed to a midwife in London. I have safely delivered hundreds of babies."

Just then, a clerk approached the seated magistrates with a letter. He went to the governor, handing him the letter and whispering in his ear. Winthrop's expression turned to one of concern.

"The court shall adjourn for a brief respite, but shall return at half past the hour," said Winthrop.

I watched as the magistrates filed out of the courtroom. The assembly chattered away, all wondering what the reason might be for the court's adjourning.

I took a deep breath and swallowed, but my throat were so parched that I could not. "Please, Constable," I said, turning to the constable next to me. "Might I have a sip of water?"

He scrutinized my face, then looked about, then back at me. "I suppose so." From out of his pocket he produced a flask. "Just one sip," he instructed.

I held the flask hungrily to my lips. Immediately I was filled with the warmth of scotch, the likes of which I had not tasted since I was in London. I coughed, startled by the contents, then quickly handed the flask back to him. "You are most kind to share that," I said, wiping at my mouth with my shackled hands.

He laughed heartily, and I could tell it was at my expense. "Not at all! Might be the last good drink you ever have on this earth!" And again he fell to laughing at his own jest.

"Aye, you might be right," I admitted with resignation.

The sadness in my voice snuffed out the rest of his laughter.

"It has been brought to this General Court's attention that Goody Jones be not of the name Jones, nor her husband at that."

At this, I did gasp. Who could have learned this, and how? London is a bustling city of tens of thousands, unlike Boston. Clearly someone had found it most recently—the information must have been contained in the letter presented to the governor before the magistrates adjourned. I quickly glanced to Thomas, whose usually serene expression had gone pale and stricken. How? How could this knowledge—how could this one secret that we shared—come all the way from London?

"Margaret Jones, is your real name not Margaret O'Byrn?"

*So that cat's been let out of the bag.* Thomas had insisted, when we left London, that we change our surname to Jones. He so feared that the trouble in London with Lady Wembly would follow us to the New World. He thought "Jones" so common and nondescript that it would never be questioned. And it hadn't, until now.

"Her husband, Thomas, he has always had the Irish lilt. Nothing Welsh in his voice!" exclaimed Magistrate Dudley with a note of glee, as though he had discovered some new scientific formula. "Are you or are you not Margaret O'Byrn?"

"My true name is Margaret Drinkwater, come from the village of Reading, west of London."

The court went into an uproar. The constable called for order.

"Are you saying that you and your husband Thomas are actually of the surname Drinkwater, not Jones?"

"Oh, no, I tell you that I am Margaret Drinkwater. That was my true name, before I were married."

Magistrate Dudley looked as though someone had insulted his very honor. "Do you mean to say that your true name is your maiden name? This is blasphemy. There is no name truer than your husband's, which you took when you were wed. Your maiden name ceases to exist."

I raised my brows at him. "Do you mean to say that I was nothing before my husband made me his wife? I was somebody, my own person. 'Twas love that persuaded me to become a wife."

"Goody Jones," said Winthrop, leaning forward in his seat, "it was God's will that you wed Thomas Jones, not your own."

"I will grant you, Governor, that the Lord did bless me when He had Thomas Jones enter my life," I said, giving my sweet husband a nod. "But it was my heart and my own mind that made the decision to bond myself to him in matrimony."

More outrage from the courtroom. The elderly Endecott looked as though I had kicked the air from his lungs. "Such words are akin to those of the late Hutchinson, who was banished from this colony and died under the knife of savages!"

"I have heard of this Anne Hutchinson. She, too, were a midwife, banished from this place for speaking her mind too freely and for having the audacity to be a woman who strove to educate other women. Heretic, indeed." I spat upon the floor.

"Silence! Silence, woman!" shouted Endecott.

I laughed aloud, a giddy madness taking over me. "Of course it would be you, Magistrate Endecott, to bid me be silent. You were the one responsible for her banishment! I am no fool. Though these things transpired before I came to this shore, I am well aware of your dealings."

"Maggie." I heard Thomas call my name. I would know his voice out of a throng of thousands. The sound of it—deep, gravelly, with purpose, his Irish lilt melting over my name like a honey drip—it was most dear to me. His voice resonated, and silenced the court. I turned to look at him. He caught my gaze and shook his head ever so slightly, and I swore I could feel his hand upon my knee, squeezing me in that familiar way he was wont to do, when I spoke too much and must mind myself. I should have been angry—I was often angry when he would do so to me, for it made me feel a chided child. But when I searched his eyes at that moment, I saw such sadness and defeat.

I did not deserve so good a husband as he, I never did. And he did not deserve to have such a burden for a wife.

"Goody Jones," called Winthrop's baritone, dragging my attention away from Thomas. "There are reports out of London that you were apothecary to Lady Wembly of Kent. Is this true?"

My past had hunted me down, even to this tiny, remote corner of the world. And I was tired of running when it was Lady Wembly's own hand that had slit her husband's throat, not mine. Why should I run? I knew myself to be a sinner, but this sin, as well as the sin of maleficium they tried to pin upon my breast, were no sin of mine. And I would fight against them with every last breath within me.

"Aye, Governor, Lady Wembly was a patron of my apothecary shop. As were a great deal of the gentry, if I do say so."

"Lady Wembly is dead."

I started at this. "I did not know this, Governor, as I have been in Massachusetts these past two years."

The courtroom was silent, hanging upon each uttered word.

"Indeed, the unfortunate Lady Wembly of Kent affronted our Lord and Savior, taking her own life in August of 1646." Winthrop stroked his goatee, as though he contemplated his own words. "She was under house arrest at the time, for the murder of her own husband, Lord Wembly of Kent. Are you aware of his murder?"

I could feign ignorance. But why should I? It mattered not what I should say, the crime would be pinned upon me.

"Aye, I was aware, as was all of London. Most unfortunate. I assume that Lady Wembly was under house arrest because she was not of sound mind. And of course, a lady of the gentry. Such mercies are never handed out to the penniless."

The crowd erupted, but with laughter and agreement. It took me by surprise. But I remembered, most of them here in Massachusetts had left behind England in order to build a new society based on godliness rather than acres of land and piles of gold.

The constable called for order. When the court quieted, Winthrop continued.

"Save your musings, Goody Jones. Or Goody O'Byrn, more like?" He smiled at his own witty remark. "It seems that Lady Wembly had dosed herself with a tincture of your making before she flew into a madness that killed her husband."

The crowd muttered in excitement. This was the best entertainment they'd had since before crossing the Atlantic.

"Did you use some maleficium in the making of this tincture? What evil was within that bottle, Goody Jones?"

"Indeed, Lady Wembly often procured from me a tincture made from Saint John's Wort. It was a tincture I often prescribed to those who were experiencing melancholy or grief. It helps to lift the humors. It's an age-old recipe, handed down for generations. 'Tis a well-known treatment, you might ask any herbalist, apothecary, or physician for something to lift the spirits and they would have some formula or tincture containing Saint John's Wort for the purpose."

"Indeed, Goody Jones, but there must have been something evil within yours, or else all of England would be murdering its spouses!" Winthrop exclaimed.

"Nothing evil at all, Governor, I can assure you. What I can tell you is this: I instructed Lady Wembly to take only ten drops of the tincture within her cup, no more than that. But she informed me that she would take half a bottle with her claret. When I told her that I would no longer sell her the tincture because she was abusing it, much to her own danger, she informed me that she would have me arrested for swindling her. And, Governor, I would not take the chance, for who would believe the word of a woman herbalist over a lady of the gentry? Money talks, does it not? Is that not why we are all here?" I gestured with my shackled hands round the room. "Are we not here to escape the corruption and Godlessness of England?"

Again, I had the court on my side. I took fuel from their shouts of agreement.

"So aye, I unwillingly gave Lady Wembly the tincture, under much duress. I knew she was an unstable woman, that she were prone to fits of melancholia and mania. But again, were I to be accused of swindling her and I were to say this about her, it would have been seen as an insult, and an insubordination to the gentry, would it have not?"

Again, a chorus of approval.

"Was I supposed to follow Lady Wembly to her Kent estate, to be sure that she did not get up to mischief? I knew her to be melancholy because Lord Wembly brought his fifteen-year-old mistress to their estate. Lady Wembly had to share her roof with her husband's whore. That would make any woman go mad, would it not? To live in such an ungodly manner?"

Shouts of approval rang out. The constable banged his staff for order.

Winthrop loudly cleared his throat. "The fact remains, Goody Jones, that your mithridate caused the murder of a lord of the peerage."

"Did it? Was it I who put the blade in Lady Wembly's hand and forced her to slash her husband's throat?"

"Without your tincture, Lord Wembly might still be alive this day, as well as his addle-minded wife."

"Mayhap, Governor. I cannot speak to God's will. Nor can you. Nor can I speak to God's will when He allows a lord to force his wife to live under the same roof as his whore."

"Hear! Hear!" shouted Samuel Stratton, and others joined him in chorus.

"Order, order!" The constable's pounding of the floorboards was like thunder.

"Governor," called Bellingham, "I must intervene in the trial's proceedings here. The General Court is gathered here to cast judgment on the charge of witchcraft against Goody Jones. What does the tragic death of a lord and lady in Kent have to do with the proceedings of this court in Massachusetts? It would seem a matter for England, not a matter for Massachusetts."

Some muttered approval. I was most thankful to Bellingham for his endeavor to bring an end to this line of questioning.

"Governor, how has it that this tragic story of Lord and Lady Wembly comes to your attention this day? I find myself wondering how this information came to you in such a timely manner."

"Goody Jones, it is not for you to question the court," chided Winthrop.

"Was this in the contents of the letter you were presented earlier? Is that why the magistrates adjourned for a brief respite?"

"One more question out of you, Goody Jones, and you will be held in contempt of this court and shall spend the night in the stocks!" warned Winthrop.

I drew in my breath. I would not be humiliated, to spend the night in the town stocks. But still, I wondered, how was it that the story of Lord and Lady Wembly had followed me all the way to this courtroom? I searched round the assembly, my eyes seeing both familiar and unfamiliar faces. But then my heart stopped when I saw her staring at me. My mind turned over as my shackled hands felt for the bulge of the tiny poppet within my skirt pocket.

Goody Longfellow, née Widow Hallett, sat at the edge of the courtroom beside her young milksop minister husband, a smug smile of satisfaction teasing her lips.

# CHAPTER TWENTY-FOUR

*4. Some things which she foretold came to pass accordingly; other things she could tell of (as secret speeches, etc.) which she had no ordinary means to come to the knowledge of.*

—*John Winthrop, journal*

"The court now summons Goody Morris, please take the witness stand."

For the briefest moment I felt relief, for the Goody Morris I knew I had helped to birth a beautiful son some months before. In fact, never had I seen such a head of dark curls upon a newborn, and I recalled joking with the mother that perhaps the father was a Spaniard, much to the mother-in-law's horror. I smiled a little, recalling how, despite how long she labored, the young mother had had a good laugh, for which I was most glad.

But to my chagrin, it was not the young mother Goody Morris, but Goody Morris the elder mother-in-law, whom I never took a liking to. She was a town gossip, always meddling into others' business and spreading rumors about. On this day, as she swore her oath over the Bible, she looked wan, angry, bitter, her face pinched, dark circles beneath her sunken eyes.

"Tell the court, Goody Morris, of how you are acquainted with the accused."

"Very well," she said with conviction. "Everyone knows that she is intemperate and wild."

"Please, Goody Morris, keep to the details of your acquaintance."

"Aye, she came to my home once, to assist my daughter-in-law in her first birthing." She stopped, awaiting more questions.

"And did the birth go smoothly, without incident?"

"Took a while for the young thing to birth the boy, but aye, she was delivered of a healthy boy."

"So for what reason have you come to stand before the court?"

"I've waited a long while to tell this," she said with a satisfied nod. "I have disowned my daughter-in-law. My son seeks to divorce her. He learned that she consorted with a blackamoor sailor from Portugal."

The court went to chattering in excitement, for who doesn't love a good bit of scandal?

"What has this to do with Goody Jones?"

"I'll tell you what! When my daughter-in-law gave birth, the baby come out with a mass of black curls, the likes of which I've never seen on a baby. Goody Jones felt the same, and said so. But then she said something that she could only have known if she could see secrets. She must converse with the Devil. She said, 'Why I'd say the father was a Spaniard!' Lo and behold, it were true, the father of the child was the blackamoor my daughter-in-law consorted with!"

"Goody Jones made a comment that perhaps the father was a Spaniard?"

"Aye, that she did!"

"But the father was Portuguese?"

"Spaniard, Portuguese, pfft," Goody Morris said with a dismissive wave of her hand. "Both the same really."

"Goody Jones." Dudley turned to me. "How did you have this intimate knowledge of young Goody Morris? Did she impart this to you whilst she labored?"

"Indeed she did not," I said, then shook my head. "Goody Morris here takes what was meant to be nothing but a simple observation and jest and creates mischief where there is naught! She thinks I came by some secret knowledge by working with the Devil? This court has sunk very low indeed if it shall accept such paltry nonsense as evidence."

"You shall not insult the integrity of this courtroom," scolded Dudley. He then turned back to Goody Morris. "Where is young Goody Morris now? You say your son seeks to divorce her because of her adultery."

"Aye, indeed, Magistrate. She's gone and run off with the blackamoor! Took the babe with her, good riddance."

For a moment, it was pleasing to know that young Goody Morris followed her heart's desire, uniting the child with its true father. And then I laughed as a humorous thought came to me. This was the second instance we'd heard of young Massachusetts wives abandoning their husbands for foreign sailors. Perhaps Massachusetts men were lacking in some way, I pondered.

"It's not just my daughter-in-law's secrets she knew. I've heard it told that she knew there was discord within the marriage bed of Goodman Mason and his wife, and that she gave him a tincture to remedy the situation without him ever uttering a word. How could she have known such secret, intimate details?"

The court murmured, some laughed.

"She is out of line, that old shrew is!" shouted Goodman Mason, who had stood up, pointing at Goody Morris. "How dare she speak of such things about me? It's her should be put in the stocks, for speaking slander!"

"Indeed," agreed Winthrop the Younger, "such information should be struck from the court record. Goody Morris, please refrain from speaking hearsay."

Goody Morris pouted like a chided child. I chortled under my breath.

"She could also tell when a woman was with child long before others knew, sometimes before the mother herself knew."

I could not argue against this.

"Is it true, Goody Jones? That you knew women were with child before everyone else? How did you have such knowledge? Did you speak with the Dark Lord to gain such knowledge?"

"There's no need to speak with the Dark Lord, as you say, to have such knowledge. I was trained by my own grandmum, to know the signs in a woman. They get a certain rosiness to their faces, they look as though they've not slept well. They decline food and drink, and often vomit. And their breasts swell, and some complain that they are sore. This is no knowledge only Satan holds. This is knowledge that most of us have if we only take a moment to consider a person, to truly care about their well-being, as I do. If being observant and caring deems me to be skilled in dark arts, then so be it."

The constable banged his staff upon the floorboards to call for order as the courtroom grew chatty and restless.

"The court shall adjourn this day, to reconvene tomorrow. This night, the accused, Goody Jones, shall be examined for signs of witchcraft, using the method employed presently in England, as prescribed by the witchfinder Matthew Hopkins in his treatise."

At this, Endecott produced a book, holding it up for all to see as though it were the Bible itself.

My heart rolled over within me. They would try every trick they knew to bring an innocent woman down, wouldn't they? I heaved a weary sigh.

The constable took note and grinned. "No sleep for you this Monday. You shall be watched the whole night through," he said with a certain glee.

"And none for you either, perhaps," I said ruefully before I could catch my own tongue. He looked stricken, not so cocksure anymore. This, too, would come back to haunt me, to be sure.

# CHAPTER
# TWENTY-FIVE

*5. she had (upon search) an apparent teat in her secret parts
as fresh as if it had been newly sucked, and after it had been
scanned, upon a forced search, that was withered, and another
began on the opposite side.*

—*John Winthrop, journal*

It being closer to Midsummer, the afternoons stretched longer, and
the daylight was for having well into evening. I held my head high as
I was removed from the jail on Monday by the constables and taken
to a simple home across the way. In the front room there were a large
hearth, whitewashed walls, and one simple table in the center of the
otherwise-bare room. Lead-paned windows lined both the front-facing
and side-facing walls, allowing for much light to enter the starkness.

The constable from the courtroom grabbed at my shackles and
pulled them toward him. I winced at the sudden abrupt movement
against my chafed skin, but I stared him in the eye as he fished in his
pocket with his free hand. Producing a small key, he went to work
unfastening the shackles I'd worn since this misery had befallen me.

I brought my wrists up before my face, inspecting the damage done
by the shackles. The skin was bleeding in places, swollen and angry. I

looked upon my own wrists as though they belonged to someone else, as though they were separate from me.

A chuckle from the constable woke me from my contemplations. I looked at him; he, too, got a good look at my wrists and seemed to take delight in their wretched state, in the pain that seemed like someone else's and not my own.

"Not very pretty now, lass," he said, laughing again at his own words.

I tilted my head so that he might look me in the eyes again. He did so, his smile fading into a sneer. I held his gaze and he stared back as though he were the designated protector of righteousness and I a filthy whore. There were silence between us. Who would blink or look away first?

In my mind's eye I envisioned the constable in his bed, tossing and turning, tormented by nightmares, in a sweat as though caught in the grip of fever. "Oh, aye, you'll not sleep a wink tonight," I said, and I willed it to be. I made a wish upon the heavens that he never sleep well again.

His cocksure posture melted before my eyes, his brows lifting and his jaw dropping slightly, as though I had imparted some very unfortunate news to him.

Never in my life had I wished ill will on another. My grandmum had told me countless times to never, ever, do so. "Evil deeds come back times three," she would admonish, pointing at me with one knobby finger, then holding up three before me. I had lived the whole of my life upholding this code of honor. Nor did I ever create a brew or mithridate that might be used to evil purpose. But where had my honorable ways gotten me? To this point in my life when I was condemned as a hand of Satan? The absurdity of it all was causing my morality to disintegrate like a lump of sugar in hot tea.

But I knew something to be very true of men. If a man took delight in the suffering of another man, or woman, or child, he was a man capable of much malice. If I were to take away his sleep, he would be less likely to unharness his cruelty upon the world. I would clip those evil wings.

The door opened, and three women entered, each with a lantern. One also held some sort of looking glass that could magnify objects.

"These women are here to inspect your body for signs of witchery," said the constable, seeming relieved that he was no longer required to be alone with me.

"Who are you?" I asked the women.

The three looked away.

"That's not for you to know. This is the way of it," said the constable as he made his way out the door.

With the click of the latch, the three women set to work, placing their lanterns and the looking glass upon the table. They then circled me.

"We shall disrobe you and inspect your body for the signs of witchcraft," said the eldest of the three. None would look me in the eye.

"Have you done this before? Are the three of you experts upon such matters?" I asked, wanting to know why, in particular, these three women had been chosen for the task.

"You are not to pester us with questions," the eldest said, now looking me in the eye. "Hold your arms out."

The three busied themselves with undressing me, and I was surprised by how efficiently and gently they did so. How odd it all was, as though I were a bride being prepared for my marriage bed. When my skirts and chemise were about my feet, I stepped out of the circle as though I were about to enter a bath. I would not shudder before them. I would not feign modesty. I was proud of my body, always had been, whether clothed or not. If these three were here to inspect me, I would gladly show them. I stood tall, arms by my sides, putting one leg before the other, as though I were a horse being appraised.

"Now you must sit upon the table and lie down."

"Very well." Slowly I approached the table, then rested my backside against it. With my arms, I pulled myself up, onto the table, and stretched myself out for their viewing.

The three stood over me, two of them holding the lanterns while the eldest began to inspect my hands and arms with her looking glass. She moved slowly, taking her time, studying every inch of me. Gently she spread my fingers apart, closely examining the skin between each, the looking glass held close to her eye, making it appear huge and fishlike. As she went about her business, the two with the lanterns were still, unmoving. One stared across the room at some fixed point. The other, the youngest one, I noticed, stole furtive glances at my belly, my breasts. I cared not, she could look all she wanted. I'm certain she had never seen any woman but her own self naked.

After a long while, I was asked to turn over onto my belly. I did so, my skin growing sticky and damp with sweat in the late-afternoon heat, the pull of it against the hard wooden surface slightly stinging. I lay flat, my head turned to the side. Along the floorboards and walls, the sun's rays created a pattern through the lead panes of the windows, and I watched as it slowly moved and crawled as the sun set.

It seemed a very long while I lay upon my belly. There was silence in the room, but for the occasional "Hmm," uttered by the eldest. "Go to your back again, and bring your knees up and spread them apart," she said with authority.

Ah, this was where we were headed. I thought of the mark upon my inner thigh, close to my cunny. I knew it would bring trouble upon me. And to think, for so many years, it had been a source of delight for my husband, who would gently kiss it and mutter "Sweet little heart," before he would bring his lips to my cunny. I was blessed to have known such a love as my husband. Few women were so lucky, I knew it to be true. As the eldest's cool fingers spread my cunny lips apart to inspect me, I thought that these women would never know such delights as I had known, and how pitiful that be, to be given a body, a vessel capable of so much pleasure, yet the knowledge hidden away, never to be discovered. Much like a horde of gold buried in the earth, never to see the light of day.

The eldest moved closer with the looking glass, grasping my other thigh roughly as she tried to get a better vantage point. I winced as her thumbnail dug into my flesh as she studied the mark upon my other thigh.

"A devil's teat," she declared, as if there were no doubt to this.

"Lord bless us, keep us safe," the youngest muttered.

"Don't worry, I won't bite you," I said, and I laughed at my own words. Often when I found myself in a quandary, I would seek out and find the humor, because it were better than dwelling upon the misfortune of it. This had always come natural to me, as it did in this moment. Besides, I had begun to resign myself to the fact that this court would see me hanged no matter how they might justify it. My earthly days were numbered. But I no longer fretted about this, for soon, I reasoned, I would be united with my Bess. She needed her mother.

"We shall have to report that she has a devil's teat upon her inner thigh," said the eldest.

"I was born with this mark," I said in a clear voice.

"Likely story," said the youngest with a sharp tongue that took me unaware.

"Have you perfectly milky skin without a mark?" I challenged her. "Blessed girl, if so."

"Quiet! You are not to speak," said the eldest. "If it is true you were born with this mark, then the Devil had you chosen as his hand before you were born."

"Perhaps?" I challenged.

"Martha." The silent one spoke finally, her voice raspy and low. "Have you the witch pricker?"

"Aye, of course. What sort of witchfinder would I be if I had not?" Her harsh rebuttal took the lot of us by surprise.

"What is a witch pricker?" I asked quickly, endeavoring to hide my sudden fear.

She had not let go of my right thigh. With her free hand, she produced a small shiny object from within her cleavage. It looked to be a bodkin or darning needle of some kind. She held it before me as though it were a beloved weapon. "'Tis this!" She smiled with pride, flashing dark, rotting teeth. "If this should be a witch's teat upon your person, it shall not produce blood when I jab it. If blood should come forth, then it is not a witch's teat."

Slowly she brought the pricker toward my mark. "Prudence, hold still her leg."

The youngest obliged, taking tight hold of my thigh, holding the skin taut for the purpose of the pricking.

I steeled myself, taking a deep breath as the cold needle touched my skin. But no pain followed. Martha made as though she pushed the needle into my heart-shaped mark, and it looked as though it slid beneath my skin, but I felt nothing. Had I gone numb with fear? "I feel nothing," I said.

Martha drew out the needle. Silently we all stared down at my mark, awaiting the answer. Seconds felt like an eternity. My flesh looked indented from the press of the needle, but nothing came forth. There was no blood to be seen.

"There's the proof of it," said Martha as though she had known what would be the answer all along.

And with this realization, I exclaimed and stared up into her eyes. It all made sense now. I hadn't gone numb with fear. "The needle didn't puncture my skin! The pricker is tricksy, it's some sleight of hand! 'Tis false! You lie!" I shouted.

Martha removed her hand from my right thigh. My skin smarted where her thumbnail had been.

"Look upon her other thigh!" cried the youngest, pointing to where the thumbnail had been. "Another mark grows!"

Martha returned with her looking glass, inspecting. "Yes, it would seem so."

"Stupid cows!" I shouted, quickly sitting up, causing the three women to jump away in fear. I studied the red blotch where Martha's thumbnail had been. "This is from your thumbnail upon me. See how it is crescent shaped, like a nail? Ridiculous! You are all being deceived! I am being deceived!" My voice grew louder, I quaked with rage.

"You shall not speak!" yelled Martha, sounding shrill and nervous now. "We shall go and alert the magistrates to the two teats upon her thighs, and that the one did not bleed when pricked," she said to the other two. "You, get dressed and wait."

After the three exited the room, I slammed my fists against the table in a fury, causing the sores upon my wrists to open and bleed. "There's the blood, proof of my innocence!" I yelled out to an empty room. And then I broke into laughter because what else was there to do? This was madness. As I snatched my chemise and pulled it roughly over my head, I muttered insults at the women. I stepped into my skirts, fastening them, and then busied myself with cinching my stays.

The door opened abruptly, another constable stepping into the room. When he saw that I was not yet decent, he quickly averted his gaze. "My apologies!" he quickly shouted as he backed out of the room. After all I had been through, after what I had just experienced, I cared little. It mattered not. With a rough tug, I cinched my stays.

"You may come in now," I said, as though I spoke to a dressmaker. What a folly it all was. In my frustration, I unplaited my braid, shaking my hair free, rubbing at my scalp, which tingled with heat and anger.

The constable returned, averting his eyes for a moment again, as though he feared I might have lied and disrobed once more.

"And who are you?" I demanded, taking my hands from my hair and putting them on my hips.

He bowed slightly, then straightened and cleared his throat, perhaps realizing that he need not bow for a prisoner. "Constable James Baldwin."

"And what's to be done to me now? Shall I have to strip to my skin once again for you? For the magistrates?"

He shook his head, putting his hands before him in protest. "No, Goody Jones, that was women's work, for women's eyes only."

"Then what?"

"I'm to watch you through the night. This is the examination method."

"Watch me for what?"

"To see if any familiars should come to you."

"Familiars?"

"The Devil in the shape of an animal." He spoke to me in a calm, soft voice, as though he spoke to a child, or a woman in mourning.

"And how can a familiar come to me if the door and windows are closed? Shall it magically appear?"

"As you can see," he said, pointing toward the front door, "the door has been left ajar, for the purpose."

"So how do we proceed? Are we to stand all night, staring at each other like this?" I gestured with my hands.

"Nay, Goody Jones, you are to sit upon the floor with your legs crisscrossed beneath your skirts. And I shall sit here in this wee chair." He walked to the corner of the room, where a simple chair sat. He took it by the back and walked a few paces toward the table, then gently placed the chair down. He unbelted his sword and hung it upon the chairback, then slowly sat himself down, heaving a sigh. "Go on then, Goody Jones, sit yourself down, else I shall have to call in the other constables."

# CHAPTER
# TWENTY-SIX

*6. In the prison, in the clear day-light, there was seen in her arms, she sitting on the floor, and her clothes up, etc., a little child, which ran from her into another room, and the officer following it, it was vanished. The like child was seen in two other places, to which she had relation; and one maid that saw it, fell sick upon it, and was cured by the said Margaret, who used means to be employed to that end.*

*—John Winthrop, journal*

There was naught else to be done. I did as I was told, seating myself on the floorboards. I crossed my legs before me and tucked my skirts over them. "And this is how I must remain through the night?"

"Aye, that is the way of it."

"Shall be a long night, then," I said, looking out the window and noticing that night had descended.

Constable Baldwin nodded pensively, considering my words. "Aye, it shall."

For a brief moment, I was reminded of Thomas, for Baldwin had the same observant, quiet manner. He gave me a sad smile.

I liked him. He was a good man, I could sense it. He was only following orders. I'd heard the slight Scottish lilt in his voice. "Are you a Scot?"

He contemplated my words, wetting his lips with his tongue. He was not young, nor was he old. He was stocky and, as he removed his hat and placed it upon the table, he revealed a balding head fringed with blond wisps of hair. "You've a good ear."

He rose from the chair and approached me. I flinched, surprised by his movement. He moved the lanterns left behind by the women closer to my person. "There, I can see you better now," he said in his calm, soothing voice. He then returned to his place upon the chair, resting one boot upon his other knee, crossing his arms before him.

"Do you believe in witches, Constable Baldwin?" I shot at him.

He nodded. "Of course. The Devil is most cunning in his methods."

There was silence.

"Do you not believe in witches, Goody Jones?"

I considered his question. "Indeed there exists evil in the hearts of some men and women, and some choose to act upon the evil. The Devil speaks through them."

"Does he speak through you, Goody Jones?"

"What do you believe, Constable Baldwin?"

He sat in silence. In the darkness of the room, I could barely make out the shape of him upon the chair. "I believe that in a righteous, God-fearing place such as this, all are innocent until their guilt can be proven without question."

"Well said." I rubbed at the back of my neck—the whole of my body ached from my time in prison, from this day of examination. "Do you believe that all men and women are capable of being corrupted by their own selfish desires, even in this place?"

"Yes, indeed."

A night breeze blew through the ajar door, bringing with it the briny scent of ocean as well as the sharp, bitter perfume of the yellow marsh marigolds that ran rampant beside the wetlands. I inhaled deeply and closed my eyes, pretending for the briefest moment that I was back within the walls of my hearty garden in Charlestown.

"Beautiful weather this eve," he said, watching me from his dark place.

"Constable Baldwin—"

"James. Call me James. If we are to spend the night together, call me by my Christian name."

There was silence between us, but then I guffawed.

"How like lovers," I said, laughing.

"Nay, nay, I'm a married man, I am, Goody Jones."

I laughed aloud again, and the sound of it echoed in the bare room. "Call me Maggie, please, if we are to spend the night together."

We laughed again. I could sense he knew this task to be absurd, but he would do his bidding.

"And if nothing should transpire this night," I said, "what shall you report to the magistrates?"

"I shall report that nothing transpired, Maggie. I am a man of honor. God sees all."

"Indeed He does. I have thought on that often, whilst in my jail cell."

"May He watch over us, keep us on our righteous path."

"Amen." I rested my chin upon my hand, elbow upon knee. "I hope He sees all that goes on here, what goes on in His name."

There was silence but for the sound of the wind outside the door, the distant shouts from the wharves at the end of King Street. I heard the shrill, distant evensong of bats. I longed to be home, safe, within the arms of my Thomas, my *Rí*. He was my sanctuary, my rock in rough seas. Without him, I felt as though I were adrift, held at the whim of the winds and the tides. As I thought of Thomas, a tear spilled down my cheek. I quickly dashed it away.

"You may close your eyes and rest, Maggie. So long as you remain seated as you are, I've no qualm with you resting."

"You are kind, James, I thank thee."

My head lay heavy upon my hand, my elbow upon my knee. I closed my eyes, breathing through my nose. I knew that there would be little sleep to be had that night, but quickly I fell into slumber, awaking with a start when my elbow slipped off my knee and I almost toppled over.

"Do be careful, Maggie. I am sorry it must be this way."

Drowsily I muttered back, "As am I, and I'm sorry it must be you to have to stay awake for this folly."

"'Tis no folly if it be God's will."

"Mmm," I said with a roll of my eyes, stretching my back before hunching over again, hands resting in my lap.

I know not how much time passed. I awoke one moment to see James beside me, gently replacing a candle within one of the lanterns. Startled, I could not remember where I was at first.

He placed a hand softly upon my shoulder, as though I were a startled dog. "'Tis just me, Maggie, replacing the candle here. Worry not."

I sniffed at his comment. "Worry not? Because you shall report that I am no witch?"

He removed his hand from my shoulder and went back to his seat in the dark corner of the room. "The night is not yet over, Maggie."

I shuddered slightly at his words, and at the cool sea air coming through the ajar door. I tilted my head to the side, stretching my neck, trying to massage away the aching pain between my shoulder blades, to no avail. The jittering pain within my joints I knew to be more than fatigue. This was the onset of a fever, an ill humor. I brought my fingers to my forehead. I burned. There would be no more sleep this night.

As though he read my thoughts, James spoke. "Tell me of your family."

"Family?"

"Aye, you husband, your children?"

"My husband, as I'm sure you know, is Thomas Jones, a cabinetmaker, joiner."

"He must be a busy man, with such a skill in great demand here."

"He prospers."

"Is he a Welshman?"

I smiled; how many times had we been asked this same question? "Nay, he's an Irishman, come to England as a child."

"How about you, Maggie, where are you from?"

"A village called Reading, west of London."

"I know of it."

"And you, James? From where in Scotland are you?"

"A little seaside town in Argyll, Port Appin."

"You are far from home."

"Mmm," he muttered, "we all are, are we not?"

I shivered again, the familiar tastes of iron and copper in my mouth, as it always was when I was in fever. "How did you come to Massachusetts, James?"

"That's a long and twisting tale."

"I like long and twisting tales, and I'm not going anywhere this night. You have my undivided attention."

"Aye, very true." He nodded. "I fought with the Covenanters, under the Campbell Clan."

"Oh aye," I replied with a sigh, disappointed. He was another Puritan, doing the Lord's work, examining a witch.

"This was less about religion and more about loyalty," he said, for he must have understood my assumption. "Campbells had been kind to my family for generations. My great-grandfather had sworn allegiance to them. So when the call was put out, to defend the clan against the MacDonalds and Camerons, I did what I was sworn to do."

"You were a soldier. Where?"

I heard his deep sigh, as though he were reluctantly trying to choose the proper words. "I fought with the Campbells at Inverlochy, some three years ago."

"Against the Royalists?"

"Aye."

"That did not end well for your side, from what I remember hearing in London."

"It did not. I barely escaped with my life."

I heard his shuddering breath. "So, after defeat you left your home and came here."

"Mmm," he agreed, scratching at his beard. "When a man watches his brethren be slaughtered by his fellow countrymen, it changes the way a man sees his country." He paused, crossing his arms over his barrel chest. "The River Lochy was crimson from the blood. I hid underwater, beneath the corpse of my brother."

I would not speak. This man was revealing something intimate to me.

"I survived by barely moving. I would raise my lips to the loch's surface and take gulps of air, beneath his blood-soaked tartan. I was forced to taste my brother's blood, in order to escape with my life, and return to my wife and children."

"War is terrible." I shivered, feeling foolish for saying something so obvious in the face of his tragedy.

He laughed a little. "Men know of no other way. 'Tis their very nature."

"Alas, you speak the truth."

There was a moment of silence.

"Have you any children, Maggie?"

She was not with me in this place, thankfully. She was not with me anymore, I knew this, but I did not. She had been a force, a flame of life, nothing could make her vanish forever. She would be with me again. I would be with her again.

"I had a child, Bess."

"Just the one?"

I paused. I clasped my hand tight, hoping to feel Bess's chubby fist within mine. I clasped my other hand, hoping to hold the forgiveness for my past.

"She is all that God saw fit to let me keep." There was no lie in this.

"Is she gone?"

I did not respond.

"We have lost two boys, my wife and I have. The grief is unspeakable. They were taken by the pox."

I fought my tears. She was still with me. She had to be. If she were not, the pain of it would kill me.

"Is that what took your daughter?"

"Nay, scarlatina."

"Ah. Pity. How old was she?"

"She is fourteen months, she is."

He did not respond.

I could suddenly smell her breath—like milk and fresh eggs. I squinted my eyes, trying to banish the tears. I brought my fingers to my lips, and they were not my fingers, but her cheek, so soft, so plump, so like silk. The sob escaped from me, low, breathy.

"If you would like to tell me more about her, I am glad to listen."

How was it that such a kind man was here to watch and judge the state of my soul? Was he real? Who sat in that dark corner, really? Was he real like Bess was real? A shiver went through me again. The fever had its fingers round me.

"But I understand if you wish not to. I cannot yet speak of my boys."

"She is everything that is most beautiful and pure in my life. She is what comes from true love. The truest love."

"Your husband is dear to you."

"He is more than dear to me. He is everything that is true and good in my life. I do not deserve him."

"Ah. Fortune has smiled upon you then."

"Aye, in this aspect, I am richest of all."

"It would be wise to keep this to yourself. It would be seen as ungodly by some here."

"Fie upon them."

He cleared his throat. "Tell me more about Bess."

Another sob came from me. "What would you like to know about her?" It hurt to speak.

"Who did she favor?"

"You mean, who *does* she favor."

There was a pause. "Of course."

"She is my own, there is no doubt. She has this unruly dark hair, these blue eyes too big, too disconcerting to some. She has my temper."

He smiled. "How so?"

I proceeded to tell story after story of my Bess: the time she howled when I took away her spoon of honey, the manner in which she yells at her wooden blocks when they do not stack as she would like, how voracious her appetite was as an infant, how it is as a toddler, how I would never deny her the honey spoon.

We laughed together, despite—or because of—our exhaustion. I spied the sky lightening through the windowpane. It would be dawn soon. My time with James would end. Surely he would vindicate me.

"Once, my eldest," said James, who cautiously allowed himself to speak of one of his departed sons, "when he was about two, he and I encountered Governor Endecott at the blacksmith's. The governor pinched his cheek. Jacob, he—" James laughed. "He grabbed at the old governor's hand and shrieked at him as if to say, 'You'll not be pinching my cheek, old man!'"

"I'd have paid a shilling to see such," I said.

With the growing light of dawn, I could now see more of James than just his dark form. I watched as he passed a trembling hand over his eyes to hide his tears. "By God, I do miss them."

"They are still with you, wherever you go, I'm sure, like my Bess," I said, for I knew how great the pain was.

"Aye?"

"Aye. Bess is with me always. She has been here all this while," I said, bracing myself against the chills that racked me. "I'll never leave my Bess alone. What sort of mother would I be?"

James did not respond. He just studied me, awaiting more from me.

I laughed a little, more tears spilling. "My husband says he does not see her. How can he not?" I asked James, holding out my hands before me, beseeching. "She is a bright spark, a force, a light in my dark world. Do you see how she brings the light into this room?"

James did not answer.

"My Bess! Do you not see her?"

And my Bess, I knew she was with us, had been with us. She hid beneath my dingy skirts, the little elfish thing! "Aha! She hides!" I lifted my skirts with a great swooping gesture, they billowed up before my face, and when they cascaded back down to the floor, Bess stood before me, before us. Bess! My own! Naughty girl, hiding all this while! I took her hands in mine, exclaiming with joy. "My Bess! Do you not see her too, James? Look at her hands in mine, my strong girl! She walked before her first birthday, did you not, my sweet girl?"

There she was, standing before me, looking up into my eyes, her dimpled cheeks rosy and flush. She smiled wide, as though she had not seen me for a long while, her mouth agape, flashing her four teeth. "Mama!"

"Mama! Oh! Did you hear?" I crushed her to me, buried my nose into her curls as smooth and soft as ermine fur. "Oh my own! My own!" My voice was muffled in her hair.

"Maggie?" James rose from his chair, a look of bewilderment upon his face.

I put her at arm's length so that I might look upon her again. How had I been so blessed, that God put this child in my life despite my sins, despite my neglect in years past? Surely he could not take away a child so beautiful, so full of light. "Just look at her, James! God did not take her from me! She has been hiding all this time, the little sprite, beneath my skirts! Look at how she smiles and laughs at us, such fools we are!"

James blinked a few times.

"Do you not see? Do you not see?" I beseeched him. "Look here, her dark curls, look here, the shape of her round cheeks, the dimples, look here, her lips like rubies, look here, her plump little hands in mine!" I lifted my hands so that he might see better. "Do you not see?"

James's mouth quivered, he seemed overwhelmed, at a loss for words. His eyes were wide with disbelief.

"Pray tell, you see her! Please! Please! She is here! She is here!"

She took her hands from mine, toddling away.

"No! Bess! Don't leave me now, not now! Don't leave me, Bess!"

She giggled and ran on her chubby little legs, away from me.

"Come back, Bess!" I yelled, tears streaming down my face. I went to move, to go after her, but I was frozen. My legs would not work. I fell to trembling, the copper taste filling my mouth. "Come! Bess! Come back to me! Don't leave me!" I looked to James. "Catch her, James, catch her!"

Bess dashed out of the room, to the back kitchen.

"Please, James!"

"Lord bless us." He stumbled after her, out of the room, the sound of his boots upon the floorboards resonating.

I covered my face, sobbing into my hands. The tears were endless. They would never end. "My Bess!"

From the kitchen I heard a shriek. James came back to the room, supporting a young kitchen maid who still shrieked, mouth agape, eyes wide.

"The maid, she saw Bess too!"

"Where is Bess?"

"She disappeared!" James exclaimed, breathless. "The maid here, she took a fright. I told her I followed a little girl, and at first she did not see, but then she did, and she shook and fainted, she did." He put the maid in the chair on which he'd sat the night through.

The maid's eyes rolled back into her head, she shook, her limbs flailing and animated by some other force. The froth rose to her mouth. I knew instantly, she was apoplectic. From years of instinct, I rose and went to her. My limbs found a way, despite the tremors of fever. "James, go quickly, find a wooden spoon or other utensil from the kitchen, quickly. Go!"

James ran back to the kitchen. I put my hands upon the maid's face, tilting her head upward so that she could get more air. "Breathe, breathe," I ordered her.

James returned with a wooden spoon. I took it from him, prying the maid's mouth open with my other hand, struggling to suppress the straining tongue inside. When I had hold, I took the spoon and placed it where my fingers had been.

"What is this she suffers from? Was it the child who did this?" James asked in a panic.

"She suffers from apoplexy. We must be certain she does not swallow her tongue and choke herself. She must have fallen into a fit when Bess startled her."

James was frozen to the spot, watching as I smoothed the maid's hair from out of her face, wiped the profuse foam that came from her mouth. Her limbs began to slow and still. She bit hard upon the spoon, growling like an injured animal.

"Was like the Devil took hold of her."

I looked at James. "That's what some might say, but I've seen it time and again, and there is no evil behind it. It's a fever of the brain. And it runs in families."

Finally, the maid was still, breathing evenly. I took the spoon from her mouth. The handle was now indented with her teeth marks. Her eyes were closed. She slept.

I shook again, the ache of my muscles reminding me where I was. Bess was gone. I heaved a sigh and made my way to the center of the room, where I sat again. It were now morning, but I did not know if my examination was yet over.

James stood between the maid and me, looking back and forth between the two of us, as though trying to comprehend all that had transpired.

I stretched my aching arms above my head, hoping to ease the pain in my back with a good stretch. As I did so, I heard a sound by the ajar door. I heard it again, a low, raspy meow. I knew that sound like I knew my own heart. "Molly?"

Silently, Molly made her way round the door, her fluffy paws padding their way toward me. Gracefully she stretched her multicolored body, then sat beside me.

"Molly, how did you get here?"

"Reow," she answered as she always did, then pushed her head into my knee, rubbing her cheek against me, purring.

"Is this cat yours?" James asked. His eyes could not grow wider.

"Aye, this is my Molly. However did she get here from Charlestown?" And then it dawned on me. This—her presence, my acknowledging her, the appearance of Bess—all of this would be the crux of my earthly life.

# CHAPTER
# TWENTY-SEVEN

*Her behavior at her trial was very intemperate, lying
notoriously, and railing upon the jury and witnesses, etc. . . .*

—*John Winthrop, journal*

The day was hot, the air close, threatening storms. When I was brought
before the court once again, I noticed the cramped assembly, shoulder
to shoulder, spectators crowded outside the doorway doing their best
to gain a vantage point from which to observe. Young lads propped
themselves up upon the windowsills, their makeshift seats. The verdict
upon the state of my soul, it seemed, were more enthralling than even
the best theaters of London.

They had searched for Molly, the constables, the court officers. I
had hissed in her ear, "Be gone, Molly!" and shoved her toward the door
so that she escaped their clutches. Cleverest girl she be, she darted out
the door and down a mews before any mortal might grab hold of her.
Thank the Lord, I believed in my heart she was safe, my Molly, the very
best girl cat there ever was, ever shall be, bless her.

The constables—aside from James, who I had not seen since
Molly had entered the examination room—had roughly handled me,
as though I were a wild, frothing beast rather than a woman. Irons

clasped round my wrists once again, they tugged upon them as they led me across the street to the courthouse. The whole of my body ached and shook with fever. My mouth was parched, my head felt as though it might combust at any moment. As I was brought before the seated magistrates, the delirium took hold, for they appeared to float, suspended in the air, rather than seated upon their chairs of judgment. I shook my head and laughed aloud—how ridiculous it all was. Oh, to be back in London again, to stand upon the stone banks of the Thames at Cheapside, to hear the lapping as sloops and ships went past, to smell the rank gutters, to hear the bustle of lives lived fully, unburdened by the predestination and piety of this place. Stupid fools, Thomas and I were, to leave. Lady Wembly, the mad cow, had offed her own self. I had done nothing wrong, not in that instance.

"Be silent!" the constable ordered me, banging his staff upon the floorboards, each thump like a burning flash within my head.

"The court summons Goody Wheeler."

"Goody Wheeler," I muttered to myself, trying to place her name. "Goody Wheeler." I scanned the courtroom and then spied the eldest examiner from the prior evening. "Martha Wheeler, there she be!"

The courtroom was silent. The magistrates glanced over at me when I muttered, looking wary, as though I might summon a demon at any moment.

"Goody Wheeler," said Magistrate Dudley, "please tell the court what you witnessed in your examination of the accused."

"Very well, Magistrate Dudley." She paused, clearing her throat, glancing over at me, then back to the seated magistrates. "I was charged with the bodily examination of Margaret Jones yesterday evening, along with two other examiners who are my apprentices."

"Are you a skilled witchfinder, Goody Wheeler, such as Matthew Hopkins, Witchfinder General of Manningtree, County Essex?"

"Indeed, sir, I am. I am well versed in his treatise, *A Discovery of Witches*. I did assist in Mister Hopkins's examination of accused witches in three instances in my hometown of Bury St. Edmunds."

"Please tell the court of your observations of the accused's body."

"Go on, *Martha*," I taunted, "tell them everything you saw. Tell them how you stripped me bare and examined every inch of my flesh."

"Silence!"

"Tell them, Martha! Tell them how your young apprentice stared at the curve of my waist and hips, the fullness of my breasts and felt temptation!" The words spilled from me and I were giddy with them. I knew there was no hope for me. What was left for me? Nothing was left but to make them all aware of their folly, their crime. I would make them pay with every last breath in my body before they took my breath away from me.

"Silence! Silence!" the constable hurled at me, the crowded courtroom in an uproar over my words.

I laughed triumphantly, glancing toward the assembly. They thought me mad, possessed, I could see it. But then I saw the Strattons; Samuel's eyes beseeched me. "Maggie," he silently mouthed, and Alice, staring at me, nodding her head in encouragement, ignorant of the tears freely spilling down her cheeks.

And then there was Thomas to her left. His green eyes spoke to me, and in my mind I heard him say, "My Maggie, my wild creature, fork-tongued to the end." And then he squinted his eyes shut, trying to banish the tears that were already escaping.

My Thomas, my own, oh, how I longed to place my lips against his temple and breathe in the scent of him. There were no scent on this earth more dear to me, no music sweeter than his laughter, no touch more magical than his rough fingers upon my skin. Lord, you had blessed me indeed, putting him in my life. How the Wheel of Fortune had favored me. I smiled triumphantly, filled with gladness, knowing that my life with Thomas had been fuller and more beautiful than anyone else's in this damned courtroom. Jealous wretches!

"Goody Jones has the mark of a witch's teat upon her," declared Goody Wheeler in a clear, low voice.

The courtroom gasped.

"Can you describe what you observed?"

"Tell them where it is, *Martha*," I taunted her again.

She paused for a moment, looking stricken.

"Please, continue," urged Magistrate Dudley.

"Aye, do go on, Dudley longs to hear all the delicious details." I leered at him, then winked. The delirium and madness were storming my inner castle walls.

"Goody Jones has, upon her upper, inner thigh, a witch's teat, a mark of the Devil."

"Aye, a mark with which I was born."

"Silence!"

"The mark," continued Goody Wheeler, "was clearly visible, looking as though it had been recently suckled upon."

I shrieked with laughter. What stupidity! "Oh aye? That's right, each of these men seated before us took his turn, sucking upon the sweetness of my thigh!"

The court was in an uproar. I knew I had gone too far. I would not look over at Thomas. He had never deserved a wife such as me. I had never been worthy of such a man. He had been mistaken about me. He was mistook.

"Silence!" The constable grabbed rough hold of my upper arm, pulling me toward his red, sweating face. "Another such outburst from you and I shall make you regret you ever spoke, later this night." His breath was hot and fetid upon my ear.

I turned, my face just inches away from his. "It seems I have provoked you to unclean thoughts, if you should make such threats."

"And then," Goody Wheeler continued once the courtroom had quieted some, "upon her other thigh, just across from the teat, another reddened teat began to bloom."

"It had naught to do with your filthy thumbnail digging into my flesh, did it not!" I shouted at her, leaning forward to get a better look into her lying face.

"Shall I gag her, Magistrates?" the constable said, and I saw the eagerness in his eyes, the quick flick of his tongue over his lips. He would like me submissive, oh yes indeed, he would, the dog.

Magistrate Bellingham held his hand up, as though he were trying to subdue both the constable and me. "Please, in the name of justice, I ask you to remain quiet, Goody Jones."

"Just as you have, Governor Bellingham. Just as you have remained quiet, even though you were one of my most loyal and gracious patrons."

The courtroom rumbled, and Bellingham's eyes grew wide for a moment, then his countenance settled into something of resignation, his mouth firmly closed, a slow nod of his head. And at that moment I knew I had lost my only possible ally upon the magistrates' bench.

"Goody Wheeler," Dudley said, wanting the witness to proceed, "continue."

"And then I used my witch pricker tool, to see if the teat would bleed."

"Please explain to the court why this is necessary."

"As all skilled witchfinders know, if a witch's teat or mark is pricked and bleeds, then it is proof of innocence. A true witch, though, shall not bleed, for her blood has been thickened by Satan and cannot be extracted."

"And what was the conclusion of your test upon Goody Jones's mark?"

"It did not bleed." Goody Wheeler and I said it in unison, for I knew what her answer would be.

Jaws dropped, prayers were muttered, for it must be proof of my dark arts that I speak the same words as she, at the same moment. That's what fools would believe.

"It did not bleed because the 'witch pricker' tool of which she speaks is a folly, prevarication, if you will. I know it to be. It did not puncture my skin, but only appeared to. The needle receded into its encasement. It's naught but a false method."

"Silence!" demanded Governor Winthrop. "Are you insinuating that this court employs trickery in its proceedings, Goody Jones? Do you speak against this court? Does the Devil have your tongue at this very moment?"

I shrugged, a rude gesture meant to further vex the governor. I wanted to be done with this performance. I wanted for them to take my life so that I might finally rest, escape the clutches of fever, hunger, pain.

"I only speak the truth of *my own* observation."

"Goody Wheeler," said Dudley, "have you anything else to add to your examination?"

"That is all, Magistrate."

"That is all."

Martha Wheeler made her way back to the assembly from the witness stand, never looking at me once. She couldn't look at me, knowing I spoke the truth. Pity, that evidence could not be used in this trial, of course.

"The court now summons Constable James Baldwin."

For a brief moment, I felt hope, but then tempered myself. Though he had been kind to me, though he were a good man, I were a fool to think he might not speak of what he had witnessed. And what he saw was damning, in their eyes.

Constable Baldwin made his way to the witness stand without haste. He looked to me when he reached the stand. His eyes were puffy and red like a man's who had not slept. He appeared as though he witnessed the mighty moose of these woods for the first time: awed, fascinated, fearful.

"Constable Baldwin, please tell us about your observation of the accused."

He cleared his throat, looked at all of the magistrates before speaking. "I did observe Goody Jones through the night as I had been bidden to do by this court. I watched her from dusk until dawn."

"Proceed with your observations, please."

"Most of the night was without incident. Goody Jones sat upon the floor with her legs drawn up before her, as is prescribed by the law."

"And then what happened?" Dudley urged, as though he were a child longing to learn the end of a story.

"Not long before dawn, Goody Jones began to speak of her little daughter, who passed some months ago. She spoke of her as though she still lived, as though she were with us in the room. At first I thought this was just a distraught mother's way of making peace with her grief. But then I saw it was something more than that."

"What do you mean by that?"

"I mean, it felt as though there were something beyond us at work."

"Satan?"

"I am but a constable, I cannot speak to what forces were at work."

"Did you feel threatened? Did it feel like malice at work?"

James considered for a moment, then looked to me, then back to the magistrates. "Nay, there were no malice, for she spoke only of her poor, deceased daughter."

"Go on, Constable."

"The more Goody Jones spoke, the closer the air felt in the room."

The courtroom muttered and stirred, clinging to his every word.

"And then Goody Jones said, 'There she be!' and with a great swoosh of her skirt, the shape of a child appeared."

Gasps and exclamations rang out from the assembly. And then a hush descended.

"A shape?" asked Dudley.

"Aye, I cannot explain it." James shook his head as though he were trying to clear his thoughts. "I know not if it were a vision, a spirit? But I swear upon my life, a tiny little girl appeared before us. I know it sounds like nonsense, like the pretense of a child's imagination, but I stand before the court and swear this is what I saw."

"And what happened to this vision of a child you speak of?"

"After a moment with her mother, she ran from the room, into the kitchen."

"Did you follow?"

"I did indeed. And I asked the scullery maid in the kitchen if she had seen the child, and she said she did, then fainted before me, into a fit."

"Did you proceed to follow the vision?"

"I went to the back door, where the child had run, but when I looked out to the back garden, I saw nothing, not one soul."

"Is the scullery maid here? Can she be brought before the court?" asked Endecott, almost breathless.

"She is unable to bear witness, for she is an invalid, unable to leave her bed, not awake," said the courtroom constable.

"Aye, she then fell into a fit, at which I brought her back into the room with Goody Jones, beseeching her to help the maid, for I knew her to be skilled in physic," explained Baldwin.

"And then what happened?"

"Goody Jones immediately tended to the maid, bid me find a wooden spoon, which I quickly did. She then pried open the maid's mouth and placed the spoon handle upon her tongue in order to suppress it."

"So that she would not swallow and choke upon her own tongue."

All the magistrates turned their attention to me.

"What was it that ailed her? Was it a dark humor?" asked Winthrop.

"She were apoplectic."

"Had she become possessed by a dark force?" asked Endecott.

I shook my head and stared at him as though he were daft. "Do I look like God? How am I to know the reasoning behind His work?"

"Blasphemous!" hissed Endecott.

"But was it His work or Satan's work?" asked Winthrop.

"I cannot speak to that. I can only speak to what I know from my training in physic. There are some who succumb frequently to apoplexy, for reasons unknown, but it often is familial."

"She did subdue the maid, Magistrates," said James.

"And once the maid was subdued, what happened?" Dudley knew of course, but he just could not wait for the last detail, the last nail in my coffin.

"After Goody Jones had subdued the maid, she returned to her place upon the floor, awaiting the end of her examination. And within a few moments, a cat entered the room."

The crowd erupted. This was the drama they had sought.

"A cat? Can you describe the cat, and what it did when it entered the room?"

"The cat were very large and plump, with a great, furry coat of many colors: black, brown, gold, ginger. She had a low, gravelly meow, and she went straight to Goody Jones, rubbed up against her."

"Goody Jones, are you familiar with this cat, or perhaps the better question is, is this cat your familiar, your imp of Satan?"

I guffawed. "There be nothing impish about my cat. Aye, she is my cat, and her name is Molly."

"Did you summon her as Satan so clearly has summoned you?" asked Endecott.

"Indeed no. I've no idea how she came all the way from my home in Charlestown to Boston."

"All the more reason to suspect that Satan is at work here, for a cat to travel across the river all the way to Boston!" exclaimed Endecott.

I shook my head. I was sick of his pious, self-righteous outrage. "You really are enjoying yourself at my expense, are you not, Governor Endecott?"

"Silence!"

There was a tug upon my hair, drawing my head back sharply. The sensation sent bolts of pain through me. My braid was within the constable's fist.

"Magistrates, I, too, have something to say regarding Goody Jones," his voice boomed.

"What is it, Constable Johnson?"

"This woman," he said, and I noted he still held my braid in his grasp, "she told me yesterday that I would not sleep well, that I would be plagued with nightmares, and indeed I was all of last night. I did not sleep a wink and I had terrifying visions, I did."

I smiled triumphantly. There was some, little, justice.

The courtroom was abuzz with chatter.

Governor Winthrop stood. "I believe the time has come for this trial to adjourn. We shall recess in order to decide and declare a verdict."

And with that, the magistrates all rose and left to the adjoining room. The courtroom erupted with conversation and discussion, everyone eyeing me with suspicion, eyeing me as though I were a creature come to prey upon them all.

Again, I felt the sharp tug upon my braid. "You'll get your due, whore of Lucifer."

I turned my head to meet his gaze. "And I wager you wish it were you to give me my due."

He only chuckled and licked the corner of his mouth.

"Trouble is, when you try to do so, you will not be able to."

"Oh aye?" he asked, the smile leaving his face.

"If I were able to bring nightmares upon you, imagine what havoc I might wreak upon your prick."

He let go of my braid, only to quickly strike me across the face. "Filthy trollop."

Most in the courtroom looked on, satisfaction upon their countenances. But some appeared outraged.

And before I knew it, there was a large hand wrapped tightly round Constable Johnson's throat, taking him by great surprise.

"Touch her again, you'll not live to see your children grow."

Thomas tightened his grip and Constable Johnson struggled, a panicked, wild look in his eyes.

"Understand?" Thomas asked calmly, but with force.

Constable Johnson managed a nod, at which Thomas let go of him. The constable choked for air, rubbing at his throat, coughing. "You'll be tried for that."

"For defending my wife? Let's see how that goes over with a jury of men."

"Thomas," I said, pleading. I did not want him to sully his hands. He was better than this. He was better than me. He did not deserve this.

His green eyes looked down into mine, and I saw so much within them, a great conflagration of emotion and pain, I had to look away. I had done this to him. I was to blame. He could have had another, he could still be back in England, a cabinetmaker in some prospering village with a brood of children, sons to carry on his name and trade. But alas, he had me, and my intemperate mind, my forked tongue, my impetuous spirit, my shame—all of my shame.

"Thomas," I said again, lifting both shackled hands to touch his disheveled goatee. His eyes closed, like a cat giving in to a caress. He pressed my fingers to his lips hungrily, then looked into my eyes, searching me. He put his hand to my forehead, the rough palm covering the whole of it. His touch instantly eased my pain.

"Maggie, you're feverish. No wonder you've . . ." He trailed off, his hand sliding down from my forehead to my cheek.

I kissed his palm. "What? No wonder I've spoken without care? You should know I don't require a fever to speak plainly."

"Aye." The ghost of a smile played at his lips.

Just then the constable, who had finally gained his composure, stood tall and banged his staff upon the floorboards. The magistrates filed back into the room and took their seats.

I looked back into Thomas's eyes. He still held my face. "This is where it ends," I whispered.

He shook his head, now holding my face in both his hands, as though I were everything he owned in the world. "Nay, it does not end here, Maggie."

The constable shoved him away from me, and the feel of his fingers slipping from my face was like the feel of plunging into icy waters. I shook mightily.

"Order! Order!" called Dudley. "The Honorable Governor Winthrop shall read the verdict."

A deliberate and heavy hush fell over the assembly. The governor stood, his tall frame, his dark visage looming over the courtroom.

I quaked in my shoes. I did not fear my own mortality, not at all. But I feared the manner in which we would meet. But I would not let them see it. They would not win. I stood tall, held my chin up high, and stared right back at each magistrate.

"Winthrop, Endecott, Dudley, Hibbins, Nowell, Bradstreet, Pynchon, Winthrop the Younger, and Bellingham." I let my gaze linger on the last one; he looked away. "What is the verdict?"

"Margaret Jones of Charlestown, on the charge of witchcraft, you have been found guilty."

The crowd roared; some with elation, others with despair, anger.

"The date of execution is set for Monday, June the fifteenth, when you shall be hanged by the neck until you are dead, so help us, God."

The din of the courtroom grew. The air within me came out with a great exhalation. *And so this is how I shall meet my end.*

"God's will be done!" shouted a woman's lithe voice from a seat near the magistrates.

I looked to see from whom it had come.

Widow Hallett, newly Goody Longfellow, panted, eyes wide, looking as though she were experiencing some spiritual rapture. Her hands slid over her protruding belly as though she hugged her unborn child.

I do not remember the manner in which I was escorted out of the courthouse and to the King Street jail, down the steps to my damp, fetid cell. But when I was shoved, tripping over the cobblestone floor and falling to my knees, I recall the blinding pain that went through the whole of me. But I bit my lip and drew blood—I would not let them see me weep.

For almost four weeks I languished in jail, allowed to see no one but for the constables who brought me paltry food and water and exchanged my privy buckets. Why must I wait? Be done with it! Fevers came and went, haunting me like a ghost. Mad thoughts, angry thoughts, would fill my mind, followed by nothing, when I would concentrate on the rhythm of my steady, shallow breathing. How I longed to see Thomas, to press my lips against his temple and inhale his scent. The longing was like a physical pain at times, and I wept silently, kissing my palm, pretending it was he I kissed.

The night before I was to be executed, I heard the sound of footsteps. I hoped that perhaps, on my last earthly night, I would be granted one last moment with my Love. I raised myself from the lousy hay that was my bed, only to see Constable Johnson unlocking my cell. He leered at me as though he were a spider just discovering its trapped prey.

He struck my face with the back of his hand and shoved me to the floor. "Get down on your knees and lift your skirts, you filthy whore."

The pain made my vision fill with stars and sparks. I heard the sound of his trouser laces hissing as he quickly undid them.

"I'll teach you a lesson," he said, his breath coming quickly.

I watched as he worked away, to no avail. "Doesn't look like it will be much of a lesson."

"Silence that Devil's tongue of yours, else I'll fuck your mouth."

I laughed despite my dire circumstance. "With what? Seems as though I pegged you rightly back in the courtroom. You're all talk. See my *witch's sight* at work?" I fell to laughing again.

The blow he let loose upon my face caused my jaw to pop, and I struggled to set it right, using my shackled hands to right it. The pain was furious, and I howled when I set it back in place. "Hit me again, and I will scream so all of Boston shall hear me." I found the strength to stand and face him. I could not hide the satisfaction from my face as I smiled.

"Stop looking at me," he said with bated breath. "Look away, bend over, and lift your skirts." He struck me across the face again with his free hand.

"She shall not!"

I steadied myself against the cell wall, catching my breath, waiting for the world to stop spinning before my eyes. Who had spoken? I heard the footsteps, as did Constable Johnson, who struggled to lace up his breeches before anyone see them unfastened.

But it was all for naught. Governor Bellingham stood at the cell door, taking in the whole of the scene, a look of disgust upon his face. He moved toward Constable Johnson, who still held his breeches laces in his fingers. "What is this, Johnson?"

I swore I could hear the slow wheels churning within Johnson's thick head as he searched for words. "Uh, she made move upon me, tried to undo my breeches, she did, evil whore!"

The world still spun slightly, but I managed to laugh. "You flatter yourself, Constable! Was this the dream you spoke of some time ago, which kept you awake?"

Bellingham looked at me, sympathy and sadness in his countenance. He then turned back to Johnson. "You are hereby dismissed from your post as constable of the General Court."

"Oy?" Johnson's face scrunched up as though Bellingham had spoken in a foreign tongue.

"Reece, Baldwin," Bellingham shouted toward the steps. "Come at once!"

Immediately their steps echoed down the stairs to the cell.

When they reached the cell, Bellingham gestured to Johnson. "Have him shackled. He will be brought up on the charges of licentiousness and assault. Better yet, put him in the stocks for the night."

I sighed in relief. For a moment I feared he would be housed in a nearby cell, where he might torment me with his words. But Bellingham had made certain that my last earthly night would at least be peaceful.

"I didn't do it! I swear it!" I heard Johnson's fretful protests fading as the constables brought him away to be locked in the stocks.

I watched Bellingham as the cell grew quiet. "Why are you here?"

"Your husband is upstairs, waiting to see you." He paused, his eyes scanning my face, my body. "Thank the Lord I did not have him come with me. We would have had a murder to be dealt with as well, I reckon."

"Aye." I nodded. "You would have."

"Did he violate you?"

"Nay, he is all bluster. He couldn't fuck a sheep if he tried."

Bellingham stared wide eyed at me, then smiled, shaking his head. "It would seem not even a pending execution will soften that forked tongue of yours."

I stood tall. "You know me well, Bellingham. I'll not meet my Maker silently."

"Nay, you won't." He considered me. "You are a most ferocious woman, Maggie Jones."

"I am," I said, looking down my nose at him. "That's why this place will not suffer me to live."

"Indeed, you speak the truth of it. And I am most sorry it must be this way."

"Oh, aye, save your false pity. You weren't sorry enough to stand for me." I spat upon the floor. "Leave me be and let me see my husband one last time."

While Bellingham went back up the stairs to summon Thomas, I stood in the silence of my jail cell. I looked to the pile of molded hay that had been my bed for weeks. In and out of fever, when sleep would finally come, it came, carrying with it the same nightmare again and again, haunting me over and over. My secret to keep, my secret over which I triumphed in my brief time in the world of the living. I mused, each of us must, within our mind's eye, see what we assume will be our final hour upon this earth. A bed—a real bed, not some pile of straw—surrounded by our family, gazing upon what God granted us so that our names might live on. Indeed, this is the ideal for most of us. Perhaps for soldiers it might be a heroic death upon a battlefield. Mayhap for ships' captains, a watery grave is most fitting. For the clergy, to be taken whilst in the midst of prayer? For a mother who knows she shall pass in birthing, to gaze upon and hold the fruit of her womb before her soul ascends.

I always thought my final moments on earth might be within my garden, surrounded by the sharp, green scent of herbs reaching skyward from their roots. The damp, rich soil might be my final pillow, the feel of a cat's whiskers tickling my weathered, wrinkled cheek, the sound of children and grandchildren, their voices and laughter echoing from the house, from the fields beyond. And the distant sound of Thomas sawing, sanding wood, the steady, patient rhythm of it. I always knew I must die before he did, for God would not be so cruel as to take the sun from my life. I could not bear to go on without my Thomas.

So in this way, God has been kind to me. The Wheel of Fortune has favored me in Love. And if one must choose one aspect of Fortune's Wheel, Love be the sweetest of all.

The cell door opened, Bellingham entered first, followed by Thomas. Key in hand, Bellingham approached, unlocking and removing the shackles from my wrists. As he tossed them aside to the cell floor, Bellingham said, "My dear wife bid me to allow you one last night with your husband, without shackles binding you. I cannot deny her. I could not return home to Winnisimmet and look her in the eye if I did not do her bidding."

"Love is most persuasive," I said, smiling at Thomas.

Bellingham made a quick exit, locking the cell door behind him.

"And now you are a prisoner too," I said, wondering if Thomas would come to me, or if I were to go to him. Neither of us moved.

Thomas looked into my eyes, then faltered and looked to the ground.

"Lord above, do speak, Thomas." I longed to hear his voice, which was always like a soft caress to me.

He looked as though he might speak, then closed his mouth, turning away from me.

"You are angry with me," I said, trying to close the silence, the gap between us.

"Nay," he said, shaking his head, still looking away from me. "I am angry, but not with you."

"Don't waste your anger on this place. You are better than all of them. You must promise me that after I go—"

"I am angry with *myself*, Maggie!" He yelled at me, jabbing his finger into his own chest. His eyes were wide, he looked like a man teetering on the brink of lunacy.

I started at his fury. "Do not blame yourself—"

"For the love of God, Maggie, for one moment, can you not speak?" His words were like a blow. "I'm sorry," I said immediately.

"It is *me*!" he shouted, pounding his hand flat against his chest. "I am the one who should apologize! What a sorry excuse I am for a man, for a husband."

"No, Thomas, don't—"

"Hold your tongue, woman, and let me speak, that's all I ask. Our time is waning, do you not realize that?"

I nodded, wishing he would come to me, but knowing I should not go to him for he wanted to speak.

"Do you know what it's been like, to watch my wife's name, her livelihood, her very existence, be dragged through the mud and the filth of their pious hypocrisy? Knowing that there was nothing I could do? Knowing that you and I were helpless victims? I stood in that courtroom each day and with every moment it was like someone had taken a knife to my balls and cut just a little more, until I stood there unmanned, a helpless, useless beast!"

The fury in his voice echoed off the stone walls. I took a step toward him, arms held out, but he put his hand before him, halting me.

"Nay, let me finish," he said, his voice lower, raspier than ever I had heard it. "This was all my doing, all of it. You shall be hanged for my sins."

"What? Thomas, that's madness, don't think that—"

"No, Maggie, listen for once," he said, his wild eyes searching mine. "I am the one who insisted we leave London when we were guiltless. I did so out of fear, cowardice, because I couldn't bear the thought of losing you. But look, God shall have His way, one way or another, for here we are, standing at Death's door." He paused, raking his hands through his unkempt locks, gritting his teeth. "I am the one who allowed us to come to this place, though I knew in my heart it would not suit us, that we would not fit here. But you persisted, and I gave in to you, in a moment of weakness, I gave in to you, when I should have listened to my own judgment. You have always said, I'm easily persuaded, easily taken in by those who don't deserve me."

"Aye, because I don't deserve you. I never have!" I shouted, pointing at my own chest.

He shook his head, a wry grimace upon his face. "Hold your tongue, Maggie. 'Tis my turn to talk and I'm not finished. I should have packed us up and left this place the moment I heard someone call you a 'cunning woman.' But I did not. I was afraid to embark once again and start over. Stupid coward and fool."

"I was stupid as well, I should have heeded you when you told me of your doubts."

"It is a man's place to be the shepherd of his family, and I have failed. I am no man."

I took another step closer, reaching out to touch his face.

He flinched as though I approached with a hot iron rod. "You did not deserve such a sorry man for a husband. I am pathetic, and I am weak, and I am a sinner and I am not worthy of your love, I am not worthy of the title of your husband."

"Thomas, you speak madness."

"Hold your tongue, woman!" he shouted. "You do not know the sins that lie within my heart. I have been most undeserving of your love and trust. I have brought this down upon you, my sin has. I have been false with you. I must confess to you before you are gone from me. I will not be able to live with myself if I do not confess to you." He descended to his knees before me. "And I know you will hate me, and I know I shall lose your love, but I prefer to risk that than to have deceived you to your last breath." With this he shuddered, his face grimacing as though he fought back tears. I saw his Adam's apple strain and bob in his sinewy throat as he struggled to compose himself.

What in the world did he speak of? Bewildered, I tried to guess how he might have deceived me. My husband was not a gambler, nor a drunkard, nor a thief or rogue. Did he make love to another? I knew his nature well, and he was governed by love—if such could be called a weakness, that was his. But I didn't care. I cared not if he had bedded another, though the thought of it made me ache and heave in pain. The thought of his mouth on another was enough to have me smash a rock in two with nothing but my blinding fury.

"I must tell you of my sin, Maggie," he said, taking hold of my hands within his roughened palms and fingers. "Please, let me do this."

"You've bedded another," I said, afraid to meet his eyes.

He sat before me, bowing his head to the side so that he might look into my eyes. "Please, Maggie, let me tell you. I know you are intuitive, but allow me to tell my tale."

"Go on, then," I said, plopping down upon the hard floor, taking a deep breath so that I might steel myself for what I was about to hear. I knew I must hear it, and I did not fault him for being fallible, knowing full well of all the dishonor I had brought down upon him. Dishonor now, dishonor before he even knew me. I had secrets too. "Tell me, Thomas."

"I was unfaithful to you. I sinned with another."

"I care not."

"You shall when I tell you all. She tricked me, somehow. I am not blameless, I went willingly, but she fed me a tincture, a poison—"

"What? Who?" In my mind I ran through a list of all the women I knew who might be able to devise such a tincture and I could not think of one. But as though it spoke to me, I felt the shift of the little poppet within my pocket. I had almost forgotten about it through all my trials. "Widow Hallett."

He went still. "How did you know?"

"Only she could."

"Mary Doyle told me, Maggie, she told me that she discovered a chaa pouch of some kind in the kitchen, that the widow had steeped in my ale before serving it to me."

"An herbal infusion," I said, thinking through all the ways one might poison another in order to seduce. I preferred to think on this than to think about my husband fucking that cunning fox. "What did it taste of?"

"It were sticky sweet in the ale, slightly smoky, with an acrid taste at the end."

"Spanish fly, mixed with wormwood, maybe juice of poppy. Were you dizzy?"

"I felt as though the earth undulated beneath me like sea waves."

"Did your cock seem to take on a life of its own?"

He paused, looking away in shame.

"You don't need to answer that."

"I'll not. It was the lowest point of my life."

The thought of his cock inside her ignited me like dry kindling. I jumped up in a sudden fit of rage. "How could you? Damn you!"

He remained seated upon the floor. "You are right to be angry."

"Don't tell me what I'm right or wrong to do!"

"I won't."

I paced the room, gritting my teeth. "The Spanish fly will cause a man such a cockswell that nothing can abate it but to fuck to oblivion. You must have given her a good romp, pumped up with Spanish fly!

302

And lo, she's round with child! The timing of it all aligns! I knew she was with child before she married the minister! That's your bastard, not that preacher husband's!"

"Don't, Maggie, please. I hate myself enough. I had to tell you. I hate myself for it. You do not deserve such a husband as me. You can damn me to hell. I don't deserve your love."

*I don't deserve your love.* Had I not thought the same, so many times, when I thought of Thomas? It seemed as though the heavens finally aligned for us in this our final hour. "You don't deserve me, I don't deserve you."

"You deserve better than me."

"No, it's you, you deserve better than me. I have deceived you all along. Evil deeds come back times three."

"What are you speaking of, Maggie?"

The revelation awed me. "I deceived you. My evil deed has come back times three: Bess was taken from us. You were seduced. I am to hang in the morning."

Thomas looked perplexed. He shook his head slightly as though trying to make sense of my words. "Maggie, what are you talking about?" Then he looked as though he had solved a riddle. "Do you speak of the Irish harpist, back in London? I know about him, I know you kissed him. Was it more than that?" He searched my face. "I care not, Maggie. You were young and passionate. I had neglected you with my long hours in apprenticeship. It matters not. What was done is done . . . though the thought of that harpist's hands upon you is enough to make me tear down these walls."

I could not help but laugh, for I had a similar reaction just moments ago when I thought of his hands upon another.

"It matters not, Maggie," he said, smiling hopefully for the first time in a very long while.

If only it were so simple. If only my deception were nothing more than a thoughtless moment of passion with another dark Irishman. "It is not that. It was only a kiss. I speak of something more."

"Who was it?"

"It is not so simple as that. If only it were so trivial as an act of passion."

"Maggie, what more could you possibly speak of?"

This was the moment I had dreaded from the moment I had set eyes upon him and knew I loved him more fiercely than any before. "You shall hate me."

"Never, Maggie, it isn't possible. Please, tell me."

Slowly I sank to the floor and sat before him, looking down at my hands upon my lap, then up into his beautiful green eyes. "I sinned before I met you. I deceived you from the moment we met."

His brows drew together as he considered my words. "I never asked you to tell me of your life before me, to tell me of how you had been wounded."

I nodded. "It's true. You only asked me where I was from, what my life was like as a child. I was not a child when these things happened."

"But you *were* a child, Maggie. I knew you had been used ill before me. Such things should not have happened to a child."

"But they do, more often than not."

He leaned toward me, placing his lips upon my forehead. "I know, Maggie. You have nothing to hide from me."

"You thought me a virgin, upon that great White Horse of Vale. I was afraid to destroy the goodness in which you held me."

He shook his head. "I've told you before and I shall tell you again. I knew you were no virgin and it mattered not. Someone had stolen your innocence. I could never give that back to you. But I gave you back your pride, did I not?"

"You showed me that there were worthy men in the world, good men of fortitude. I was scared to death of losing you, of losing such a man."

"And lo and behold, your good man of fortitude now," he said, spreading his arms out. "I was untrue to you, unfaithful."

I considered him for a moment. Nothing outside us mattered anymore. I would not speak any more about my greatest shame. How absurd and trivial, his fear of confessing to me. None of it mattered, none of it. It was all silly, worthless nonsense in the face of our love. Some things were better left unsaid. If no one spoke of them, then perhaps they no longer existed. No, that girl no longer existed.

"That girl no longer exists," I said aloud, like a proclamation, willing it to be, for if she did and if he knew, my greatest shame would taint them both. I lifted my chin with purpose. "We are equals now," I said, placing my finger upon the bridge of his thick nose, trailing it gently down to the tip.

He took my finger and placed it to his lips. "None of it matters, Maggie. I love you, I love you more today than I did yesterday, more than I did when I asked for your hand in marriage."

"Love makes us daft," I said with a wry laugh.

"Love makes us whole. Love makes us rise above." He placed his lips on mine and gently kissed.

We heard the distant chatter of constables upstairs. Thomas glanced to the tiny window above my cell. "Dawn approaches." He shivered. He broke into a sob, hiding his face behind his hands in shame.

"Thomas, don't cry. I need you to do something for me. I need you to do something for Bess, and for yourself."

He wiped roughly at his face with his fingers, taking a deep breath. "What is it, Maggie, what do you want of me?"

"Go from this place."

"You do not need to ask me twice, Maggie. I'll go from this place and damn it to Hell."

"Go from this place, Thomas, and make a new life. When I am gone, do not be weighed down by sadness."

"Aye, Maggie, worry not, please. I'll go, and I'll take all of our belongings with me. I'll not leave one piece of our lives in this godforsaken place. I'll take your hope chest, even, wherever I go."

At his mention of the hope chest, I recalled the chest he had crafted for me back in England, a wedding gift so dear. Within it were wedding linens, the green gown I wore the day we were married. But then I remembered, my diary, my writing, my letter, which I had stashed away, within the folds of my green wedding gown. *Oh dear God, no!* I had written the letter in haste, in panic, in an act of confession, a confession of my greatest shame—and perhaps purest gift—but I would not bring myself to tell him now, now that I would be tainted by this label of witch. I had declared, had I not? That girl no longer existed. She could not come to light now, not like this.

"Be rid of this life, be rid of every vestige of it—of me!"

"Silence, Maggie! Shut your mouth for once! Stop talking nonsense!"

"You heed me!" I could feel my lips cracking with each plea. "Every trace of me must be destroyed. Promise me you shall be rid of it all—sell it, burn it, I don't care!"

"You talk madness!"

"Nay! I dread the thought of you keeping some part of me and being dragged into some lonely abyss, for innocence . . . a life—your life, to be tainted by this stain upon mine! Swear to me you shall do as I ask. Swear it!" The panic rose within me as I gripped his hands in mine.

The ferocity of my words seemed to stifle his protest. Slowly and reluctantly he nodded. "I shall."

"I'm so sorry, Thomas. I'm so sorry, for everything."

Footsteps descended the jail steps. The realization of what was to come hit me like a fist. I struggled for air, sobbing. How I loved him. He was the very best of men, my Thomas, my own.

"Do not cry, Maggie," he said, wiping my tears with his rough fingers, though he cried too. "Don't let them see you weak, not now, not after all this, my Maggie." He kissed me with a hunger, I kissed him back. He pulled away, held my face within his hands so very dear to me. "I'll be with you until the very end. Be proud, my Maggie, be proud."

# CHAPTER TWENTY-EIGHT

*The day of her Execution, I went in company of some Neighbors, who took great pains to bring her to confession & repentance. But she constantly professed herself innocent of that crime: Then one prayed her to consider if God did not bring this punishment upon her for some other crime, and asked, if she had not been guilty of Stealing many years ago; she answered, she had stolen something, but it was long since, and she had repented of it, and there was Grace enough in Christ to pardon that long ago; but as for Witchcraft she was wholly free from it, and so she said unto her Death.*

*—John Hale, A Modest Enquiry Into the Nature of Witchcraft*

The constables ushered Thomas away, out of the cell, out of my life.

I stood there, bewildered, bereft. The loss of him was more painful than any other I had felt before, as painful as when I had lost my babe, as when I had lost Bess. The bile surged within me, the pain so great, I doubled over and retched upon the floor a great quantity of clear liquid. I could not recall the last time I'd eaten. There was nothing left within me, nothing left without.

I heard the sound of many footsteps and the cell door opened again, as I retched one last time. I looked to see a large congregation, perhaps a dozen or so men and women, and one young boy, entering my cell, staring at me as though I were some horrible aberration. I supposed I was.

"Goody Jones." A man who looked to be a preacher, holding a Bible, spoke to me. "We've come from our congregation north of here, in Beverly. We have traveled far, in order to beseech you to confess that you are guilty of witchcraft."

I wiped at my mouth with the back of my hand, watching as the congregation clasped their hands in prayer, even the young, wide-eyed boy. I looked upon him, poor wretch, to be dragged here to witness this crime. "Bless," I said softly, giving him a half-hearted smile that split my dry lips and caused them to bleed.

He trembled, hiding his face in the skirts of a woman I can only assume was his mother.

"I swear to you all," I said slowly, my parched throat sounding like a frog's croak, "I am innocent of witchcraft."

There was a general sigh of disappointment.

"Perhaps, Goody Jones." The preacher spoke in a sudden, hopeful tone. "Perhaps you are being punished at this hour for some past misdeed or sin?"

His words took me by surprise—had he seen into my soul? Were he so intuitive? Was it perhaps he who used dark arts and saw my deepest secret?

"Do you . . . do you know of something? Do you know of something about me, my past?" I asked, fearful that perhaps, somehow, he were Lucifer in disguise and had come to punish me.

"Nay, Goody Jones, I know nothing of your past, but I see that perhaps I have reminded you of some past sin that you must repent for now?"

I shook my head slightly. He knew nothing.

What could I tell them? They meant no harm to me. They had come in good faith and with good intention, to try to help me save my soul, these strangers. To give them nothing would be cruel. But never would I speak of the purest gift that was my greatest shame.

I thought quickly. "When I was a girl, only a bit older than this one here," I said, gesturing to the frightened boy, "I stole a silk ribbon in the village shop. I had to have it. It summoned me with its shine and softness. It had mesmerized me. I sought it out, and in seeking sin, sin found me. But how could something so beautiful—so pure and tiny a thing—be sinful?" I dashed a tear away with my grimy fingertips. "But it was. And I confessed to no one but our Lord and Savior. And He did punish me for it, and rightfully so."

The congregation seemed to hang on my every word.

I continued, "But I have repented for this, long ago, and there were grace enough in Christ to pardon that long ago. I go to my death with a clean conscience." And I smiled again, for it were true. Christ knew my sins. I could go in peace.

"Very well, Goody Jones," said the preacher, sounding disappointed. "Might we say a prayer for your soul?"

"I would like that very much. I thank thee," I said, bowing my head and clasping my hands before me.

The prayer was brief, and when it was over, the congregation filed out of the cell. I watched the last of them go, but then a form lingered by the cell entrance.

"Who goes there?" I asked, straining to make out who it might be.

The form stepped into the cell, hands removing a hood.

"Lo and behold," I said. "You've come to pray for me, Goody Longfellow?"

She approached me quickly, grabbing hold of my arm, her face just inches from mine. "I've come here not to pray, but to send you to your grave with some knowledge."

"Aye, for you could not live with yourself if you didn't have the satisfaction of telling me before I die, is it not true?"

"I carry his child," she hissed, smiling triumphantly. "He shall be mine, rest assured."

I laughed in her face. "You carry his bastard. And rest assured, he wants never to see you again."

She let go of my arm, shoving me away, gritting her teeth. "You wait and see. Oh wait, you cannot!" She laughed, amused by her own joke.

"Such behavior is very unbecoming of a minister's wife. Does he know the child is not his?"

"Ha! He is a simpleton, he knows nothing of how women's bodies work or how babies grow."

"That's a pity, for you."

"Did you know it was I who told the magistrates of your unfortunate flight from London? Are you surprised?"

I had been right, I had known it must have been her doing. "Not in the least bit. Nothing surprises me now."

She looked quite pleased with herself and would not give up so easily. "Lady Wembly is my great-aunt."

I could not help but laugh. "What a small world this is. And somehow, it all makes sense. Lady Wembly was a lunatic who favored potions and posits. It seems to be a familial trait."

Her triumphant smile faded. "And no one shall ever know. I've won this game."

"You speak callously about life, as though it were a game of cribbage."

"In your case, yes indeed."

"Ah, well, I've one last wager to make. Come, give me your hand."

She looked unsure and cocked her head to the side.

Roughly I grabbed her hand. She gasped in surprise. I let go and then fished for the tiny poppet I had held in my pocket all this while. I shoved it in her palm. "Here's my wager: evil deeds come back times three."

She looked down at the poppet, her mouth agape.

I grabbed hold of her chin and brought her face to mine. "You used dark arts to wish me dead, and so it seems Lucifer has granted your wish. Lucky girl! But mark my words, evil deeds come back times three. Lucifer will come back for you, the child, and your husband. When you wager with the Devil, he will come back to get his due!" And with that I pressed my mouth upon hers to seal the deal.

She stumbled away from me, eyes wide with horror, casting aside the poppet before she fled from my cell.

I looked at the poppet upon the floor. She stared up at me, smiling as though her work was done.

# CHAPTER
# TWENTY-NINE

*And in the like distemper she died. The same day and hour she was executed, there was a very great tempest at Connecticut, which blew down many trees, etc.*

—*John Winthrop, journal, June 15, 1648*

The summer air was close and heavy, the wind whipped off the sea and thrashed at my skirts, my face, my hair. The sky was ominously both light and dark. A tempest brewed over this land. Of course it did, for this land, this place at the edge of the world, was about to execute a woman for the sin of being a woman.

I stood upon the cart, beneath a verdant, towering maple tree. My hands were bound behind me. The rope was strung over a solid branch, the noose tied expertly, dangling above my head. I gazed upon it. Ah, so that's how it was done. No wonder I had failed at fifteen years old. But here I was now, come full circle.

They muttered some nonsense from the Bible. The crowd was sprawling, silent as they stared on.

"Have you any last words, Goody Jones?"

I nodded. "Aye, indeed I do."

"Lord help us," I heard Endecott mutter. The magistrates stood at the front of the crowd to oversee my execution.

"Indeed, Goodman Endecott, Lord help you, all of you, this day. For you are about to execute an innocent woman. You are about to execute an innocent woman for the crime of being a woman, a woman who lived fully, spoke plainly, listened intently, observed acutely, intuited wisely, loved passionately. I am too much for this world of yours, this *Jerusalem upon a hill*." I spat upon the ground. "I am a force that makes you quake!"

At that, the wind came from the ocean in a great gust, howling through the tree branches above me, followed by the low, growling rumble of thunder. I breathed deeply, smelling the dampness, the salt air. I closed my eyes and thought of the ocean, the blue-gray expanse that separated me from my past. Then I thought of the smoky-clouded sky, which separated me from my daughter. My heart lifted, I smiled, knowing that so very soon, I would at last be united with her. I would hold her again in my arms and press my lips against the silky softness and warmth of her cheek. There was nothing, nothing I desired more at that moment than just that, to kiss her and breathe in her scent. Oh, how I ached to do so—it had been so long! The beauty of this realization made me gasp in delight.

"Enough," said Winthrop, signaling for the executioner to place the noose round my neck.

"She is innocent!" shrieked a woman, and I knew instantly who it be. Alice Stratton, my dearest friend, standing up for me to the very end. "She is innocent, and all of you know it! You, Magistrates, shall have innocent blood upon your hands!"

The crowd erupted in chatter, just as the executioner walked to the front of the cart and took hold of the reins.

The cart slowly moved ahead, my shoes sliding against the floorboards of the cart. My eyes scanned the crowd, and immediately I found my Thomas, my own.

"Goodbye, *mo Rí*."

# EPILOGUE

Thomas finished the last journal entry, exhaling with a shuddering breath. Tears spilled down his cheek; one coursed down to the tip of his nose and plopped audibly onto the last page of Maggie's diary. It startled him, and he went to wipe the tear away with the side of his palm. As he did so, a loose piece of parchment danced its way out of beneath the final page, and dangled precariously—invitingly—at the edge of the binding.

Surely, it must be another of Maggie's disorganized bills of receipt, or a note from a thankful new mother. He took hold of the paper and spread it open upon the back cover of the journal. It was Maggie's hand, but harried, messy, and ink blotched, unlike her neat prior entries. He took note of the date atop the letter.

*May 12, 1648.*

Thomas knew this to be the day of Maggie's arrest. Had she known it would happen? What was this?

*I write this down as my confession, for it weighs heavy on me at this hour, when I sense my life shall be my own for only a moment longer. Thomas, I could not bring myself to tell you this, for it would have been the ruin of us, that I had kept this from you for the whole of our lives together. Here I confess to you, my greatest shame, and purest gift.*

*Eight weeks after I had been violated by not one but two, my grandmum asked me to drink the Pennyroyal tea. I forced it down, but my monthly blood did not come. She told me there were things she could do, to make the babe go away, but I refused. I saw it as my punishment for my sinfulness, my stupidity.*

*I said to my grandmum, The child should not die because of my mistake.*

*She said, We shall find the babe a good home.*

*At fifteen I gave birth to a baby girl. I nursed her three times before my grandmother took her from my arms. I never saw her again.*

*I wept for weeks. My heart was shattered in a thousand pieces. I tried to hang myself from the rafters where we dried herbs, but the knot didn't hold. I fell to the floor, dazed, staring up at the Rosemary and Rue, Chamomile and Valerian, and the rope, swinging above me like a pendulum.*

*When I came to the Winship Farm, my breasts were still bound, to stop the milk.*

*When I would go in the darkness of morning to the cows, their moans of relief as I took their milk would make my breasts ache and I would silently weep into their hot bellies.*

*Thomas, I have two daughters. One, Bess, is with me each day, though you cannot see her. The other, if the Good Lord saw fit to let her flourish, was given to the Wells Family, near Reading.*

*I have sinned in that I kept this from you. I feared that after having kept her a secret so long, you would hate me, and I would have died with a heart cut in two, if you should hate me. I also kept her secret because—sweet babe—she did not choose to be born of such sin and suffering, such evil and violence. She was a pure gift, and I would not have her be tainted by my greatest shame.*

*I should not write this. I should cast this into the fire, and perhaps I shall. Perhaps this is all for naught. But let this parchment bear witness to my deepest, most sinful secret. If it should come to your hands, I pray that you will find it in your heart to forgive my deception, my dishonesty. I love you, love you, love you . . .*

*Eternally Yours . . .*

"Maggie! My God!"

Thomas's heart convulsed and turned over within his chest. The breath within him had been stolen by this piece of paper.

"Maggie." He let the parchment and the journal from which it had come fall to the floor. He covered his face with his hands. "My God, my Maggie." He hunched forward in the chair, rocking to and fro. The pain of the discovery, the knowledge that she believed she must keep this secret from him or else he would cast her away, it was too much. To think she had suffered with needless shame. Damn not just one, but two—*two*—vile men, that they had wrought such suffering upon his Love.

He bolted up out of the chair, causing it to topple over. He stared round the darkened room like a man gone to lunacy, like a beast caged after a life of freedom. Realizing that his other half had carried this burden and hidden it from him—he knew immediately he must act to make it right, to seek the justice stolen not only once but twice now, from his Love. Somehow, he must set it right and just again. How? He felt adrift, lost in his surprise and confusion.

He breathed to steady himself. He picked up and righted the chair, rested his arms atop the back of it as he pondered. He knew one thing for certain—Barbados would not be his next destination. Barbados was a death sentence. This was why he had thought to go there, to get as far away from this place as he could, even if it meant going to Hell, because he had not known how he could go on without his Love, his Life.

But this? "A child!" he said, still dumbfounded. He laughed in delight. Perhaps he really was going mad? No, this was elation. This was purpose. This was his life handed back to him. He would do this for his Maggie. He would make this right. He owed it to her, having never known how she carried this burden of a secret.

He would go elsewhere and thrive and make his way in the world so that he could make this right. How? He knew not at this moment, but he had faith enough in himself and his hands to make this right. This was how he would lift the secret burden from Maggie, take it from her shoulders and shift it to his own. He was Maggie's husband, Maggie's king. "I swear it, Maggie. I swear it."

### Two years later, Swindon, Wiltshire

As I rode east, away from the village of Swindon, the morning fog was just lifting. I could see the road before me, perhaps some fifteen yards, before the fog shrouded the rest. Despite the morning damp, it promised to be a fine day, the sun rising, eventually burning off the rest of the mist.

About two hours into my journey, the fog was gone, the sun shone upon the countryside. The air was heady with the scent of wildflowers and damp earth. I was making good time. I would reach my destination well before dusk. At one point, I passed a battalion of the New Model

Army, making its way west toward Bristol. No doubt they were bound for Ireland. Not satisfied even with the taking of the King's head, Cromwell still waged his Protestant war against the Royalists and Catholics. There were few who had not heard of the bloody siege of Drogheda. Even the nuns were not spared. God damn this war, all wars. In the end, it were always the powerless and the innocent who suffered most.

How grateful I was to have my home in the New World, away from the conflicts between landowners who had owned too much for too long. Maryland prospered, and Catholics were allowed to live in peace. I was proud to call it home, proud to own acres and acres of land, dark with rich soil that stretched to the mouth of the Chesapeake.

I had rid myself of Massachusetts as soon as I could. Samuel and Alice Stratton had urged me to go, and still to this day we corresponded. Many times I had invited them to Saint Mary's City, to be my guests, and they promised they would. Some months ago, Alice Stratton, also, had been accused of witchcraft, for she freely spoke out against the magistrates and General Court, claiming they had the blood of an innocent woman upon their consciences. She had not abated in her defense of her dearest friend. In the end, the court had no evidence against her, but that she would never let them forget how her best friend had perished at their hands.

Samuel had also informed me, some six months after my arrival to Maryland, that Goody Longfellow had died, along with her child, in birthing. I knew the child was mine, but reasoned and believed it wasn't mine. It was the work of her Evil, that had used me as its tool. I understood now, in a small way, how it feels to be taken, to be raped. One week later, in his grief, Reverend Longfellow had taken his own life. The news had shaken me, but also was in some way a relief, a satisfaction to know that, in the end, the Widow Hallett's evil deeds had caught up with her.

After some time riding, I dismounted so that I might piss by the roadside bushes. As I relieved myself, I looked northward, at the rolling hills of Wiltshire. My breath caught in my chest, for I could not believe my eyes. There, well in the distance, I could distinctly make out the faint outline of the Uffington White Horse.

In haste, I refastened my breeches, then took a few steps onto the farmland in front of me. I stared at the white horse, placing my hands over my aching heart. I closed my eyes. I could recall every detail, every moment of the first time I had made love to Maggie upon the neck of the white horse. I opened my eyes, smiling. How blessed I have been in my life, to have known such a love, to have been bound to such a woman as Maggie.

It was late afternoon when I reached the village of Reading.

I asked the innkeeper the way to the Wells Farm. He knew it well, said it was one of the largest in the area, and gave me directions. And so I set off, north of the village, to fulfill my vow.

It was almost dusk when I came upon the path that led to the Wells Farm. As I rounded a corner, I saw before me a large, thatched-roof home and neighboring barn, surrounded by acres of farmland not unlike my own in Maryland. As I approached the front gate of the house, I saw a figure, tending to what looked to be peony bushes. A gardener, perhaps? When I reached the front gate I tethered the horse to the hitching post. The gardener was bent over, hard at work.

"Good day," I called. "I've come to call upon the Wells family. Are they at home?"

The figure stood tall. A woman, with a straw bonnet perched upon her head. She put her hands to the small of her back as she stretched and turned to face me.

My heart seized. It were Maggie, Maggie when we were first married.

"Good day," she called, making her way toward the garden gate.

I could not speak. I was overcome: the pain in my chest, the shock of seeing young Maggie again.

As she came closer, I grasped the fence post to steady myself. She was smiling, and it was then I saw the dimples in her cheeks. "Bess!" I whispered.

Her smile faded when she saw the state of me, a frown of concern taking over. "Pray, sir, are you unwell?"

"I am," I said, trying to catch my breath, disbelieving what was before my eyes.

"Oh, sir," she said, quickly opening the gate and coming to my side to assist me. "Shall I bring you some ale?"

"Aye, please," I said, panting.

"Come, this way," she said, leading me to the base of a large willow tree. "Rest here and I'll fetch you a cup." She ran off to the house.

I took deep gulps of air, trying to steady myself. In, one two three. Out, one two three.

She approached, tankard in hand.

I knew it were her—how could it not be?

"Here, take this," she said, handing me the tankard. She studied me for a moment, then sat beside me, beneath the tree. She placed her hand upon my shoulder. "Better now?"

"Aye," I managed, still staring at her.

She considered me, as Maggie would. "Last year we had a lot of men come past this way: soldiers, deserters, wanderers," she said. "The family decided we must always share a bit of our ale, for these are trying times for many."

"'Tis kind of you," I mustered.

She blatantly stared at me, and she were so like Maggie, I could not help but laugh.

"Why do you laugh?" she demanded.

"You remind me of someone."

"Ah," she said. Then she glanced back toward the house. "Did you tell me your name? I cannot remember."

"Thomas O'Byrn," I told her.

"Do you have business with us, Mister O'Byrn? Have you come to see my father?"

How was I to answer? There was never any fooling Maggie, she always wanted me to be direct. Perhaps her daughter was the same.

"No, I've come a very long way to see you."

She started at this, eyes wide and disbelieving. "Me? Whyever for?"

"What is your name?"

"Constance," she said, now eyeing me warily.

"I do not come in malice, Constance," I tried to reassure her.

"State your business, Mister O'Byrn."

"Thomas. Call me Thomas. I knew your mother."

She instinctively moved away from me. "You must have known her when she was very young, for my real mother died giving birth to me. The Wells family adopted me as an infant, out of kindness and charity."

"Is that what you were told?"

"Yes, it's the truth. All I know of my real mother is that her name was Margaret Drinkwater. Her grandmother—my great-grandmother—passed not long after I was given to the Wells family."

"I knew Maggie Drinkwater."

Her eyes narrowed. "Were you her lover? Are you my real father?"

"Alas, no." I would not lie to her about her origins, but nor would I tell her straightaway.

"Then how did you know my mother? It isn't possible."

"Your mother didn't die giving birth to you. She indentured herself to a dairy farm near Uffington. She was a dairymaid. And that's where I came to know her, came to love her."

By the time I had finished telling the story, it were dark. Constance sat before me, her dark eyes wide, her mouth quivering. One tear escaped, quickly coursing down her cheek to her chin.

"They hanged her. Yet she was innocent."

"Indeed. Innocent, as I suspect are many a woman hanged for witchcraft here in England."

She looked down at her hands upon her lap, then back up at me. "How did you find the strength to go on?"

I sat tall, reaching my arms in the air to stretch after sitting on one spot for so long. I mulled over how to give a simple answer to so difficult a question. "I swore to myself that I would do right by Maggie, that I would find you and tell you the story of your mother." I smiled at her. She blushed and looked away, and again, my heart raced for the hundredth time, to see young Maggie again. I could have gazed upon her for the rest of my days, but I feared I overstayed my welcome. "Will your family be looking for you? It's night."

She shook her head, waving her hand dismissively. "They've always treated me like one of the servants. I have been reminded daily, ever since I can remember, about how I must be grateful to their charity. Suffice to say, I grow weary of it."

I laughed. This was proof of nature, not nurture, for Maggie would have said something quite similar. "How old are you, Constance?"

"Mistress Wells tells me I am about twenty-five years."

"Why are you still here? Why haven't you married?"

"Are you calling me a spinster, Thomas?"

"I suppose I am, yes."

"Many have tried, but the Wellses have forbade me to marry. They prefer me here. Especially now that Mistress Wells suffers in her lungs. I think they'd like me to be her nurse, as I'm free labor, you see."

"But what do you want, Constance?"

"I try not to think about that, especially now that I'm too old to marry."

"That's nonsense and you know it. You'd have your pick in Maryland."

"But I am not in Maryland. I am here in England."

I swallowed and cleared my throat, trepidation filling me as I said softly, "You are welcome to my home, in Maryland."

She stared at me, then blinked a couple of times, shaking her head dismissively. "There's a war going on, Thomas. You've been gone for so long, across the ocean, you forget. That changes things. The world is unsafe."

My heart sank, but I knew it to be irrational that a young woman would up and go with a strange man from a foreign, faraway land. I got up and went to the tethered horse, fishing inside the saddlebag until I grasped what I came here to give. Walking back to her, I held it before her. "I vowed to myself that I would do this, that I would provide for you."

The leather sack of coin plopped into her outstretched hand. The heft of it told her she need not look inside. In the darkness, I could see her mouth fall open in surprise.

"Go and marry, Constance. Live your life."

"I—I don't know what to say. I don't deserve this." She choked back tears.

"I would have done the same for my own daughter, my Bess," I said, feeling the ache of my heart whenever I said her name aloud. "You are the closest thing I have."

"Thank you," she said, two tears escaping down her cheeks.

I knew not what else to say, I was overcome. I had dreamt of meeting this girl since I had read Maggie's letter. And now here I was, fulfilling my vow.

"Goodbye, Constance," I said, placing my hand upon her mass of dark curls. The feel of them upon my palm caused my heart to roll over. I made my way to the impatient horse pawing the ground.

"Wait," she said, following me. "Have you a place to stay?"

"I have a room at the Sun Inn."

"Ah, you should have chosen the Fox and Crown."

"Tomorrow I'll make my way back to Bristol, where my sloop awaits. I want to head back before the hottest days of August, when the seas can be most unpredictable."

"How far you have traveled. I am indebted to you, Thomas."

"You owe me no debt," I said as I mounted the horse. "It was I who had the vow to keep."

∞

"Looks to be a fine day to launch," said Captain Davies.

Oddly enough, the Welshman, the captain of the ship *Welcome* that had purged me from its hold after Maggie's murder, had sought me out a year ago when he learned I had come to Maryland. We had become fast friends, and I had offered him enough coin to become the captain of my sloop.

"Indeed, it does," I said. I stared out toward the ocean and then back to the harbor of Bristol, thinking of the rolling hills beyond, and a young woman so like my own Bess. The Lord giveth and the Lord taketh away. I found myself now a man without a mission. I had fulfilled Maggie's final wish. Suddenly, I felt as though I had no direction, no purpose. My heart sank, and I felt very much alone.

I awoke from my dreary contemplations to the feel of Molly rubbing up against my boots.

"Reow!" she yelled up at me, looking greatly displeased that I had left her alone for some days.

I scooped up her chunky, fluffy body, and held her in my arms as I looked out at the sea. "'Tis just you and I now, Molly," I muttered into her fur. "We shall grow old together, my fine lady."

"Captain Davies." A dockworker waved his hands to get his attention. "There's someone here to see your boss."

"Oh aye? Who? We are about to pull anchor here!"

"This lass, here."

"Davies, wait!" I shouted, hope filling my heart. I ran toward the starboard side of the sloop, to Davies's side, Molly still in my arms.

"Good day!"

And there she was, waving her arms wildly in the air.

"Constance?" I asked, to be certain my eyes did not deceive me.

"Aye! Might I join you, and your cat, on your journey to Maryland?"

"Ha!" The joy surged through me. "I would be honored!"

I turned to Davies. "Have the men help her board."

Davies scratched his chin, looking confused. "Who is the lass?"

I felt the tears come to my eyes. "She is my daughter."

# AUTHOR'S NOTE

Years ago, a person in the publishing industry told me to "write a book about some famous man's wife, daughter, or sister." I immediately bristled at this notion and thought how about I write a novel about some famous woman's husband instead?

The brief historical record of Margaret Jones was known to me already, as I had stored it in my mind's disheveled filing cabinet many years before while doing postgraduate research. From it, I also knew that Margaret Jones had a husband, Thomas. Was Margaret Jones "famous," since she was the first woman hanged for witchcraft in Boston? Maybe. But the inspirational flame was kindled regardless—and it didn't matter whether she was famous enough. In writing *The First Witch of Boston*, I did my best to make her so, and through bringing her to life on the page, I tried to honor her spirit and the spirit of all the women like her who are nothing more than a maligned blip in the historical record or, worse yet, forgotten and lost to history altogether.

And what of the hence anonymous husband, Thomas? I wondered what sort of man was married to such a woman as Margaret Jones. What kind of husband would stand steadfastly beside his wife—even after the dark accusation upon her then came to fall upon him as well? He was a fascinating puzzle to solve and portrait to paint. I then set out to draw two characters who were believable and true to their time, as well as ours. There are themes that are universal human experiences, for better or for worse: childbirth, motherhood, fatherhood, kinship, love, desire, jealousy, pain, loss, violence, rape, and death. In doing so, the hopeless romantic in me created a couple very much devoted to each other in all ways of a happy marriage.

Puritan settlers in Massachusetts were by no means unanimous in their godliness, piety, stoicism, and behaviors, despite the enduring legacy created by nineteenth-century historians and writers (looking at you, ghost of Nathaniel Hawthorne). The colony at the edge of the world needed more than just ministers and politicians; it also required skilled laborers and craftsmen to build and sustain it. Puritan leaders learned soon enough that they would have to allow for these less pious, slightly unsavory settlers out of necessity—a necessary evil, so to speak. It is these people whose stories fascinated me most.

One does not have to look very far into the few, precious, primary sources of these settlers before it becomes apparent that many in the Massachusetts Bay Colony were far less pious, and far more fallible, lusty, and therefore relatable to us today. Terms of endearments for wives left behind upon wills and estate inventories; poetry and verses expressing love, devotion, longing; even ministers' sermons that raptured about the soul's communion with Jesus in the afterlife, likening it to the sexual capitulation to a bridegroom. Court records detail all sorts of illicit, premarital, sexual "incidents." And above it all was the oftentimes hypocritical judgment of those who hoped to socially climb, and those who, in order to remain in power, must hold in place a system to somehow control the masses and keep them in line.

How uncanny this all feels, some four hundred years later. History, and human nature, repeats patterns without fail. As not only an author and student of history but also as a woman, I am compelled to shine a light on the persecution of women who might have been overt, bold, and confident in an increasingly overly conservative political climate.

# The Facts

Margaret Jones, midwife and healer of Charlestown, Massachusetts Bay Colony, was found guilty of witchcraft by the Massachusetts General Court and executed by hanging on June 15, 1648. She was the first person tried for witchcraft in Boston, but not the first in New England. Alice Young of Windsor, Connecticut, was tried and executed for witchcraft on May 26, 1647.

Only two definitive primary sources on the lives of Margaret and Thomas Jones exist: the entries dated May 28 and July 28 from *The Journal of John Winthrop, 1630–1649*, and a brief mention in Reverend John Hale's *A Modest Enquiry Into the Nature of Witchcraft*, written in 1697. The quotations at the opening of each chapter in Part II of this novel, which detail each charge brought against Margaret Jones, as well as the results of her "examination," are direct quotes from these texts.

There exists, in the Massachusetts Court Records and Deputies' Records, an entry for May 18, 1648, a nameless reference to "the witch now in question . . . that a strict watch be set about her every night, and that her husband be confined to a private room and watched also." It is safe to assume this record refers to Margaret and Thomas Jones, given the date and method of examination. One other contemporary source, Samuel Danforth's *An Almanack For the Year of Our Lord 1648*, makes mention of the date of execution of Jones on June 15, 1648.

We do not know if Margaret and Thomas Jones had any children—there is no mention in the historical record. But I took the liberty of giving them the gift of Bess, who was inspired by the story of another innocent woman hanged for witchcraft, Alice Lake. Alice, of Dorchester, was found guilty of witchcraft and executed in June 1651. According to a letter dated December 1684, between Reverend Nathaniel Mather and his brother, the president of Harvard College, Increase Mather, Alice Lake claimed to have been visited by the ghost or spirit of her deceased child, whom she greatly missed. I found that briefly recorded detail so moving, as it made me pause to consider how women at that time, on the edge of the known world, might cope with such immense grief.

The event detailed in the prologue, of Thomas Jones's travails on the dangerously listing ship *Welcome*, is based on Governor Winthrop's journal entry dated July 28, 1648. Such an amazing tale, told with such earnest authority, was great fun for a fiction writer to flesh out. It is possible that Thomas Jones, husband of Margaret Jones, may be same Thomas Jones listed in Thomas Bellows Wyman's *The Genealogies and Estates of Charlestown, 1629–1818, Vol 1*. That particular Thomas Jones is listed as a butcher from Norfolk County who arrived in Massachusetts in 1637, but it shows his wife as Abigail Wise. The same list shows a Margaret Jones, "executed for witchcraft at Boston, June 15, 1648," wife of a "Captain" Thomas Jones. Of said "captain," nothing more is recorded.

Samuel and Alice Stratton, the steadfast, loyal friends of Thomas and Margaret, were real. They lived in Charlestown and, shortly after Margaret's execution, relocated to Watertown in Middlesex County. As Thomas mentions in the epilogue, both persisted in trying to clear Margaret Jones's name and were brought to trial before the General Court and fined for doing so in October 1649. As found in Middlesex County Court Records, Folder 2, and as transcribed by historian John Demos in *Entertaining Satan: Witchcraft and the Culture of Early New England*, Alice was tried for slander for saying that Margaret Jones "had died wrongfully . . . and her blood would be required at the magistrates' hands." Samuel stated that any magistrate could be bought and paid for, and both were duly fined by the General Court, which made a point of recording that they were being "most merciful" to the couple. The two agreed to pay the fine, but the following year, they are once again mentioned in the court records, this time for not paying the fine as they had agreed to do. It appears they were loyal friends through and through.

While many of the characters in this novel are fictional, of my own making, there are also some real people I included from my research.

One is Samuel Maverick, whom Thomas mentions, with much disdain, as the owner of Noddle's Island (present-day East Boston). Maverick did indeed employ enslaved Africans. There exists an account in the travel journal of John Josselyn, who was briefly a guest of Samuel Maverick's in 1638. Josselyn says he heard crying and discovered it came from an African woman enslaved upon Maverick's plantation. When he asked why she cried, she told him she would be raped, by order of Maverick, who desired more enslaved people. It is heartbreaking to read, and forever imprinted in my memory now. For more specific information regarding this woman and these enslaved people of Noddle's Island, as well as the enslaved Africans throughout seventeenth-century New England, I would highly recommend the scholarship of historian Wendy Warren.

The members of the General Court in 1648, as listed by Margaret Jones on the first day of her trial were, of course, real people, some of them original founders of Massachusetts Bay Colony. Richard Bellingham did own a hunting lodge across the Mystic River from Charlestown, in Winnisimmet, in what is now known as Chelsea, as well as the ferry service between Charlestown and present-day Marginal Street in Chelsea. Though Bellingham purchased the Winnisimmet lands from John Maverick of Noddle's Island in 1635, and was said to have spent his summers on this land rather than at his townhome on Tremont Street in Boston, the actual hunting lodge was not built until 1659. For the sake of good storytelling, I took the liberty of placing the hunting lodge in Winnisimmet in 1647, twelve years before it actually existed, though Bellingham did, indeed, spend time upon his land there at that time.

Speaking of Chelsea, I grew up in Chelsea, Massachusetts. My elementary school was a few blocks away from the site of Richard Bellingham's house, and I had to walk by it to get to a dear friend's house. Growing up in Chelsea in the 1980s, one was steeped in two unavoidable things: crime and history. I had a keen affinity for the latter, thankfully. The Bellingham house—or the Cary House, as it was known to my friends and me—was a source of endless fascination, and we would tour it again and again to hear the amazing ghost stories and urban myths that surrounded such a historical site stuck in the middle of an impoverished city. I'm certain that this place helped to inspire my love for seventeenth-century Massachusetts history.

Later on, I went to pursue my MPhil degree at Cambridge University and focused my dissertation on the lives of indentured servants and their chances of socioeconomic upward mobility in seventeenth-century Massachusetts as compared to former servants in East Anglia and South Carolina. It was while delving into the passenger lists of the ships of the Great Migration of the 1630s that I became intimately familiar with the lives of many early settlers. Each of their stories holds some fascination for me, even to this day. It was through this postgrad research that I first happened upon the story of Margaret Jones, the first woman tried and executed for witchcraft in Massachusetts. I knew that, someday, I would circle back to her and do my best to give her a story, give her a voice.

Was Margaret Jones a witch? I suppose that depends on what your definition of a witch might be. Was she a woman who had a wealth of knowledge on how to heal and use herbal remedies, knew how to assist women through their labors and see them safely delivered of their children? Did she intuitively understand her patients' ailments, their pain? Did she believe in the power found within nature? Most likely, yes, and unfortunately, at that time, on the edge of the world, such knowledge and skill in a woman were regarded suspiciously. She, as well as the thousands of other women and men who were tried and executed on charges of witchcraft and sorcery throughout the colonies and Europe, and those who are still persecuted on such charges round the world even to this day, all of them deserve vindication.

# ACKNOWLEDGMENTS

Some authors' accounts of their road to publishing success are stuff of fairy tales. Others have stories like twisted, tangled yarns, and some are Tolstoy-esque in their duration as well as their suffering. I'd like to think my own publishing tale is a mix of all three of these. But one common thread in every author's tale is the vital and valued help, constructive criticism, and encouragement they received in their publishing journey, without which they might not have had the fortunate opportunity to write an acknowledgment in their novel's final pages.

To the Lake Union Team: Chantelle Aimee Osman, you've actively championed my vision, making sure it stay intact and true—I'm forever grateful. Jenna Free, I'm so thankful for your keen eyes and attention to detail. Jen Bentham, thanks for keeping it all together. Many thanks to the Art Department at Lake Union, who took the time to consider my outside-the-box cover notion and made it a beautiful reality.

To Danielle Marshall, my original acquiring editor at Lake Union, thank you for taking a chance on me, and thank you for your unwavering encouragement. Also, I am indebted to you for recommending me to my amazing literary agent, Danielle Egan-Miller of Browne & Miller.

It's true, I have the World's Best Literary Agent. Danielle, I'm so grateful to you for all of your time and your dedication to helping me make this dream a reality. Your counsel has been invaluable. Our impromptu Zoom meetings are the most fun. Also, so many thanks to Mariana Fisher, Foreign Rights Manager at Browne & Miller. Your insight and your thoughtful feedback in the eleventh hour are greatly appreciated.

Of course, when writing historical fiction, a novelist is nothing without the most valuable assistance and guidance of dedicated historians, archivists, and librarians. A heartfelt thanks goes out to the amazing team at Massachusetts Historical Society, especially Dan Hinchen, Livia Zarge, and Brandon McGrath-Neely. The three of you were so kind and helpful to me as I conducted my research. I'm indebted to the research and scholarship of many historians, especially John Demos, Richard Godbeer, Malcolm Gaskill, Wendy Warren, Laurel Thatcher Ulrich, David Hackett Fischer, Carol F. Karlsen, David D. Hall, Mary Beth Norton, John M. Murrin, Christopher Hill, Lawrence Stone, and Keith Wrightson, who, many years ago, was also examiner for my MPhil dissertation at Cambridge.

I am grateful for the contemporary writings of the following: the physician, herbalist, astronomer, and botanist Nicholas Culpeper (1616–1654); the naturalist John Josselyn (1608–1675); the herbalist John Gerard (1545–1612); botanist Thomas Johnson (ca. 1600–1644); and astronomer, minister, and poet Samuel Danforth (1626–1674).

To author Olivia Hawker, I'm indebted. It was a fateful night at the Historical Novel Society Conference 2023 in San Antonio when I decided to work up the courage to read a love scene aloud to a room of strangers—and Jamie Ford—at an after-hours cold read. Apparently I impressed Olivia, so much so that the next day she told her editor, Danielle Marshall, about me, and then the two proceeded to chase me down in the ladies' restroom of the Marriott Hotel. It's the stuff of legend and rom-coms, and that's really how it went down. Olivia, thank you for believing in me, and thank you for all of your counsel and advice. Don't forget, I owe you dinner!

I am forever grateful for Rocky Mountain Fiction Writers, without which I'm not sure I'd be writing this acknowledgment. This amazing organization took me in as a naive writer beginning her first manuscript back in 2004, and the knowledge I gained about the writing process and all its inner workings from its members has been invaluable. My heartfelt thanks to the Southwest Denver Thursday Night Critique Group: Kathy Reynolds, Mindy McIntyre, John Turley, Ed Hickok, Liesa Malik, Kathy House, Joy Jarrett-Meredith, Kevin Wolf, ZJ Czupor, Sue Hinkin, Martha Hussein. And of course, I honor the memory of the amazing Grammar Jedi, Mary Ann Kersten. Always encouraging, always laughing, always spotting split infinitives and dangling prepositions, always fighting the patriarchy, I can feel her presence as I write this. How blessed and lucky I am to have known such an amazing woman.

To Karleen Koen, thank you for deciding to lead an Artist's Way Class in the Houston Heights on the brink of the pandemic. You gave me hope and inspiration when I had very little of either. Your wisdom, your kindness to me are so greatly appreciated.

To Diana Gabaldon, who kindly read the first ten pages of this manuscript back in 2016 and said, "You need to keep going with this." You probably thought it wasn't a big deal that you said that to me, but believe me, it was a very, very big deal. It kept me going. I'm most grateful to you.

To my author friends, the fellow writers who always have each other's backs, who always are there to celebrate successes and dry tears of rejection: Gwen Florio, Katie Moretti, Eliza Knight, Donna Thorland, Jason Evans, Nancy Bileau, Kris Waldherr, Piper Huguley, Zenobia Neil, Paulette Kennedy, Shawntelle Madison, Lauren Willig, Veronica R. Calisto—I'm lucky to call all of you friends. To Heather Webb and Aimie Runyan, the both of you have been by my side through thick and thin, always believing in me and encouraging me when I couldn't catch a break. Love you, friends.

To my awesome therapist, Karen Pennebaker, I'm indebted to you for keeping me accountable and motivating me to get back in the saddle.

To my friends who always encouraged me and assured me I was not delusional: Lisa Polcaro, Jamie Cole, Erin McLaughlin, Caren Mote, Sommer Louis, Helen Read, Jane Kelly, Josh Frey, Elizabeth

Wallace, Alex Talbot, Stephanie Crochet, Jennifer Solak, Joan Dwyer, Dawn Spencer-Hurwitz, Amber Jobin. Thank you all for your support, friendship, and love through all these years. A special thanks to Matthew Silas, who, many years ago, told me via AOL Messenger (ha!) to stop reading and start writing, dammit. Glad I took your sage advice, dear friend.

To my beloved kitties: Princess Zora, and my Other Husband, Kodi, always nearby, always purring, always sitting on the reference books I used most frequently. And especially to the late, great, Moll Fluff Flanders, the inspiration for Molly the cat in this novel. She was a grand dame, and the angels smiled upon me the day I found her at the Friends For Life Animal Shelter and thus became her devoted servant.

To my family, especially my mother-in-law, Charline Mize, for always holding down the fort when I would travel to writing conferences. I could not have pitched my novels so many times had you not been there to take care of the kids while I was gone—thank you so much. To my mom and dad, Ann and John Catalano, I'm so grateful that you always encouraged me to follow my dreams, no matter how impractical, ridiculous, or wild they might have been. Ma, thank you for being my #1 beta reader and listening to all my crazy ideas. I love you both very much.

To my kids, Theo and Gigi, thank you for always inspiring me in some little-yet-big way each day, and for believing in me. I love, love, love you both so much.

And finally, to my husband, Robert. I could never find the right words to summarize the depth of my gratitude to you, my love for you. Through all the days, both bright and dark, you have been by my side, steadfast, always holding my hand and always telling me that I could make my dreams come true. Your belief in me never faltered, even when I stopped believing in myself. The stars aligned when you and I met. Thank you a thousand times over.

# ABOUT THE AUTHOR

*Photo © 2024 Jennifer Evans*

Andrea Catalano is a historical novelist who holds a master of philosophy in historical studies degree from University of Cambridge, UK. Originally from the Boston area, she currently lives in Texas with her husband, children, two fluffy cats, and many, many books. Find her online at www.andreacatalanoauthor.com.

Printed in Dunstable, United Kingdom